Praise for Sisters, Ink

"Excellent! Rebeca captures the craziness of women's lives, even while showing their commitment to each other and their craft of scrapbooking. A fabulous story of romance and family ties. I highly recommend *Sisters, Ink*."

Stacy Julian
Founder, Big Picture Scrapbooking
Founding Editor, *Simple Scrapbooks* magazine

"Fun . . . funny . . . fantastic! Rebeca Seitz has brought together scrapbooking and sisterhood in a lively romp, with a love for going home again."

Eva Marie Everson
Coauthor of *The Potluck Club* series

"I am tickled to know there is another book coming soon. I honestly thought to myself, I hope I don't have to wait too long for the next book, now that I have made these new friends!"

Lisa Brennan
Bazzill Basics Paper

"Every woman wants a friend to confide in, laugh with, cry with, and just be herself around. When the friend is a sister, it's even better. Add scrapbooking, family, and a guy, and things are sure to get interesting and wonderful. That's exactly what Rebeca Seitz has done in this fun novel. I enjoyed it so much, I can't wait for the next installment to see what else the sisters are up to!"

Ginger Kolbaba
Author of *Desperate Pastors' Wives*

"An enchanting tale. *Sisters, Ink* is written with a perfect balance of humor, candor, and a sprinkling of romance. The story embraces sisterly love through a conduit of art, emotion, spirituality, and diversity. *Sisters, Ink* is a genuine, engaging read for sisters, women of faith, and scrapbookers alike. I reached the last page with an enormous smile on my face."

Becky Fleck
PageMaps.com

"I don't know much about scrapbooking—edgers, brads, and all those doodads—but I do know a good story when I see one. And that's what Rebeca Seitz delivers with this tale of faith, romance, and four sisters' shared love of scrapbooking. A delightful combination!"

Tamara Leigh
Author of *Splitting Harriet* and *Perfecting Kate*

"What more can any woman want? *Sisters, Ink* weaves the love of sisters, the fun of scrapbooking, and a romance as sugary and tingling as *Sweet Home Alabama*. A must read for those who love southern fiction."

DiAnn Mills
Author of *Leather and Lace* and *When the Nile Runs Red*

"*Sisters, Ink* is warm, fun, and so easy to relate to! I connected immediately to the sisters & the family."

Kerri Wickersheim
Marketing Director, Scrapbook Adhesives by 3L

SiSTERS, INK

Rebeca Seitz

B&H
PUBLISHING GROUP

Nashville, Tennessee

978-0-8054-4690-6

Published by B&H Publishing Group,
Nashville, Tennessee

Dewey Decimal Classification: F
Subject Heading: SCRAPBOOKING—FICTION \
SISTERS—FICTION \ GOD—WILL—FICTION

Publisher's Note: This novel is a work of fiction.
Names, characters places, and incidents are either products
of the author's imagination or used fictitiously. All characters are fictional, and any similarity to people living or
dead is purely coincidental.

1 2 3 4 5 6 7 8 9 10   12 11 10 09 08

For my patient, gentle husband, Charlie,
without whom I cannot imagine life or love.

Acknowledgments

There are so many individuals that contributed to making this novel. I'm certain I'll leave someone out, but the effort should be made.

First, to my editor Karen Ball. We've shared a lot of laughs and lows along the way, lady, and I'm a better woman for them. Your involvement in my life is a gift for which I am not worthy but will always be grateful.

And to my "new" editor, David Webb. I love your genteel, intelligent, quiet presence and strength on this project. Working with such a respectful, knowledgeable person is a joy and has made this process a pleasure.

To the promotions team at B&H, thank you for your belief in *Sisters, Ink* and your hard work in finding unique ways to promote it. Robin Patterson, you're a talented lady and I'm thankful for your experience (and fun conversations!) along the way.

To Chef Oscar at the Ritz-Carlton in Naples, Florida. Thank you for taking time out from the festivities at Jim and Grace's to share your culinary genius with me. Your wisdom made up for my lack of knowledge in the kitchen so that Joy could shine!

To the team here at Glass Road PR, I know it's not easy having a boss who is also committed to writing novels. I appreciate each of you for your dedication to the growth of this firm as a haven for Christian novelists and artists. It's a blessing to work alongside each of you.

To my fabulous assistant, Darcy Skelton, thanks for your attention to detail and willingness to do just about anything that's asked of you. You make my life run smoothly! I'm so glad you found your One and Only!

Finally, to my little one, Anderson. I know you can't read this yet, little guy, but Mommy is so very, very grateful for you. Thanks for playing with Daddy so Mommy could write—and for giving me hugs and smiles every time I came downstairs and back into your world. God's got plans for you, precious son, and I'm honored that one of them was making me your mom.

One

Tandy's purple stiletto heel tapped in perfect rhythm to the pulse that threatened to leap out of her neck. She stared at the phone, willing it to ring and someone on the other end to declare this a joke. Her boss did *not* just call her into his office. *Now.*

The smooth tones from her CD player of Ol' Blue Eyes crooning "I Did It My Way" mocked rather than soothed her. She had to calm down, but Meg's idea of music soothing the savage soul was not working. Fingers shaking, Tandy snatched up the receiver and dialed her sister. Calm, stoic Meg always knew what to do in a crisis. From falling off the swing set to supplying Oreos and caffeine the night before Tandy's bar exam, Meg was a pro at handling crises and keeping her three sisters' lives humming.

A busy signal sounded, and Tandy slammed the phone back down. Of course Meg would be on the phone right now. Why on earth couldn't that woman understand the helpfulness of call-waiting? Tandy could hear Meg's gentle, persuasive response now: *Why would I stop talking to one*

1

person before our conversation ended, T? It's rude, and I just won't have it in my house.

Grabbing the receiver again, Tandy punched in Kendra's numbers, jumping when yet another hawk flew into her window. Why did Orlando have to have a courthouse with perfect nooks and crannies for building a nest? Ever since the completion of this new structure, hawks circled attorneys in the BellSouth building across the street on a daily basis.

Kendra's melodic voice floated over the line, its harmonious tones the same as in childhood: *"You have reached the voice mail of Kendra Sinclair . . ."*

Tandy slammed the receiver down again and glared at the circling hawks. Of course Mr. Beasley was angry. He had every right to be, really. That fat deposit in her checking account every other week meant the continuation of her dedication to keeping their clients *out* of jail. Certainly it meant she wouldn't hand the prosecution the very evidence they needed to obtain a conviction. She fiddled with the purple and black silk scarf tied around her neck.

Would Joy be any help at all in this situation? Joy might be the baby sister, but her quiet strength could come in handy right now. Except that Joy loved to talk and Christopher Beasley was waiting. The thought of him in his office high above the hawks, tapping his long fingers on the glass top of a heavy mahogany desk, didn't allow for long phone conversations.

Tandy's office phone rang and she jumped. "Tandy Sinclair."

"Tandy, it's Anna." Tandy smiled, thinking of the gentle lady seated a few floors above her. "Mr. Beasley's on his third cup of coffee."

Her smile vanished. "Oh, no, Anna. Couldn't you

have dawdled a bit? You know how he gets with caffeine overload."

"And you know how he gets when I dawdle. You've got maybe three minutes before he asks me to get cup number four."

"I'm on my way." Tandy pushed back from her desk and stood up. "Thanks, Anna."

"No problem, sweetie."

Tandy dropped the phone in its cradle, her gaze darting around the room for something, *any*thing that would prevent the next ten minutes.

If that idiot Harry Simons had been one iota less smarmy, this predicament could have been avoided. His outright ogling of her figure had been bad enough, but certainly that was not the first time Tandy had been forced to ignore a man's unwanted attentions. They all seemed to believe her red, wavy hair was a sign she'd fulfill their wildest dreams. Heck, Mr. Beasley had probably even made that assumption at some point, as evidenced by his swift promotions landing her in a cushy corner office of Meyers, Briggs, and Stratton.

Tandy swigged caffeine and paced the office. It wasn't even Harry's condescension. His superiority, rooted in maleness, made no effort to hide the belief that a brain resting between the pierced ears of a thirty-year-old *female* graduate of Yale School of Law somehow negated its existence. That idiocy didn't even raise her blood pressure. She fingered her pearl earrings and grimaced as a hawk glided to rest on the ledge outside.

No, she would have been fine, and Christopher Beasley would not at this very moment be preparing to fire her, except for one innocent little lunch with small-minded Harry. Why, oh *why*, had she agreed to go to lunch with the lizard? Honestly, his head rivaled the shape of the geckos that ran in and out of every flower bed in Central Florida. Come to think of it, his eyes were shifty like a gecko, too. Was the single life getting to her so much that she'd date a lizard? She stopped and tapped the window ledge. Meg and Kendra were on her case to date more, but who had time to meet people after spending sixty-five hours a week at the office? She sighed. The sisters just didn't understand life in the city.

"You guys have got it easy," she said to the hawks. "Circle, eat, rest, repeat. With the occasional head bang into a window to keep us lawyers on our toes." She shook her head.

Well, it didn't matter now. Mr. Beasley awaited her presence, and it would only get worse the longer she stood here. Her heels sank into the plush pearl-colored carpet as she crossed the office, ignoring the latest sacrifice to her black thumb, a nearly dead African violet. She opened her office door and cast one last glance at what, in about ten minutes, probably would not be her office. Oh well. Maybe she could take the plant to Anna.

She picked up the violet. At least the charade of defending a slimeball who made fun of an old homeless man to make himself feel big would come to an end. And the day was still young—she could hit the beach before the lunch rush hit I-4.

Shoulders thrown back, chin up, Tandy made her way down the hallway and entered an elevator lined in the obligatory mahogany, brass, and mirrors, testimony to Christopher's desire never to rock a boat even in the decoration of his law firm's offices. She eyed her reflection and saw steel in the brown eyes staring back. Cutting Harry off at the knees in public wasn't the best financial move she could have made. How would she buy food for Cooper? Or pay his vet bills? Keeping an old basset hound with arthritic knees and hips in comfort was a pricey endeavor. Still, it had been worth it to see the shock on Harry's face when she announced *in her loud voice* the impending completion of his career. From a 9 x 9 prison cell, that cardboard box would look like heaven.

She checked her chignon, tucking in a stray curl and smoothing the rest down. Picturing Harry's smug, pudgy face behind bars did way more to calm her pulse rate than Sinatra's crooning. The elevator dinged, announcing her arrival to Christopher Beasley's penthouse lair.

Tandy took a deep breath, tightened her grip on the sagging violet, sent up a prayer of thanks that she'd picked the Ann Taylor suit today—must look sharp when being fired—and stepped across the threshold.

"He's waiting for you." Sympathy shimmered in Anna's blue eyes. The Orlando sun shining through the window made Anna's hair glow like a fresh pearl.

Tandy set the violet down on Anna's desk. "Thanks, Anna. It's been good knowing you. I wonder if you might coax this little guy back to life?"

Anna raised her eyebrows. "Tandy, how many times do I have to tell you? You're a danger to plants." She smiled and wagged her finger. "You taking them in isn't an act of kindness. You leave the greenery to us old chicks."

Tandy laughed. "Yes ma'am." She took another breath. "I guess I should go in now."

Anna sobered. "Guess so."

"Still on cup number three?"

"I just took in cup four. I doubt he's taken a sip yet, though. He's slowing down."

"Thanks for everything, Anna."

"You're welcome, honey. Take care of yourself. And you call me if you need anything, hear?"

Tandy nodded, only now realizing that losing her job also meant losing Anna's kind wisdom. She blinked hard. Crying at work would not do. She stepped to Christopher's door and knocked.

"Come." His deep voice bellowed through the door, and Tandy's pulse kicked up again. This was it. For the first time ever, Tandy Sinclair was about to be fired from a job. When she'd moved to Orlando to take this job and declare war on the city that took her childhood, Tandy never would have guessed she'd become a beach bum herself.

"Tandy, sit down, sit down." Christopher stood, gesturing to a chair and patting the telltale stripes of his Ben Silver tie. "Seems we have a little situation on our hands." The hawks circled one story below his window, the tops of their feathered backs lit by the sun.

Tandy sat down and nodded.

Christopher's padded leather chair creaked with his weight. He settled back, propped his elbows on the arms, and templed his fingers. "Harry tells me he's headed for a prison cell."

She nodded again.

"He also tells me that would be your fault."

Another nod. This must be what bobbleheads felt like.

"And he says he's ready to sue this firm for inadequate representation unless I do something about it."

She quirked an eyebrow. Score one for Harry.

"I've assured Harry that there must be some misunderstanding since you're one of the most capable attorneys this firm has seen in quite some time. So, please, Tandy, explain to me how one of our biggest clients, someone for whom you serve as lead counsel, suddenly finds himself facing jail."

Tandy tilted her head. He was giving her an out, bless him. Leave it to Christopher Beasley, king of calm and proper appearances, to smooth the choppy waters and restore her professional boat to proper order. An image of Harry's sneer popped into her mind, though, and the thought of backtracking fled like money from her wallet during a trunk sale.

She smiled and adopted her lawyer voice. "Well, Mr. Beasley, I appreciate your belief in my professional abilities, but it seems Mr. Simons has some rather extreme positions regarding personal values that led me to determine he is, in fact, guilty of the crime for which he has been accused. When I asked him directly, he admitted as much to me."

It was Christopher's turn to raise a brow. "He told you he embezzled funds from Hope House?"

Tandy nodded. "Yes, sir. I advised him I could not put him on the stand, as I would be suborning perjury, but he refused to listen. It was either let him lie to the court or remove myself from his case. I chose the latter."

Christopher swiveled his chair and stared out at the courthouse. What she wouldn't give for a hawk to barrel into the glass. Anything to break the tension. Losing this job wouldn't be the end of the world . . . just of her bank account, for the time being. She really didn't want to lose the paycheck, but Harry gave her no choice.

The man wouldn't listen to reason if someone etched it in a brick and threw it at his head.

She thought about their lunch again, seeing the hump-backed old man picking through a dumpster across the street. His coat had been threadbare, but Tandy knew too well the value of a coat, threadbare or not, on the streets. The priceless nature of every layer between skin and street. How the three bites of cheeseburger he found wrapped in its foil was enough to fill his belly for an entire day.

Harry's voice had faded into the background of restaurant chatter as Tandy's mind flew back to the seven years she spent living in a box with her mother. Before she met Marian and Jack Sinclair. Hearing the trains rumble past where they camped. Begging people for money. Searching for a dry place when it rained, for a piece of food that hadn't already been discovered by bugs. Watching her mom bob and weave as she walked, that scary light in her eyes that was both mesmerizing and terrifying because it meant Mom wouldn't make sense.

Tandy knew now her childhood had been stolen the first day her mother lit a match beneath the bowl of a pipe.

"Stupid junkie. Probably lost his job because of some drug habit." Harry's voice joined a thousand other voices that still kept her awake on too many nights. "Bet he *chooses* to live like that. Easier than getting a job and working for his money like the rest of us."

Tandy looked at Harry sitting there in his three-thousand-dollar pin-striped suit, black crocodile shoes, and platinum cuff links with the Brooks Brothers insignia. Thought about reminding him that his money came from his *father's* hard work and planning but decided against it. Harry was, after all, a huge client.

"Oh, probably not, Harry. You'd be amazed what some of the people living on the streets have been through." She sipped her water and willed her blood not to boil at the stupidity of the man before her.

He sneered and pointed a stubby finger at her. "Don't be naïve, Tandy. That man could get a job flipping burgers at McDonald's just as easy as sit out there with a cup in his hand, begging me to part with my cold hard cash that I worked very hard to get."

Silence was about as possible as finding a pair of Ferragamos in a size ten. On sale. Never gonna happen.

"Harry, how would he get a job? I doubt he owns any clothing other than what's on his back. What would he wear to a job interview? Where would he get enough sleep in one sitting to be awake for an entire shift? What address would he even put on his job application?"

"Why, Tandy, I didn't know you cared so much about our fair city's homeless degenerates." His voice, so patronizing and smooth, grated. It fought with the pockmarks on his face to portray a polished image. "I'd think, with such convictions, you would have a hard time taking my case."

"Why is that, Harry? You didn't embezzle from Hope House. Which means you didn't take money from the mouths of homeless people. Which means my awareness of the plight of the homeless works in your favor." She took a sip of her water and tried to relax.

He wagged his finger at her. "Tsk, tsk, tsk, Tandy. There goes your naiveté again."

It took her a second to catch on. "Excuse me?"

He grinned, and for the first time Tandy knew what *jowls* meant. "I think we both know what I'm saying."

"I certainly hope not. Because if you're confessing to taking money from a homeless shelter, I can't put you on the stand. I'd be suborning perjury."

Christopher cleared his throat, snapping Tandy back into the present. He swiveled around to face her. "I'm in a predicament, Tandy. Harry Simons brings a lot of money to this firm, been with us for years. That must count for something. Yet I find myself struggling with the thought of firing you since I understand the ethical dilemma you faced."

A tiny smidgen of hope blossomed in her heart.

Christopher placed his palms down on his glass-topped desk, an act of finality. "And yet I see no course of action but to terminate your employment with Meyers, Briggs, and Stratton. Anything less would cause serious repercussions in our relationship with Harry Simons."

She fought to breathe normally. Blinked to hold back tears. Her savings account was basically nonexistent, which meant she and Cooper better start looking for a big refrigerator box to call home. Or maybe finding Cooper another family to live with would be a better idea. One of the sisters could take him. Meg, or maybe Joy. Kendra would be a last resort. She was as good with pets as Tandy was with plants. Well, except for Kitty, but cats are self-sufficient.

A hawk slammed into the window, making Christopher jump and spill the coffee sitting on his desk. "Dadgum it! Anna!"

Anna came rushing in, saw the mess, and snagged a roll of paper towels from the cabinet by the door without a word.

"You've got to call somebody about these hawks, Anna. They're ruining my concentration!"

"Yes, Mr. Beasley. I'll make the call today." Anna shot Tandy a sideways glance. Tandy grinned. Seeing the unflappable Christopher Beasley in a snit was worth getting fired— almost. Anna sopped up the mess and left the room.

"Now, where were we?" He pushed paper around the desk, checking to ensure all the coffee was gone.

Tandy cleared her throat. "I think you were firing me."

Christopher stopped arranging paper and looked up at her. "Right, right. Well, I don't think we have to be that drastic. How about a leave of absence?"

Thank heaven for hawks.

"A leave of absence, sir?" Not to look a gift horse in the mouth, but, hey, it had to be asked.

"Yes. I think that will mollify our good friend Harry." Christopher nodded and patted the desktop, warming to his idea. "I'll let him know you've taken some time to think through your behavior and will come back to the firm when you've gotten some perspective. Say, two months?"

Two months? She calculated the amount in her checking account and began deducting bills. With no extracurricular spending at all, it might work. Two months to find something else or learn how to eat crow. Okay, maybe this was a good thing. There was no immediate need to take another boring job in a legal firm. Two months was a ton of time. Figuring out her professional passion should be a snap. She could almost see Meg's eyes roll at that thought.

"Thank you for that, sir."

Christopher smiled. "It's the least we can do. You've been a good employee. I just wish this mess hadn't occurred."

Poor Christopher. Conflict between an employee and a major client. He must have been up all night figuring out ways to smooth ruffled feathers.

She shrugged. "These things happen for a reason, I think." She stood up and held out her hand. Christopher took it with his own limp one and made a motion that might optimistically be called a handshake.

"Good luck, Tandy. We'll see you back here in two months."

"Thank you." She turned on one Ferragamo heel and walked out of Christopher Beasley's office. Eight weeks of nothingness spread out before her like a gift. There had to be a way to make money off of this.

She tapped her chin and watched the lights over the elevator. Maybe some tourist would want her apartment for a couple of weeks. Tourists would pay just about anything for somewhere to stay during season. A couple thousand bucks, easy.

But if someone were to stay in her apartment, where could she go? The whisper of her heart tickled Tandy's brain. Stars Hill, Tennessee's rolling countryside, Daddy's smile, Momma's painted roses, the sisters' scrapbooks . . .

The ding of the elevator dispelled her mind's image but not the idea. Stars Hill. Well, it *had* been a while since she'd been back. Three years, if memory served. And with Daddy and the sisters around, there wouldn't be any need to spend money on restaurants. Though what she'd save might be spent on scrapbook stuff. It was one thing to scrap alone and quite another to sit around Momma's old scrapping table with the girls.

Tandy exited the elevator and smiled. If she left right now, she'd be home in Stars Hill by morning.

She walked into her office, snagged her briefcase, and whipped out a tiny cell phone on the way back to the elevator.

"Hello?"

"Meg?"

"Hey, T, what's up in the big city?"

Tandy laughed. "Well, not me. I've got eight weeks of sudden vacation."

"What? What happened?"

"I'll tell you all about it when I get there."

Meg's squeal pierced Tandy's ears, and she jerked the phone away from her head. "You're coming home? To Stars Hill? Yes!! When will you be here? Wait, what happened? Did you get fired? Did something happen at work?" Tandy could hear Meg's three kids squealing now in the background. They must have caught on to their mom's excitement.

"Seriously, I'll tell you when I get there. Call Kendra and Joy. Breakfast at Joy's, nine a.m."

"You've got it, sister. James, get down off that table!" Tandy could just picture Meg's eldest. He must have grown a foot by now. "I'm telling you that child will climb on anything," Meg said.

"Go keep your kids from tearing down the house. I've got to get home, get all my scrapping stuff packed, call the rental company to let some crazy tourist in my place for a couple of weeks, and get on the highway."

"*On the road again . . .*" Meg's voice blared through the phone.

"Sheesh, Sis, are you ever going to stop with the songs?"

"Not as long as there's a breath in me." Tandy heard scuffling. "James, put your sister *down*! I am not kidding with you, mister!"

Tandy chuckled. "See you in the morning."

"Okay. Be careful and buckle up."

"You've got it."

Tandy snapped the phone closed and walked through the parking deck toward her new silver BMW 323. Man was this car going to stand out in sleepy little Stars Hill.

Two

It's okay, boy," Tandy comforted Cooper as he whined from the backseat. "I'm sure an exit will be coming up soon." She sighed as her headlights shone on a beautiful green sign declaring Valdosta, Georgia's exit two miles ahead. Cooper whined again.

"Seriously, Coop, we're almost there." Leave it to her to pick the only dog in the universe with a bladder the size of a kidney bean. She punched the radio dial, cutting Terry Gross off in mid-sentence. No worries—the Middle East would still be falling apart when Cooper finished his business. If she made it to the exit in time.

She tapped a little harder on the gas.

"Just think, Coop—" she spoke over whining that was increasing not only in volume but also in pitch—"in seven more hours you'll be running all over the place and making sure Kitty knows exactly who's boss." Cooper growled at the mention of his archnemesis.

Tandy chuckled as she swerved onto the off-ramp. "Now don't get any ideas, mister. We will have no repeats of our last visit to Stars Hill. Got it?" She swung into a parking space at the closest gas station and jumped out of the car, barely managing to snap Cooper's leash on before he pulled her across the parking lot to the nearest patch of green.

As she positioned herself upwind, Tandy continued laying down the law. "I'm not kidding with you. If you hurt Kitty again, Kendra won't let you come over anymore. And then who will make you weird homemade doggie treats?" Cooper finished his task and woofed at her. "Good, so we're clear on this?"

He woofed again and she nodded, satisfied that had been a sound of agreement rather than argument. They crossed the grass, heading back toward the car when the first notes of Kelly Clarkson's "Miss Independent" chorus sounded from her cell phone. She fished around in her pocket and pulled out the phone, making a mental note to change the ringtone before Daddy heard it and launched into a sermon about depending only on God.

"Hello?"

"So I have to hear from Meg that you're coming home? Why does she get to know everything first?"

"Hi, Kendra. And how are you this lovely evening?" She opened the car door and Cooper climbed in.

"Hi, yourself. Now why do I have to hear from Meg that you're coming home?" The love in Kendra's voice contradicted her mocking, stern tone. Tandy pictured Kendra's beautiful smile—the one that made heads turn and stopped men in their tracks—as she slid into her own seat.

"You have to hear it from Meg because I didn't tell Joy yet." She laughed as Kendra's melodic sounds of happiness crossed the phone lines.

"Yeah, whatever, like you'd tell the baby anything."

"Are you still calling her that to her face?"

"Every chance I get. Somebody's got to keep her off that pedestal she's so intent on inhabiting."

"You know as well as I do that Daddy put her up on that pedestal, and it'll take a strong man to either keep her there or knock her off."

"Don't I know it. Poor Scott's got his work cut out for him. I told him that at the wedding. So, spill. What's chasing you out of the Sunshine State?"

"Hang on, I've gotta shift." She put the phone on her lap and navigated her way back onto the interstate. "Now, what makes you think I'm running?"

"Joy's the baby. Meg's the steady one. You're the runner. Always have been. Now tell me what spooked you."

"Nothing spooked me." She fought the desire to be defensive. That would only confirm Kendra's accusation.

"Mm-hmm. You just up and decided it was a good time to drive eleven hours north and stop in at the happening town of Stars Hill. Last I checked, I still had a working brain between my two ears."

"Silly me, I'd have thought you transferred it to a canvas by now."

"I'm on to sculptures."

"What?"

"I put down the brushes and picked up the clay. I've been sculpting for a little while in between writing gigs."

"Since when?"

"Since the phone call I got from you three weeks ago."

"Sorry. You know I call as often as I can."

"More like often as you remember to, but don't sweat it. I know you're busy. If I had something important to say, I'd call you. But, since I live in Stars Hill and you live in the sunniest place in the country, I just wait for Big City Sister to call me."

Tandy laughed. "Yeah, well, Big City Sister needs a break."

"Ah, we finally get to it. The reason for the run."

"I'm not running, Kendra."

"Okay, how about you tell me what you're *not* running from, and we just call it a fast trot?"

Tandy sighed. Kendra was like a dog with a bone. No stopping her once she'd dug her teeth in. "I sort of had an altercation with a client."

"I see you've lapsed into lawyer-speak. Details, girl. I need details. Are we talking send-a-gift-certificate-and-a-nice-box-of-Godiva altercation or contemplate-my-future-in-another-country altercation?"

"Somewhere in between."

"Closer to Godiva or relocation?"

"Oh, probably right there in the middle."

"My patience for word pictures is wearing thin. I've got clay drying in front of me, and you're stalling, which means you've got something to stall about. What's up?"

Tandy told her the whole story—from Harry's idiocy and guilt to Christopher's idea of a vacation.

"I guess I wouldn't have done much different," Kendra said when Tandy was finished. "Well, that's not true. We all know I'd have taken that man down a peg or two, and he might still be talking in a falsetto today."

"Then I wish you'd been there."

"Me, too. So, that still doesn't explain why you're coming to Stars Hill. Or have you had too much of the beach to just go wait this thing out while the waves roll in and the seagulls soar overhead?"

"I think . . . I just wanted some home time, you know?" Silence hummed over the phone line as Tandy struggled to come up with the words, or admit what was already in her mind. "Kendra, do you ever wonder if maybe you somehow got off course?"

"Off course of what?"

"Life."

"There's a course? Shoot, nobody told me there was a course."

"I'm serious, Kendra."

"I know you are, honey, but I don't have much of an answer for you. Kitty and I pretty much take it day by day."

"Speaking of which, I have duly informed Cooper not to mess with Kitty."

"You tell that mangy mutt he won't be getting any more chicken-flavored biscuits from me if he so much as looks *sideways* at Her Highness."

"He is not a mangy mutt. He's purebred basset hound."

"Mm-hmm. Like I said."

"Just because your brain's wires are crossed to make you think cats are better than dogs doesn't mean my Cooper isn't a lovely specimen of canine perfection."

"Do you think lightning can strike through a cell phone?"

"Ha ha, very funny. I'm hanging up now."

"You buckled up?"

"As always."

"See you in the morning."

"You bet. Go warn Kitty."

"Already on it."

Tandy snapped the phone shut and hit the volume

button on the steering wheel in time to hear Terry Gross giving the closing credits for *Fresh Air*. She hit the scan button and listened as snatches of Air Supply followed Garth Brooks, who came before Beethoven. Radio—such a marvelous invention.

Six and a half hours to Stars Hill, Tennessee. Wonder if Meg told Daddy she was coming? Probably. Knowing Meg, there'd be a welcome banner stretched across Lindell Street and a "welcome home" sign in every business window. She pictured James working on it right now, paper stretched out across Meg's huge kitchen. Joy had probably planned an extensive breakfast complete with eggs Benedict, omelets, Belgian waffles, French toast, fresh coffee, and mixed juices, the news of which was likely already circulating through town. Residents were keeping phone lines hot over what Suzanne said Pamela said Ms. McMurty saw Joy buy at the grocery store. Petra, Suzanne's neighbor and Meg's friend, would end up calling Meg to get all the details and pass the info on down the line right back to Ms. McMurty.

If Stars Hill could do anything, it was keep track of its people.

Tandy shifted in her seat. There's something she hadn't missed. Everyone knowing her business. As soon as that sign went up across Lindell, folks would probably start telling stories of how she'd failed in the city and was coming home with her tail between her legs. Of how disappointed their momma would be if she were alive to see Tandy come home in defeat. Others would chime in with ruminations of a sickness in the family that brought her running back. They'd all have a story. Stars Hill loved stories. They were a supportive bunch if the situation warranted and they knew the facts, but that meant telling the facts.

Tandy shook her head. They'd have to make up stories because this was just a break. She'd stay for two weeks, let Daddy know she was all right, put some flowers on Momma's grave, scrapbook with her sisters, and be back in Florida in no time, sunning herself on a beach with a Diet Mello Yello in one hand and a thick, fresh novel in the other.

Three hours later Kelly Clarkson sang out again from the phone, and Tandy made another mental note to change that ring.

"Hello?"

"How far out are you?"

"Is no one in this family capable of saying hello first?"

"Hello, my dear darling sister. How far out are you?" Joy's lilting voice was soft, even over her cell phone, which was always turned to the loudest volume.

Tandy rolled her eyes. "Hello, Joy. And how are you tonight?"

"I'm excellent. A blonde is now a redhead, a brunette is now a blonde, and a truly atrocious redhead is now a very natural-looking white. I'm in the midst of choosing recipes for tomorrow and cannot decide between two dishes, one of which requires overnight baking. Thus the reason for my call. Now, how far out are you?"

"An atrocious redhead? Do tell."

"I can only assume by your refusal to answer my question that you've arrived by now. Which is just like Meg to wait until the very last minute and call me to whip up breakfast for the entire—"

"No, I'm not there yet." Tandy 'fessed up before Joy's sense of decorum was offended. "Tell me about the redhead, and I'll tell you where I am."

"But I called *you.*"

"So?"

"So, the one who places the call drives the conversation. Which means I get my question answered first."

"I'm older."

Joy sighed. "Oh, please, not the baby stuff again. I'm twenty-eight years old. At what point will you three learn I'm not a baby?"

"When you quit telling us you're not the baby. The redhead?"

Joy's sigh was louder this time. "She was seventy years old and should have said good-bye to the red a decade ago. No, that's wrong. Someone should have said 'Red is not your color' a decade ago, or whenever she first selected it, which I'm guessing could be anywhere from ten to a thousand years ago."

"That bad?"

"Think stop sign."

"Oh, bad."

"Abysmal. Do you have any idea what chemicals have to be applied to result in white rather than pink? I spent the entire session concerned she would leave my chair resembling a cloud of cotton candy rather than Angel Soft."

Tandy laughed. "I trust the Genius Hairdresser produced a snowy result."

"She was pleased."

"Since she seems to have been pleased with resembling a traffic sign for a decade, I'm not sure her approval constitutes a job well done."

"There wasn't a speck of pink or red anywhere on her head when she left my chair, and you know it."

Tandy grinned as Joy's usual calm gave way to a touch of indignance. "Oh, I know it. You're the best colorist

Stars Hill has ever seen. A whiz with chemicals. A magician with mixes. A—"

"All right, I'm amazing. Where are you?"

"I'm going through Atlanta right now."

"Oh, heavens. How's the traffic?"

"Atlantian."

"And you're talking on a cell phone? Do you have a death wish?"

"No, just a strong need to get this drive over with."

"Why don't you stop for the night? It's eight o'clock. You're not going to get here until midnight as it is."

"Worried I won't see Meg's sign?"

"How did you know about the sign?"

"Please, it's Meg."

Joy laughed. "True, very true. To tell the truth, we talked her out of it."

"There's no sign stretched across Lindell? Come on! How will I know I'm welcome at home if there's no sign?"

"By consuming a full breakfast with all the trimmings."

"Oooh, are you making your waffles?"

"I'm making a welcome-home breakfast, and that's all the information I'll share."

"Fine, then. I'll amuse myself for the next three hours with visions of your cooking."

"You do that. I'll call Meg and tell her to put the sign up."

"Awww, you're the best little sister a girl could ever have."

"One of these days I just know you'll drop the 'little' part."

"Hey, how am I going to see the sign if I don't get there until midnight?"

"Oh yes, you missed the Street Light Debate." Humor laced Joy's tone.

"The what?"

"Tanner called a town meeting and spent forty-five minutes explaining how historical streetlights would bring millions of dollars in tourism revenue to Stars Hill."

"Oh, how sad I wasn't there for Tanner and his oratorical skills."

"I can hear the sorrow in your voice. Anyway, Lindell is now lined with what I must admit are quite brilliant streetlights."

"Streetlights? In Stars Hill? But how will we communicate to the world that everyone should be home with their families by six p.m. unless the entire downtown goes dark?"

"We're still rolling up the streets."

"Ah, good idea."

"See you when you get here, Sister Dear. Drive safe."

"Will do." Tandy slapped shut the phone and tossed it into the passenger seat as Cooper whined from the backseat.

"I hear you, buddy. We'll stop as soon as we get on the other side of the city." Cooper's grateful woof made her smile.

Only three and a half more hours and she'd be in Stars Hill.

Three

Pulling into Stars Hill always felt like going back in time. The signs on the businesses around town central were hand-painted, visible from the glow of Tanner's new streetlights. Tandy pulled into a parking space and got out of the car, pulling Cooper out by his leash.

Even the air smelled different here. Cleaner. Fresher, somehow.

She tilted her head back and took in the thousands of stars in the sky, visible here, where Orlando's lights didn't obscure the view. Tulips and irises lining the entrance and steps of the library swayed in the gentle night breeze. Cooper tugged her over to the grass, and she went, noting that Emma's Attic had become Emmy's Attic but Fawcett's Fixtures was still in its usual place. The streetlights reflected off shiny silver address plates and brass fixtures in the store window, and Tandy left the library yard to cross the street and take a look. Something from Sara had expanded into the store next door to Fawcett's. Tandy leaned into the window, cupping her hands around the glass to see the jewelry, purses, scarves, and baubles Sara Sykes kept in stock. You knew you were loved if someone bought you Something from Sara.

She strolled on down the sidewalk, letting the feeling of home settle back into her bones as Cooper's nails clicked on the worn concrete. She came to the point where Oxford Street intersected Lindell and looked up to see a diner that hadn't been there before. A red sign hung above the door under a navy-striped awning, and *Clay's* was painted in matching navy letters.

Tandy's stomach flipped, and she sucked in her breath. It wasn't Clay Kelner—he was probably in prison or some foreign jungle by now—but the name was enough to conjure visions of long, loopy drives on back country roads and whispered promises in the back of Clay's dad's old blue Chevy truck. They'd lain together until dawn, making wishes on stars and dreaming in the moonlight. Daddy just about popped an artery when she came in the door at 6:00 a.m., but Tandy hadn't cared. That was the summer they lost Momma, and the only person in the world who could make Tandy believe everything would be all right someday was Clay Kelner.

The sign creaked as a breeze hit it, bringing Tandy back to the dark street in downtown Stars Hill. Enough of this. Trips down memory lane didn't get goals met or dreams realized. She took a deep breath and tried to calm down. Just the thought of Clay Kelner was enough to make the blood zing through her veins again, even if he had been wrong about everything being all right.

Cooper pulled against the leash as Tandy hustled them back across Lindell to the Beamer sitting all by itself. By now the whole town probably knew she was home.

She slipped in and buckled her seat belt, firmly pushing thoughts of Clay to the back of her mind. There were reasons she didn't live in Stars Hill anymore. She pulled out her cell phone and changed the ring tone to "When the Roll is Called Up Yonder." That'd make Daddy happy.

Slipping the phone back into its cradle, she backed the car out of its space and headed down Lindell to Sunnywood Lane. As always it dead-ended at Mockingbird Drive. Tandy turned right, keeping an eye out for deer caught in the mesmerizing lights of her car. As she guided the car left onto Old Crockett Road, she rolled down the window and inhaled the country scent of fresh-turned dirt. Somebody must be planting corn. April in Tennessee fields was all about getting the seeds in the ground.

White fence line sprang up on her right, and Tandy drew in her breath. Home was at the end of that fence line, but Momma wouldn't be waiting in the kitchen. Tandy's heart twisted at the thought. No matter how many years passed, the longing for Momma to be at home cooking in her kitchen, full of assurances that all was right with the world as she added a dash of salt or sugar to a mix, or upstairs scrapbooking, turning a picture this way and that to get the layout perfect, never really went away.

At a break in the fence, a wooden gate painted black with a large white *S* in the center greeted her. She grinned at the sign hung just below and to the right of the *S* reading "Welcome Home, Tandy."

Much better than Lindell Street.

Rolling down her window, she keyed in the gate code at the lock box and watched the big wooden panels swing open. Daddy waited down that winding gravel path. Daddy and a lifetime of memories.

She kept the car in second gear the whole way down the

drive, steeling herself. Cooper, ever tuned to her moods, whined and leaned in from the backseat to nuzzle her elbow. "It's okay, boy. We're fine. Just wishing for something we can't have."

She parked the car and popped the trunk. Cooper bounded out the door and up onto the porch as Daddy came out the front door.

"Well, there's my girl! I'd just about decided those Atlanta folk got you!" He was wearing the sea-green cotton shirt she'd given him for Christmas last year. It matched his eyes, which she noted hadn't lost their sparkle. Creases lined his face from squinting against the sun as he planted acres and acres of corn, soybeans, and winter wheat year after year. He grabbed her up in a bear hug, and she was crushed against his big chest. *Daddy.*

"Hey, Daddy." She squeezed him back. "How's the planting going?"

"Corn's in the soil, but we're still plowing seeds of the Spirit every chance we get."

"So Grace Christian hasn't put you out to pasture yet?"

"Honey girl, it'd take a bigger congregation than Grace Christian's got to put me out of the pastorate."

"Meg told me you were having a little trouble." She walked around to the trunk and pulled out her bags.

Daddy followed her and picked them up, then led her back to the porch. "Did she now?" The third and fourth step creaked, as always, reminding Tandy of the nights she'd forgotten to skip them and been caught sneaking back in. Amazing how she'd always been able to get out but rarely back in. "Sounds like she might have forgotten to mention the congregation is growing and the trouble lies at someone else's door. It just spills on down the hallway to mine every now and again."

"Ah, the new music minister. What's his name again?"

They walked inside the house, and Tandy fought the urge to glance into the kitchen as Cooper ran ahead of them up the stairs. Daddy went straight on through a living room whose couch was covered in a quilt Momma made the last year of her life. Its country charm somehow blended perfectly with the swirls of red and gold in the Persian rug that covered walnut hardwood. Daddy's leather recliner stood sentinel by the couch, as always, and Momma's smaller version was still tucked away in the corner beneath a reading light.

Tandy saw it all in a glance as they made their own way to the stairs.

"Kevin Summers. He's from over in Hohenwald."

"Let me guess. He wants to sing something that was written after 1960, contains a melody, and may actually cause someone to think of worshipping Jesus as they sing."

"Close. He mixes new stuff with the old."

They turned into her old bedroom, and Daddy hefted her bags onto the trunk at the base of her bed. Another quilt stitched by Momma, this one with Dutch girl dolls wearing dresses of pink and green, covered a queen-size bed. Tandy walked over and ran her fingers across the fabric worn soft from years of use. Cooper jumped up on the low chair in the corner, circled a few times, then settled down.

"Do you ever think of her, Daddy?"

"Every hour of every day." He set down the suitcases and came over to hug her.

Tandy hugged him back, wishing Momma had been there to see her succeed in the city. Momma always knew Tandy could make it on her own. She'd said so tons of times. The first day Tandy walked into the Bank of America building in downtown Orlando, she'd taken the first steps to fulfilling Momma's dreams for her.

Daddy stepped back and sniffed. "Well, let's get you unpacked. The girls'll probably be here soon since word's already all over town that you're here."

"Too late. There was a sign."

Daddy grinned. "On Lindell?"

"Thankfully, no. They stretched it across the front gate."

His chuckle was deep and low, and she knew if her head was still on his chest she'd have felt the vibration down to her toes. "Been too long since you've been home, honey girl."

"Yes sir, I think you may be right. But the sisters aren't coming over tonight. I talked to Joy. She's having one of her breakfasts in the morning."

"Really? Well, I'll make sure not to consume another thing before the morning then. Want me to give Cooper-Scooper there a quick turn around the yard before bed?"

Cooper lifted his massive head as if he knew he was being discussed.

"That'd be great. I think I'd fall asleep on the front porch if I had to do it."

Daddy walked over and scratched Cooper between the ears. "Come on, buddy. Let's go do your business before your momma here conks out on us." He and Cooper, tail wagging, left the room.

She took a deep breath. Orlando, with its tall buildings and beautifully coiffed, nipped, and tucked people, seemed a world away from this room full of country honesty and wisdom. This was a good decision, hanging out with Daddy and the sisters for a few days while she regrouped. Coming home more often was going to be a priority from now on.

Her gaze traveled to a four-drawer chest by the adjacent bathroom door. Roses and irises covered the chest. Irises because they were the Tennessee state flower. Roses because the only way Momma said she could count on them to be around from season to season was to paint them on a surface that wasn't moving. An image flashed in her mind of Momma out in the front yard, kneeling beside this very dresser, paintbrush in hand, face screwed up in concentration.

"Why don't you just buy a new chest?" Tandy asked.

"Because I don't need a new chest," came Momma's eversensible reply.

"Sure looks like it."

Momma sat back on her heels and studied her work. "You might be right about that."

Ashamed for making Momma question her talents when she'd done nothing but be kind to Tandy since they met, Tandy burst forth with, "No, I meant if this one was all right you wouldn't have to be painting it. It'd be just fine the way it is."

Momma cocked her head and turned her studied gaze from the furniture to Tandy. "Well, the inner workings of this chest function just beautifully. The drawers open and close without any effort, and all the drawer handles are still firmly attached. But this chest has seen more than a few years of use, and it's got some scratches here and there. Even a dent in the wood where one of your sisters threw something or other during a tantrum." She pointed out the dent with her finger.

"So I thought about it, and I decided I like knowing those

scratches and dents are there. Means this piece has some history, some life, to it. So I don't think I'll get rid of it. No, I'll just help it look a little better so everyone else can see the beauty I see."

Tandy focused back in on the present-day dresser, realizing now Momma had been talking about more than refinishing furniture. All of the sisters had come to Daddy and Momma with cracks and dents. Their new parents polished them up and sent them out into the world.

She walked over to the dresser and ran her fingers across it as she'd done with the quilt before.

Welcome home.

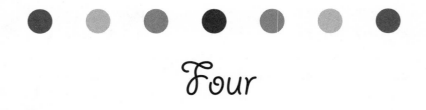

Four

Sunlight poured through the window and onto Tandy's face, bringing her out of a dream she shouldn't be having. It must have been that diner that reminded her of Clay. She hadn't dreamt of him since her first week in Orlando. It was only the diner and being back home that made her do so now.

She sat up in bed and looked around the room again. Cooper was still asleep, curled into a ball on the chair in the corner. Or as much of a ball as sixty pounds of basset hound could make, anyway. Stretching lazily, the knots in her shoulders that had built during the long hours of driving made themselves known. Wonder if Stars Hill had a massage therapist now?

She slid out of bed and headed for the shower. Maybe the hot water would wash away the cobwebs in her brain. "When the Roll Is Called Up Yonder" began to play and she hesitated. Had she accidentally picked up someone else's cell phone at a rest area? Walking back into the bedroom, she remembered changing her ring tone last night just in time to snatch the phone up before it went to voice mail.

"Hello?"

"Oh, wonderful, you're up." Joy's voice, as always, was too kind and chipper for morning.

"That's the rumor." She made her way to the bathroom.

"Breakfast will be served within an hour. Think you can be here in that time frame?"

"If the knots in my neck untie themselves long enough to let me have a shower then, yeah, I'll be there in an hour."

"Should I call Taylor for you?"

"Who's Taylor?"

"He's the amazing masseur I told you about over a year ago. The man has magical hands, Tandy. I had knots on top of knots in my neck before I went to see him."

"What in the world did *you* have to be so stressed about?" She turned on the shower, closing the curtain to let the space heat up.

"Excuse me, Big City Sister, but maintaining crowns of glory in the perfect shade and style isn't without its stresses."

"Oh, I'm sure. We can't all be blessed with shining ebony hair and a porcelain complexion like *some* sisters I know. So Taylor's a godsend, huh?"

"Like you wouldn't believe. Shall I call him and get you an appointment?"

"I'd love you forever."

"You're going to love me forever anyway, but this will ensure your undying gratitude, so I'll make the call. Could you get something from Mother's studio before you come over?"

Tandy's heart seized. She hadn't planned on going into Momma's scrapbooking studio so soon. "I guess. What do you need?"

"I left my *Simple Scrapbooks* magazine over there when we were scrapping last week, and I'm dying to finish it. I think there's a layout in there that would be perfect for pictures of the Iris Festival. I left it on the table."

"Sure, I'll get it."

"Wonderful, thanks. See you in an hour!"

"Bye." Tandy flipped the phone closed and tossed it through the bathroom door and onto the bed. The prospect of a breakfast at Joy's *and* magical hands being scheduled for her at this very moment made Tandy smile despite her dread. It was good to be home for a while. Maybe she and the sisters could spend some time scrapping together, just like they did when Momma was around.

Twenty-five minutes later Tandy slid her feet into black slides and snapped a leash on the now-awake Cooper. The taste of Joy's homemade waffles, piled high with cream and strawberries she'd almost certainly picked over at Flippen's Orchard, was enough to make even the most confirmed night owl look forward to a morning. She tugged Cooper off the chair and all but skipped down the stairs. Daddy was sitting in his recliner when she bounced into the living room.

"Hey, Daddy, can you give Coop a quick walk? I've got to grab something out of Momma's studio for Joy, and then we can head on over there for breakfast. You're coming to breakfast, right?"

He put down his newspaper. "Of course I'm coming. You think I'd miss a breakfast by Joy?"

She chuckled. "I doubt it." She handed him the leash and bounded back up the steps. Walking to the end of the hallway, she opened a door and climbed another set of steps that led to the finished attic. They had all grumbled at one time or another about the long climb, but Momma said it showed their commitment to scrapping if they were willing to exert all that energy just to get to the studio.

She snapped on the light via a switch at the top of the stairs, and the sight of the studio took her breath. A huge square oak table still sat in the middle, the perfect height for standing and working. Daddy and Momma built that table together, taking nearly a month to make it. Spotlights that she'd helped Daddy hang shone down on the workspace and on the Peg-Board that ran along one wall. Embellishments of every size and shape hung from silver hooks. Four paper stands were full of 12 x 12 and 8½ x 11 paper. Two large metal storage cabinets on either side of the studio held adhesive and tools.

Tandy's cramped scrapping space back in Orlando could never compare to this.

Small, circular windows let in the glorious sunshine, and dust particles danced in its light. How many hours had been spent around that table cutting, gluing, distressing, inking, talking, and arguing? Any event of significance—from football games to homecoming week, from beauty pageants to parades—was scrapbooked right here. Even mundane, everyday existence on the farm was preserved for generations to come. A huge ear of corn that Daddy grew. One of the elm trees blazing with fall color. The four sisters jumping in a monstrous pile of leaves. It didn't take much for Momma to break out her camera.

Tandy walked over to the table, running a finger along its grain. Her throat cramped with longing for Momma, and she ground her teeth. Scrapping in this room, breathing in Momma's scent and the memories they made, both hurt and pleased her. Scrapping in Orlando was dry and functional, a way to capture the continuation of her life. She stopped, staring at the wall as realization struck.

She didn't scrap there the way she did here.

Dust motes danced along in the light, falling with an ease and grace that ignored the tumult in Tandy's mind. She breathed deep and watched them fall.

Shaking her head, Tandy noticed the magazine Joy had mentioned laying on top of the table. She picked it up and, not quite sure of the thoughts swirling in her mind, headed back down the stairs.

"Hey, Daddy!" She made her way out into the sunshine. Tandy lifted her face to the sky and, arms outstretched, twirled in a circle just as she'd done as a child. Cooper barked at her strange behavior and began running in circles.

"You're gonna make the dog sick." Daddy nodded at Cooper. "You look just like you did the day we brought you home from second grade."

"I remember that day. I was so happy that I'd *never* have to go back to school."

Daddy chuckled. "And I was stupefied trying to figure out how I'd make you go back."

"Well, you'd said if I didn't like it I didn't have to go back, and I took you at your word."

"Yes, but I never thought you'd hate it so much you would hold me to that. I thought you'd go, make some friends, and be excited about it."

"Please." She stopped and looked at him. "Those kids had been in school together for two years. They'd decided who was who and what was what, and they didn't need some homeless Florida kid coming in and messing things up."

"I suppose you're right about that. But it all worked out, right?"

"Hmm, I guess it did." She walked toward the car. "But I'll bet dollars to doughnuts no parent of any child in that class would have guessed I'd end up an attorney in a high-rise in Orlando." She slid into the leather seat of her Beamer and watched as Daddy let Cooper into the back, then folded himself into the passenger seat.

"Now don't be judging people you haven't seen for a while, Tandy. Some of those parents were nice to you."

"And others saw me for what I was: the daughter of a druggie homeless woman who couldn't care enough about herself or her child to find shelter and food."

Daddy's strong hand covered her own on the gearshift. "They saw a hurting child whom we loved. The smart ones, the ones who mattered. That's what they saw."

She harrumphed. Enough with all this emotion. "Water under the bridge, Daddy." The car slid a little as she turned and raced down the gravel drive. "So tell me what's going on in Stars Hill."

"Well, we got some streetlights, but you probably saw those last night."

"Yeah, I heard Tanner held court for forty-five minutes."

"Seemed more like forty-five hours. By the time he finished, we were all derelict townsfolk who should have had the decency to raise streetlights decades ago."

She laughed. "What else?"

"Emma finally passed her shop on down to Emmy."

"Saw that, too." She saw his raised eyebrows and shrugged. "I may have stopped in town on the way in just to get a feel for the place again."

"Ahh, I see. Did you notice anything else?"

No way was she mentioning Clay's Diner. On the off chance—very, very off chance—that it was *the* Clay, that bit of information had no business floating around in her heart or her brain.

"Nope, that's about it."

Daddy let out a breath he'd been holding. "Good. Good. Well, I guess there's nothing much new to report."

Did Daddy still have a thing against Clay, even after all these years? "Nice to know y'all kept things pretty much the same for me."

"We're here to serve."

"Very funny."

"I guess it's news that the Iris Festival is in two weeks."

"Y'all are still having the Iris Festival?" Visions of floats full of local beauty-pageant royalty, the fat mayor, Tanner, in all his glory, and the high-school marching band played through her mind. Oh, and funnel cake. Lots and lots of funnel cake.

"Yep! This year will be the fiftieth Iris Festival parade in honor of our lovely state flower. You going to be around long enough to enjoy the festivities?"

"More than likely. We'll see how it goes."

"You know you don't want to miss the funnel cake."

This man knew her too well. She grinned. "I'll see if I can work it out so I can stay for the parade."

"I'm sure your sisters would love that."

"Though my waistline might hate me for it."

"Your waistline is a bit too much on the lean side as it is. Do they not have food down in Florida?"

"Of course we do. We keep it in tiny one-ounce jars and only consume a full jar in a twenty-four-hour period. Keeps our bodies fit for bikinis."

"So long as you're eating something, I guess that's all that matters."

"Exactly. Why, I'll probably be full after just one bite of Joy's waffles."

"No room for muffins?"

"I doubt it."

"Hmm. More for me, I suppose."

"I guess I should have grabbed my hollow leg before we left the house."

"Can't believe you didn't have the foresight to do such."

"Me, either." She succumbed to a fit of giggles, and Daddy joined in the laughter. "Oh, Daddy, I've missed talking to you."

"Me, too, honey girl. Me, too."

"I've just been so busy with work and everything that I haven't had time to call like I mean to."

He patted her knee. "I'd like to say it's okay, but I'd be lying and we both know it. I miss you, too. Are you sure you're happy down there in the big city?"

"Aside from the one-ounce rationings, yeah, everything's going well." She wondered at the lack of truth in her words. Then again, everything *was* going well. This was a small hiccup in an otherwise perfect career path. Momma would be proud of all Tandy had accomplished.

"So this is just a visit home?"

"Of course."

"Tandy."

"Oh, good grief. What did Meg say to you?"

"Meg didn't say anything. She didn't have to. You coming home in the middle of the night with barely any notice spoke volumes. What's going on? Can I help? Are you in some sort of trouble?"

"No, not really." Heaving a sigh, she told him what had happened back in Orlando, omitting Harry's name, of course. "I thought I'd come up here and spend some time thinking, you know? Just a couple of weeks to clear my head and refocus on my job."

He nodded. "Okay, I'll buy that for now. But I think you need to be thinking harder about whether you're in the right job before you focus on it."

"What's that supposed to mean?"

They pulled into the creatively landscaped entrance of Joy's subdivision, Sugar Valley. "I'm not sure, Tandy. You've been so distant since you moved down to Florida, and I worry about you, is all. You know me. I want you home in Stars Hill."

"Well, I can only sue Tanner on behalf of the townsfolk so many times before I'd be out of business, Daddy." She swung the Beamer into Joy's driveway. A stunning three-story home rose before them, its blonde bricks glowing in the morning sun like a dream, black shutters firmly anchoring it to reality. Gumdrop bushes rose from the earth as if sheltering the house from the wind, and a crepe myrtle's long arms of just-blooming pink flowers swayed gently in the breeze. Tandy followed the circle of the driveway, coming to a stop in front of the sweeping staircase that led to a massive mahogany front door. She put the car in park and turned to Daddy.

"I understand, Daddy, I do. But you know I've always dreamed of returning to the city, of making a name for myself there. Momma and I talked about it all the time."

"I know." He sighed. "I guess I want to make sure you're not in Orlando because you think that's where your mother would want you to be."

"That's ridiculous, Daddy. I'm there because it's my dream to succeed there."

He held up his hands. "All right, all right. Just ignore the ramblings of an old man then."

"You're not an old man."

"No, I'm a *hungry* man, and there are waffles in there—" he jerked his thumb over his shoulder and toward the front door—"like you *can't* get in the city."

"You're right. Let's go." She opened her door and heard the playful splashing of water over rocks coming from a fountain situated in the center of the circle drive. Pulling Cooper from the backseat, she took in the surroundings, appreciating anew Joy's lovely home.

"You're here!" Tandy turned to see Kendra flying down the steps, her gold-and-black-striped caftan billowing out behind, along with a mane of dark-brown spiral curls. Her caramel-colored skin glowed with a health that can only be reached by consuming grains and figs and anything from a whole foods market. They met at the middle landing, and Kendra swept Tandy up into a perfumed embrace. "I can't believe you're here!" Kendra's gold bangle bracelets clinked as she stepped back and held Tandy at arm's length.

"In the flesh."

"Well bring that flesh on inside. Joy's made a feast to make Martha Stewart salivate." They turned to walk up the rest of the steps. "Hey, Daddy," Kendra tossed over her shoulder.

"Hey yourself, kiddo. Why don't I get hugs like that when *I* come over?"

"'Cause I see you nearly every day. Tandy here I only see once in a blue moon."

Tandy ignored the dig and chose to feel special instead.

They walked through the front door and into a marble-floored entryway. A grand staircase rose to the right, begging for comparisons to the grand homes Sherman razed on his trek through Georgia. Raising her gaze, Tandy saw light reflecting off the hundreds of glass teardrops suspended from a black iron chandelier. Small statues and busts graced the built-in nooks around the foyer.

Kendra pulled her along through a hallway in which she could have fit her entire apartment and on whose walls were hung Jack Vettriano originals. Tandy remembered Joy loved the artist because he had risen from such humble beginnings to become the sought-after painter he was today. Cooper's nails clicked on the hardwood floor as he followed them on to the back of the house and the kitchen.

Meg looked up from her place on a stool at the kitchen island when they entered. "You're here!" She flew around the island and gripped Tandy in a hug. "I thought Kendra was hearing things again. I mean, who can hear a car on the driveway all the way back here?" She tucked a long, blonde lock of hair behind her ear.

"I have skills," Kendra said.

"Skills which seemed to have failed you the first five times you were sure they'd driven up." Joy came from the sink to give Tandy a hug as well.

"I'm so glad you're home," Joy said in that graceful, soft voice that had served to break up more than one fight among the sisters over the years. Light from another wrought-iron chandelier reflected off of Joy's shining hair. Her skin, no doubt a genetic gift from her birth mother in China, was flawless. Her blue eyes, so rare for those of Asian descent and possibly the reason her mother abandoned her, sparkled with restrained energy.

"Me, too. And thanks for the sign." Tandy looked at Meg.

"You're welcome. James and Savannah helped, I'll have to admit."

"Speaking of which, where are my niece and nephew?

And where's Hannah? She has to have grown a foot by now."

"Oh, she has. They're up in the playroom." Meg pointed to the ceiling.

"Ah, I see." Tandy reached out and snagged a grape from a bowl in the center of a large kitchen island topped with black granite. "So, tell me, are things as dead here in Stars Hill as Daddy says, or is he holding out on me?"

The sisters' faces all froze as they turned to stare at Daddy.

"You didn't tell her?" Kendra's voice boomed through the room. "Are you *kidding* me?"

"Tell me what?" Tandy frowned.

"I didn't think it was worth mentioning." Daddy shrugged his shoulders. "I think Cooper probably needs to go out." He took the leash from Tandy's hand and headed for the back door.

"What wasn't worth mentioning?" Tandy looked from sister to sister.

"I can't believe he didn't tell her. Did I tell you he wouldn't tell her? I told both of you he wouldn't say anything." Kendra waved her big hands toward the door, bracelets tinkling.

"Kendra, maybe he just didn't want to make waves or upset Tandy," Meg said. "She hasn't even been here twenty-four hours. It's not like he's going to announce it the second she drives up."

"Upset me about what?"

"Or maybe it truly *isn't* worth mentioning." Joy took a basket of muffins from the island and gently placed it on the breakfast table that sat under a nearby bay window. "That's my vote."

Tandy slammed her hands down onto the hard granite surface of the island. "That's *it!*"

The sisters turned to look at her.

"Somebody tell me what's going on. *Now!*"

"Oh, Tandy, stop being so dramatic. That's Kendra's bag." Meg nodded toward their flamboyant sister.

Tandy closed her eyes. Had she stepped into a dream or a nightmare? She took a deep breath and tried again. "Fine. I'm calm. Now will someone please tell me what you all seem to know that I don't?"

Joy came back to the island and took the bowl of fruit, pirouetting back toward the breakfast table, every inch a ballerina. "It's nothing to be excited over, Tandy. Clay opened a diner downtown since your last visit, and we thought you should know before you go wandering around down there. That's all."

Tandy's stomach hit her toes. If it was a big enough deal for them to have discussed who would tell her and how, then it *had* to be Clay Kelner. Opening a diner would be hard to do from a jail cell, so maybe he hadn't become a felon or followed through with his military dreams. Unless he served his time and now he'd come back home to make something of his life . . .

Either way, all she had to do was avoid downtown for the next two weeks. "Just to be clear, we're talking about Clay Kelner, right?"

"What other Clay would there be?" Meg cocked her head.

"I don't know. Maybe another Clay moved to town by now."

"If it was another Clay, why would we care if you knew?" The ever-logical Meg.

"I have no idea sometimes how you three think together. So I can assume it's Clay Kelner?"

"You would assume correctly," Joy said. "Breakfast is ready. Somebody go get Daddy and tell him Tandy knows and she didn't spontaneously combust."

"I'll get his sorry behind." Kendra headed for the door, a woman on a mission. "He should have told her the minute she drove up. Imagine if she had gone downtown this morning!"

"It's okay, Kendra. I've been over Clay for years. He's old news. I'm fine. He made his choices. I made mine."

Kendra slid open the glass door leading out into an expansive backyard. "Daddy! You can come in now!" She closed the door and turned back toward the room. Her dark eyes bore down on Tandy. "When's the last time you saw Clay?"

"You know, of course."

"You haven't seen him since then?"

"Nope. Not even for a millisecond."

"Wait, wait." Joy held up her hands. "You haven't seen or talked to Clay since the night you left town for college?" All three sisters looked at Tandy as if she'd sprouted a third ear.

On her forehead.

Tandy stared at the black granite, its speckles reminding her of the stars that night. A scene played vividly in her mind. Sneaking back into the house at 4:00 a.m., she'd been caught. And Daddy, too tired from fighting the battle to join his wife in death, didn't even fuss at her. He'd just looked at her with worn-out eyes that said more than anything his mouth and tongue could ever conjure. Tandy had been angry. Angry that he was still so depressed two months after

Momma's death. Angry that he didn't care enough anymore to punish her for coming in late. Angry at cancer for taking Momma before Tandy had been able to share any portion of adulthood with her. And angry at Clay Kelner for . . . well, no need to go there.

"No, I haven't."

"Girl, that is some *dedication*. You've been holding that grudge for ten years?" Kendra shook her head.

"I'm not holding anything. I don't even think of him anymore. And if I don't think of him, then why would I talk to him?"

"The lady's got a point, girls," Joy said. "Besides, it's too lovely of a morning to waste talking about such divisive issues. These muffins are going to get cold."

"And woe to the person who lets any of Joy's food get cold." Kendra circled the breakfast table, pulled out a chair, and plopped down. "You don't have to call me twice."

"Me, either." Tandy took her customary chair beside Kendra. Meg sat down to Tandy's left.

"Meg, should we get James and Savannah?" Joy asked.

"Oh, no. They had oatmeal before we left the house this morning. As good as your breakfasts are, they don't warrant testing the patience of two young children."

"Good point. Daddy, if you'll take a seat then we can get started," Joy said.

Daddy sat down across from the girls, and Cooper flopped down at his feet. Joy came and stood behind an empty chair. "Tandy, welcome home. I'm sorry Scott couldn't be here, but he had a showing this morning."

"Not a problem. The real estate business stops for no one, right?"

Joy smiled and nodded. "Daddy, if you'll say grace for us, please?"

Daddy bowed his head and offered thanks for the food, requesting a blessing on their days and guidance for their paths. The deep tones of Daddy's faith rolled over Tandy. Her throat filled up as it had in the scrapping room, and she swallowed hard. God was easier in Orlando. She could keep him at arm's length by standing anonymously among thousands of people in a mega-sanctuary. Daddy finished his prayer with a heartfelt amen.

"So, Joy, is Scott still enjoying being a realtor?" Tandy asked as they began passing bowls heaped with eggs, grits, sausage, muffins, and biscuits around the table.

"He loves it. As soon as he got his broker's license, he was off and running. He outgrew his first office, is now in his second, and is thinking of moving into a larger space by the end of the year."

"Wow! Who knew there was so much real estate to sell in sleepy Stars Hill?"

Joy nodded. "That's what one would think. It turns out, however, that a lot of the folks from Nashville are moving outside of the city. People are working from home or traveling to the office only two or three days a week. The rest of the time, they prefer to be away from the hustle and bustle."

"I can identify with that. Every morning when I'm sitting at a standstill on I-4, I wonder why I'm doing it."

"Why *are* you doing it?"

Tandy squirmed a bit in her seat at Kendra's question. "You know why. I'm an attorney. If I want to succeed, I need to be in a big city. And I'm familiar with Orlando, so it's a logical choice."

"You could succeed right here," Meg said.

Tandy snorted. "I highly doubt there's enough legal business in Stars Hill to keep me busy."

"One could have said that about real estate," Joy said. "But Scott would beg to differ."

"Y'all, she hasn't even been home twenty-four hours," Kendra said. "How about we let her remind herself why she loves Stars Hill before we give the full-court press?"

Tandy shot Kendra a grateful look.

"We're not pressing her." Meg waved a forkful of egg in the air. "We're just letting her know she's wanted here if she decides to get out of the city."

"And I thank you for that." Tandy smiled. "Really. But I'm happy in Orlando." Happy may have been stretching it a bit, but it was close enough.

"So long as you're doing what you're called to do, we're fine with it," Daddy said as he slathered honey on a biscuit.

"Thanks, Daddy." She poured lemonade from a glass pitcher that had oranges and lemon slices floating in the top.

"Oh, before I forget, did you retrieve my *Simple Scrapbooks* from Mother's studio?" Joy said.

"I did. It's out in the car. I'll get it after breakfast. Man, going up there sure brought back some memories." She stuffed a forkful of eggs in her mouth before blurting out anything else.

Meg nodded. "I know. There's just something magical about Mom's studio. I mean, I can't be nearly as creative in my own place as I can there, you know? I think she must have sprinkled some artsy dust around or something."

"Let's go with 'or something,'" Kendra smiled, "and pretend you haven't lost your mind."

"No, I know what she means," Joy said. "I can scrapbook for hours here at the house and still not end up with as lovely a layout as I would have if I'd just gone over to Mother and Daddy's house."

"Fess up, Daddy. What was Momma's secret?" Tandy stabbed her eggs again.

Daddy chuckled. "I wish I knew, girls. She just had that special something about her, and I guess she left it behind in that room for you girls to use."

"Then we'd better not let it go to waste, right?" Kendra raised a hand. "Who's up for scrapbooking tonight?"

"Oooh! Count me in!" Meg threw her hand in the air. "Daddy, can I bring the kids? Do you have time to watch them tonight?"

"If I don't, I'll find something to keep them busy, I'm sure."

"Great!"

"That's two of us." Kendra dropped her hand and went back to her food. "Anything to avoid a deadline. My editor is breathing down my neck, but if she can't find me, she can't threaten me, right?"

"Who's the article for?" Tandy asked.

"I'm doing a series for *Southern Living* about art in the South. It's one article a month for twelve months, and I'm four months into it."

"That sounds exciting!"

Kendra nodded. "Most days, yeah. But I'm really jazzed about this new sculpture, and every time I sit down at the keyboard to write the article, I think of something to do with the sculpture, so I'm getting nothing written."

"Well, I suppose I can scrap tonight if Scott doesn't have plans for us," Joy said. "Let's say, oh, seven?"

"Seven it is," Tandy broke apart a biscuit. "Is that okay with you, Daddy?"

"Fine as frog hair, split three ways."

"Perfect!" Tandy reached for the jar of homemade strawberry jam. "Joy, this breakfast is divine, as always."

"Oh, it was nothing." Joy shook her head. "I'm just pleased you're home for a bit." Her small mouth curved into a smile.

"Speaking of being home, have you made plans for today yet?" Meg asked as she bit into a muffin.

"I thought I'd walk around downtown, see what's changed, that sort of thing."

"So you're going to check out Clay's diner." Kendra took a big bite of waffle.

"No, that's not what I meant."

"Mm-hmm. Who do you think you're fooling?" Kendra swirled another bite in syrup. "We all know you still have a thing for him."

"I do *not* have a 'thing' for him. I just wanted to see downtown again. What's so wrong with that?"

"Nothing's wrong with that if you're really interested in downtown," Meg said. "But this is Big City Tandy we're talking to, and we know you couldn't care less about what's happening in Stars Hill. You're going down there to see Clay, and I think it's marvelous." She held out her arms and began to sing. "'*S wonderful, 's marvelous . . .*"

"Meg, stop it. Everybody's life is not a song."

"Sure it is! You just may not know the tune yet. Though 'As Time Goes By' is a pretty good try."

Tandy cast a pleading look down the table. "Joy, help me out here."

Joy shook her head, her sleek hair swishing against a

slender neck. "Wish I could, sister dear, but I'm on their side. I think it's about time you spoke with him."

Tandy pushed back from the table, her appetite gone despite the sumptuous food laid before her. She folded her arms across her chest, then unfolded them when she realized it made her look defensive.

"I'm not interested in having a conversation, in having *anything* with Clay Kelner. I'm here for two weeks. Period. Then it's back to work and life and none of that has anything to do with Clay. Got it?" She drilled each of them with a look.

Kendra laughed. "Whatever you need to tell yourself, sister. Just keep saying that when you're standing under the Clay's sign in a little while."

Five

Later that day, having dropped Daddy off at home, Tandy and Cooper made their way again downtown. It looked different in daylight but no less charming. A banner announcing the upcoming Iris Festival parade now hung across Lindell. If the sisters kept at her about Clay, it might be worth missing the parade to escape to the anonymity of Orlando. She drove under the banner and turned into the library parking lot.

Tugging Coop's leash, she walked one block over to Broadway. Not to avoid Clay's Diner, of course. The Color Shoppe still sat at the end of Broadway. She and Momma had spent more than a few hours in there working out wallpaper and paint schemes for different rooms in the house. A new business stood next door, and she squinted to make out the painted window still a block away. Looked like an interior design business. Had The Color Shoppe opened an addition, or was some competition in town now? She shrugged and walked on.

The beauty salon, Styles On Broadway, looked like it had gotten a major makeover. A quick glance inside the plateglass window revealed a décor updated to reflect the current obsession with all things Tuscan. Brown and mustard yellow seemed to be the colors of the day as women occupied every available chair, covered in capes of swirling earth colors and tended by hair stylists dressed all in black.

She walked on and passed an upscale children's clothing store that looked new. Making a mental note to see if they had anything appropriate for James, Savannah, and Hannah when she didn't have Cooper with her, Tandy came to the end of the brick sidewalk. She sighed. Lindell beckoned her. What right did Clay have to keep her from enjoying her hometown anyway?

Turning on her heel, chin high and back straight, Tandy tugged a now tiring Cooper back the direction they had come.

When they passed the library parking lot again, Cooper whined and pulled her toward the car. "Come on, buddy. Just a little farther, and we'll head home to that comfy chair and a rawhide I've been saving since Florida."

She glanced up the street and saw the sign swaying in the breeze, brashly proclaiming the home of Clay Kelner's culinary pursuits.

Why was this so hard? Clay was back in town. Not a problem. So they'd parted ways in a less than amicable manner. He shouldn't have left for the military in the first place. Why bother, when here he was, back in town and the owner of a diner—which he could have done from the very beginning. Though if he had, Orlando might never have become her home. In the end, perhaps the incompatibility of his dreams and hers meant something. Otherwise, she'd be right by his side in there, flipping burgers, taking orders, and—

"Tandy? Tandy Sinclair?"

No. Her heart clenched at the voice coming from behind. She balled her fists, the leash handle digging into her skin. *No. No. No.* Red dots appeared behind her eyes as she squeezed them shut, not ready for this. Not even *close* to being ready for this.

"It *is* you!"

At the sound of the voice now in front of her, her eyes popped open. "Hi, Clay."

Oh, great.

He looked good.

His deep-blue T-shirt was stretched across a chest that had filled out more than she remembered, and black curls brushed his ears. Sea-green eyes were open wide and sparkled with humor. Strong fingers curled around the bottoms of two paper grocery bags.

Cooper woofed.

"Hey, cute dog!" Kneeling, Clay set the bags down and scratched Cooper's ears. The dog laid down, rolling over to offer his belly.

Traitor. "Yeah, I think so." She tried to sound lighthearted but came off strangled instead.

He looked up at her and she swallowed hard. No need to let him know her heart had relocated to her throat. Or that the sight of him loving on her dog was making her consider the life of a waitress.

"How long have you been in town?"

"Got in last night."

"Everything okay? I saw your dad yesterday and he seemed fine. The guardians?"

"The sisters are fine. I'm just visiting for a couple of weeks."

He stood and raised an eyebrow. "Two weeks?"

"Yeah, no big deal. I hadn't been home in a while, and Daddy was threatening to call the National Guard."

"I can believe that." They stood in awkward silence, years of unspoken words choking the air around them.

"So, you have a restaurant now, I guess." *Aren't you brilliant, Tandy? Great conversation starter.*

"Oh! Right. Can't play soldier forever, remember?"

"Sounds like wise words."

"I think so, too."

She started. He thought so, too? "You didn't when you first heard them. I seem to recall someone telling me how awesome it would be to travel the world on the government's dime and never be tied down to one place very long."

He blew out a breath and took a step toward her. "I was a dumb kid. I think we both know that."

She stepped back. "What I know is I've gotta get back to the house in time to scrap with the sisters. So I guess we'll just have to have that conversation another time." *As in never.* "Besides—" she nodded to the plate-glass window and began backing away—"you have customers waiting."

"Tandy, come on." His eyes—eyes she'd tried so hard to forget, eyes now framed by the faintest of lines—softened.

"Don't, Clay." She shook her head, pulling Coop along and away from a past that had no future. "Just don't."

She turned and darted across the road, running to the safety of her Beamer as fast as Cooper allowed.

This was a mistake. Stars Hill, missing Momma, seeing Clay—it was all a mistake. A weakness she'd indulged. A universe spinning with emotion and mess. She shifted hard and backed out of the parking space. It would be dumb to leave tonight and drive eleven hours back to Orlando. But first thing in the morning should be soon enough.

"Coop, you ready for some sand and sun, boy?" She checked the rearview mirror and saw Cooper cock his head at her. His *Are-you-nuts?* look was hard to miss.

There were tourists in her apartment. And Meg would have her head on one of Joy's engraved silver platters if she left before spending some time with James, Savannah, and Hannah. Maybe a couple more days would be all right. If she didn't come downtown and only spent time at home or one of the sisters', there was no chance of running into . . . anyone. The rental company could let her tenants know she was coming back sooner than planned and they'd need to find a hotel.

"Okay, a couple more days. Then we're out of here. That's a good plan, right, Coop?" He turned his sad basset eyes her way, and she smiled. "Sorry I made you run. It won't happen again, I promise. Because we're going to stay far, far away from Lindell. Pretty soon you'll be back in sunny Florida lying on the beach and ogling the poodles." Coop harrumphed and plopped his head on his massive paws.

She maneuvered her way through town, relieved to see the white wooden *S* within just a few minutes. Taking the driveway much faster than the night before, she slid to a stop and popped open the car door. What to do for the next few hours before the sisters arrived with their scrapping stuff?

She got Cooper settled inside and, hands on hips, looked around the bedroom. "Coop, we've got half the day ahead of us. What should we do?" The dog lay his head down and closed his eyes. Okay, so something not involving an exhausted basset hound.

Her lime-green scrapping tote screamed from the corner

of the room. But scrapping alone wasn't fun, and the thought of going into Momma's studio without the emotional protection of constant conversation was even less so.

Leaving the house wasn't an option either since there'd be a slim chance she'd run into . . . people. People who'd want to know why she was here, how things were in Orlando, and when she was going back.

Which meant word of her impending departure would be all over town before breakfast, ensuring the sisters' swift disapproval and Daddy's disappointment.

She sighed and rubbed at the base of her skull. *Was this worth the headache?* Still rubbing her tight muscles, Tandy turned and left a now snoring Cooper. There was nothing stopping her from checking out the barn and seeing if anything had changed in her absence.

Her cell phone rang just as her foot hit the ground outside. She flipped it open without checking the caller ID.

"Tandy Sinclair."

"You ran into Clay?"

"Hi, Kendra. How's the writing coming?"

"About as good as your love life. What'd he say?"

"Sheesh, that was fast even for Stars Hill. I haven't been home ten minutes yet. How'd you find out?"

"I have spies all over the place."

"You're not going to tell me?"

"I think the concept of spying means you don't know who's watching."

"Well, it was no big deal, so retract your claws."

"My claws are put away, honey. I think it'd be great if you two hooked up again."

"Is this the same sister of mine who once slept outside my bedroom door to keep me from sneaking out and meeting him?" Tandy turned past the back of the house and continued toward the barn.

"You were eighteen and stupid and so was he. I was only doing my sisterly duty."

"And now?"

"Now I think you two might be good for each other and you should let him off the hook."

"When did you become a turncoat?"

"I'm not a turncoat. He wasn't good for you before. He is now. I'm only keeping your best interests at heart."

"How is it in my best interest to reconnect with the man who broke my heart ten years ago?" She put one foot on the bottom rung of the ladder leading to the hayloft and her favorite reading spot.

"Because if he broke it, that means he at least touched it, and—correct me if I'm wrong—no man has done that since."

Tandy fumbled on the ladder, the truth of Kendra's words hitting home. She grasped hold of the rung at her face and held on. "Oh my gosh. You're right."

"Of course I'm right."

"You're right! How have I not had a serious relationship for an entire decade?"

"Because you're still hung up on a man from ten years ago?"

"I'm not, Kendra. You know I'm not." She got to the top of the ladder and crawled to the corner. Snuggling back into the scratchy hay, she twisted and squirmed until it formed a nest. "I've been over him for years."

"Okay, let's say you're right and not delusional. Why haven't you found a man then?"

"Because I've been busy! College, then law school, then

moving, then work. When would I have had time to date, much less form a serious relationship?"

"Plenty of women find men during their college years and get married."

"Goody-goody for those women. I wasn't one of them."

"Because you weren't over Clay."

"Because I was holding down three jobs and taking overloads of classes to graduate early."

"That, too. But you could have dated."

"When? I slept four hours a night, Kendra. I didn't have time to do anything but go to class, work, and sleep. I don't even remember half my time at college. It's all just one big blur."

"A blur that lacks a man."

"I don't see you doing so much better, sister."

"Hey, this is not about me. I'm doing just fine, thank you very much."

"So you're dating? Who?"

"No one in particular." Kendra's voice took on an air of nonchalance, and Tandy knew she'd hit on something. Stars Hill upbringing meshed with lawyer instincts, and Tandy grinned. Time for a cross-examination. Stars Hill style.

"Does this unparticular man have a name?"

"I think it's *imparticular.*"

"No, it's not. It's *unparticular.*"

"Are you sure?"

"Positive and nice try, but I'm not getting off the subject. Who is he?"

"Nobody from around here and nothing serious, so not worth mentioning."

"Wow, three negatives in one sentence. It must be serious."

"It's not serious. Unlike you and Clay. You two could be serious."

"No, we can't, Ken. It's over. It was over a long time ago."

Kendra's sigh was long. "It doesn't have to be over."

"Yeah, it does. I've moved on. So has he. He has a diner, for crying out loud." Forget cross-examination. Time to put this topic to bed once and for all.

"What does the diner have to do with anything?"

"Think it through." She ticked off the logic on her fingers. "Let's say the universe shifts and I lose my mind and decide I should try to fix things with Clay." She tapped a second finger. "I go back to him." Tapped a third finger. "Things work out peachy." Because how else could they possibly work out? This was *Clay*. "We decide to get married." *Do not think of that.* "Then what?"

"Then you live happily ever after."

Tandy dropped her hands to the hay and squeezed the phone tighter between her shoulder and ear. "Where?"

"What do you mean, where?"

"I mean, where would we live?"

"Here."

"In Stars Hill?"

"Why not?"

"Oh, I don't know. Maybe because I have a life and career in Orlando? Because I've worked hard to establish that life? Because living eleven hours from my husband might not make for the best marriage?"

"Why couldn't you just move here?"

"Why *would* I move here?"

"I thought you two were married."

"Kendra!"

"You said it! Not me. Why wouldn't you move back to

Stars Hill if the man you loved and were married to lived here?"

Tandy picked a piece of hay from beside her knee and began breaking it in little pieces. It didn't matter if she gave Kendra a million reasons. Her sister would never understand the dream she and Momma shared. She wouldn't get that Tandy couldn't make a name for herself in tiny little Stars Hill. Even if, by some miracle, things were to start up again with Clay Kelner, it could never be a forever thing. Because her forever was in Orlando and his, as far as she could tell, was right here.

"Tandy?"

"Yeah, Kendra, I'm here." Her voice sounded old and tired, and she knew it.

"Look, ignore me. You know I like to debate just for the sake of debate. Keeps things lively."

"I know, I know."

"Forget what I said about Clay. He's history."

"History, huh? What happened to him being right for me?"

"What do I know, right? I'm a thirty-three-year-old single black woman who sculpts and ignores a writing deadline with no words to deliver to my editor. I'd say I'm the last person you should listen to for advice."

Tandy chuckled. "Good point. So I'll see you in a bit to scrap?"

"Better believe it."

"Okay, then."

"Hey, Tandy?"

"Yeah?"

"I'm sorry I made you sad. And you know I'm happy you're home."

"I know. Thanks. See ya in a little while."

"See ya."

Tandy flipped the phone closed and fell back into the hay. The image of Clay as he'd looked today floated into her mind, and for just a minute she allowed herself the luxury of enjoying the picture. Why was he back in Stars Hill, and why, of all things, did he own a diner? They'd never talked about him wanting to own a diner, and they'd talked about *everything*.

At least she thought they had.

He was her best friend, her rock when all else seemed to be shifting. The image in her mind morphed into a younger Clay. Her mind filled with the sight of him in a black suit, green tie slightly askew, and curls running rampant over his forehead. Daddy and the sisters sat in the front row at the funeral home, and she'd pulled him to the chair beside her without hesitation. No way could she get through this day without his strong hand anchoring her to earth. If he let go, she'd just float away to the clouds to find Momma.

His hand carried her through the graveside service, too. Tugging her up out of her seat when it was time to stand and back down when it was time to sit. Her ears closed up, refusing the words of good-bye that the minister spoke over Momma's casket. All she knew was the feel of Clay's warm hand in her icy one and the sure fact that, if she never heard another sound on earth, she'd always have his hand.

A mouse skittered across the loft, startling Tandy out of her reverie. She shook her head to dispel the images of years past. No use thinking about them now. Momma was gone and, shortly thereafter, her surety that Clay Kelner—and, by extension, any new man she ever encountered—could be trusted. He wasn't supposed to leave her.

But he had.

It didn't matter that she'd left first. She only went because the sight of him leaving her behind wasn't allowed. And he was going to leave her behind. She knew it. And so did he. Their fate had been decided the day the military recruiter came to Stars Hill High and told the senior class they were looking for a few good men. Clay was a good man. Well, good for them. Not so much for her.

She crawled back across the loft and swung a leg over the ladder. No more thinking about Clay Kelner. No point in it. Life in Orlando was good—and would be great again as soon as this little hiatus was over and she was back in her office jumping at hawks, both winged and suited.

She rolled to her side in the hay and snuggled in for a nap, which she wouldn't need if she hadn't spent half of last night dreaming of Clay Kelner.

See? The man was nothing but difficulty.

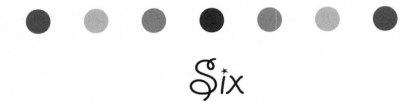

Six

Tandy jumped from the last rung of the ladder to the ground.

"There you are."

Tandy spun. "Daddy! You nearly scared me to death."

"Last time I caught you coming down from there, you weren't alone." He tilted his head and squinted up at the hayloft. "Anybody else in here I should know about?"

Tandy felt the blush rise from her neck to her cheeks. "Of course not, Daddy. And even if there was, I'm a grown woman."

"Not so grown you need to be rolling around in haylofts."

"I don't roll around in anything."

"Glad to hear it."

"Why are we talking about this?"

"I think you opened the door, oh, about eleven years ago."

"Tell me you're not going to push the Clay-Kelner-as-Perfect-Man-for-Tandy theory, too."

Daddy stuffed his hand in a pocket. "I suppose that depends. Who else is pushing the theory?"

"Kendra."

Daddy chuckled. "I don't think I'll bet against her."

"Good thing she recanted her theory then."

"Did she now?"

"She did." Tandy walked toward the barn entrance, tucking a curl behind her ear and mentally vowing to have a Clayless remainder of the day. "And I'd appreciate it if you would, too. I'm not looking for a relationship, and even if I were, it wouldn't be with Clay. We're history."

Daddy held up his hands as he walked beside her back toward the house. "Message received. Loud and clear."

She stopped and turned to face him. "Really?"

"Yep. Feel free to stay single until I join your mother in heaven. Just take the wedding money out of your inheritance."

"Very funny, Daddy. Don't joke. I may take you up on that."

"Somehow, I doubt it."

They climbed the porch steps and went inside. "I think I'll make some snack food before the sisters get here," she said.

"Have at it. Cookbooks are where they always were, and I just went to the grocery yesterday. You should have everything you need."

"You don't want to help?"

"Oh, I think I'll head upstairs and catch a few minutes of shut-eye. Get some rest before the grandkids get here."

"Smart man."

"I try." Daddy turned and headed up the stairs. Tandy took a deep breath and entered Momma's kitchen.

Momma could do two hobbies really well: cook and scrap. She'd said the two went together like biscuits and gravy because you always needed something to nibble on when you were scrapping.

Tandy opened the cupboard and pulled down Momma's *Proud as a Peacock* cookbook. The cover, bearing the image of the aforementioned bird, was curling at the corners. Smudges of recipe ingredients were evident here and there. She flipped to the dessert section and saw Momma's loopy notes in the margin of nearly every recipe.

"Good for about 2 hours," one note said and Tandy chuckled. She'd need at least a four-hour recipe for tonight. If they were still scrapping after four hours, they'd just have to order pizza.

✂ ✂ ✂

TWO HOURS LATER five dozen peanut butter buckeyes lay on waxed paper, their chocolate coating drying, and Tandy grinned. Scrapping, sweets, and the sisters. It was going to be a good night.

"Yoo-hoo! Anybody home?" Meg's voice rang through the house as little towheaded James came barreling into the kitchen.

"Mom! She's in here. And there's chocolate!"

Tandy scooped him up in a hug and twirled in a circle. "When did you get so big, little man?"

"Last year, in kindergarten."

"Well, could you not get so big so fast, please?"

"Mom says I grow like a weed. But I'm not a weed. I'm just a James."

"And a handsome James at that."

"Daddy says I'm handsome, too."

"He does, does he?"

James nodded, his chocolate-brown eyes serious. "Yes. I don't lie. Because then I'd be like the Rumor Weed, and I'd rather be like Larry Boy!"

Tandy threw a questioning glance Meg's way as her sister came into the kitchen. "Larry Boy?"

"VeggieTales. He's addicted to them."

"I just love VeggieTales! Vannah loves them, too. Except when the Frankencelery comes out. He's kind of scary." James giggled, and Tandy's heart melted.

"Why is Frankencelery scary?"

"'Cause he's just got these things coming out his head," James reached up and made pulling motions above his hair. "That's how they control him. And Vannah thinks they'll come put them in her head, too. I just love you." He squirmed, and Tandy sat him down on the floor. Before she could blink, he grabbed a buckeye and scampered out of the kitchen.

"I just love you too, buddy!" she called to his retreating figure, then turned to her sister. "When did he start saying, 'I love you'?"

"He said it one time when he got in trouble. I was so surprised and touched, I didn't punish him. Now he thinks it will get him out of everything. I swear I hear, 'I love you' fifty times a day."

Tandy laughed. "Hey, enjoy it while you've got it."

"I *just* think I will."

"What's all the funny happening up in here?" Kendra said, coming into the kitchen.

"Tandy just had an encounter with the lovernator." Meg popped a buckeye in her mouth.

"I'm telling you, you better stop that little man before he tells some first grader he *just* loves her."

"Kendra, you're nuts. And besides, we homeschool."

"Mm-hmm, I'll remind you of this conversation when he's eighteen and married to some little girl he met at a homeschool event."

"Don't listen to her," Tandy said. "She gives bad love advice."

"You gave Tandy bad advice?"

Kendra stuck her nose in the air. "I only give good advice. I have no idea what she's talking about."

"Then it had to be about Clay."

"And now we're moving on." Tandy started gathering buckeyes. "Help me put these in tins, girls."

They pulled tins from cupboards and began loading the buckeyes in, one at a time.

"How many hours' worth did you make?"

"Four."

"We're going to run out."

"Then we'll call for pizza."

Meg and Kendra looked at her, then doubled over in laughter.

"What? What's so funny?"

"Oh, girl, you've been gone too long." Kendra wiped a tear from her eye.

"What do you mean? All I said was—" Tandy stopped and slapped her forehead, "—that we'd order a pizza in a town that doesn't have pizza delivery."

"Yep, that about covers it," Meg said.

Tandy shook her head. "Then we'll have to make the buckeyes last. Which isn't going to happen unless we get our big rear ends upstairs and put our hands to work on some layouts."

"Amen, honey!" Kendra said. "Let's get to the scrapping!"

They each grabbed tins and drinks and made their way to the staircase as Joy came in the door.

"Hey, you're just in time! We're heading on upstairs."

"Don't let me stop you then." Joy joined in the back of the line as they all trooped up the stairs.

"Ugh, one of these days we need to install an elevator or something," Kendra complained.

"Love in an elevator . . ." Meg sang.

"That was too easy," Joy said.

"Hey, don't knock Aerosmith. They're legends. Besides, there's a song for everything in life."

"No, there isn't."

"Of course there is."

"You're crazy."

"And yet, still right."

They came into the studio, and Tandy noticed Daddy had put her scrapping totes on Momma's side of the table. She took a deep breath. Conversation, busyness. She could get through this.

"Okay, name a song for Atlanta," Tandy said.

"Just an old sweet song," Meg crooned, *"keeps Georgia on my mind . . ."*

"You did *not* go there. Michael Bolton? Is he a legend, too?"

"In some circles, yes. But I was channeling Willie Nelson."

Kendra rolled her eyes. "My turn. Bet I can stump you. Name one for finding the perfect diamond."

Meg didn't hesitate. *"A kiss on the hand may be quite continental, but diamonds are a girl's best friend,"* she sang, jumping up on the table, crossing her legs, and ducking her head Marilyn Monroe-style.

"Diamonds?" Joy shook her head. "Kendra, give her a challenge at least."

Kendra crossed her arms and tossed her hair. "Fine. How about doing dishes?"

"I can bring home the bacon," Meg belted out, *"fry it up in a pan."* She hopped off the table and sashayed around the room. *"And never let you forget you're a man,"* she held up an imaginary microphone, *"'cuz I'm a woman!"*

"Oh, for the love of Pete. Finding a good pair of shoes?"

"These boots were made for walkin'"—she changed the sashay to a purposeful walk away from them—*"and that's just what they'll do."*

"That was a great song before Jessica Simpson ruined it," Tandy said.

Meg dropped the act and came back to the scrapping table. "I know. I'm still mad at her over leaving Nick."

Joy shook her head. "I don't understand why you keep up with celebrity marriages."

"Come visit Orlando for two weeks," Tandy said. "You can't help but know what's happening in Hollywood."

"Wait! Wait!" Kendra held up her hands. "I've got it!"

"Got what?"

Kendra turned to Meg, a gleam in her eye. "Bet you can't name a song for getting a skin rash. There's nobody who would sing about something like that."

Meg grinned and leaned across the table. She sang in a sultry voice, *"I've got you . . . under my skin."*

"Oh no, you did not just break out Ol' Blue Eyes for a skin rash," Tandy said. "That's wrong in so many ways."

Meg straightened and laughed. "Never doubt my lyrical powers."

"Lyrical?" Tandy smirked.

"It's a word," Meg defended.

"Yeah, but not in the way you meant it."

"Yes, it is."

"It's about as much of a word as *imparticular*."

"But that's not a word."

"It should be," Kendra butted in.

"No, it shouldn't. You should just say unparticular."

"But *imparticular* sounds better."

"It sounds dumb."

"Are you saying I'm dumb?"

"No, I'm saying the word *imparticular* would sound dumb if it came into common usage. Why are we talking about this?"

"Because Kendra's dating an *imparticular* man." Tandy pulled a photo box out of her tote and began thumbing through the sections. The other sisters each pulled a similar photo box off the shelf.

"You're dating?" Joy came back to the table and set her box down. She, too, began thumbing through prints. "Who?"

"No one." Kendra pulled a grouping of photos from her box.

"Then I have to ask again, why are we talking about this?"

"Now we're talking about it because Kendra's lying." Tandy selected a group of photos. Reaching across the table, she snagged one of four paper cutters. Hers still had the purple paint she'd spilled on it her senior year of high school, making it easy to find. "She told me today she's been seeing a man."

"Who are you dating?" Meg asked. "And why don't we know about him?"

"I'm not dating anyone in particular," Kendra said.

"Oh! So he's *imparticular!*" Joy said.

Kendra snapped her fingers and pointed at Joy. "Exactly, little sis."

"So if he's *imparticular,* why were you talking about him with Tandy?"

"I wasn't. I was talking to Tandy about Clay."

"Even better," Joy said. "Now is a much more appropriate time to discuss this. I heard you ran into him downtown."

"Nice to know the Stars Hill grapevine is still thriving like a stubborn weed. So everybody in town is talking about this now?" Tandy finished cutting a photo and pulled the blade holder up.

All the sisters looked up from their photos and cutters. "Pretty much," Meg said.

"Oh, for Pete's sake. Is it so dead in Stars Hill that—"

"Do you really need to finish that sentence?" Kendra's eyes widened. "Remember, this is the town without pizza delivery." She popped a buckeye into her mouth, then walked over to the wall of paper towers and bent low.

"I talked to the man for all of fifteen seconds. This is not news."

"Fifteen seconds of conversation with a boy that this whole town watched you fall in love with in high school. In Stars Hill, that's news," Joy began laying photos out on the table, moving them this way and that to decide on a layout.

"Then help me make it un-news."

"How would we do that?" Kendra chose a few 12 x 12 sheets of red paper, then one each of patterned paper with the same shade of red. She came back to the table.

"I have no idea. But I don't want to be the topic at every-body's dinner table."

Joy leaned back to eye her photo grouping. "You could date him." With her melodic voice, the suggestion didn't sound as ridiculous as it should have.

"Wouldn't that make everybody talk more?"

Joy shrugged. "I'm not certain. Maybe, maybe not. I think they're talking now because they wonder if something *might* happen."

"Like what?"

"Like a replay of ten years ago." Kendra pushed her bracelets up her arm and began layering prints on the solid background.

"No way people remember something that happened a decade ago."

They all three stopped scrapping again and looked up at her.

"They remember that?"

Kendra's cutter sliced through the paper. "Like it was yesterday. It's not every day we have two people going at it in the middle of Lindell Street."

"And then, ten years later, one of them opens a diner at the very spot the event took place." Meg went over and reached up to pull a Becky Higgins sketchbook from the top of the bookshelf. As she slid it off, something large and green came with it. Meg jumped back, went off balance, and landed on her backside. "Ack!"

All the sisters looked up at the commotion.

Tandy sprang from her stool and ran around to help Meg up off the floor. "What was that?" She looked back to see what had fallen. "Oh my word, I haven't seen this in years!" With reverent care Tandy picked up the object.

Kendra came around the table for a closer look. "Is that Momma's old Polaroid?"

"It is!" Tandy wiped a bit of grime off the corner of it with her shirt. "And it's even got film in it."

"You're kidding me." Joy came to crouch down by her three sisters. "Well, would you look at that? It does have film!"

"We should take some pictures with this thing."

"Oh, Tandy, it probably doesn't work anymore." Joy went back to the table, and Kendra followed suit.

"Kinda like my backside." Meg wiped the seat of her pants where she'd fallen. "It's not the cushion it used to be when we were kids. This floor's *hard*."

Kendra chuckled. "If you'd get some padding back there like the rest of us, you wouldn't be at such risk of hurting yourself."

Meg grimaced at her and went back to her stool, then settled on it gingerly.

"I bet it does work." Tandy pulled a face at Meg. "The camera, that is, not your backside." She brought the old camera back to the table and set it down.

"Let's try it out later." Meg thumbed through the sketch-book looking, they all knew, for a layout to fit all her pictures on. "Right now, let's get back to Clay and the strategic positioning of his diner."

"Somebody tell me he didn't put his diner there for any reason other than it was the only space open on Lindell."

"The old bookstore was vacant, but that's not a very good location." Meg turned pages.

"I think he did it for looooove," Kendra said.

"Kendra, this is not a Lifetime movie. This is my real life, and everything doesn't work out all happy and perfect in the end." Tandy refocused on her pictures.

"Why not?"

"Are you serious?"

"Maybe. Meg got her happily ever after. And Joy did, too. Why not us?"

"Whoa, sister—" Meg set the guidebook down—"marriage is not happily ever after. It's happily ever sometimes and difficult every other time."

Kendra wrinkled her nose. "I love it when married people try to tell me how fortunate I am to still be single."

"Look, I'm not saying one is better than the other, but there are advantages to both."

"Yeah, yeah, but one of *my* advantages isn't lying down next to a fine man every night after tucking in my three beautiful kids."

Meg wasn't backing down. "No, it's getting to go to bed whenever you want and staying up all night working on a sculpture if you feel like it without worrying about being too tired to get your kids ready in the morning."

"Point taken." Kendra nodded. "But I'd go to bed every night at the same time for what you've got."

"I'll remind you of that when you've been married as long as I have."

"Deal. Joy, you're awfully silent about this. Everything okay with Scott?"

Joy looked up from her eyelet setter and nodded. "Of course. We're wonderful. He's working hard, and I don't see him as much as I'd like, but other than that we're wonderful."

"Good," Tandy said. "Because I think there's a law somewhere about only two sisters having messed up love lives at one time. Wouldn't want to disturb the fabric of the universe or anything."

"The universe is in good standing," Joy said with a smile.

She went and pulled a bottle of fabric flowers from a shelving unit hanging off the Peg-Board. "I just adore these little flowers now."

"Me, too. I've got them all over my scrapbook," Kendra said. "It's beginning to look like a flower child put it together."

"I don't think I've used them much yet," Tandy said. "Let me see."

Joy handed over the glass bottle, and Tandy tipped it up in her hand. A few flowers in bright turquoise, pink, orange, and yellow fell out. "These are pretty."

"I'm using them on a lot of Savannah's pages," Meg said. "I love the ones by K & Company."

"Me, too."

Tandy looked up at the wistful tone of Joy's voice. "Are you sure you're all right?"

Joy's bright blue eyes widened. "Why wouldn't I be?"

"I don't know, but you sounded funny just then."

"Funny how?"

"Funny like you're hiding something."

"No, not a thing." Joy's gaze dropped to her layout, and Tandy admired her sister's shock of black eyelashes on pale skin before going back to her own work.

"If I date Clay, people will still talk about whether or not we'll keep dating."

"Or get married," Kendra said. "This town loves a wedding."

"Don't I know it," Meg and Joy said in unison, then laughed.

"Then dating him isn't going to help. What if I just stay away from him?"

"I don't see how that will help," Meg said.

Tandy glared at Meg. "If they don't have anything new to say, then they'll go on to the next interesting thing."

"Are you planning on giving them another interesting thing?"

"The Iris Festival is in two weeks. They'll focus on that!"

"You may have a point there," Joy said. "They're planning a doozy of a parade and even a live concert the night before."

"A live concert? Who's playing?"

For the third time the sisters stopped their scrapping. This time, though, they looked at one another. An uneasy feeling started in the pit of Tandy's stomach. "You guys have got to stop doing that. You make me think I'm about to get hit by a bus and you're trying to figure out which one of you should tell me."

"You're planning on coming to the Iris Festival?" Kendra asked.

"Is there a reason I shouldn't?"

"Let's find out." Kendra leaned forward and locked gazes with Tandy. "The band is Clay's."

Tandy's forehead wrinkled. "Clay has a band? I don't understand."

"He plays with a couple other guys. They go to Nashville sometimes and play a gig. It's nothing major. At least, I don't think it's major. But his band is playing the Iris Festival."

The uneasy feeling grew into a lead weight. Tandy leaned on the table and thought fast, trying to hide her thought process from Kendra's laser eyes. She took a deep breath. "Then I don't see a reason to miss the Iris Festival."

"If this is some sort of reverse psychology—" Kendra peered at Tandy—"it's working."

"No psychology. Just pragmatism. If Clay's busy playing music, then the town can't expect us to talk or not talk to each other. There won't be anything for anybody to observe and discuss. It's perfect."

"Your definition of perfect needs a little work," Meg said. "Are you telling us you have no feelings at all for Clay Kelner?"

Tandy walked over to the window and looked out. Everything seemed perfect and placid except for the soft wind rustling new leaves. She could lie, she supposed. But the sisters would know, and they'd be on her in a heartbeat.

"I'm telling you that I don't have any feelings worth acknowledging." She turned from the window and walked back to the scrapping table.

"What does that mean?" Meg asked.

"It means you always have a special feeling for your first love. Clay was my first love, so it's logical that I would still feel *something* for him. But it has nothing to do with the present and certainly nothing to do with the future. It's a fondness for the past. That's all."

They stared at her as if she'd stabbed herself with an eyelet setter.

"Just so we're clear—" Meg said and Tandy braced herself—"you're still in love with Clay Kelner."

"I didn't say that."

"Right. You just said you love him."

"I said I'll always have a special place in my heart for him because he was my first love. That's not the same as being *in love* with him."

They continued to look at her.

"Girls, stop looking at me like that. You're freaking me out."

Meg whistled the theme from *The Twilight Zone*.

"Meg, cut it out. I'm not living in another dimension."

"No, but you may have lost your mind."

"Why?" Tandy threw her hands in the air. "Because I don't want to start a relationship that can do nothing but end badly? Because I don't trust a guy who broke my heart ten years ago? Because I'm having a conversation about this after *fifteen seconds* of conversation, which he has, by now, totally forgotten but which this town is calling my sisters about within the hour?" She picked up a piece of paper and a distresser and savagely ripped down the side of it. "Which of these reasons lumps me in the category of another dimension?"

"Whoa, girl! Put down the distresser and step away from the table," Kendra said.

Tandy realized she was sounding a bit hysterical and got herself back under control. This is why she didn't like emotion—it crept up on you and sandbagged your plans when you least expected it.

"We didn't mean to upset you."

"Oh, Meg, I know you didn't. But you're all making such a big deal of this when it isn't. I ran into Clay unexpectedly today. We talked for fifteen seconds. He said hi. I said hi. Cooper barked. That was about it."

"I heard he scratched Cooper's ears and belly."

Tandy rolled her eyes. "Yes, Cooper and Clay bonded in the five seconds of doggy love they shared. Do you hear yourself? If anything is weird here, it's this conversation. Man, I forgot how small towns work." She blew out her breath and tucked her curls behind her ears.

Silence reigned for a few moments until Meg sighed. "You know what? You're right. We'll not mention Clay again unless you decide you want to talk about him."

Tandy sent up a prayer of thanks for her peacemaking sister.

"Thank you." She made eye contact with each sister. "I didn't come home to find a man, and I don't need this right now, all right?"

Kendra and Joy nodded, and Meg picked up her scissors. "All right, T," Meg said. "Then let's get to scrapping. We've got about three hours of buckeyes left."

Each woman went back to her layouts, and Tandy switched to autopilot. As she cropped photos, she wondered if the sisters could really hold true to their promise of no Clay talk the entire time she was in Stars Hill. And why was she sad they wouldn't be talking about him anymore?

She placed pictures of the ocean on her layout. Short waves, their edges a frothy white, were laying on the shoreline, frozen forever in time. Tangled seaweed formed a jagged border between the beach and ocean, the only reminder of a storm that had moved through the night before. All else was calm, the water now so clear she could see bits of shell beneath if she held the picture to the light. A light-blue sky refused even the faintest wisp of cloud.

Tandy set the picture down and wondered at her uneasy feeling in the face of such a serene picture. When realization struck, she sat back on her stool and stared. For the first time in three years, she noticed what was missing in her prints.

People.

Seven

Later that night, her stomach full of peanut butter and chocolate buckeyes, Tandy lay in bed staring up at the ceiling. If she stayed until the Iris Festival, chances were pretty high she'd run into Clay. Two weeks was a long time in Stars Hill. What should she say? Would it be presumptive to tell him she wasn't interested?

Was *he*?

She jumped as something hit her window. Cooper raised his head and growled low in his throat. If Cooper was growling, then that wasn't her imagination. But hawks and burglaries didn't happen in Stars Hill.

Several somethings hit her window, sounding like small rocks or pellets. Cooper jumped down off his chair and went to the window. He stretched his big barrel body up onto the wall and whined at the window sill.

A memory of Clay outside that same window eleven years ago made Tandy bolt upright. Surely not.

She threw off the covers and slid her legs off the bed. Tiptoeing to the window, she peeked out into the side yard.

There, illuminated beneath the soft yellow light from the barn, stood Clay Kelner.

Tandy's heart skipped a beat.

The window creaked as she raised it, and Tandy glanced back to her closed bedroom door. Daddy would have a fit if he saw Clay out in the yard. Cooper let out a short bark.

"Shh, buddy. It's okay." *I think.* Clay Kelner was standing outside her window throwing rocks to wake her up. Well, she'd been awake anyway, but he didn't know that. She stuck her head out the window.

"What are you doing?" She hissed the words, holding a finger up to her lips, then pointing down to the back corner of the house. Daddy's window.

Clay motioned for her to come down. She shook her head. He motioned again. She shook her head again. He put his hands on his hips, which should have been a womanly gesture but on him seemed threatening. He held up one finger. What did *that* mean? Wait a second? One more try? What?

He made the motion again for her to come down. Again, she shook her head no. Clay threw up his hands in a gesture that clearly meant, *Well, I tried.* Tandy began to breathe easier. His staying power must have waned over the years.

Her eyebrows knit, though, as Clay strode over to stand in front of Daddy's window. He held up one finger again and understanding dawned. She had one more try or he would wake Daddy up.

She held up her palm, hoping he knew that meant hold on, and shut the window. Shoving her feet into house slippers, she snatched a sweatshirt from the corner of the bed to ward off the April night air. She paused in the hallway, biting her lip and trying to remember which of the stairs creaked. Her sleep-deprived brain wasn't awake enough to help.

The banister was cool and smooth under a hand Tandy realized was shaking. Clay Kelner. After all these years. She tested each step, careful to stay on the far side to prevent creaks. Cooper's nails clicking on the hardwood were the only sound to betray her stealthy approach to the front door. With a hope that Daddy's hearing was not as good as it used to be, she turned the knob and slipped out.

Clay, hands tucked in the pockets of faded jeans, stood waiting at the bottom of the porch steps. She tiptoed down—skipping the creak out of habit—and stood in front of him. Heat and memories thickened the air between them. The moonlight caught his eyes as he looked at her for a long second. Her feet squeaked on dew-heavy grass as she turned and headed for the barn. No sense talking in the front yard and waking Daddy up. Clay followed her, his steps heavy and sure in the silence.

As soon as they got to the barn, though, he cupped her elbow and turned her around.

"What are you doing here?" she said.

"I needed to talk to you." His deep voice brought back memories best left buried.

"In the middle of the night? What time is it?" She stuffed a lock of hair behind her ear.

"It's about two in the morning. And, if you'll recall, I tried to talk to you in broad daylight, but you ran off."

"I didn't run off. I needed to get home." She crossed her arms over her chest, not caring if he interpreted it as a defensive move. Cooper sat rigid at her feet, staring a hole through the one making his momma tense.

"You were running, and we both know it. It hasn't been so long that I've forgotten you're a runner."

Twice in two days she'd been called that, and the knowledge that people had labeled her as such weighed heavy enough to make her hang her head. Couldn't they call her a fighter instead, like Kendra? A survivor, like Joy? Why a runner? Cowards ran.

"What do you want, Clay?" The defeat in her voice made Cooper whine, and she crouched down beside him to give a reassuring pat.

Silence stretched, causing her to look up.

Big mistake.

Time really had been good to Clay Kelner, she noticed now. His eyes, formerly wild with a desperate longing for adventure and excitement, had allowed kindness to replace impetuousness. A small gleam let her know that his fun-loving side was still there, but it looked like life had tempered the immaturity right out of him. Laugh lines cut deep into the tan skin beside either eye, and Tandy was surprised to find herself warmed by the thought that he had been happy.

And jealous of whoever had caused it.

She stood up and walked over to the old AM/FM radio in the far corner of the barn. She sent up a silent prayer that Meg's belief in the calming power of music would hold true. Turning the dial, she searched through static until WSIX out of Nashville came through.

Clay's presence behind her was almost overwhelming. Her past, right there within arm's reach. A past that had both healed and hurt. A past that, if she was smart, would stay just that.

"Tandy, what happened in Orlando?" His voice rolled over her shoulder. It had coaxed so many secrets from her in high school. The truth of her birth mother, her fear of never fulfilling Momma's dreams, of being scared to leave the safety of Stars Hill, of hating the uncertainty of emotion, of needing to have some sense of control over her own life. He'd heard it all.

And none of it had kept him here.

She straightened her spine and turned, glaring at him. "Nothing happened. I just hadn't been home in a long while and thought it was time for a visit."

"So it's going to be like that between us now? I get the Stars Hill party line?"

"I don't recall you valuing anything else." Her gaze broke and wandered around the barn. *Steady.*

"What does that mean?"

"Whatever you want it to mean, I guess."

"Tandy, come on." He reached out and touched her arm. She stepped back, bumping into the table on which the radio sat. Keith Urban's gravelly voice crooned, *"Tonight I wanna cry . . ."*

It only leads to more tears, Keith. Better to move on.

"Tell me what happened, Taz." His pet name for her, what he'd called her since the day he learned her initials— TAS. Tandy Ann Sinclair. He'd decided her whirlwind nature was perfectly suited to the cartoon character. Back then it made her feel accepted. Loved for who she was. Now it only reminded her of the frivolity and uselessness of love. Her shoulders slumped and she shook her head.

"It really wasn't anything, Clay. Just gave me a good reason to come see Daddy and the sisters."

He studied her as Keith sang on, *"I've never been the kind to ever let my feelings show. I thought that being strong meant never losing my self control . . ."*

Why had she turned the radio on? Oh yeah, Meg.

"Okay, Tandy." He backed away a few steps and held up his hands. "You don't have to tell me. But you know me well enough to know I'm going to find out anyway. Either you can spin it to me now or I can listen to the Stars Hill version. Your choice."

That was a choice? Stars Hill could make a fender bender into a twelve-car pileup overnight. They had the sisters advising her to *marry* Clay, for Pete's sake.

"That's not fair."

He grinned, and she saw the face she'd held so many times. The one she'd let slip past her hands and into her heart.

"Fair, no. Effective? Yes."

She blew out her breath and tucked more curls behind her ears. "I had an incident with a client. A big client."

"Big enough for me to know him?"

"Big enough for my boss to know him."

"Ah. Go on."

She shrugged. "He talked to my boss. My boss talked to me. Here I am."

"You were fired?"

"No, no, nothing like that. I can't believe you'd think I got fired! What *is* it with people?"

"Okay, you didn't get fired. Then why are you here?"

"Just taking a little time off to let things blow over."

"What was the incident?"

"Just a misunderstanding, really."

"You were forced to take leave over a misunderstanding? Sounds like Orlando's a tough city."

"It can be."

"So what'd he misunderstand?"

"How do you know it was a he?"

"Because I know you, Tandy. Women you can handle. Men? Well, sometimes."

"You know me from a decade ago, Clay." *And it almost killed me when it ended then. Please don't try to know me now.*

He shrugged. "Fair enough. Tell me what *she* misunderstood."

"It was a he."

He threw back his head and laughed.

"Shh! You're going to wake up Daddy!"

"Oh, please. Your daddy couldn't hear a cat yowling in heat from out here. Don't try to change the subject. What did he misunderstand?"

"The motivations of his attorney."

"Are you going to make me pull this out of you? Because I should warn you, I had a nap between the diner and here." He sat down on a bale of hay at his feet, and Cooper, the traitor, padded over to him. Clay scratched Coop's ears and looked up at her. "I'm good for at least a few hours, but I was hoping you wouldn't make me work this hard to get a feeling out of you."

Clay had always been tenacious when he wanted something. Too bad she hadn't fallen into that category. She hopped up onto the table by the radio where Big and Rich were kicking into a guitar solo.

"He was guilty, but he wanted to testify."

"And you wouldn't let him."

"Of course not."

"And that got you put on leave?"

"It may have had something to do with how I found out he was guilty."

"Finally, we're getting to it. How'd you find out?"

"He told me."

"Just out of the blue he says, 'Hey, Ms. Sinclair. I may have forgotten to mention that I'm guilty. Just thought you should know'?"

"Not exactly."

"Then quit making me play twenty questions and tell me what happened. It must have had some effect to make you this hesitant to tell me."

She met his eyes and saw caring, acceptance. Oh, what was the use? Two weeks would be over before she could blink.

"We were at lunch."

"You were dating a client?"

The jealousy in his voice gave her pause. Did he care if she had been?

"Does it matter?"

"Maybe."

"Then, no. Not really."

"Not really?"

"It was just lunch."

"Just lunch for you or just lunch for him?"

"Both, I'd guess. A break in the workday."

"A break."

"Why are you repeating everything I'm saying?"

"Because you keep giving me more when I do. So, a break?"

She raked her hands through her hair. This was getting out of hand. "Yes. A break for lunch with a client because I hadn't brought anything to eat at my desk that day. Do you want to know what happened or not? Because, unlike some people, I *didn't* get a nap today."

Cooper woofed at her.

"Why do you eat lunch at your desk?"

"What?"

"You said you did this because you hadn't brought anything to eat that day. Do you eat lunch at your desk every day?"

Tandy paused, thinking. "Yeah, I guess I do. I hadn't thought of that."

"You don't go out with friends? Ever?"

"I have a few times. There's this woman, Anna, in the office who's very nice." She smiled at the thought of sweet Anna, who no doubt had a blooming African violet on her desk by this time. "I'd rather eat fast and get back to work. I don't have time to replay everyone's conquests from the night before and decide why *he* hasn't called yet."

"Ah, I get it. No attachments."

"No *mess*."

"Okay, okay." Clay leaned back on his elbows in the hay. "You're at lunch with a client for convenience sake and . . ."

The image of Anna vanished from her mind, replaced by the hump-backed man in an overcoat. "And there was a man across the street."

"Your boyfriend?"

She glared at him. "No."

"Sorry. Of course not. Go ahead."

"He was, um . . ." She searched for a way to describe the scene without degrading the homeless man any further. "He was . . ." Her eyes trailed up to the ceiling, grasping for a phrase. "Well, it was like . . ."

"Was he homeless, Tandy?" Compassion soaked his words, and she looked across the hay-strewn floor at him.

"How did you know that?"

"The look on your face. It's the same one you got when we found that baby kitten abandoned by its mother and my dad said it would never live."

"He had no right to be so cold. And I'll remind you that kitten made a great recovery."

"Yes, he did. And he's been increasing the cat population of Stars Hill ever since." Clay sat up and leaned toward her. "My point is that you let your feelings out when it benefits something in need. I'm guessing your jerk of a non-date made some comment about this man."

"Yes." She was only halfway surprised with this guess.

"To which you replied."

"How could I not? That man did nothing to deserve scorn or ridicule. He was just trying to find some dinner. Not bothering anybody. How could I, how could anyone, say awful things about a man in that condition?"

"Being you, you couldn't. Which, of course, means you're now in Stars Hill having been put on leave."

She blew out a breath she didn't know she'd been holding. "Yes."

He stood up and came to stand in front of her. She stared down at his dusty brown boots, feeling his nearness, yet longing to lean into the safe, warm circle that was him.

"Taz."

Her head came up and the understanding in his gaze was so much like the old days yet so much deeper that she could do nothing but look.

"I'm glad you're home." He put his arms around her. She let herself lean into him, knowing it was weak of her. She had the ability to stand on her own two feet now, to fight it out in the world, to chase after an identity and mission without needing to depend on others.

But, for just a second, she promised herself, she'd stop and enjoy the guilty indulgence of leaning into him. Of forgetting that he'd hurt her. That he'd left her for his own dreams. That, when the rubber met the road, he'd run after his mission and she'd chased hers. For a long minute on this cool southern night, Tandy wanted to be held. To have no purpose. No fight. Just this feeling.

In the morning, she thought, as the warmth of his skin touched her cheek through the cotton of his shirt, she could stand and fight again. Even pretend this moment hadn't happened. Maybe even avoid him for the next two weeks. Go back to doing what she was supposed to do, fully armored in self-reliance.

His big hand covered nearly the entire top of her head as he ran it down her fire-colored curls, over and over. The thump of his heart beat a steady rhythm beneath her ear, telling a story—false, she knew—of a dependable, consistent man. That wasn't Clay.

At least, not the Clay she knew. He was a rabble-rouser. A man dedicated to squeezing as much life from this world as humanly possible. Focused on sacrificing himself for a greater good, even if the sacrifice meant hurting the ones he professed to love.

The memory of his rough words, spoken by the same voice that now murmured assurances and compassion to her, made her push back abruptly from the drug of him.

Instant cold invaded without his arms around her. She risked a look at him.

"I need to get to bed."

He grinned and her cheeks flamed.

"*Alone*, of course. I meant it's late and I should get back inside."

He ran his hands down her arms, cupping her elbows and looking her in the eye. "I know what you meant, Taz. You haven't talked to me in a decade, either, remember. I may be just a little different from the man I was before."

Believing that would get her a one-way ticket back to Stars Hill and off the train of her life's goals.

"Good for you, if that's true." She hopped down off the table and sidled around him. "Come on, Coop." Slapping her leg to get the dog's attention, Tandy turned and walked from the barn.

It was a moment, that's all. One moment.

She didn't look back.

Eight

"Morning, sunshine." Meg's voice pulled Tandy from a hazy dream about beaches and diners.

"Morning." She rubbed sleep from her eyes and stood up, watching Meg open the blinds. Sunlight poured in through the windows. "What time is it?"

"About nine, lazy bones. Daddy thought it was time you got up."

"Nine in the morning? Wow. I must have been tired." She checked the clock on the nightstand. "Hey, what are you doing here?"

"James woke up wanting his Aunt Tandy. He wouldn't hush about it all through breakfast. The only way I could get him to eat his pancakes was to promise a trip over here."

"Pushover." Tandy grinned.

"Only when what they want is good for them. You up for some niece-and-nephew time today?"

"You bet! Any plans made yet?"

"Well, Savannah wants the playground and James wants a ride into Nashville for Chuck E. Cheese." Finished with the windows, she turned and threw her hands in the air. "Your call."

Images of last night, the barn, and Clay rushed in on her. Nashville was a good idea.

"Chuck E. Cheese it is."

"Seriously? You want to drive all the way in to Nashville?"

"You say that like it's fourteen hours away. It's a little over an hour, Meg."

"Says the woman who doesn't routinely spend time in a van with three small children."

"How bad can it be?"

Two hours and fifteen miles from Nashville later, Tandy was eating crow. "I don't know how you do this and stay sane."

"Do what?" Meg filled a sippy cup for the second time with white grape juice while steering with her knee.

"This!" Tandy waved her hand to encompass the three children laughing hysterically at a DVD playing on the flip-down screen installed in the ceiling. Someone was singing about a lost hairbrush. "They're beautiful, but they're so full of energy I'm exhausted before we even get out of the vehicle. And why are they singing about a lost hairbrush?"

Meg laughed. "VeggieTales. It's the silly song on that video, 'O, Where Is My Hairbrush?'"

"That's an actual song?"

"Oh, yeah." Meg nodded, smiling. "You should listen to the Silly Song Countdown. Jamison and I laugh our heads off when we watch it."

"You are one strange woman."

"Probably. But you wait until you have kids, and we'll see how many lyrics you learn."

"What makes you so sure I'm going to have kids?"

Meg glanced from the road to Tandy. "You're not?"

"I don't know. But dating someone and getting married might come in handy before I do."

"No prospects in Orlando? I'd think there it would be *'raining men! Hallelujah! It's raining men!'*"

"None for me, thanks. Nice song, though."

"Thanks. You're not seeing anyone? Even casually?"

"Formally, casually, pin-striped, or button-down. Not a soul."

"On purpose?"

"Of course not on purpose, Meg. I'm busy at work. I don't have time to meet someone, let alone put time into building a relationship." The echo of her conversation with Clay made her squirm.

"That sounds like 'on purpose' to me."

"It should sound like focusing on my career to you."

"That, too. I'm not sure those are mutually exclusive, though."

"Right now, they are."

"What about seeing someone while you're in Stars Hill?"

They neared the exit for Cool Springs, and Meg veered onto the off-ramp.

"Is there a cadre of new men in town? Because I remember a Stars Hill devoid of possibilities."

"Only when your sole possibility is Clay Kelner."

"I'm *not* dating Clay." Her voice was louder than she intended.

Meg's puzzlement was that of a cat catching the scent of a mouse while on a leisurely stroll through the field. "I didn't say you were. I was talking about high school."

"Oh, well, that was then." Tandy pulled down the visor and checked her makeup in the mirror. The scent of deception hung in the air.

"Tandy Sinclair, are you seeing Clay again?"

Tandy snapped the visor shut and turned in her seat. "When would I have had time to see Clay? I was with you and the sisters all day yesterday and am now on my way to Nashville with you."

"And yet, not an answer to my question. Are you seeing Clay?"

She'd seen gray fur and was pouncing. "No."

"Have you seen Clay?"

"You know I ran into him in front of the diner. Speaking of which, you didn't tell me which townsperson clued you in. Was it Mrs. McMurty?"

"No, Petra was eating in the diner and called me. Stop trying to change the subject. Have you seen him other than that time?"

She could lie, but Meg would know. Tandy's lies were about as good as Bill Clinton's, but she lacked his Teflon exterior. "Maybe."

Meg pulled into the Chuck E. Cheese parking lot and threw the van in park. James and Savannah squealed when they saw the big, bright mouse on the building. Hannah, not yet old enough at eight months to be excited about the mouse, threw her hands up and chortled her own glee for her siblings.

"Mom! Let's go get some coins! I just want to ride everything!" James was out of his booster seat and pushing the button to open the door.

Tandy unbuckled her own seat belt and made a swift exit. She opened the sliding door on her side to get Hannah out of her car seat as Meg poked her head in from the other side to release Savannah.

"Don't think this conversation is over."

"Wouldn't dream of it." Tandy pulled Hannah out and propped her on a hip, formulating a plan for how to spend the day with the kids instead of being grilled by her sister. She'd been back in town for less than three days and already Clay was causing trouble in her life again. It was no good. Even if he'd changed, and that was open for as much debate as the reason for the war in Iraq, he was Stars Hill. And her life was Orlando.

Stars Hill was great, it was Daddy and the sisters and memories of Momma. But she couldn't prove her worth there or attain the dreams she and Momma discussed.

For the next three hours Tandy chased James and Savannah all over the popcorn-strewn carpet of the gaming area, stuffing their tickets into her bulging pockets. Whack-a-Moles fell beneath their bopping sticks. Plastic frogs climbed walls as their water-gun spray hit the go button. Pac-Man ate thousands of pellets, gobbling up ghosts and extra points, then spitting out the coveted paper proof of a game well played.

No matter how Meg tried to restart their conversation, Tandy found a new game for James or Savannah to try. Hannah fell asleep an hour into it, forcing Meg to either walk around carrying her sleeping form or hang out in the booth guarding the pizza while Tandy, James, and Savannah played.

Tandy hadn't had this much fun in way too long. Though a resident of the East Coast home of the Magic Kingdom, she was realizing how very little of the magic bled over into her everyday life. This place was a drop in the bucket compared to what they would see at Disney and Epcot, but James and Savannah didn't seem to be lacking an ounce of enthusiasm or excitement. They pulled her across the floor, two tiny engines tugging an adult object growing slower and more immovable as the day progressed.

Fun was exhausting. Tandy sat down on the ski-ball alley beside where James attempted shot after shot at the ten-thousand-point ring. "Having fun, buddy?" She smiled at the screwed up concentration on the six-year-old's face.

He rolled the ball hard down the alley. Tandy watched it bounce hard at the end, glance off the ten-thousand-point ring, and land in the five-thousand-point hole instead.

"I was just so close, Aunt Tandy! Did you see? Did you see?" He hopped up and down, blond hair bouncing.

"I did! Good job!" She picked a scarred wooden ball up out of his stash and offered it to him. "Try again."

James's face pinched together, and he took a few practice swings with his arm. With that kind of focus, the little guy would have no problem making it in life.

"Oof!" The breath went out of her as Savannah jumped into her lap.

"See me!" Savannah said in her tinny three-year-old voice. "See me!"

"I see you, sweetheart."

"No, *swing* her," James said, rolling the ball down the alley.

"Oh! Swing you! Okay. But only for a minute. Aunt Tandy is old and tired."

Both kids giggled. "You're not old, Aunt Tandy," James said.

"I'm not? Are you sure about that?"

He bobbed his head in confidence. "Yep. 'Cause if you was old, you'd have kids like us."

Tandy ignored the tiny stab of pain. "Maybe not, James. Some people end up not having any kiddos, you know. And some people don't ever get married, either."

James and Savannah both looked at her in confusion. "Why not?" James said.

"Well . . ." Oh, how to explain life to someone whose frame of reference was a singing cucumber and a talking tomato? "Some people don't want to get married and have kids."

James forgot the wooden balls and climbed up in her lap beside Savannah. "But why?"

She thought hard, shifting on the uncomfortable lane. Truthfully, she wanted to get married one day and have kids, but there *were* people who chose to live a single life or a life with no children. Tandy knew that, even applauded it. But her reality didn't fall into that category. And, not having the desire, she sat helpless to come up with a justification for it.

"I don't know, James."

A flash went off to her right, and they jumped. "And thank goodness for that," Meg said rising from her kneeling position, camera in one hand and a sleeping Hannah on the other arm.

"Oh, hey, didn't see you there," Tandy said. "You could have jumped in, you know."

"I wanted that shot for my scrapbook. And, besides, I wondered about your answer, too." Meg held out her hand and James took it. "Come on, munchkins. Time to head back home. Daddy will be back and looking for dinner soon."

"But I don't want to!" James planted his feet and pulled back against Meg's hand. "I just want one more game."

Meg turned and knelt down in front of him. "James, Mommy said it's time to go." Her voice reminded Tandy of Momma's. When had that happened? "Now we can either spend five minutes playing more games or five minutes cashing in your tickets for some prizes over at that counter." She pointed with the hand that wasn't holding Hannah toward a glass case filled with plastic trinkets.

"Ooh! Prizes!" James bounced up and down again, taking Meg's hand and pulling her over to the display. "I just love prizes!"

"Nicely done, sister."

Meg threw a smile over her shoulder at Tandy. "You learn what works."

Nine

Halfway back to Stars Hill, with lime-green whistles and plastic red harmonicas nestled in the crooks of sleeping children's arms, Meg turned down the radio and went back on the hunt. "Did you see Clay last night, Tandy?"

"Yes." No sense running. Tandy winced when she even thought the word. No wonder they called her a runner.

"When? Where?"

"He threw rocks at my window at two a.m. I had to go outside or he was going to wake up Daddy."

"Yeah, right." Meg divided glances between the road and Tandy's face. "What happened?"

"Nothing much. We talked. He asked me why I was in Stars Hill. I told him I was taking a break from work and coming home to see everybody."

"That's it?"

"Isn't that enough?"

"I don't know." Meg leaned back in her seat and focused on the road again. "Did he say anything about, you know, you two?"

"As in, did he ask me to get back together? Come on,

Meg. I know you're a romantic, but it's been ten years. We're different people now."

"Just because you're different doesn't mean you aren't still right for each other."

"We weren't right for each other then."

"Are you kidding me? The whole town knew it. Momma got calls daily. Mrs. McMurty had picked out your china."

"Except for Clay. And I'm pretty sure he would need to be in on the secret."

"Oh, he knew it, too. He was just young and dumb and thought you'd follow him anywhere."

"No, he wasn't dumb enough to think I'd give up my own dreams and goals to traipse all over the world with a soldier and his glorified death wish."

"He didn't have a death wish, Tandy."

"Yes, he did!" She took a breath and calmed down. "Yes. He did," she said in a softer voice. "He was determined to join the service and take the most dangerous job he could find."

"I think he'd tell you the word was *adventurous*, not *dangerous*."

"In the military it might as well be the same thing. And how was I going to go to college? Then law school? Have a career? Have *my* dreams?"

"He gambled on those things meaning less to you than being with him."

"Then he only loved the version of me in his head."

"That may be. But it wasn't an unreasonable assumption."

Tandy turned in her seat, eyes wide. "Hel-*lo*? Remember me? Tandy? The one with a mission?"

Meg sighed. "I know who I'm talking to."

"Then you should know how *un*reasonable his assumption was. How could you say that? Do you really think I'd let Momma down like that?"

"Let *Momma* down?"

"Let everybody down. You know what I mean."

"I'm not sure I do." Silence reigned for a few seconds. "T, did you *want* to become a lawyer, move to Orlando, rise to the top of the legal food chain, live on your own, make a name for yourself, and all that jazz because of yourself . . . or Mom?"

"That's a ridiculous question."

"But still a question."

"Not one worthy of an answer." Tandy leaned over and turned up the radio.

Meg turned it back down. "Humor me."

"Why?"

"Because if you think you're fulfilling some dying wish of Momma's, then I've got a sermon for you."

Tandy sighed. "Of course I want those things, Meg. You think I'd let somebody like Clay Kelner go if I didn't want something more? Is that how little you think of me?"

"You know I have all kinds of respect for you, T. I've got enough respect to know you'd sacrifice your own desires if you thought it would honor Momma. You've always been that way. Heck, it's why you're here in Stars Hill, right? You sacrificed your job for a homeless man. You're an amazing woman and everybody knows it. Except, sometimes, maybe you."

"Oh, yeah, I'm just fabulous." Tandy waved a hand in the air. "Belle of the ball. Talk of the town. The city can't get enough of me, I'm just so wonderful."

"In a lot of ways, you are."

"Yet you're the one with a husband and three kids. Joy's the one with a husband and the perfect Martha Stewart home. And don't even mention Kendra because I don't think she wants to be married, so she's happy, too."

"Are you not happy?"

"I don't know!" Tandy put her hand over her mouth. Where had *that* come from? Of course she was happy! She had a great career, an apartment, a dog, a *life*. What was there to be unhappy about?

Clay's voice swept through her memory like a summer breeze heavy with sunshine. Until she'd seen his name swing from that sign on Lindell, contentedness existed, if not happiness. And it would come back as soon as her eyes saw the "Welcome to the Sunshine State" sign in ten days. Ten short, awfully long, days.

"I'm happy, Meg. I may not have everything you or Joy or Kendra has, but I've got a whole lot more than a homeless girl from the streets of Orlando can hope for."

"Do you have more than the daughter of Marian and Jack Sinclair could hope for? Because that's you, too, Tandy."

"Momma and Daddy were more than I deserved. They gave me the chance to do something with my life. And I'm not going to let them down."

"They also gave us love, Tandy. And Momma would want you to share that with someone else."

Tandy reached over and turned the radio back up.

This time Meg let it go.

Ten

As they drove down Lindell, Tandy looked out the window. "Hey, when did Emmy put in scrapbooking supplies?"

"Oh! That reminds me!" Meg swung the van into a parking space in front of the store. "I've got to see if they have the new Cricut cartridges yet."

"I'll stay here with the kids."

Meg nodded and dashed toward the glass door bearing the name *Emmy's Attic.*

Seconds later Kendra popped out of the store. Tandy opened the van door. "Hey! What are you doing down here?"

"Ran out of clay ingredients." Kendra stuck her head in the door and peeked toward the back. "Meg said y'all went to Nashville?"

"Yeah, James wanted Chuck E. Cheese."

"Sucker." Kendra grinned.

"Have you looked at him when he begs? That child will break hearts in a few years."

"I know. I feel bad for Meg and Jamison. Can you imagine how many girls will be calling their house at all hours?"

They laughed. "So did you get your supplies?"

"Yeah. I'm trying to finish a sculpture in time for the Iris Festival competition. Ran out just as I was making some progress."

"Isn't that always how it goes?"

"In our lives, yeah." Kendra winked. "What are you doing for dinner?"

"I hadn't thought that far ahead. I haven't talked to Daddy since this morning, though. He may have something planned."

"Oh, he's got something planned, all right." Kendra's smile rivaled the Cheshire cat's.

"What?"

"Didn't he tell you?"

"No, which seems to be a running problem around here."

"He goes over to Heartland now."

"No!" Tandy glanced down the sidewalk to see if anyone was within hearing distance.

"Yep. And don't bother looking around, everybody knows. Every Friday night, like clockwork, you'll find him cutting a rug on the dance floor."

"Daddy? Our daddy?" Tandy squeaked.

"The same."

Tandy shook her head like a diver getting water out of his ears. "Daddy goes country dancing every Friday night."

"You heard me."

"And the deacons of Grace Christian haven't done something about it?"

"Other than join him, no."

"The *deacons* are at Heartland too?" Tandy sat back hard in the seat.

"I asked the same thing. Daddy said, and I quote, 'David danced before the Lord.'" Tandy's eyes grew wide at that and Kendra put her hand over her heart. "I kid you not."

"David, as in the Bible? King David? That David?"

"Yep. I went home and looked it up and, sure enough, Daddy's right. David danced before the Lord when he was overcome with happiness. His wife lit into him for it, though."

"Wonder if Momma would do the same to Daddy?"

"I doubt it. Momma loved to dance. Don't you remember them dancing in the living room together?"

"Yeah, but they didn't dance in public."

"Momma told me once they danced all the time in public before Daddy took the pastorate at Grace Christian."

"You're lying!"

"If I'm lying, I'm dying. No joke. Daddy didn't want to upset folks, though, after he started preaching. So they quit going." Kendra sighed. "Bet Daddy wishes now they'd kept it up."

Tulips swayed in the cool breeze as they thought about Momma and Daddy dancing.

Tandy remembered one night when she'd been awakened by the sound of music. Tiptoeing out of her room, she found the sight of Daddy and Momma, swaying together in each other's arms. Patsy Cline sang in the background. Momma noticed her and motioned for Tandy to come over.

Tandy had only been with them for six months by then, not long enough yet to fully trust that Momma and Daddy were as nice as they seemed on the outside. She walked over to Momma, knotted red hair hanging to her bony shoulders, nibbling on a fingernail already bitten to the quick. Momma scooped her up and said, "Tandy sandwich!" Daddy put his arms around them and, suddenly, she was squished between them both just like the creamy middle of a sandwich cookie.

"Earth to Tandy." Kendra snapped her fingers in front of Tandy's face. "You with me?"

"Hmm?" Tandy blinked. "Sure, yeah, I'm with you."

"Groovy! Then I'll pick you up around 7."

"Pick me up?"

"Unless you want to show up with Daddy. I didn't figure you could get ready in time for him. He leaves right at 5:45 to be there when Heartland opens at six."

"We're going to Heartland?"

"That's what I said. Are you with me or not?"

What else did she have to do on a Friday night in Stars Hill? If Meg was going home to make dinner, they wouldn't all be getting together to scrap again in Momma's studio. "Why not?"

"Okay, see ya at seven, then." Kendra turned to go.

"Wait, can you sit here with the kiddos while I run inside? I ran out of adhesive last night, and I think my paper supply is dwindling."

"I'd never stand between a scrapper and her supplies." Kendra pulled Tandy's door open wider and made a sweeping gesture like a butler. "Your store awaits, milady."

Tandy giggled and stepped onto the sidewalk. "Thanks, Ken." She entered the store, impressed by the changes Emmy had made since taking it over from Emma. An immense scrapbooking section stretched the entire length of the store. In back, above a double doorway, hung a sign that read *Scrapbooking Classroom*.

Circle racks of Kaleidoscope and Basic Grey paper drew her in. She turned the wire racks, snatching up several sheets of almost every option. The swirls of red, blue, and brown were going to look fantastic with her pictures. And the cards she'd make with the leftover scraps would be color-suited for pretty much any purpose from birthday to anniversary to thank you.

The thought of cards sent her toward a Peg-Board full of card kits hanging in the hues of the rainbow. At the far end were columns of cards and envelopes in basic colors like tan, black, white, and ivory. She pulled ten ivory, ten white, and six tan from their stacks, adding them to her growing armload of product.

Remembering the discovery of a distressing tool last night, Tandy prowled around the store until she found the little pink disc with the white cursive words *Heidi Swapp* on it. Using Kendra's distresser last night had added just enough dimension to make the paper leap off the page.

Falling back into a world she now realized she'd been neglecting, Tandy overloaded her arms in a matter of minutes. She went in search of a basket.

"Tandy Sinclair! As I live and breathe!" Emmy Dotson stood behind the register, ringing up Meg's sale. She clapped her small hands, reminding Tandy of James's face at Chuck E. Cheese, and came scurrying around the counter. "Get over here and give me a hug, girl! It's been too long!" Emmy voice was the biggest thing about her. Not more than five feet tall and small enough to still shop in the Juniors section, Emmy's size gave no indication of her energy. Tandy leaned down to hug her and smelled caramel and apples in the fabric of her white apron.

"Hey, Emmy. I love what you've done with the place."

Emmy stepped back from the hug and looked around the store as if seeing it anew. "It's getting there. I swear

Momma would have turned this into a nursing home if I'd let her." She touched Tandy's shoulder and leaned forward. "Told me I was crazy to bring in scrapbooking stuff and I needed to stick with the basics of sewing and painting. But I was having none of it. I told her, 'Momma, either let me do this, or I'm taking my idea and going down to Sara Sykes.' You should've seen how fast that woman changed her mind." Emmy snapped her fingers. "Like a dog smacked by a cat's paw, she backed off and told me it was on my own disrespectful, foolhardy head if it failed."

Emmy waved a short arm around the room. "But it didn't! We started out with about half this much stuff, and everybody kept coming in here wanting more. Pretty soon, it just about took over the store. Momma finally said I might not be as foolhardy as she thought, though she didn't say a word about the disrespectful part, and gave me full ownership of the store. Now she's down in Florida sunning herself on a beach half the year, and I'm in here working myself silly making caramel apples and fruit punch for the nightly classes."

Tandy rushed to get a word in. "I noticed you had a classroom over there. Who teaches?"

"Your sister teaches sometimes for us—" Emmy turned and looked at Meg. "Oh my stars! I completely forgot about you, Meg." She darted back around the counter and continued ringing up Meg's sale. "Let's see, where was I? We just lacked the paper, right, Meg?"

"You've got it." Meg smiled and winked at Tandy.

"Anyway, Meg here teaches some of our classes, and Kendra and Joy have both taught for me, too. It's pretty much the Sinclair School, I guess, except, you know, Meg and Joy are married so they're not Sinclairs in name anymore."

Emmy punched buttons on the register and filled a bag with products.

Tandy knew this could go on for another half hour if she let it. She stepped to the counter and set down her supplies.

"Look what all you found! Did you see the new letters from K & Company? They've got glitter! I put clear embossing powder on them and then use my heat gun." Emmy leaned across the counter and spoke in a whisper, though Tandy had seen no one else in the store. "Seals in the glitter. Makes it so it doesn't spread all over your page over time. Just a little trick I figured out."

She leaned back and finished up Meg's sale.

"Thanks, Emmy," Meg said. "Tandy, I'll wait for you in the van. I'm sure Kendra's wondering what's happened to us."

"Oh, are the little ones out there? You know you can bring them on in here, Meg. They can play over there with the crayons and colors." She waved to an area that Tandy now saw was set up as a children's play station. Legos and balls filled three baskets while dolls and doll clothes filled three on the opposite wall. A blank television screen was set within a built-in bookcase lined with DVDs.

"Thanks, Emmy," Meg said. "But they fell asleep in the van, and I hated to wake them up." She backed toward the door as she spoke. "I'll see you later!" She pushed the door open with her backside and escaped into the April sunshine.

"So, Miss Tandy, what's going on in the big city?"

"Oh, not much. Just working hard, I guess."

"You're still working?" Emmy cocked her head, looking for all the world like a little wren contemplating a worm. "I thought I heard you were in between jobs."

"Where in the world did you hear that?"

"Come to think of it, I'm not sure. Maybe Mrs. McMurty? Or Sandra Hanover." She shrugged and resumed ringing up Tandy's purchase. "But you give me the skinny, and I'll make sure to correct anybody who says otherwise. You know this town. Everybody knows everybody else's business and just loves to share it with anybody who will listen. Why, I had Mrs. Crowley in here last week telling me my momma was surfing waves and wearing a bikini like she'd lost her mind down there in Florida. I thought she'd caught the Alzheimer's or something and went running to a phone. But, no, turns out she had told Edna Johnston about a girl in a bikini on the beach who had a, shall we say, wardrobe malfunction, when she fell off her surfboard. Now how that turned into my God-fearing, respectable momma wearing a bikini is anybody's guess. But there you go. So you just tell me what happened to make you come home, and I'll get it straightened out for you."

Tandy forced a smile. Emmy had a good heart and meant well. "I'm afraid there's not much of a story, Emmy. I just wanted to come home and visit with the sisters and Daddy for a while."

Emmy finished her scanning and looked at Tandy. "It's gonna be hard to get folks to repeat that. No juice to it. No meat to sink your teeth into." She glanced at the window on the register. "It's $21.67. So nothing happened to make you come home?"

Tandy handed over her money and picked up the bag of product. "Nope. Just a boring old visit. Tell the townsfolk I'm sorry to disappoint." She backed toward the door as Meg had done earlier.

"I'll try, Tandy. You hurry back in now, you hear?"

Tandy nodded and pushed through the door onto the sidewalk. She yanked open the van door, nearly falling into the seat and slamming it closed.

"Do you still have both your ears?" Meg asked.

"What?"

"Your ears. Did she talk one of them off?"

"Very funny. I can't believe she's still like that."

"And this was a good day."

Tandy's look of shock was as genuine as Cooper's the day they'd gone to PetSmart and found his food brand was discontinued. "It's worse?"

Meg started the van and pulled onto Lindell, nodding. "Mm-hmm. One day I got to hear the entire story of Brent's colonoscopy. You haven't lived until you hear a woman describe her husband's invasive medical procedure."

"Ewww. So she and Brent are still married then?"

"Yep. Former cheerleader. Former football player." Meg lifted a shoulder. "Guess it was inevitable."

"She's got good product, though."

"I know, that's why she's successful in spite of herself. She had every single one of the three new Cricut cartridges. And did you see that Kaleidoscope paper?"

Tandy held up her own bag. "Yep."

Meg glanced over and laughed. "Great minds think alike."

"Now that I've got more paper options, I'm itching to scrapbook again. Think everybody could find some time tomorrow?"

Meg tapped her finger on the steering wheel, thinking. "Joy's cutting my hair at nine in the morning. Then Savannah's got gymnastics at ten."

"She's in gymnastics class? She's three!"

"Yeah, but they can start as soon as they're potty trained now. She loves it, so we let her go. She'll come home and do somersaults all over the living room until she falls asleep."

"That's too funny."

"It *is* pretty cute. She'll do a half turn and then just lay out in the floor in a dead slumber. I've got a layout of it I'll show you tomorrow."

"Cute." Tandy pushed down thoughts of her own personless pictures. "Okay, so how about noonish?"

"Works for me."

"I'll ask Kendra about it tonight, and you talk to Joy in the morning, okay?"

"Deal."

"Oh, and see if she managed to get me an appointment with Taylor. These knots are only getting worse."

"Will do."

They pulled through the gates and drove up to the house. Tandy gathered up her purse and bag, pulling on the door handle.

"Hey, Tandy?" Meg's soft voice made Tandy pause and turn.

"Yeah?"

"I'm sorry if I said something to hurt you today. You know, earlier."

Tandy smiled. "Hurt me? Of course not. Don't worry about it for a second. We're good." She backed away. *Hurting isn't something I do anymore.*

"You're sure?" Meg narrowed her eyes, unconvinced.

"Absolutely. Good to go." Tandy kept backing.

"Okay, if you say so. See ya tomorrow?"

"See ya." She turned and trotted up the porch steps.

✂ ✂ ✂

INSIDE, A NOTE was propped up on the middle step. She picked it up and read,

> *Gone up to the church for a while. Be back around*
> *4:30. I've got Coop.*
> *Love,*
> *Dad*

She stuffed the note in her pocket and climbed the rest of the stairs, a small smile on her face. Cooper was probably running between the old mahogany pews, sniffing out every corner, chasing down dust bunnies and ladybugs. Grace Christian had endured a problem with ladybugs ever since she could remember. Like the hawks of Orlando, the creatures refused to go anywhere else, no matter what measures they took.

Several Sundays she'd sat on the front pew with Momma, watching a ladybug crawl all over her hand for the half hour of Daddy's sermon. Momma said God loved the color of her hair so much he'd made a fun ladybug to match it. That way the rest of the world could see the beautiful color, too.

Entering her bedroom, she tossed the Emmy's Attic bag on her Dutch doll quilt and headed for the closet. Heaven only knew if she'd brought something suitable for Heartland. Hangers clacked together as she considered and discarded each option. Finally, a yellow silk skirt presented itself. Its wide ruffles fell gracefully, and Tandy remembered how they'd shifted in the ocean breeze the night she wore it to a dinner for the firm. It was a bit dressy for Heartland, but if she wore a white cotton button-up and could find her old boots, it would work. If she decided to dance, the length would be perfect, hitting just at her knees.

She laid the skirt and shirt out on the bed and heard Daddy's truck pull up outside. A few seconds later Cooper's welcoming woof sounded downstairs, and she went to meet them.

"Hey, Daddy! Everything ready for Sunday service?"

"Ready as it's gonna get," he said, coming down the hallway and turning into the kitchen. She followed him in. "How was Nashville?"

"Still there," she said.

"Good to know."

"So Kendra tells me you're going dancing tonight."

"That child has a mouth the size of Texas." He pulled a bowl of chili from the refrigerator.

"She says you go every Friday night."

He spooned chili into two bowls, then put one in the microwave.

"We thought we might join you tonight."

At that she got his eyes. "You and Kendra?"

"Yes, Kendra and me. Who else would I go dancing with?"

"After last night's visitor, I wasn't sure."

Tandy felt her face turn fourteen shades of red. "Visitor?"

Daddy smiled. "Don't go making it worse by lying about it, Tandy. If I'd had a problem with you talking to Clay Kelner, I'd have come out to the barn and said so."

"Why didn't you?"

The microwave beeped, and he pulled the bowls out, stirred them, then put them back in.

"Because I thought it'd be good for you two to talk by yourselves for a little while."

"I thought you didn't like Clay."

"I don't like what Clay did to you back in the day. I don't know the man well enough to have an opinion about the present."

"You think he's changed?"

"I guess that depends on what part of him you're referring to." The microwave dinged again, and he pulled the bowls of chili out. Carrying them across the kitchen, he motioned with his elbow for her to follow him. She grabbed spoons from the utensil drawer and followed. "If you're asking me about his wanderlust, I'd say a man with the itch to travel in his bones doesn't open up a diner in a town the size of Stars Hill. Owning a business pretty much locks you into a location."

"True." She sat down and took a bite of chili.

"You're going to choke on that."

"What? Oh." She bowed her head and tensed up, waiting for him to say grace.

"Thank you for this food, Lord. In your Son's name, amen." He took a bite of chili, and she relaxed again. "Now if you're asking me would he hurt you again, then I don't have an answer. Nobody would. Including Clay."

"Daddy, I didn't come home to start a relationship. This was just supposed to be a time to kick back, relax, see you, see the sisters, get some scrapbooking done, that kind of thing."

"I know, honey, but you should know by now that what we plan isn't always—shoot, is *rarely ever* what happens in reality."

"Are you telling me to pursue a relationship with Clay Kelner?"

"No. You do whatever you think is right about that. It's your life, your choice. But I'm telling you not to dismiss the idea because of the boy he was ten years ago."

"I'm dismissing the idea because, as you just pointed out, he's here. In Stars Hill. And my life is eight hundred miles south of here. I have a career at a firm that I like and I'm being promoted in. I could be a partner in a few years."

Daddy grinned. "There you go again, planning things."

"What's so wrong with planning things? Isn't that what you and Momma taught us to do? How many times did you tell us to chase after our dreams, think big, don't let our past dictate our future, and all that?"

"You're right. We did tell you those things. But there's a balance, Tandy, a flexibility that you need to factor in. Dream big. Make a plan for achieving your dream. But if something comes up that makes you want to alter your dream or reach it in a different way, don't dismiss it just because it isn't in the original plan." He took a bite of chili and chewed.

She scooped chili and considered his words. "And you think I should reconsider things because of Clay?"

His spoon clinked the side of the bowl as he set it down. "I don't know, Tandy. Tell me this, why do you live in Orlando?"

"Because I *work* there, Daddy. And you *know* why else."

"Tell me."

"Why are we getting into this?" She stood and snatched up her bowl.

"Because we should have a long time ago, and I'm a little late to the party."

"I needed to go and confront what happened to me." Jerking up the faucet, Tandy ignored the spray of water bouncing out of the bowl and onto her shirt. She grabbed the dishrag and scrubbed the dish.

"Why?"

"You know why. You were there when Momma said it."

"I was there when your momma said a lot of things, Tandy."

"Then you'll remember she said it was important that I not let fear make my decisions for me." She turned the water off and put the bowl in the drying rack. "So I don't. I live in the very city that took my childhood. No, I don't live there; I *succeed* there." Pulling a red gingham towel off its rack, she dried her hands.

"And this is your purpose?" Daddy continued eating, his back to her.

"Excuse me?"

"This is the reason God created you?"

"Well, it's a whole lot better than believing he created me to live on the streets, be adopted by loving parents, and lose one to cancer before I even went to college." She froze. *What?*

Daddy had stilled. He turned in his chair and met her eyes. "Tandy, honey, I can't pretend to understand why God let your momma die when and how she did. But I'm also not going to pretend this life you have in Orlando is all he or I want for you."

"What is so wrong with my life? I have a successful—"

"I know, I know." Daddy held up his big, calloused hands. "You're an attorney with an office in a firm other attorneys would give their left arm for. But where's the love in your life, Tandy? The faith? The things that matter?"

I couldn't just go lay on the beach for two weeks. No, I had to come here. "I need to go get a shower and get ready," she said. "I'll see you at Heartland."

She left the kitchen, back as straight as the line from Daddy to heaven and steps as firm as his faith. When she entered her bedroom, the painted dresser mocked her with the love Daddy said was missing from her life.

She had plenty of love. It was just wrapped around a memory that blocked a dream she couldn't chase.

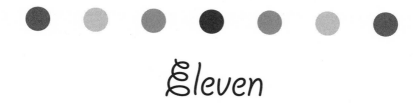

Eleven

Girl, what are you *doing?*" Kendra stood in the hallway, hand on hip, eyes raking up and down Tandy's body.

"What?"

"Are you trying to make every man in this town want you? Or just upstage me?"

Tandy glanced down at her outfit. "In this? It's not a big deal."

"Says the woman who has obviously forgotten that the number of available men in this town hovers around the temperature of Buffalo in winter." Kendra looped her arm through Tandy's and walked them toward the front door. "And here you are strutting all over the place in those boots and tan legs. Good thing I carry my tan year-round, or I'd be in trouble tonight."

Their laughter accompanied them into the cool night. "We taking yours or mine?" Kendra eyed Tandy's car. "Because if I have a vote, I'll take a Beamer any day."

"Mine it is." They settled into the gray leather seats, and Tandy started the engine. Gretchen Wilson's voice poured from the speakers. *"I'm here for the party . . ."*

"Sing it, girl!" Kendra's laughter rang out, and off they went.

Fifteen minutes later they parked in the white gravel lot beside a steel building. A white metal sign with rust on the corners hung by chains above a door. "Heartland Dance" it read in looping red letters. Chevy, Ford, and Dodge pickup trucks crowded the lot with an occasional Toyota here and there. With the exception of her Beamer, not one car could be seen—luxury or otherwise.

"What is this, a truck convention?"

Kendra laughed and the wind caught her long spiral hair. "You've been gone so long, you're forgetting your roots. Come on!" They linked arms again and crossed the gravel lot, weaving in between row after row of pickups.

Tandy wondered if this was such a good idea. Everybody in there had probably spent the past two days talking about her return. They'd dissected her relationship with Clay and retold the story of him leaving her to join the military. She stopped in her tracks.

"What's wrong?"

"I may have changed my mind."

"What?" Kendra ducked her head to catch Tandy's gaze. "Why?"

"I'm tired. I, uh, don't feel much like dancing."

Kendra stood in front of her and put both hands on her hips. "Tandy Sinclair, what are you running from?"

Tandy looked up. "I'm not running. I just don't feel like walking in there right now."

"Why not?"

"Kendra, come on! You know those people have spent the past two days talking about me. If I go in there, I'm just going to keep the rumor mill going."

"So?"

"So? What do you mean, 'so'?"

"I mean, who cares? So they talk about you. Big deal."

"Easy for you to say."

"Tandy, I am the only black girl in an all-white family living in a tiny town in Tennessee. I'm an artist in my thirties and unmarried. I am as far from normal around here as it gets. Do you think these people don't talk about me? Half of them think I'm a lesbian, and the others think I have a husband and child I'm hiding in Nashville. Oh, and there's a 2 percent contingent that says I've been married several times secretly and sworn off men *and women* for good."

"You're kidding me."

"I am not."

"Then why do you stay here?"

Kendra shrugged. "Why wouldn't I? The way I look at it, if they're talking about me, then they're not talking about somebody else. And who cares what they think of me anyway? It's a small town with not a lot to do. I get that, and I'm happy to give them some entertainment. They've given me a great place to live."

"You're something else." Tandy shook her head.

"And don't you forget it." Kendra took Tandy's elbow and turned her back toward the entrance. "Now get yourself in there and have some fun before I tell folks I'm not married because I'm moving in with my sister in Orlando. You better believe they'd have some fun with that one."

"I'm pretty sure that's blackmail."

"Sue me." They reached the door, and Kendra put her hand on the knob. She paused and looked Tandy in the eye. "But I have to warn you, I have a sister who's an attorney; and she'll crucify you in court, she's so good."

Tandy grinned. "Thanks."

"You're welcome. Ready for some fun?"

"You bet."

They walked through the door, and Kendra veered off toward the left side of the room. Tandy followed, taking in the worn wooden floor, the thud of boots pounding it in rhythm, the sound of a steel guitar from the raised platform at the other end of the room. The noise was almost overwhelming but not quite. Small bulb lights were strung with no pattern here and there around the room. Metal folding chairs lined the walls and were grouped in occasional clusters. Everywhere she looked, Tandy saw smiling faces and tapping feet. A little of the tension left her shoulders. Maybe they weren't *all* talking about her.

Kendra plopped down on one of the chairs and motioned for Tandy to do the same. "I think we'll wait for a line dance," Kendra yelled over the din.

Tandy nodded. Dancers packed the dance floor. Skirts flared as couples executed quick turns. Cowboy hats spun in shades of brown and black. Some of the older women wore the traditional country garb, their mates in bolos and string ties. Younger adults danced right alongside them in Seven jeans and Nine West boots.

"I can't believe how many people are here!" she hollered at Kendra.

Kendra nodded. The song came to an end, and everybody clapped. Opening notes for "Boot Scootin' Boogie" sounded, and a cheer went up from the crowd.

Kendra stood. "Oldie but a goodie!" She held out her hand. Tandy allowed herself to be pulled from the chair and onto the dance floor. People were lining up and, on cue, started lattice stepping to the right. Tandy fumbled a few times, but by the third set through remembered the steps and put some enthusiasm into it. Kendra nodded her encouragement.

Tandy twirled and stomped, loving the feel of a boot heel beneath her foot again. She never wore boots in Orlando. That was only for the horse farmers that lived way outside of town or over in Ocala. Or for teenagers growing up on a farm in a little Tennessee town. But these boots, molded from years of wear, felt like gloves for her feet; and, before she knew it, she was moving to the dance with barely any thought. She'd worried they wouldn't fit. But they did. Perfectly. Her laughter rang out.

The band kicked into another line dance, and everybody adjusted their steps to the new song. Tandy didn't know this one. It was new. But it wasn't hard, and a few turns into it she had it down, mostly. Even when her feet stumbled and she bumped into someone, they laughed with her and exaggerated their own steps to show her how.

By the end of the second song, Tandy was loose, relaxed, and in need of some water. She tapped Kendra on the shoulder and pantomimed drinking. Kendra nodded and shooed her on, showing she wasn't ready for a break yet. Tandy turned and made her way through the crowd, trying not to disrupt the rhythm of the participants.

She stepped off the floor with a sigh of relief and headed for the concession stand.

"Bottle of water, please," she said to the kid behind the counter. Hormones were wreaking havoc on the poor guy's face, and her heart went out to him. She smiled as she handed over her dollar for the water, and he grinned back, revealing a mouth so full of metal she wondered if he had a hard time making it through the detector at the airport. Clear braces must not have made their way to Stars Hill.

She unscrewed the cap and took a swig of water, grateful for the liquid relief as it flowed down her throat. Swallowing, she tilted her head left and right, stretching the muscles in her neck.

"Well, hey there," a deep voice said from her side. She turned to see a tall man with scruffy brown hair and a very wide forehead. "Remember me?"

She squinted. The light in here wasn't the greatest, and he didn't look all that familiar. "I'm sorry. I don't think so."

"It's Eric! Eric Hoffstetler!" He patted his chest with a big, beefy hand, and she remembered her old classmate.

"Eric! Hey!" She leaned over and hugged him. "How are you?"

"Good . . . can't complain . . . heard you . . . town."

She caught about every other word over the din of music and stomping boots but did her best to interpret. "Yeah, just visiting Daddy and the sisters for a few days. So how's Kathy?"

His face clouded over. "She's good. Living in Nashville now."

"Oh, I'm so sorry. I hadn't heard."

"It's okay. Me and Ricky are making it fine while she's finding herself or whatever."

"Did you two have any more kids?"

"Nope, just Ricky."

"He's about ten now, right?"

Eric puffed up. "Eleven. Born just a few weeks after graduation, remember?"

She wasn't sure what to say to that.

"Oh, right. You were gone by then."

He scuffed the toe of his boot on the dusty floor as they let the music and noise swirl around them.

"You want to dance?"

"Oh! No, I'm just doing the line dances. You know. I'm here with Kendra."

She looked out on the floor as the song changed to a two-step. Kendra was nodding her head and smiling at a man in a black Stetson, white oxford, and black jeans. He put his arm around her waist, and they danced off.

"Looks like Kendra's not sitting this one out," Eric said. "Come on. It'll be fun."

She'd come this far. Might as well go ahead and enjoy the place as much as possible. Besides, Eric Hofstettler and romance belonged together like chick peas and chocolate— never gonna be a good combination.

She nodded, set her bottle of water on a chair, and put her hand in his offered one. "Okay. Let's go."

He pulled her out on the dance floor, and she surprised herself by remembering how to two-step. They didn't talk, just moved to the rhythm of the music. Tandy again felt herself relaxing and looked up at Eric.

He was smiling at her. "Guess you haven't forgotten how we dance around here."

She grinned. "It's like riding a bike. You don't remember how, but your body does if you try."

He nodded, his hand on her waist guiding her around the other couples.

"You're pretty good at this."

"Ricky and I come pretty much every weekend."

"He's here?" She looked around the dimly lit room. "Which one is he?"

Eric gestured with the hand that held hers. "He's the tallest one in that group of kids over there."

She scanned the walls and spotted a miniature version of Eric. She turned to focus back on Eric and caught sight of Clay.

He stood behind the line of chairs, his green eyes heavy on her. A rushing sound went through her head, blocking out the pounding music and reminding her of waves crashing on the rocks. She froze, stumbling over her feet when Eric's steps moved on without her.

"You okay?" He stopped and balanced her with his hands. Couples continued to twirl around them.

She swallowed, looked at Eric, and began to hear the guitar's twang again. The rushing noise receded. "Yeah. Yeah, I'm fine. Guess it's not as easy as I thought." She laughed and took his hand again.

"Just like riding a bike. You've gotta fall off sometimes. Trick is in the getting back up."

"Good point." Focusing on his eyes would keep her from looking anywhere else. "Before I fall off again, tell me what's been going on around here."

"Hmm. Cheerleaders won the state championship again."

"Nice to know they're still bringing home the trophy." She congratulated herself for carrying on a mundane conversation while Clay's gaze bore holes into the back of her head.

"Junior high's getting a new gym."

"I'll bet Ricky is excited about that."

"Yeah. He's great with a basketball." The pride in Eric's voice made her smile and really pay attention.

"And football?"

"He's not too bad on the gridiron, either. Still a little early to tell."

"Like father, like son, I'll bet."

Ricky's back straightened further under her hand, and his chest puffed up a bit. Her eye strayed across the dance floor and caught sight of Kendra being dipped by the tall guy with the black Stetson. Kendra looked her way and grinned as the band ended the song with flourish.

Tandy turned her attention back to Eric.

"Thanks for the dance, Tandy." He let go of her hand and took a step back.

"You bet!" Awkwardness crept between them. "Guess I'll go finish that water now." Ducking her head, her boots clopped on the hardwood, carrying her to the corner of the room and the bliss of an isolated chair. She took a drink from the water bottle she'd snatched up along the way. Getting out of here was at the top of the priority list. It wouldn't be long before Clay made his way over here, and then the entire town would have something new to talk about tomorrow morning over breakfast.

Her searching gaze darted around the room, looking for Kendra or Daddy. There! Daddy sat in the corner talking to some woman Tandy didn't know. Which was impossible since Tandy knew everyone in this town, but that woman didn't look like anybody Tandy knew. Her red—not auburn, *red*—hair was cut to about half an inch all over her head and stood up in little spikes. A round face of pale skin contributed to the shock of the red. Her posture, hand on hip with one foot forward and leaning in to hear whatever Daddy was saying, communicated an intimacy Tandy didn't find appropriate right here in front of everybody. Even in front of nobody.

A white peasant blouse hung low on her shoulders, cinched in at the waist. Her blue skirt of crinkly fabric looked full, probably designed to swirl around her legs while she danced, and ended in brown leather boots that resembled Tandy's except for some ornament Tandy couldn't get a clear look at from here. As the woman tapped her toe, the light occasionally glinted off the piece of embellishment, whatever it was.

Tandy stared. Most likely Daddy had offered the woman an invitation to Grace Christian in a few days. That had to be why he appeared so interested in the words coming from her mouth. Tandy watched as the woman laid her small hand on Daddy's arm and laughed. Daddy put his hand on top of hers and joined in the joy.

That doesn't look like a church invitation. She got up to investigate and felt a hand on her own arm.

"How about letting him have his fun?"

Clay's voice shocked her ears into that roaring silence again.

She shook her head to clear it of both the roar and the image of Daddy and that woman. This town, these people, this *noise* was too much. "Excuse me?"

Clay nodded in Daddy's direction as the band began a slow Gretchen Wilson tune. "He's just having a little fun talking to Zelda. And I'm guessing by the look on your face you were headed over there to put a stop to it."

"Of course not." She shook her arm free of his hand, which he stuffed in the pockets of some very snug jeans. "I just wondered who she was and all." *And what she's doing flirting with Daddy in the middle of Heartland.* At least Tandy wouldn't be the only thing everybody talked about in the morning.

"She's Zelda Norman and she's fine. Not a barracuda. Not a hussy."

"I didn't say she was any of those things."

"Yes, you did."

"No, I didn't."

He laid a hand against her cheek, his eyes softening as their gazes locked. Blood froze in her veins, savoring the heat of his palm, memorizing it. There would be plenty of time in Orlando to chastise herself for the feeling. "Your face, Tandy. It tells everything you don't want to say."

Being known by this man, this one, this part of her past that aligned with the happiness of Momma and a safe place to live, took her breath. He was a gift of a man, but one better given to a different woman. One without her history or her plans for the future. Her dreams lay in Orlando, a big city that hurt her but in which she could live without hurting now. The triumph of that would make Momma proud.

Even if Clay no longer lusted for the adventures of military life that prevented her from being his, he seemed to have traded that for a life here in Stars Hill. Once again he'd chosen a path that she couldn't possibly follow.

The room closed in on her as she realized she was reliving it all.

Clay stood tall, his honest eyes now framed in laugh lines, his shoulders a bit more broad.

And his feet on a path not wide enough for her.

Twelve

The band ended their song, and Tandy vaguely heard them announce a ten-minute break. Prerecorded music played but not at the volume of the band. Conversations buzzed around her. And still she stood there, surroundings forgotten, staring into eyes that for years had held the promise of hope and a future.

Clay's thumb grazed her cheekbone, eyes questioning hers.

She didn't have the answers. "Clay."

"Hmm?"

She didn't know what she'd intended to say. Just needed to affirm his name, a name she hadn't spoken all through college or law school or her years in Orlando. Not allowing it to cross her lips, she realized now, hadn't prevented her heart from beating it.

She shook her head slightly, unable to get past the emotions crashing over her. She felt like the little bits of broken shell left behind on the shore. Jagged. Edgy. Scattered. Adrift.

"Tandy, we need to talk."

Her head shook, automatically negating the idea before it left his mouth. She'd been saying no to this chaos of emotion for so many years in her mind, it didn't seem possible to do otherwise. His hand slid from her cheek to her neck and rubbed the muscles tightened into knots there.

"Think, Tandy. This is me. This is *us*."

"There is no us." Fear and uncertainty turned her voice husky, but the words sounded right. "There is no us." More sure this time.

"Yes, there is. And I know you enough to know that your words don't match your reality. We need to talk."

The giant wave crashed again, and in her mind she gathered all the sharp bits together, her efforts frantic yet fruitful. She stepped back from him. "I can't, Clay. You're Stars Hill. I'm not." Backed another step.

He came toward her. "See, that's something we should discuss."

Loose curls bounced around her face as her head shook vehemently back and forth. "No. It's pointless to discuss things that aren't going to change."

"Then let's talk about why they can't change."

"Tandy!" Kendra appeared at her side, stepping between her and Clay. "Girl, I just about lost you over here in the corner. Come on out to the dance floor. The band's about to play 'Devil Went Down to Georgia.'"

Tandy looked into Kendra's sparkling brown eyes, her relief sighing out through dry lips. She glanced toward the stage where the band was, indeed, taking their positions again. She turned back and caught Clay's eyes over Kendra's head.

Kendra grabbed her arm, and Tandy looked at her again. "Come on! I know you remember this dance."

"What?" Kendra's words bobbed on the surface of the waves in her head while Clay stood there, his eyes begging her to do *something*, though she wasn't sure what.

Kendra put her hands on Tandy's shoulders and shook. "Earth to Tandy! 'Devil Went Down to Georgia'!" It registered with her this time, and Tandy's mind filled with images of her and Kendra in the front yard, practicing the steps over and over. They'd told Momma they were going to be Coyotes. Thankfully, Momma had as much interest in movies as Tandy did in sitting still, so they'd gone on practicing for weeks. It had been Meg who finally explained to Momma the meaning and job description of a Coyote. Their practicing came to a screeching halt.

"Come on!" Tandy allowed Kendra to pull her through the rows of chairs and back up onto the dance floor. The opening notes of the Charlie Daniels Band's signature song sounded, and Tandy's feet moved of their own accord. Her skirt didn't provide pockets to hook her thumbs in, so she just put her hands on hips instead.

"The devil went down to Georgia, he was looking for a soul to steal," the band leader's deep voice intoned the words that set Tandy and Kendra's feet to stomping. *"He was in a bind, 'cause he was way behind, and he was willing to make a deal . . ."*

She bit her lip, thoughts of Clay receding, concentrating now on the steps, kicking up her knees, then planting the balls of her feet and spinning. She and Kendra had modified the dance from the movie, filling in the gaps they couldn't see on the video and embellishing the ones they could see.

Other dancers noticed them, stopped what they were doing, and turned to watch. Tandy briefly thought about what they'd say the next day, but the dance required too much thought, so she let it go.

"Fire on the mountain, run boys, run . . ."

They were getting to the really hard part. Tandy reached up and pulled her hair off her neck, twisting and holding it in place as she and Kendra turned and kicked.

The fiddle player kicked into those notes few in the world could play well, and Tandy sneaked a glance up at Kendra. Her sister nodded once and smiled, then they broke into intricate steps to match the fiddle. Her ankles burned as she used them to twist her feet back and forth, moving across the dance floor without ever lifting her booted feet, changing directions each time the fiddle changed directions on the scale. Her hip joints were on fire, but Tandy bit her lip, stifling the grin of triumph, and stayed with it.

They were almost to the end. Johnny was about to beat the devil and win a fiddle of gold in the process. The notes and frenzy of the music doubled, reflecting a triumphant joy. Tandy and Kendra followed suit, sweat rolling down their faces and onto their necks.

The song ended with two victorious chords, and Kendra and Tandy matched them with two strong thumps of their boots on the hardwood. Applause broke out around the dance floor, and Tandy realized that everyone in the room had been watching her and Kendra.

"Guess we've still got it!" Kendra held her hand up for a high five. Tandy slapped her hand and hugged her, choosing to ignore the attention around them.

"Man, I've missed you," Tandy said. "I've missed *this*." Her heart swelled with love for the beautiful sister at her side.

"Back at you." The band went into a two-step number, and couples began filling the dance floor again.

Kendra hooked her arm through Tandy's and walked off the dance floor.

"Thanks for saving me back there," Tandy said.

"Looked like maybe you needed an escape route."

"Something like that."

"You know, sis, you've got another week and a half here. There's nothing saying you can't enjoy him while you're here." Kendra laughed at her own joke.

Tandy thought about that for a second. Could she love him and leave him the way he'd done to her? She'd turned love off before. Surely she could do it again.

"It's a thought."

Kendra stopped laughing and stared at her. "A good one?"

"Maybe."

"You can't be ser—"

"I'm telling you girls, your momma would be proud." Daddy's voice caused Kendra to shut her mouth in haste.

Tandy chuckled. "She'd be telling us to get our behinds off that dance floor and our noses back in our schoolbooks."

"Or that," Daddy nodded.

"So who's your friend?" Tandy tilted her head toward the corner where Zelda stood sipping from a cup.

Daddy's face turned the slightest pink. "That's Zelda Norman."

"Daddy's got a thing for her," Kendra said.

"Kendra Sinclair!" Daddy's voice boomed above the music.

"What? I'm just giving it to Tandy like it is."

"Are you dating her, Daddy?" This was unbelievable. He wouldn't do that to Momma. Her panicked gaze darted between Daddy and Kendra, searching for an explanation.

"No, no, nothing like that. We just dance together occasionally and talk."

"And she comes over." Kendra gave a sly smile as she readjusted her bracelets.

"To our house?" How could Daddy betray Momma like that? Granted, it had been ten years since Momma passed, but still.

"Only twice. You know your sister, she loves to exaggerate," Daddy frowned at Kendra.

"Don't get all Disapproval Daddy on me. I think it's great you have somebody to talk with, dance with, and share dinner with."

"You have dinner with her?" Tandy had trouble wrapping her mind around this. Daddy. With someone other than Momma. Someone with short, spiky red hair that represented the furthest thing possible from Momma's long, flowing locks.

"Every now and then," Daddy said. "But it's nothing serious, Tandy. I don't want you to worry."

"What should I not be worried about?" Lawyer mode kicked in and Tandy went on the attack cross-examining the hostile witness. Fists to hips, toes pointed toward the witness, shoulders thrown back. No doubting who held the authority.

"Well, nothing." Daddy looked at her warily.

"Nothing as in what?" Eyes wide, face forward, getting in his space. "Dinner? Visits to the house? Flirting with her in front of the entire town? Which of these is not something that's characteristic of your relationship with *Zelda*?" The name caused a bitter taste in her mouth, and she pointed at Daddy's chest.

"Oh, Tandy, chill out. He's not replacing Mom or anything."

"And you!" Tandy turned on her flamboyant sister, bearing down on her. "I can't believe you didn't tell me about this when it started!"

"Whoa, girl, don't go judicial system on *me*." Kendra held up her hands. "You want to get mad, go ahead and direct that toward Meg. She knew about it first."

Tandy stopped in her tracks, thrown. "Meg knows?"

Kendra nodded. "Joy, too."

Her shoulders slumped, hands falling by her sides. "How long have you all known? And why didn't somebody call me?"

"Tandy, nobody called you because there was nothing to say." Daddy shrugged and put his arm around her waist. "I don't call you every time I make a new friend, and you don't call me, either."

So this was punishment for not calling often enough? If they hadn't shared this, what else had she been left out of? "So Zelda is just a friend?"

"Yes."

"A friend who comes over and eats at our house, at Momma's table."

"Yes."

"A friend you dance with and laugh with."

"Yes."

She felt the tension in Daddy's arm. He wasn't going to back down from her on this. And the sisters must have approved because Zelda sat in the corner waiting on Daddy's return. They had approved without even calling her. She closed her eyes and tried to accept that.

"Fine, then." She turned to Kendra. "I've had about all the fun I'd like for one night. You ready to pack it in?"

"Pack it in? We've barely been here an hour!"

"I can take you home," Daddy said.

"No, I don't want to cut your time with Zelda short." She waved a hand in dismissal. Let them have their fun. What did it matter? "Y'all go on, and I'll just get some fresh air."

With that, she headed for the door before either of them could protest.

Thirteen

Outside the night passed clear and crisp. Tandy tilted her head and took in the dazzling sight of a sky so covered in stars it seemed they'd fall down for lack of space. A cool breeze swept around her legs as she walked the length of the parking lot. Hopping onto the hood of the Beamer, she lay back against the windshield and crossed her legs at the ankles.

Hiding out beneath the night sky. Meg would call that a great title for a country song. Her feet bounced in rhythm to the drumbeats coming through Heartland's steel walls. She'd come back to Stars Hill to think about her career. At least, that's what Mr. Beasley had said. But thinking about her career would mean acknowledging that it didn't fulfill her the way she'd thought it would. She drummed her fingers against the windshield. Winning cases didn't produce the emotional high anymore. Like the drugs that held sway over her birth mother for years, the body craved more and more stimulation to achieve the same state of excitement. It hadn't proved enough.

Her world had somehow become about defending the

likes of Harry Simons. He'd seemed like the ideal man at first glance. Well dressed, well spoken, well heeled, well groomed. A perfectly put together package. His philanthropic endeavors intimated an interest in helping the plight of the homeless, and Tandy had allowed herself to believe that there might actually exist another man like Clay Kelner. He wasn't as good-looking as Clay, of course, not even in the same ballpark—check that, stratosphere—as Clay. But on paper it appeared that Harry Simons possessed a heart.

What a difference a few minutes facing the object of his philanthropy revealed!

Tandy took in a deep lungful of the night air, expanding her lungs in an effort to break the vise that she felt gripping her heart. Orlando could get lonely, but it was also easier. Nothing to be emotionally tangled with other than Cooper. And so long as the kibble remained constant, he wasn't going anywhere. Shoot, even if it ran out, he'd just sit his big basset rear right down by hers until they'd both died of starvation.

"Figured it all out yet?" Clay's voice should have surprised her. It didn't.

"Not quite. But give me a few minutes, and I'll see what I can do."

The car tilted a bit as he leaned against it. "Mind some company?"

Did she? "Guess not."

It tilted more as he scooted backward across the hood then swung his legs around to mirror her position. Lacing his fingers behind his head, Clay leaned back against the cold windshield.

"Okay, I have assumed the appropriate position. What's the first item up for dissection?"

"You mean discussion?"

"That too."

Tandy sighed. "Dad's got a friend."

"I thought we already went through this and you were going to let him have his fun."

"Maybe I should have."

"But you didn't."

"I did. I will. I just can't help feeling he's somehow betraying Momma."

"Don't you think your mom wouldn't want your dad to make friends? To live his life?"

"No, I know they discussed it. I heard them. Momma even told him to go find some other woman and marry her after a while."

"I don't think your dad's anywhere near marrying Zelda, if that helps."

"It does. Some."

"Good. So on the topic of Zelda, you've decided to understand that your dad is also a human being and would like to have conversations with members of the opposite sex within his own age range."

"I don't remember making a decision. I thought we were discussing."

"Dissecting."

"Whatever." She rolled her eyes in the darkness.

"What else is there to know?"

"I don't know."

"Let me try again. What else about Zelda is bugging you?"

"That she isn't Momma?" Tandy turned her head to look at him. She took in his profile, bathed in moon and starlight. Even the heavens loved to highlight the beauty of Clay Kelner's face.

His Adam's apple bobbed as he swallowed. "He gets to have emotion in his life without her, Taz." His soft voice imbued the words with meaning.

"I know that." She stopped, confused that she didn't know it until he said so. "I do. I know that."

He turned to look at her. "You do?"

"Of course. Like I said, Momma told Daddy to get married again. I assumed that meant he'd need emotion in his life after her." She looked back up at the stars and crossed her hands over her abdomen.

After a minute Clay turned to the sky again and said, "She really is a good woman. Zelda. I checked her out when I first saw them together."

"You what?"

"I did some digging. You don't have to put forth a lot of effort in Stars Hill to find out about someone."

"You do if you want the unembellished version."

"Point taken. I did my homework. She's okay." His voice sounded sure.

"Why did you check out a woman my dad was spending time with?"

"Maybe I hoped the information would come in handy someday."

"Like when I came for a visit and asked you to give me the dirt on her."

"Like that." There was that surety again.

She pushed up onto her elbows and looked over at him. "I don't get you, Clay Kelner."

He turned his head toward her and grinned. "About time you admitted that."

Her groan gave the only warning before she punched him in the arm. "Why do you have to be so confusing?"

"Hey!" He grabbed her wrist before she could hit him again, holding it in place while keeping his fingers gentle on her skin. "I know your mom taught you not to hit people."

"People, yes. But I think she'd make an exception for you."

"Your mom liked me and you know it."

"My mother did *not* like you. What world are you living in?"

"The one that says when your girlfriend's mom tells you to take good care of her daughter, it means she trusts you to do just that."

"Momma never said that to you."

"Two months before she died."

"That'd make a great Lifetime movie, but it never happened." She tried to pull away from all this feeling, but his easy touch held her fast.

"Yes, it did. I came over to the house to see you, and you weren't there. Your mom was sitting in that rocker on the porch, sipping lemonade. I told her it was too cold and she needed to get back inside, and she told me she didn't need taking care of but that I should take good care of her daughter."

Tears sprang to Tandy's eyes and, before she could think to blink them away, tumbled down her cheeks. Momma had been trying to take care of her, even when it was obvious her time was coming to an end. But why tell Clay to take care of her? It didn't make sense.

Except that Momma had no way of knowing that Clay would up and leave a few months later. The day Clay Kelner joined the service, he'd betrayed Momma just as surely as he'd betrayed Tandy. She jerked her wrist out of his grasp.

"I thought you were a jerk before. Thanks for confirming it."

"What are you talking about?" He raised up on his own elbows and stared at her, eye to eye.

"You told Momma you'd take care of me. Does that include running off and leaving me in your dust? Because I can tell you, I didn't feel taken care of."

"I asked you to come with me."

"You knew I couldn't."

"I knew you could do anything you wanted. And I thought you'd want to come with me."

"No." She shook her head and blinked through the tears, praying they would stop so she could get control again. "I told you Momma's dreams, my dreams, Orlando. You knew that wouldn't work with your soldier life and so you left me. You knew I couldn't come with you, which is why you left." Her voice broke on the last word and she gulped in air. "You're just like her. It's great to have Tandy around until her deadweight is holding you back."

"Just like who?"

"Until you need to go running after some stupid idea that's going to get you killed anyway. But you don't care about that. All you care about is chasing down that thing in your head. Finding it and consuming it so you'll feel good."

He sat up all the way and leaned over her. "You lost me, babe. Who am I like?"

"Except that when you consume it, it's not going to last. You're just going to need more and more until one day you catch it and it kills you." She was sobbing now, a voice in her mind telling her to stop and get some control even as another voice told that one to shut up, that it was about time some real emotion made its way to the surface. Maybe she was schizophrenic. Or tired. She turned on her side and curled up into a ball, hiding her face behind clenched fists. Who cared anyway?

Gentle hands wrapped over her fists, thumbs moving in circles. She felt it, and couldn't believe she'd lost control in front of him. Lost it in a way she'd been proud not to have done before he left or since.

"Are you talking about your birth mom?" His gentle voice soothed her, stealing its way through the crevices of her darkness and burrowed down inside her mind. "Tandy, you have to know I didn't *want* to leave you behind."

She snorted.

"I didn't. I begged you to come with me."

"You knew—"

"I knew you would have to sacrifice, yes, but I thought that you would. I thought coming with me would mean more to you than going right to college and becoming a lawyer. I really did."

She sneaked a look over her hands at his face. "Then you didn't know me."

"I did know you, but you changed when your momma died. I still don't know why, but you did." Sadness etched itself into the corners of his eyes, and his smile held no happiness. "I couldn't get you to feel anything anymore. It's like you just decided to die right along with her."

"That's a horrible thing to say!"

"And a horrible thing to watch." He kept rubbing her hands. "I thought if we got away from Stars Hill for a while . . ." He sighed and kissed her knuckles. "I don't know what I thought."

"I wish we *had* gotten away. Just for a little while." It was dumb. Putting herself out there like that.

His hands tightened on hers. "Me, too."

The silence of past regrets weighed them down to the windshield. She thought of the family they might have by now. A little girl with her red curls and his green eyes. A little boy with his black hair and her stubborn spirit. Kiddos for Daddy to spoil and play with. A home near the farm that rang with laughter and love and shared dreams. She forced the images from her mind. She had her goals and he had his. They didn't go together then. And they didn't go together now.

She came to a sitting position on the hood, crossed her legs Indian-style and faced him. "We were kids, Clay. Babies at eighteen. Probably not a good idea to judge either of us on decisions we made then."

He took one of her hands in his. "There's nothing saying we can't start over now, Tandy."

Gravel crunched beneath the tires of a passing truck. Here lay the chance to be with the man who knew her. A man who called Stars Hill home. Her mind turned to those dark days, sitting by Momma's side, planning her future as Momma grew paler and paler, thinner and thinner. Cancer was patient in its killing.

"Clay, I have a life in Orlando."

"I know that. The whole *town* knows that. And I know that I can't ask you to move here when we haven't even seen each other in ten years. I guess I don't know what to ask you for."

The silence settled in again. Someone left the dance hall, music spilling out the door like tinkling glass. Kendra's words echoed in her mind: *There's nothing saying you can't enjoy him while you're here.* It was wrong, she knew. Relationships weren't something to be cavalierly tossed aside like that.

But she'd be spending the next nine days in Stars Hill anyway. It could be nine days of new memories to keep her company on long Orlando nights. Nine days of fun with him. Nine days of conversation with him. Nine days. If she took lots of pictures, the scrapbooking alone would get her through the next year. Maybe then she could come home again, depending on her schedule at work. She'd have people in her pictures again.

Nine days.

She squeezed his hand. Like he'd done for her the night she'd told him about the first seven years of her life. It had been the first time she'd let the wall down around her heart. If ever she'd do it again, it'd be for him.

"We've got nine days, Clay. How about we just enjoy that?"

"Tandy Sinclair isn't making a plan for the next ten years?" His teasing tone took the bite out of the commentary.

"Just for the next nine days." She turned and looked at him. "Thought I'd try something new."

He blew out a breath. "Nine days, then."

The silence felt welcome now, an acknowledgment of what they had. And, for now, it would have to be okay.

"You know, if we count today, we have ten days." His teasing tone made her smile.

"Tonight is almost gone."

"You know what they say. Almost only counts in hand grenades and thermonuclear warfare."

"You soldiers, always with the weaponry jokes." She playfully pushed her shoulder into his.

"Yeah, well, we make them because they're true. We've got—" he let go of her hand and pushed a button on his watch, and a green glow emanated from its face—"three hours and twenty-seven minutes before midnight and I, for one, don't intend to waste them." He slid off the hood, then reached for her hand. She gave it to him without thinking, and he pulled her across the metal as well. She dropped to the gravel, grabbing at his arm for balance.

"Hey, easy there, soldier."

He turned and tugged her back across the parking lot. They weaved through the beat-up trucks back to the door of Heartland. "There's good dancing to be had in there, and we're not missing another minute of it." He threw open the door, and the whine of a steel guitar washed over them. "Come on!"

Fourteen

The little brass bell tinkled out her arrival as Tandy burst through the salon door Saturday morning. They had three hours until scrapping time, and Tandy felt lighter than the chemical-laden air around her.

Four hours of sleep shouldn't be enough to feel this good, but memories of Clay's arms around her, twirling around the dance floor, made up for lack of sleep. It made up for lack of a whole lot, she could admit. Not everything. But a lot. Her heart felt new and stretched, like a muscle learning to move again.

"Believe it or not, I'm walking on air," Meg sang from her position in the chair in front of Joy. She cut her eyes at Tandy in the mirror, a black cape draped around her shoulders. Joy was combing and snipping the pale blonde locks.

"Sing all you want, sister, I don't care." Tandy twirled in a circle, collapsing in the chair to Meg's right.

"One night of dancing and the world is her oyster," Joy said.

"I could have danced all night, and still have begged for more," Meg sang.

"She goes from Joey Scarbury to *My Fair Lady* in three seconds flat," Tandy slid down in the seat. "There's got to be a way to make money off of that."

"Or get her committed." Joy snipped some more. Tandy pulled out her small digital camera and, before Meg could realize it, snapped off a picture.

"Hey!"

Tandy shrugged, slipping the camera back into her pocket. "I need pictures to scrapbook."

"Yeah, I noticed a distinct lack of humans in your latest work in progress," Meg watched Joy in the mirror.

Tandy winced. "I know. What better moment to supply people pictures than my two dear sisters engaged in the art of beauty?"

"Man, she's laying it on thick today," Joy said.

"She must want something big," Meg nodded.

"Stop moving your head." Joy combed the thick locks straight again.

"I don't want anything from either of you. Can't a girl just be happy?"

Meg threw up her hands, careful to keep her head still. "Fine by us."

"Did you come by, then, just to show off your happy self?"

"Yep."

"You're kidding." Meg strained her eyes up to the mirror to see Tandy.

"Nope. Well, that and I could use a trim."

"I knew it," Joy said. "And I've got roasted *coq au vin poulard* in the oven."

"You've got what?"

"It's a dish Scott and I had down at the Ritz-Carlton

in Naples. They served these wonderful young spring vegetables and pan *au jus* with it. It was to die for."

"If you say so." Tandy scrunched her nose. "I'm not sure I can pronounce that, much less try to cook it. What's the occasion?"

"No special reason. I just thought Scott would appreciate a nice dinner after a long week of work."

"Mm-hmm. When are you guys going to give me a niece or nephew? Meg here can't carry all the load."

"Actually, we've decided to start trying." Joy's cheeks turned pink.

"What?! That's great!"

"I'm not sure I'm ready to have my body all stretched out and waddle around like a walrus, but we do want to have children, so I suppose I must resign myself to the process."

"Trust me, baby sis, it's worth every single stretch mark." Meg smiled. "And I'll remind you of that when your little one is screaming his or her head off because you've just run out of Cheerios."

Joy took in a deep breath, then nodded.

"And, hey—" Tandy kicked the counter and threw her head back as the chair swung in circles again—"maybe if you become a mom, we'll quit calling you the baby around here."

"A woman can hope." Joy pulled a hair dryer from its holder. She switched it on, drowning out further conversation. Ten minutes later she switched off the dryer and unclasped the cape. Meg stood up and turned her head from side to side, appraising the new cut.

"Thanks."

"Anytime. Tandy, your turn."

"Never mind." Tandy continued twirling in circles. "I'll just get it done next week sometime."

"If you need a trim, then you need a trim. My dish can wait a little longer without going dry."

Tandy shook her head. "No way am I getting between you and the creation of my next niece or nephew. Besides, I need to run over to the grocery and get back home before we scrap."

"If you're sure." Joy didn't look convinced, but her raised eyebrows signaled hope.

Tandy hopped up from her chair. "Positive. Oh, before I forget, did you call Taylor?"

"I did. He's out of town until after the parade. I'm sorry."

"Oh well. I'll figure out something else." She stood up. "See you girls in a few hours!" She wiggled her fingers over her shoulder in good-bye, heading out the door toward the small market on Lindell.

The sun baked its heat into her T-shirt as Tandy crossed the street. Stars Hill and sunshine. A glorious night dancing in the arms of a man her heart knew. Tandy couldn't wipe the grin off her face no matter how many times she tried.

And why try?

She stopped short, standing on the sidewalk in front of the library. Why? Because something inside was reminding her that this much happiness was dangerous. She bit her lip, trying to put a finger on the cause of disquiet.

Because it always ends. Her birth mother's words, spoken through the slur of cheap scotch, were a torrent of rain on this sunny day. As much as Tandy wanted her mother to be wrong, life had proven the truth in those words.

But life also showed that sometimes it could work out, right? Momma and Daddy were proof of that. Okay, not a great example because that ended, too. Meg and Jamison! It worked out great for them. Meg might be exhausted a lot these days, but she was also happy. And Joy and Scott! They were going to be even happier in a few months when Joy announced the conception of their first little one.

Satisfied, Tandy began walking again. When the thought of returning to Orlando threatened the sunshine, she pushed it in the same direction as her mother's rain cloud.

✂ ✂ ✂

TWO AND A half hours later, Tandy and Kendra were in the kitchen putting together sandwiches for the adults and mini-pizzas for the kids. Cooper sat by the counter, intent on every piece of food, waiting for any morsel to drop.

"You are shameless," Kendra said to the dog.

"He's just smart," Tandy shot Cooper a loving look. "He knows if I'm in the kitchen, it'll likely end up as messy as Paris Hilton's rap sheet."

"So it's not begging so much as waiting for the inevitable?"

"Exactly." Tandy dropped a pepperoni, and Cooper snatched it up with his teeth. "See?"

"You did that on purpose."

"Cynic."

"Food dropper."

"What time is it?"

Kendra looked at the lime-green watch on her wrist. Yesterday's watch was red. Tandy smiled at the color of Kendra's life.

"We've got about fifteen minutes before Joy, Meg, and the kids get here."

"Okay, then let's pop these bad boys in the oven." She slid a cookie sheet full of mini-pizzas into the hot oven, then turned the timer to twelve minutes. "How are those sandwiches coming?"

"Almost done." Kendra slapped a piece of bread on top of the sandwich in front of her. "There. Finished."

"Perfect. Now we can get to scrapping as soon as they get here." She glanced out the window and saw Meg's van pulling down the driveway. "Speaking of which . . ." She gestured outside, and Kendra's eyes followed her hand.

A minute later James and Savannah came through the front door. "Aunt Tanny, Aunt Tanny!" Savannah came screaming into the kitchen and barreled right into Tandy's legs. Tandy saw a streak of blonde hair as James went running down the hallway. She heard him calling out, "Granddaddy! I'm here!"

"Well, hey there, sunshine." Tandy scooped Savannah up for a hug. "You hungry?"

Savannah nodded her head, causing her short little blonde pigtails to bounce. Pink ribbons were tied around each one. "You sure are looking pretty today."

"I did 'nastics."

"You went to gymnastics?"

"Yep. And we rolled." She wiggled, and Tandy put her back down on the floor. Immediately the little girl began doing somersaults.

"Wow, look at you!" Kendra clapped.

"Look out, Olympic committee, here comes Savannah!" Tandy clapped, too. Savannah finished her flip, jumped up, and joined in the applause.

"Yea!" she said.

Meg came into the kitchen, a sleeping Hannah in her arms. "Hey."

"Hey, yourself," Tandy said. "Ready to do some serious scrapping?"

"Absolutely. Let me just go lay her down, and I'll come back to help carry up the food."

"Sure. Do you need some help?"

"No, I've got it. You've got her for a second?" Meg nodded her head toward Savannah.

"Yep. Go." Tandy shooed Meg out of the kitchen.

"Granddaddy!" James was still walking through the house, his little voice carrying.

"He's out in the barn," Tandy called back. Savannah resumed her somersaults as they heard the front door open and slam shut.

"Granddaddy!" James's voice carried through the windows from the front yard.

Kendra shook her head. "That child is attached to Daddy like fuzz on a peach."

Tandy looked out the window. "Hail, hail, the gang's all here."

"Joy?"

"Coming down the drive."

"Then let's get this party started!"

Tandy nodded. "Yeah, because I have a feeling I'll have a hot date tonight."

"You and Clay looked as tight as my jeans after a Chinese food binge last night."

"We've got nine days. Might as well use them."

"And then what?"

"What?"

"After nine days," Kendra said, "then what?"

"I go back to Orlando, and he stays here."

"You're just going to walk away from him?"

"Weren't you the one telling me last night to love 'em and leave 'em?"

"I was kidding, Tandy. I didn't think you'd *do* it." Kendra reached up and adjusted the brightly colored scarf in her hair.

"Well, I did." She heard the defensiveness in her tone and made an effort to correct it. "I'll be here for nine days, regardless, Ken. It makes sense to spend time with him."

"He makes you happy?" Kendra quirked an eyebrow. "This setup makes you happy?"

"It's more than that. Yeah, he makes me happy. But he's Clay. He's, you know, Clay."

Kendra sighed. "I know. But you be careful, sister. In about nine days it's going to hurt like a thousand Band-Aids ripped off at once."

Tandy bit her lip and stared out the window at nothing. "I know," she whispered as Joy came into the kitchen. Meg followed on her heels.

"Hannah's down, James is out with Daddy, and," Meg looked down at Savannah on the floor, "this one is about to watch some VeggieTales. I'd say the time for scrapping has come!"

Tandy shook herself free of the melancholy. There'd be time enough for sadness later. Like eight hundred miles' worth.

"What are we waiting for? Grab a sandwich and get your behinds up those stairs!"

They filled plates with sandwiches and chips, snagging drinks from the refrigerator, then headed up the stairs to the scrapping studio. Meg stopped along the way and put in a video for Savannah.

Each girl settled into her scrapping station. Tandy kept her sandwich in one hand while she resumed arranging photos she'd laid out last night. Too keyed up with energy to sleep, she'd come up here and grouped her pictures in preparation for scrapping today. The remembrance of last night made her hands still on the prints.

Dancing with Clay, being with Clay, was easy as breathing. She'd forgotten how they could finish each other's sentences, debate with humor, have intelligent conversation. Every song seemed more perfect than the last, and she'd tried to record every single second in her memory banks. They hadn't talked much, just reveled in the feel of being together again.

Kendra snapped her fingers. "Earth to Tandy."

Tandy blinked and noticed the sisters staring at her. "Sorry." She smiled and went back to pushing pictures around into various layouts.

"Hey, Ken, how's your sculpture coming?" Meg asked. "Think it'll be ready in time for the Iris Festival?"

Kendra shook her head. "I don't know. I worked on it this morning, but there's something that's off about it."

"What are you sculpting?" Joy eyes were intent on her layout. "You haven't told us much about it."

"I have an image in my head of this woman running, but she's caught." Kendra waved her hands in the air, her gold bangles clinking together as she outlined the shape of the sculpture. "She's fighting and struggling, and there are wisps and tendrils around her, weaving in between her arms and legs, holding her back in their tangle."

"Wow. Sounds intense."

"It is." Kendra sighed and dropped her hands to the table. "Which is probably why I'm having such a hard time with it. Every time I work on her, she exhausts me emotionally."

"Do you think you'll finish her?"

"I hope so. If I could figure out what she's running from, what those tendrils represent, it might help. Or figure out if she *wants* to get away, then I would know her facial expression and could start on it."

"Why wouldn't she want to escape?" Joy applied rub-on letters to circles of chipboard.

Kendra shrugged. "If she doesn't want to leave what's holding her back, then she wouldn't want to get away."

"But then why run at all?" Meg pushed a distresser up and down the edge of paper striped with brick red and dark brown. "I mean, if she wants what's behind her, why doesn't she just turn around and quit running?"

"Because she wants what's in front of her, too." Tandy's voice was soft. Kendra's ability to tap into Tandy's mind had always amazed the entire family. They shared no blood relation, yet their hearts and minds were as connected as identical twins. "She wants them both."

"Sounds like you got your facial expression," Meg said.

Kendra nodded, her eyes on Tandy. "Yeah, it does."

Tandy gave a half laugh. "Glad I could help."

"Okay, we've got Kendra's sculpture back on track," Joy said brightly. "How about you, Meg? Do the children have any floats to ride in the parade this year?" She reached for a roll of glue dots, then began applying the chipboard pieces to her layout.

"Savannah's riding on the float for Lakewood Gymnastics."

Meg finished distressing the paper and applied adhesive to its back. "But I got out of serving on the float committee this year."

"How'd you manage that?"

"Pretended I was Winona Ryder and they were a shoplifting charge. If celebrities can pay their debt to society in checks, so can I. Lakewood Gymnastics is now the proud owner of fifty new floor mats."

"Nice," Joy said.

"I thought so."

"Does Grace Christian have a float?" Tandy cut some ribbon and applied it across her page.

"No." Meg pulled a paper piercer from the tool turnabout in the center of the table. "They're serving free ice cream during the festival, though."

"Sounds like a mess in the making." Tandy uncapped a journaling pen and bent low over her layout.

"Oh, yeah." Meg began sliding her finished layout into page protectors. "But you know Daddy. He loves a good mess."

"That'd be why *we're* here," Kendra said and the sisters nodded.

Tandy left her chair and walked over to the pegboard. Selecting a set of rub-on letters in dark brown, she walked back over to the table. Her layout—pictures of Cooper at the beach—was coming along well. Cooper's big basset eyes looked up at her from a shell-strewn patch of sand. His paws were covered in grains of sand, and his ears were tipped in it as well from dragging the ground. She smiled. People would be nice, but Cooper was a good substitute. Most days.

The phone on the wall trilled, and Kendra jumped up to grab it.

"Hello? Oh, Clay, hi!"

Tandy's head jerked up and her eyes locked on Kendra, who was now twirling the phone cord around her finger.

Kendra laughed. "Well, you weren't doing too bad yourself out there."

Another pause.

"Yeah, she's here. Hang on, and I'll get her for you." Kendra held out the phone, and Tandy's eyes opened wide.

"Phone," Kendra said.

Tandy went over and took the phone from Kendra's hand. "Hello?"

"Tandy?" His voice made her smile. She turned her back to the sisters to hide her reaction.

"Last time I checked."

"Whatcha doing?"

"Talking to you."

"You know, it's a good thing I like a sassy woman."

"Good for whom?"

"By the look on your face last night, I'd say you."

"Must have been the bad lighting."

"Yeah, I guess that was it. No way were you actually enjoying yourself or anything. That was some other woman dancing with me, singing along to the songs, right?"

"Must have been."

"Good, then I need to let you go and correct a few conversations happening here."

"Here, as in the diner?"

"Yep. Seems we're the talk of the town."

Tandy groaned. "Please tell me you're lying."

"I'm lying."

"Wait, are you lying now or were you lying before?"

"Tell you what, you do me a favor, and I'll make sure the folks around here talk more about the Iris Festival than you and me." Tandy heard conversation in the background and pictured a roomful of diners leaning as close to the phone as they dared, as desperate for an earful as paparazzi for a money shot.

"Why don't you just make them hush out of the goodness of your heart?"

"My heart's not that good. Come on, it's just one little favor."

"Then why are red flags flying in my head?"

"Do these red flags have black boxes?"

"What?"

"Red flags with black boxes. One signifies a tropical storm. Two means a hurricane warning. You live in Orlando and don't know these things?"

"When the weather turns bad, I turn on the television. The man who gets paid thousands of dollars to tell me a hurricane is coming tells me a hurricane is coming. No need for flags."

"What's the fun in that? Takes all the guesswork out of it."

"I know. We're funny like that in Florida."

"So, can I get a favor?"

"Are you going to stop asking if I say no?"

"You've known me this long and still have to ask?"

She sighed, deliberately drawing it out. "What's the favor?"

"First you have to agree to it."

"Hang on, let me go check." She clunked the phone against the wall and stomped away, knowing he'd hear her steps on the floor. The sisters looked up from their scrapping and watched her with questioning looks. She held her finger to her lips for silence, then walked back to the phone. "Nope, I looked and looked but not one single pig was flying."

The sisters laughed behind her.

"Sassy women. God's gift to mankind."

"The favor?"

"Right. Well, I play in a band; and before you make fun of me, we're not half bad. It's something fun to do, and we even make a little money at it."

"So I heard."

"You knew I played in a band?"

"It's Stars Hill, Clay. If I wanted to, I could find out what you had for breakfast this morning."

"Good point. Okay, normally on Saturday nights I hang out with Darin, our bass player. Except tonight I wanted to be with you, not Darin."

"Sounds like a logical choice."

"But I can't just call Darin and cancel last minute. We've hung out nearly ever Saturday night since the band started."

"Darin's girlfriend is okay with this?"

"I'm sure if he had one, she wouldn't be. But his ex split over a year ago, and dating hasn't been at the top of his to-do list."

"You guys just get together every Saturday and, what?"

"Not much. Play pool. Hit a movie. Whatever."

"Okay, I'll bite. What's the favor?"

"Think you could get Kendra to go out with us tonight?"

"You're kidding me."

"It's either that or you, me, and a third wheel. I don't know about you, but I'd much rather find something to keep

Darin's interest than spend all night sitting on his couch, just the cozy three of us, watching the *Modern Marvels* marathon."

"A smart woman would say no to this."

"Good thing I like sassy instead."

"Hang on. I'll go see if she'll come. But I'm warning you, if she hits me, you pay the hospital bill."

"Deal. But duck if you can, okay?"

"Got it. Be right back." Tandy let the phone fall again and walked over to the scrapping table. Joy looked up from her layout. Meg sat down her eyelet setter. Tandy waited until Kendra finished tying a knot in a piece of ribbon and met her gaze.

"I don't like that look," Kendra said.

Tandy blinked. "What look?"

"The one that says you're about to ask me to do something or say something I don't want."

Tandy broke and made her way around the table to Kendra's side. "Please, Ken, it's just one little favor, and it'd mean the world to me, and dating him was your idea anyway."

Kendra turned on her stool and put one hand on her hip. "I told you I was kidding." She reached forward and poked Tandy's chest like a robin pecking the ground for worms. "You did it anyway, so don't be laying that at my feet anymore."

"Okay, fine. It was all me. Just do me this favor."

Kendra quirked an eyebrow. "Will we end up in jail?"

"Not unless the night goes way better than I anticipate."

"What is it?"

"Clay spends Saturday nights with his band mate, Darin.

He doesn't want to flake on Darin last minute, so he wants you to double-date with us."

"A blind date? Tandy, how old are we?"

"Old enough to know better, I know. But also old enough to do great, wonderful, fantastic things for each other even when we don't want to." She leaned forward and placed a hand on Kendra's arm. "Please, Ken. If you hate him, we can leave. I promise. Unless your unparticular man would object."

"I told you, I don't have a man, *imparticular* or otherwise."

"Then please, please, please, can you do this for me?"

"Another one bites the dust . . ." Meg sang without looking up from her work.

Joy laughed. "Oh, Meg, stop."

Kendra turned back to Tandy. "What does he play?"

"Bass."

"Hmm, bass is good. Shows he's got some rhythm in him, some art." She paused a second longer.

"You're killing me here, sis."

"Okay, I'll do it."

Tandy jumped up and down. "Yes! Thank you! You are the best sister ever!" She circled the table again and went for the phone.

"What are we, chopped liver?" Meg asked.

"Y'all are great, too," Tandy said, snatching up the phone. "Okay, Clay, she said yes."

"Wow, remind me never to go up against you in court. Those powers of persuasion must be intense."

"I'm murder in a courtroom."

"I can imagine. So I'll pick you up around six, and we can swing by and pick up Kendra afterward. Does that work?"

"Like Julia Roberts on Hollywood Boulevard."

His chuckle sent warm shivers through her. "See you tonight."

"See ya." She hung up the phone and stared at it, then turned to see Kendra walking over to the window.

Kendra's hand went to her hip, and she peered through the glass.

"What are you doing?" Tandy walked over to her.

"I know you said you didn't see any—" Kendra's eyes darted back and forth—"but I'm pretty sure *something's* flying out there that shouldn't be if I just agreed to go on a blind date."

Meg and Joy laughed as Tandy laid her head on Kendra's shoulder and looked outside. "Thanks for doing this."

Kendra leaned into her. "That'll teach me to make dumb jokes about seizing the day. Or nine days, as the case may be."

Fifteen

Any chance you can come down off the cloud long enough to tell me where we're going?"

Kendra's question just barely got through Tandy's pleasant fog. "Hmm?"

"Tonight. Where is this blind date taking me?"

"Oh, I didn't ask."

Meg and Joy giggled and kept their heads down, eyes focused on their layouts.

"You didn't ask?" The disapproval in her voice made Tandy think of the nun from *The Sound of Music*. She glanced down to confirm she wasn't wearing clothes made from the curtains.

"No, I forgot."

"You forgot?" Kendra stood, one fist planted on each hip. Tandy knew that stance. It worked in court. "How am I supposed to know what to wear?"

"Guess?"

Kendra's steely glare was louder than any amplification could have provided.

"Does this man know I'm black?" Her voice had dropped

to that quiet level reserved only for deep waters and hidden danger. "Is he?"

"Um—" Tandy's eyes pleaded with the tops of Meg and Joy's heads, but both sisters were as focused on their work as a sniper on his target—"I may have forgotten to ask."

Kendra threw her hands in the air, her bracelets jangling. "Of course you did. I mean, why would Kendra want to know any details about the guy she's going to have to make conversation with for hours on end so her sister can have fun? Did it occur to you he may not be okay with this?"

"Wait, wait. Hang on. I'll call Clay back and get some more information." Tandy scurried over to the phone. "Just hang on. I'm out of practice at this, okay? I'll get more info."

"You do that," Kendra pointed a red-tipped finger at Tandy. "You just go do that." She sat back down on the stool with a flourish, her colorful caftan billowing out, then settling in around her. Tandy had the impression of a regal princess assuming her throne.

She tapped the Caller ID button on the phone, then dialed the number Clay had called her from earlier.

"Clay's."

"Hey, I need some info on Darin."

"Did Kendra change her mind?"

"No, no, nothing like that. But we need to know where we're going."

"You girls have something against surprises?"

"Only when they render us incapable of dressing the part."

"Ah." Understanding flooded his voice. "I see. How about the Bluebird?"

"We're driving to Nashville?"

"It's just a thought. We can stay around here if you want. There's a fun jazz club now about half an hour from here."

"Hmmm, jazz." She raised her eyebrows at Kendra, who nodded. "I think we like the idea of jazz."

"Okay. Their dinner menu is good, too. We'll eat there and listen to some music, talk. Sound good?"

"Sounds great. Oh, and what'd you tell Darin about Kendra?"

"That she's your sister, loves art, sculpts and paints, occasionally writes. The basics. Why?"

"You told him she was my sister?"

"Was I not supposed to?"

"Did you tell him she was my adoptive sister?"

"Why would I specify that?"

"Because he might assume Kendra looks like me."

"He doesn't know what you look like. And even if he did—oh, wait. You mean, did I tell him Kendra's black, don't you?"

"Yes."

"I didn't think he'd care."

"Clay! That matters to some people. What if he meets Kendra, takes one look at her, and walks the other way? Didn't you think that might be awkward for her? For me?"

"No, I thought that if he didn't care about race when he got married, he probably doesn't care about it too much now."

"His wife was black?"

"Biracial, if you want to be technical. And I can't believe we're having this conversation in the twenty-first century."

"Me, either. Forget I brought it up."

"Already gone from the memory banks. Any other info you need before I see you in four hours?"

"Just one thing."

"Says the cat to the mouse."

Tandy made a face at the phone. "How'd you get so smart?"

"I dated this really hot chick in high school whose brain was better than mine. Made me sharpen my skills."

"Must have been some woman."

"Honey, you have no idea."

"See you tonight." She hung up, her heart racing like the high school days. Sometimes, when she allowed herself to think of him, she couldn't help but wonder if the pain of losing him had obliterated the flaw of him—the mundane characteristics that, if given enough time, would have driven her insane and ended their relationship anyway. She'd think hard, searching the recesses of her memory the way a miser seeks out a lost penny, but it was always in vain. Clay Kelner had his faults, but none of them would have driven them apart.

Except his need to chase after military madness and her need to succeed in Orlando.

She shook her head, the thought slinking away into the dark corners of her brain. "We're doing jazz," she called out to Kendra, going back to the scrapping table. "You need a slinky dress and heels."

Kendra held up a hand, "Say no more, I bought the perfect dress for that two weeks ago. It's a red silk number with a halter top. Might as well have *jazz* stitched right across the front of it."

"That's perfect!"

Kendra looked over at Joy, who had been watching the exchange. "She says that like it's a miracle I can put together an outfit."

Joy smiled. "Or like a woman excited to see her man."

"He's not *my* man, Joy," Tandy rushed to correct her.

Meg joined in the conversation. "The town thinks otherwise."

"How can you know what the town is saying already? It was last night, and I saw you this morning."

"I stopped at the bank before I came over." Meg flipped through a *Simple Scrapbooks*, pausing at a layout and turning down the page. "Sadie Jenkins sends you her love. She thinks you two looked—" Meg's voice adopted that of an elderly woman, and she put her finger to her lips—"just divine, Meg, div*ine*."

"Oh my word. Ms. Jenkins was at Heartland?"

Meg lifted a shoulder. "And, in addition to her love, she wants you to know she approves."

"Oh, *well* then—" Tandy rolled her eyes—"somebody find me a marriage certificate because if Ms. Jenkins has issued her approval, then it's all said and done."

"Tandy, don't be ugly." Joy echoed Momma's oft-repeated phrase.

"I'm not." Tandy winced at her petulant tone. "Like I know you're not defending the right of a woman who has been married four times and engaged seven to issue a decree on the rightness or wrongness of *anyone*'s relationship, much less mine with Clay Kelner."

"She was only being nice, Tandy," Meg's eyes were wide. "I don't think she meant any harm by it."

Tandy sighed. "I know. I just hate being the topic of town conversation." She pulled up on the end of a Clik-It and let it go, making an eyelet-sized hole in the paper on the table.

"Why do you hate it so much?" Joy asked.

"It doesn't bother you?" She reached for a copper-colored eyelet and set it in place.

"Not really. I don't love being discussed, but I take my turn like everyone else."

"Why have a turn at all?" Tandy popped the Clik-It onto the eyelet, smashing it into place. "Why can't folks just talk about their crops or church or something other than the people in this town?"

"They only talk because they care." Kendra held up a hand, stopping Tandy's retort. "I don't like it any more than you do, so don't holler at me, but hear me out. If they didn't give an owl's hoot about you or me or Joy or Meg, then what we did wouldn't be worthy of talking about. But they *do* care about us. They were the ones that stood outside Murphy's for an hour in the rain, waiting to pay last respects to Momma. And if they want to spend a little time advising us, then I say we tell them thanks for the advice and for caring and quit throwing a tantrum every time they talk."

"I'm not throwing a tantrum." She snagged a mini-hammer from the tool turnabout and smashed a wayward edge of the eyelet. The silence in the room made her look up. "What?"

"This isn't a tantrum?" Joy said. "You're pounding on that eyelet hard enough for China to hear it."

Tandy dropped the hammer back in its slot. "Okay, maybe a mini-tantrum. But I could do a lot worse."

"Heaven forbid we should witness that," Kendra said.

Tandy harrumphed and went back to her layout.

"Meg!" Daddy called up the stairs. "Do you want me to put in another video for Savannah?"

"Be right there, Daddy!" Meg stood up and walked over

to the stairs. "Y'all don't cover anything important while I'm gone, okay?"

"Of course." Joy slid a completed page into a page protector.

Sounds of tearing paper and cutters created a sense of beehive busyness.

Tandy tried to focus on the work in front of her. She was making good progress, much more than she ever got done by herself in Orlando. But images of Clay—his smile, his hands, his long jean-clad legs—kept popping into her mind. Was he thinking of her this much? Probably not. He had the diner to worry about, which left little room for daydreaming. Not like scrapbooking, which allowed time for conversation and thinking and hashing out life's problems and perils like a prospector shaking his gold pan for nuggets of truth.

Her anticipation for the coming night grew. A jazz place. Even if Kendra and Darin didn't hit it off, no one in their right mind could listen to jazz and not feel like snuggling up to someone. There'd be the sound of practiced hands sliding back and forth over a piano keyboard, playing the keys the same way love played with people's hearts. Maybe there'd be a singer, her voice with that raspy tone just right for singing the blues and the energy of jazz. Tandy couldn't help the goofy grin that crossed her face.

"I put in *Heroes of the Bible*, so we're good for an hour and a half," Meg announced as she came back up the stairs.

"Hannah sleeps for two hours?" Tandy asked.

"That's the best part of having an infant. They spend more time sleeping than anything else. I'm convinced it's how God lulls us into having more." Meg laughed and settled back in on her stool. "Now, where was I?"

"Hey, Tandy, what are you wearing tonight?" Kendra snipped a piece of ribbon from the spool.

"Hmm. I'm not sure. I didn't pack with the thought I'd be dating once I got here." Tandy sat up straighter, realizing now that she really didn't have anything appropriate for a jazz club. "You know what? I don't think I have a single thing to wear."

"Did I just hear a desperate cry for shopping?" Joy asked.

"Unless Meg's got something in her closet I could borrow."

Meg's lips lifted in a crooked grin. "Motherhood isn't really conducive to building a knock-'em-dead wardrobe, sis. I've got jeans, sweats, and three skirts I rotate for church. The good clothes are down in Savannah's closet. She's got more Hanna Anderssons than you can shake a stick at."

Joy's eyebrows rose and her hopeful eyes, their blue shocking in their Asian setting, turned to Tandy. "So, shopping then?"

Tandy's shoulders fell. "I don't have time to get to Nashville before tonight! And where am I going to find something in Stars Hill to wear to a jazz club?"

"Have you not been in Sara Sykes's shop since you got home?"

"No, I keep wanting to get down there, though."

"She added a clothing section in the back. Gorgeous stuff."

"What time does she close on Saturday?"

"Five, I think. I can run call her and make sure, but I'm pretty certain it's still five."

Tandy glanced over at the clock on the wall. "We've got four hours to get down there and find something fabulous."

"You're going right now?" Meg said.

"Joy, you up for it?"

"For shopping? You've been away too long if you have to ask me that."

Kendra snorted. "Yeah, that girl and shopping are like Nicole Richie and a camera. Can't keep the two apart."

Joy rolled her eyes at Kendra and started putting her finished layouts into her scrapbook. "I'm at a stopping point anyway. We can go now, and if you don't find something, you can go raid Kendra's closet."

"Yeah, and we can just pull up the hemlines with clothes pins so you won't look like you're wearing a sheet or anything," Kendra joked.

"Very funny." Tandy stood up and wiped her hands together. "Okay, let's hit it."

✂ ✂ ✂

A FEW MINUTES later Tandy and Joy walked into Something from Sara.

"Tandy Sinclair!" Sara came from behind the counter and walked toward her, arms outstretched. "I can't believe you took this long to come in here!"

Sara's black hair was showing gray, and she'd pulled it back into her customary low ponytail.

"Hey, Sara." Tandy embraced the slender woman.

"It's been too long since I've seen your smiling face."

"I know." Tandy pulled back and looked into Sara's face, seeing the lines the past three years had etched there. "I get so busy in Orlando, I don't realize how long it's been until I come home."

"Well, it's good to have you back. How long are you here for?"

"Just until the Iris Festival. I'll probably go home on Sunday."

"That soon?"

Tandy nodded. "It's about as long as I can stay away."

"Yes, I heard you were taking the legal world by storm. About to make partner, is the story that's floating around here."

"Oh, I don't know about that." Tandy stuffed her hands in her pockets. "But I've been fortunate at the firm."

"Well—" Sara clasped her hands at her waist—"to what do I owe the pleasure today?"

"Tandy's got a—"

Tandy cut Joy off mid-sentence. "I need a dress, Sara." No need adding grist to the rumor mill.

"Special occasion?"

"Yes," Joy said.

"No," Tandy said at the same time.

"I see." Sara looked from one sister to the other, missing nothing. "All right, let's go look through the racks." She turned and walked toward the back of the store, directing the girls to the far corner where mannequins were dressed in silk dresses of all types. "Would something like this work?" She fingered the ruffled edge of a pale green dress. Its bodice was cinched tightly around the mannequin's waist, then exploded into layers of pleated chiffon.

"Hmm, a little too froufrou, I think." Joy turned to her. "Tandy?"

Tandy nodded. "Yeah. Maybe something, I don't know, simpler?"

Sara stepped over to another mannequin and held her hand up. "Better?" This one was a lavender sheath dress with short cap sleeves and a rounded neckline.

"Too fitted. I like the looseness of that one—" Tandy pointed back to the green dress—"just not the frilliness of it. And maybe a darker color?"

Sara held up a finger. "Ah, I've got the perfect thing. Be right back." She turned and walked away, leaving Tandy and Joy to sift through the hangers of dresses.

"Wow, she has an eye for clothes," Tandy said.

Joy nodded. "My closet is full of things she selected for me. You should see this place at prom time. It's an absolute madhouse."

"I can imagine."

"Here we go!" Sara returned from the back of the store. In her arms was a midnight-blue dress. Designed to fall to the knees, it had a wide strap that crossed the chest and went over one shoulder. The fitted bodice gave way to a flowing skirt that Tandy could almost feel swishing against her legs as she danced with Clay. Sara held the dress up by the hanger and turned it to reveal a back that was brazen in its design.

The wide strap continued over the shoulder and spilled into the side fabric of the dress. It was mirrored by another, wider stretch of fabric that went across the back, connecting one side of the dress to the other. The cut-out ended in a V shape that allowed for the flow of the skirt.

"That's—" Joy started.

"It's just—" Tandy couldn't finish her sentence, either. The dress didn't reveal anything she'd have difficulty baring in public, but it was daring in its reveal of her back.

"Try it on." Sara grinned. "I've been waiting for someone with the right figure to show me what it looks like."

Tandy followed Sara to a dressing room and, after Sara had hung the dress for her, stepped inside. She quickly changed into the dress, then turned to the mirror.

The front was conservative enough, its slash of midnight blue across her chest giving a wonderful bold contrast to the soft, flowing skirt. Tandy turned to see the back, and her breath caught. Every inch of fabric fell in the perfect spot. It was as if the dress was made for her.

But that back. There'd be no mistaking her interest in Clay when he got a look at this dress. He'd know in a millisecond she'd dressed for him. Not because it was revealing of anything he shouldn't see. No, she could wear this dress in front of Daddy with not an ounce of shame. But did she want to declare this openly how much she wanted Clay to see her as beautiful?

"Tandy?" Joy called through the dressing room door. "Even I don't take half an hour to change into a dress."

Tandy took a deep breath and opened the door.

"Wow, that color is amazing on you." Joy's wide eyes glowed. "Come out here and turn around."

Tandy bit her lip, hesitating.

"What's wrong?" Joy asked.

Tandy shot a gaze to Sara, whose eyes were bright with anticipation. "Does it not fit right? We can take it in or let it out if we need to."

"Oh no," Tandy rushed to assure her. "It's not that."

"Then come out here!" Joy's tiny hands urged Tandy from the dressing room.

Tandy walked out into the viewing area, stepping up onto a slightly raised platform in front of three mirrors. She heard Joy gasp behind her.

Sara clapped her hands together. "I knew it! I knew that dress would be gorgeous on you!"

Tandy stared into the mirror, seeing the front, side, and back views all at once. Her thick red curls fell down nearly to the wide swath of fabric in back, its deep hue highlighting the stunning nature of her hair. The whole thing was as bold as if Laura Bush told Barbara Walters she wore red lace underwear to bed every night. Bolder, even.

"You *must* wear that dress tonight." Joy sounded more effusive than Tandy thought she could be. "He might die of a heart attack, but he'll die a happy man. Just be certain you turn around first."

Wrinkles crossed her forehead as Tandy looked at Joy's reflection in the mirror. "You don't think it's a little, um, audacious?"

"Of course I do. It's audacious and amazing and daring."

"Exactly."

Joy shook her head as if to clear it. "My daring Big City Sister has difficulties with this dress?"

"You don't think this should come with a sign that says, 'Please notice me'?"

"Sis, it does not need a sign."

Tandy tucked her hair back, looking again at the mirror. It'd be fun to shake Clay up a bit. Let him know she'd developed just a bit of confidence over the past ten years, no longer thought of herself as the skinny kid on the streets. But *this* much confidence?

"I don't know, Joy," Tandy said. "If Clay sees this—"

"He'll know he's the most blessed man on the planet."

"Or he'll wonder why I'm dressing up like this, making this kind of effort."

"Why wouldn't you make the effort to look nice for him?"

Tandy noticed Sara had left the dressing room. "I would. But," she lifted the skirt of the dress as if presenting evidence, "this goes way past nice. This jumps with both feet into the realm of *working it*."

"All right, it's not something I'd advise doing under normal circumstances. But this is Clay, and, though I tend to think you're setting yourself up for heartache, I was under the impression you had committed to the next nine days." Joy raised her pencil-thin eyebrows. "Having second thoughts about that decision?"

"No. I agree with you that it isn't the best situation, but it's all either of us could give each other." She held Joy's arm. "Can you understand that?"

Joy's bright blue eyes met Tandy's deep brown ones. "I don't understand it, no, but I accept that it's your decision. And if it's your decision, then I believe this dress is a must. What is the difficulty in wearing this tonight?"

"Because it might embarrass him. This is the kind of dress that demands to be noticed. To be commented on."

"Yes." Joy still looked confused.

"What if he doesn't make a comment?"

"Have you lost your mind?" Joy put her small hands on Tandy's bare shoulders and turned her once again to the mirror. "Look." She spun Tandy so that the image of her back was on the main mirror. "Do you believe Clay, or any man on Earth for that matter, could look at that and not make a comment? What are those men in Orlando teaching you?"

Tandy gave a small laugh. "Not a whole lot since I don't go out with them much."

Joy turned Tandy so they were toe to toe. She put one hand on either side of her face and tilted it down. "Then look at me. Look right here in my eyes so you will know I speak the truth." She waited until Tandy focused on her. "You are a lovely woman. Not just because you're my big sister but because you're Tandy Ann Sinclair. You're intelligent and fun and talented and professionally successful.

There is no reason for you to leave this dress behind unless you've turned into someone who cows to fear. You're scared Clay will fall head over heels for you again and that you'll do the same and you won't be able to go back to Orlando at the end of this ridiculous nine-day period that I can't comprehend." She took a deep breath and continued. "But the Tandy I know laughs at fear and does her own thing. Going out on a limb for someone doesn't frighten her; it emboldens her. She'll move eight hundred miles away to chase a dream that is not her own." Tandy moved to stop her at that, but Joy covered her mouth. "She didn't mean for you, for any of us, to give up our lives, Tandy. Momma left this earth. We did not. Daddy finally knows that and is seeing Zelda. I pray you'll learn the same in the next nine days."

Tandy pulled Joy's hand from her mouth, fighting tears. Crying in public would *not* do. "You think I don't know that she's gone? I've missed her every day for ten years. I've spent every one of those days fulfilling her dreams—*our* dreams—"

"Are they really yours, Tandy? For that matter, were they really hers? It was ten years ago."

"You sound like Daddy."

"Thank you."

"It wasn't a compliment." Tandy backed away from Joy and turned to look in the mirror. She turned this way and that, appraising the dress.

"I know it wasn't, but I choose to take it as such. Daddy and I see the same thing happening: We see you living a life that allows you to have no emotion. No love. No faith. Just work. Lets you run from any possibility of emotion. But the Tandy I know and have loved all my life," Joy placed a hand at the small of Tandy's back, "doesn't run."

The word *run* left Joy's mouth and floated around the room. Tandy had been called a runner more than once since coming home. Kendra thought she was a runner. Clay even told her she ran.

But this dress wasn't something a runner would wear. It was something a confident woman would put on and stand tall in. It told the world that the woman within wasn't afraid of putting herself out there, of having an expectation of others. If she left this dress in the store, she was giving truth to Clay and Kendra's label. She rubbed the soft skirt fabric between her fingers, breath short with the pounding of her heart.

"Okay." Her whisper was lighter than a single feather blown by the wind, but hearing it come from her own mouth was enough to grow the tiny seed of determination Joy had planted. She straightened, throwing back her shoulders and tilting her chin up slightly as she'd done a million times in court. Persuading juries was easy; winning the jurors seated in the box of her heart was quite another. But Joy had won her at least a reprieve. "Okay." Her firm tone was that of a woman who had looked the prosecutor in the eye, assessed his case, and—with a bit of shock—found it wanting.

"Sara," Joy called out, her gaze firm on Tandy, "I believe we found our dress."

Sixteen

Tandy leaned over the white porcelain sink and closed an eyelid. She brushed on dark-brown shadow, then smudged it with her finger. The new dress hung in the doorway, keeping her confidence high. That was *her* dress. Bought with *her* money. Because it was going on *her* body.

She sneaked a glance at it in the mirror, shivered, then went back to applying makeup. Clay would freak out. Her stomach fluttered at the possibility that he could not even notice. She heard Joy's words from the ride home that afternoon: *He'll notice.* Another quick look at the dress confirmed it. He might not notice her, but that dress demanded attention.

She finished her eye makeup and picked up the lip liner. The bedroom phone rang. Maybe Clay calling to cancel. Decided to spend his night with Darin, just the guys, instead of a date.

"Tandy!" Daddy's voice boomed down the hallway. "Telephone!"

Her heart hit her toes. He was canceling. "Thanks!" She made her way into the bedroom, chastising herself for letting high hopes spend hard-earned money on a dress she had nowhere to wear.

"Hello?"

"Hey, you ready yet?" Kendra's voice hummed with excitement.

"Kendra?"

"Look, I know you're mind is full of Clay Kelner right now, but surely you know your own sister's voice."

"Of course." Tandy shook her head, comprehending it wasn't Clay calling to cancel. "Just thought you were somebody else."

"Who?"

"Never mind. Not important. Am I ready? No, but I will be in about five minutes."

"Then quit taking phone calls and get finished. I don't want to sit here waiting while you primp."

"Sheesh, *sorry*. If somebody would quit calling me, then I could leave here on time."

"Yeah, yeah, I'll leave you alone. Just make sure you get here soon."

"Ready to get this over with?" Tandy tried to put sympathy in her voice but failed.

"Something like that."

"What?"

"This will probably come up tonight, so I might as well tell you. Darin called me about an hour ago."

"He called you? What for?"

"To thank me for joining him tonight." Happiness hummed across the phone line.

"Aw, that was nice of him."

"I thought so, too."

"Is this why you're hurrying me up? Did you and Darin have a love connection?"

Kendra giggled. "Let's just say I think we're going to have fun tonight."

"Not if I don't get dressed."

"Right. Go get dressed. I can't wait to see this dress."

"Joy called?"

"She did. I'm proud of you, sis. It's high time you came out of mourning."

"What?"

But Kendra had already hung up.

Tandy placed the phone in its cradle and was on her way back to the bathroom when Daddy knocked on her bedroom door.

She pulled the towel around her body and cracked it open. "Yeah, Daddy?"

"Clay and Darin are here."

"They're *here? Already?*"

Daddy hooked his thumbs in his pockets and rocked on his heels. "Yep. I'd say you need to hustle it up in there."

"Tell them I'll be right down." She pushed the door shut, whirled around, and ran back to the bathroom. Finishing her makeup routine in forty-five seconds, she snatched the dress hanger off the doorframe and pulled the fabric over her head, careful not to smash her hair. Thank goodness it had no clasp to mess with. She zipped the small zipper on the side closed and walked back to the bedroom on trembling legs.

Her shoes lay waiting in their box on the bedspread. Sara's eye for fashion had come through once again, finding Tandy pale gold slides with a strap around her ankle that echoed those of the dress. Gold filigree teardrop earrings with jewels the color of the dress finished the look. Her heels clicked on the hardwood as she went to the closet door and pulled it open.

She stared into the full-length mirror on the other side of the door. The dress was as simple and conservative in front as she remembered, hiding the hips she hated beneath the loose skirt. She dared to turn and check out the back again.

With the guys waiting downstairs and Kendra probably tapping her foot through the carpet by now, there was no time to question her decision. Besides, she had no other options to try on. It was this or nothing.

She took a deep breath and left the bedroom.

Daddy's voice floated up the stairs from the direction of the living room. The timbre of Clay's voice as he responded carried through the air, its warm tones washing over her. She smoothed the dress across her stomach and walked down the stairs.

"We'll just put the ice cream in the back, and you guys can get it as you need it." Clay was sitting on the couch, his back to her, light from the Tiffany lamp bathing his profile and turning his ebony curls blue.

"Hey, guys." She forced nonchalance into her tone. Clay and Darin turned to look at her as she came around the side of the couch, careful to keep her front side to them. "I think Kendra's probably waiting on us, so if you're ready, we can go ahead." The men stood, and Clay's eyes raked her up and down.

"You look amazing," he said.

"Thanks." Her cheeks flamed and she struggled to breathe.

"No, I mean it."

"Trust me, he means it." Darin held out his hand. "I'm Darin, by the way." He was tall. Light glinted off his bald, tanned head. Chocolate-brown eyes and a wide smile made him seem as approachable as a puppy. His broad shoulders hidden beneath a dusky-purple button-up tapered to a trim waist around which a black leather belt and pants were fixed. Kendra would be thrilled.

She took his hand, shook it. "Hi, Darin. Nice to meet you. I'm sorry you had to change your plans with Clay tonight."

"Hey, don't worry about it. I talked to Kendra earlier, and I'm looking forward to meeting her."

"Good. Then I guess we should get going." She backed up a step to be beside Daddy, still keeping her front to them. "Daddy, you'll take Coop out before you go to bed?"

"Cooper Scooper and I will be just fine. You go and have some fun." He put his arm around her waist and leaned in to her ear. "But not too much," he whispered. "Nice dress."

She grinned up at him, grateful he approved and didn't think it was too provocative. "Thanks," she whispered back.

"After you, milady," Clay swept his arm toward the hallway. As soon as she stepped forward, though, he'd see the back of her dress. And he'd already complimented the front, so even if he wanted to say something nice, he couldn't. The urge to run hit her hard.

"Tandy?" She blinked and realized all eyes in the room were on her. "You okay?"

This was dumb. It was a dress, for Pete's sake, not the end of the world. "Yeah, yeah, I'm fine. Sorry, just thought I had forgotten something. We can go." She turned around to hug Daddy bye—and heard Clay's swift intake of breath. "Don't wait up," she whispered to Daddy.

"Don't forget your raising," he whispered back and tweaked her nose.

She turned back around, not meeting Clay's eyes. "Let's go!"

She made it out the front door and onto the porch before realizing Clay wasn't with them. "Where's Clay?"

"I'm guessing he's back in the living room trying to find his eyeballs." He smiled and shook his head at her. "You are one mean woman."

"Why am I mean?"

"You could have given the guy a little warning about that dress. If he's in there having a heart attack, it's your fault."

She blushed again.

"Please tell me your sister has the same fashion sense as you."

Her confidence growing, Tandy tossed her hair and leaned against the porch post. "I don't think you'll be disappointed."

"I am never having guys' night again."

Clay came through the door looking a bit shell-shocked. He tossed the keys to Darin. "We'll meet you in the car." He turned to Tandy and crooked a finger. "Come here a minute."

She followed him to the end of the porch. Was he mad? Darin seemed to think the dress was good. She sniffed. He could just get over it if he was mad. She looked good; and, with Darin's words ringing in her ears, she knew it. If he didn't want to take her out, then there were plenty of men at that jazz place that would be happy to dance with her. She could go with Darin and Kendra. He could go on home.

They reached the end of the porch, and he spun around, planting his hands on either side of the porch railing.

"What's the matter with you?" She planted her fists on her hips.

His green eyes looked like the ocean before a storm, that much she could tell by the porch light. And he was grinding his teeth, the muscles in his jaw rolling back and forth.

"I need to get something out of the way before we pick up Kendra."

"Okay. Did I do something? You seem mad."

He stared at the wood-planked floor, not meeting her eyes. "No, I'm not mad."

"Then what? For somebody who's not mad, you sure do act like you are."

He closed the space between them with one step, his hands grazing her face, burying themselves in her hair before she realized he had even moved.

"I'm sorry. I just wasn't expecting," his eyes softened as he met hers, "this. And I wasn't prepared, and then you turned around, and I'm pretty sure your dad is in there rethinking his opinion of me."

Her arms fell by her sides. "You're mad about my dress?"

"No!" His eyes widened. "Definitely not mad. Just shocked the snot out of me, is all."

"*Shocked* is a word people use when they find out their best friend is dating their other friend's mother or something." She frowned.

"*Shocked* is a word people use when they're stunned by beauty, Tandy. You looked amazing when you came in the room. When you turned around, well, *phenomenal* doesn't begin to cover it."

"So you're saying you *like* the dress?"

"Am I the only one hearing myself here?"

"No, but you're not being very clear."

"Oh, okay, let me fix that." He dipped his head, and without warning his lips were on hers.

A part of her—the part that she let think of him every now and then—stood up in the back of her mind and cheered. His kiss was so familiar, the first kiss she'd ever had and the last one she'd ever wanted. Her hands listened to the cheering section and traced their way around his waist, thicker since their high school years, more solid somehow. She kissed him back, feeling the exact moment when he realized she was giving back to him.

He lifted his head and looked down into her eyes, his gaze roaming her face. "Darin's going to wonder where we went." His voice sounded like rocks tumbling together as he tucked a strand of hair behind her ear. "And if we're on this porch much longer, I'm pretty sure your daddy is going to make you go change that dress."

She smiled, grateful for his attempt to lighten the mood. "I'll have you know, Daddy told me this was a nice dress." She stepped backward, out of his embrace, missing his warmth but knowing the wisdom of her move. Turning, she walked down the porch, hearing his footfalls behind her. Certain now of his reaction to the view, she put a little extra sway in her hips as they crossed the yard.

They reached his car, a four-door sleek, black Dodge Charger, and he came around to open her door. "Thanks for that," he said and reached for the door handle. Before she could duck in, he leaned forward and dropped a quick kiss on the top of her nose. She all but fell into her seat.

"Told you that dress was mean," Darin said from the backseat.

She turned in her seat and looked at him. "Thanks for the warning."

They wiped their faces of grins as Clay opened his own door and slid into the car. "What'd I miss?" He looked from Tandy to Darin.

"Not a thing, ol' buddy." Darin clapped a big hand on Clay's shoulder. "Not a thing. Can we please go pick up *my* date now? Tandy says they have the same fashion sense, so you can understand my anticipation."

Clay put the car in gear and swung a wide arc. "In that case I'll have us there in about five minutes." He reached across the console and took Tandy's hand in his own, like he'd done a million times during their high school years. She clasped her fingers in his, loving the way they clicked back together so quickly.

"That gives you five whole minutes to give me the dirt on your sister, then," Darin said.

"What's Clay told you so far?'

"That she's creative, artsy, and can't stick with any job longer than six months."

"Clay!" She swatted his arm.

"What? It's the truth."

"Yeah, but it doesn't paint a very flattering picture of her."

"Sorry." He lifted his eyes from the road and looked at Darin in the rearview mirror. "Kendra's great, Darin, really."

"She seemed like it on the phone, but you still haven't told me what she looks like."

"What?" A frisson of alarm skittered up Tandy's back. "You didn't tell him *anything?*"

"Why do I feel like you're going to tell me she has a third eye or something?" Darin asked.

"I told you, it's not a big deal," Clay said.

"What's not a big deal?" Darin's voice had gone from playful to suspicious.

"Don't you think maybe *he* should make that decision?" Tandy ignored Darin's question.

"What decision?" Darin asked.

"I told you, he already did."

"Great, if I made it, then somebody tell me what it is," Darin said. "I promise I'll stand by the decision, unless I made it after severe bodily abuse, in which case I reserve the right to change my mind."

Tandy twisted in her seat to face him as best she could. "Kendra's black, Darin."

Darin's blank look made her clarify.

"Black, as in African-American."

Darin looked at her as if he was trying to figure out a riddle. "Yeah, now tell me the part about the third eye."

"She doesn't have a third eye. As a matter of fact, she has great eyes. But she's black."

"Why are you saying that like it matters?"

"It doesn't?"

"Not to me."

"You already knew she was black." His lack of reaction was enough to tell her she was speaking the truth.

He shrugged. "I guessed as much after I talked to her. Then, when I saw the family picture on the mantel at your house, I asked your dad to tell me which one was Kendra."

"So this isn't an issue?"

"Did Clay tell you about my first marriage?"

"Yes. He thought it wasn't an issue."

"Smart man. It isn't."

She settled back into her seat, the knot of nervous tension that had coiled in her stomach began to relax. "Okay. Good."

"So there really is no third eye?"

"Darin!"

"Okay, okay. Just making sure."

"We're here." Clay turned into the driveway of a rambling white Victorian home.

"Want me to go up and get her?" Tandy asked.

"Not a chance." Darin opened his door. "You kids talk among yourselves while I go retrieve the lady." He got out, and they watched him bound up the steps to the porch. Kendra must have told him how the house was laid out into apartments, one tenant to each floor, because he didn't bother with the doorbell. Just opened the weathered white door and went on in.

"Darin seems nice," Tandy said.

"He's a good guy."

"How'd you two meet?"

"We were in the service together. Joined up on the same day. Got out on the same day."

"Oh." Crickets chirped in the night as she wondered whether to ask him about his days as a soldier. Did he want to talk about it?

"You know, it wasn't what I expected it to be." He reached across and took her hand again. "Being in the service."

"It wasn't?"

"No." His thumb traced circles on the back of her hand. "I had seen all these movies and TV shows that made it seem so heroic to fight for our country, defend our freedoms, all that stuff."

"It *is* heroic, Clay."

He nodded. "It is, you're right. But when you're doing it, it doesn't feel all that heroic. It just feels like another day on the job. You get to doing your duty—delivering gas or parts or patrolling streets or whatever—and you forget that you're in the middle of a hostile environment. You get used to the feel of a gun in your hands, helmet on your head, vest strapped around your chest. It becomes comfortable. Until some guy tries to shoot you in the head, not because you've done anything or even know who he is but because of what you stand for, what flag is stitched to your uniform."

"You were shot at?"

"Yeah, we all were. Pretty much anybody who did time in Iraq has been shot at. It's just part of the job. Some of the citizens are so grateful to have us there, they come running out of their homes to bring us food and gifts. Others throw rocks, or worse."

The way he said it, like serving in a war was as ordinary as changing socks or doing the laundry, broke her heart.

"I'm sorry." She wasn't sure what she was sorry about, only that it was important to say the words.

He looked at her. She couldn't make out his features in the darkness of the car, but the heat in her chest told her he was looking at her. His hand tightened on hers, their sure way of telling the other the depth of their feelings.

"I hate what that man said to you in Orlando," he said, and she struggled to switch focus. "But if it's what made you come back here, then I'm glad he said it."

She thought about his words, decided she agreed with him. "Me, too." She glanced up at the house and saw Kendra and Darin coming out the front door. "Looks like they hit it off."

Kendra's laughter rang out across the lawn, and her hand was tucked into the crook of Darin's arm. She wore the red halter dress, but in true Kendra fashion had thrown a red-and-purple striped scarf around her neck. The ends of it trailed down her back, along with her mahogany-colored hair. Her slender brown ankles were laced with crimson-red ribbons that held a spiky red heel to her foot.

"He better not be a jerk."

Clay cleared his throat. "Judging by the looks of you two tonight, I'd say it's far more likely we men will be going home with broken hearts before the night is over."

Tandy laughed and leaned her head back against the headrest. "Doubtful," she said.

Darin walked Kendra around the car and opened her door. She allowed herself to be helped into the seat and settled back into its leather softness as Darin shut the door.

"Clay, I don't care what they say about you, you're a wonderful man," she said.

"Glad to know you approve," Clay shot back.

Darin slid into his side of the car, and Clay backed down the driveway. Tandy sucked in a deep breath, determined to remember every detail of this night and ignore the reality that made that necessary.

They headed down Lindell and out of town to Highway 64, the Dodge's motor throbbing beneath the hood.

"Tell me about this place we're going." Tandy turned her head to see his profile. "It must be new since neither Kendra nor I have heard of it."

"It's about a year old," Clay said. "The owner had a jazz bar in Atlanta, but he got sick of fighting the traffic every day, so he moved out here to the country and opened a supper club instead."

"You can take the man out of the city," Darin said, "but the love of jazz lives on."

"That's Joe's motto," Clay explained. "He's a cool cat. Plays sax and piano and tells some stories you wouldn't believe, but they're true. He worked with some of the legends back in the day."

"Like who?" Kendra leaned forward.

"B.B. King, Otis Redding, John Coltrane, Etta James . . ."

"Get out!" Kendra slapped the seat in front of her. "He played with Etta James? You lie."

"Nope," Darin said. "He tells the truth. We'll get Joe to tell you some of his stories. Maybe even see his office. That's where he keeps all his pictures from the old days."

"Get me in that office and we might be looking at a long-term thing, here."

"Don't believe her," Clay warned. "Kendra doesn't do anything long-term."

"You watch it, mister," she retorted. "I'm a woman, so I can change my mind *or* my ways at any time."

"Yes, ma'am." Clay's mock salute made Tandy giggle.

"Hey, Clay?"

"Yeah, man?"

"Remind me to find a way to get Kendra in Joe's office."

"Roger that."

Clay reached over and turned on the radio, pushing preset buttons until they landed on the easy listening station. He took Tandy's hand in his again.

They bantered the whole way and, about twenty minutes later, turned off the highway into a blacktop parking lot. A squat brick building was lit up by spotlights hanging from its roof by black iron and angled down to illuminate a white sign that read *Joe's* in flowing black script. Underneath that, in smaller letters, Tandy read, *Jazz lovers welcome. Live music Friday and Saturday nights.* "

Cars were lined up in rows, and Tandy wondered if they'd be able to get a table.

Clay pulled the car into a parking space and killed the engine. Tandy reached for her door handle, but Clay's voice halted her.

"Stop right there."

"You, too," Darin said from the back.

"What is it with women these days, Darin?" Clay said as they exited their side of the car. "Can't give us men two seconds to get around the car and open a door." He shut his door, and Tandy turned to face Kendra.

"Hey, thanks for doing this, sis."

Kendra harrumphed. "It was a favor before, but consider your debt paid. Have you looked at that man?" She jerked her finger to the back of the car where the men were coming around to open their doors. "He is f-i-n-e fine."

Tandy chuckled and turned back around. "Good to know I'm all paid up."

A rush of cool air swept across Tandy's face when Clay opened her door. He held out his hand and she took it, letting him help her out of the seat.

The two couples walked to the door, and Clay reached out to open it. He wiggled his eyebrows at Tandy and said, "After you, madam."

"You just want to check out my dress again."

"You better believe it." He swept his hand forward, and she walked on through. She turned around to get his reaction and cracked up when she saw his arm across Darin, holding back his and Kendra's entrance to get a better view of Tandy.

"You are a nutcase," she announced as they joined her in the club.

"It'd be lunacy to not take every opportunity I can to enjoy the sight of you in that dress."

Tandy rolled her eyes at him and looked around the room. Circular tables were arranged in the center of the room, votive candles burning atop their linen-covered tops. Plush upholstered chairs with black script *J*'s embroidered in the center were situated around each table. Intimate booths stood sentry on a platform around the room, their high-backed seats covered in a diamond-shaped gray pattern. The booth tables were also covered in white linen, a black script *J* embroidered in the middle of the overhang. Candelabras sat on the rail above each booth, white taper candles providing a moody ambience.

A haunting melody flowed from the black lacquer-finished grand piano at the front of the room. A microphone, in the style of the 1920s, stood by itself at center stage.

"That's Joe on the piano," Clay said in her ear. His warm breath made her shiver.

"Does he play all night?"

"No, just until eight or so. Then he'll have some performer booked to play or sing."

"Clay and Darin, good to see you boys." This from a raven-haired beauty poised behind the hostess stand, as regal as a queen holding court. "And I see you've brought some friends this time."

"Sophia, meet Tandy and Kendra Sinclair," Clay said. "Girls, this is Sophia, Joe's better half."

"I don't know about that, but I am his wife." She came

from around the stand and shook Tandy's hand, then Kendra's. "Are you ladies searching for some good jazz tonight?"

"We are," Tandy affirmed. "Clay says this is the place to come."

"He should know. He and Darin are here, what, Clay, about once a month?"

"Give or take. Who's playing tonight?"

"Jenna will be on the piano the first hour. We're not sure about the main act since Bo and Liv just called to cancel."

"Nothing wrong, I hope?" Darin asked.

"Oh, no, they're probably just living it up in New York an extra night. They played a gig there the past two weeks. You know jazz folks."

They nodded.

"I'm sure we'll work out something, though. We always do!" She went back around to the hostess stand and marked something on the paper in front of her. "Let's find you four a booth, all right?"

"Thanks, Sophia," Clay said.

"Don't thank me yet. If I can't talk Jenna into staying through the night or find someone else to come in for Bo and Liv, I'll be hitting you and Slick here up for some talent."

"Let's hope things don't get that desperate," Darin said as they stopped at the booth facing center stage.

"We'll see." Sophia gestured to the booth. "Is this all right?"

"It's perfect, thanks." They settled into the booth, and Sophia went back to her station at the door.

"You guys come here once a month?" Kendra smirked. "Aren't *you* in touch with your feminine side."

"Hey, don't knock a man's love for the finer things in life," Darin said.

Kendra placed a hand on her chest in mock seriousness. "I am so very sorry to have called into question your manliness, sir."

Darin turned to Clay. "Is she mocking me? Because I think she's mocking me."

"She might be."

"No might to it. The woman is mocking me." He faced Kendra. "Do you know the penalty for mocking a man in a jazz club?"

"A night of watching WWE?"

Darin groaned. "Ugh, I wouldn't subject my worst enemy to that. No, the punishment here is a bit less severe."

"Depending on your point of view," Clay cut in, and Darin cut his eyes at him.

"Okay, break it to me gently. What horrible act must I perform to atone for my sin?" Kendra batted her eyes.

"You must dance with me before even looking at the menu."

"That *is* harsh."

"I warned you it was a serious offense."

Kendra sighed in melodramatic fashion. "And yet, I am a woman of principle, so I must accept my punishment with grace."

Darin stood up and offered his hand to help her from the booth. She took it, and they joined a few other couples on the dance floor.

"He sure didn't waste any time," Tandy said.

"Guess she shouldn't have mocked him."

"Point taken. Are there other rules to the jazz club I should know before I inadvertently break one?"

"Too late."

"How can it be too late? I just sat down and, I promise, I've only mocked you in my mind."

"And yet you broke the rule of fellowship."

"The rule of fellowship?"

He nodded. "Whenever the party consists of two couples, both must dance or none dance at all."

"That's a rule."

He made an *x* over his heart and held up two fingers. "Cross my heart."

She sighed, mimicking Kendra's dramatic flair. "Ah, the things we do for the love of jazz."

Clay stood and led her to the dance floor. Catching Joe's eye, he nodded. Joe nodded back, his fingers dancing over the keys to the opening notes of "For Once in My Life."

"I love this song," Tandy breathed as they moved together.

"I know. I remember."

His big hand was warm on the bare skin of her back. She laid her head on his shoulder, finding the hollow there that fit better than any pillow. His heartbeat thudded in her ear, and she relaxed into his arms like a bird who'd found its nest.

Kendra and Darin were a few steps away, talking and laughing, moving in time to the music. Kendra's scarf swayed across her back as Darin turned her. Tandy closed her eyes and took in the moment, committing it to memory. From the sure firmness of Clay's arms to the soft notes of the familiar melody, she drank in every detail using every sense.

The song ended too soon, and she opened her eyes to find Kendra looking at her, mouth set in a hard line. Kendra said something to Darin, who nodded and headed back to their booth.

"Excuse us, Clay." Kendra walked over to them and pulled on Tandy's wrist. "We just need to freshen up a bit."

Clay smiled. "Oh, sure. Want us to go ahead and order for you?"

"That'll be fine. Come on, Tandy." Kendra pulled her across the dance floor toward a lighted sign that said *Ladies Room*.

"Did Darin do something?" Tandy asked as soon as they were inside the door of a dressing area furnished with more upholstered chairs and a chaise lounge. A mirror ran from ceiling to floor on one side of the room. Tandy could see in its reflection that there were two bathroom stalls around the corner. She struggled to pay attention and get her mind out of the haze of that dance floor.

"No, it's what you're doing that has me worried." Kendra put her hands on her silk-clad hips.

"What *I'm* doing? What do you mean?"

"I saw you out there. You looked like a couple of newlyweds."

"No, we didn't. At least, I didn't." She shook her head, pulling her brain into the room.

"Please, this is me you're talking to. You can bluff your way around Joy and Meg but not me. You're as crazy for him as he is for you."

"So what if I am? I'm single and an adult, and as far as I know, so is he. What's the problem?"

"Have you forgotten you're leaving here in a week?"

"Nine days."

"Whatever." Kendra threw her hands in the air. "You're going to leave and he's going to be here."

"I know this." *And I hate it, but I can't change it.*

"And still you're letting yourself fall for him this hard?"

"Yeah, I am."

They both stopped short at her admission.

"Look, it's what we've got, okay?"

"You say that like you have some awful illness that only gives you nine days to live."

"No, just a dream to go chase down." Sadness weighed down her words, the haze of happiness completely obliterated.

"What if you change your dream, sis?"

"You know I can't do that. People don't change their dreams."

"Of course they do. It's just harder when those dreams were made with someone who isn't here anymore."

"I can't, Ken. Momma and I talked about this forever. It was practically all we talked about those last couple of months. I'm not going to let her down by calling it quits because Clay Kelner moved back to town." Tandy held up her hand to stop Kendra's retort. "Don't, please. It's a ridiculous situation, I know. I get it. But it's what we've got, and that's a whole lot more than some people get, so we're going to take it. Please don't ruin it for me."

Kendra's look said everything her mouth wasn't, her exotic brown eyes bearing down on Tandy like a lab technician observing a rat and not liking the results. She shook her head slowly, her eyes still on Tandy, checking for the slightest change or weakness. When Tandy made no move, Kendra's lips thinned. "Fine. I won't say another word."

They went back out to the club, and Tandy saw Clay over by the stage, talking to Joe. Joe nodded and gave a thumbs-up, then headed back to the piano. Clay turned and, seeing Tandy, crossed the dance floor to her side.

"There you are. I was beginning to think Kendra had carted you off to another country."

"Nope. Still here." The irony of the phrase was not lost on her as Joe played the opening notes of "At Last."

Clay held out his hand. "Care to dance?"

"Won't our food be here soon?"

He took her hand and slid his arm around her waist. "I think it'll wait." Their feet moved in tandem, and all thoughts of dinner flew away as she let herself fall back into the cloud of happiness that surrounded them.

At the closing notes, she sighed and lifted her head from his chest. "Thanks for this."

"You're welcome. I like it when you're loose and relaxed. Your smile looks real."

"And it doesn't when I'm tense?"

"No. It looks like you're playing a role you didn't realize you tried out for."

She wrinkled her nose at him. "That doesn't sound attractive."

"Everything on you is attractive. It just doesn't look real."

They walked back to the table, and she sat down. A waiter arrived and placed dishes in front of them. She saw Clay had ordered something with chicken and pasta in it. The white sauce would go straight to her hips, but the dancing tonight, combined with all the calories they'd burned at Heartland, should make up for it.

"How is everything?" Sophia stood at the end of their table.

"Perfect," Kendra declared.

"Oh, good. I hate to intrude on your evening, but, guys, we're in a tough spot. I haven't been able to find anybody to fill in tonight. Jenna can come back, but she's got to pick up her little boy at nine from her mother's and take him home. She says she can be back by nine-thirty. Could one of you please fill in for just thirty minutes?"

"Kendra, you sing. Why don't you fill in?"

Kendra's eyes opened wide at Tandy's suggestion. "Because I'm certain Sophia doesn't want to lose her entire clientele."

"I remember your voice from high school," Clay said. "You were good."

"She still is. Come on, Ken."

Darin leaned toward her. "I'll play piano if you sing."

"I thought you played bass."

"I keep telling you, I'm a man of many talents." He wiggled his eyebrows at her, and she laughed.

"I can't promise stellar results—" Kendra looked at Sophia—"but if you want to take a chance, I'm happy to help out."

"If Clay says you can sing, then you can sing," Sophia said. "I'll go let Jenna know. Thank you so much!"

Sophia made a note on her clipboard and walked around the dance area to the stage steps.

"I can't believe I just agreed to sing in a jazz club. I think there's something in this glass besides iced tea."

"You'll be fine," Tandy assured her. "I've heard you sing. Your voice is perfect for jazz."

"What songs can you sing?" Darin asked. "We should probably have about seven to make it until Jenna gets back."

Clay caught Tandy's eye as Kendra and Darin worked out a song list. The heat in his eyes told her everything she needed to know about his thoughts. Amazing how they had come back together as if ten years hadn't separated them.

She remembered the long days they had spent just talking. Sitting out by the lake or walking up and down Old Crockett Road, hand in hand. He was a good listener. When she told him about being different from everyone else but her sisters, he understood the feeling. He had been the only boy without a mother in junior high. Her stories of dark days and darker nights in Orlando didn't make him flinch. Instead, he shared the dark feelings hiding at his house, the despair of his dad ever since his mom died.

He was a gem of a kid back then, an even better man now.

"Okay, I think we're set." Darin said, and Tandy came back to the present. Clay's gentle green eyes sparkled at her across the table.

The couples danced and ate, waiting for the clock to swing around to 9:00 p.m. When the hour came, Tandy saw Kendra tense up. "You're going to be great." She rubbed Kendra's arm and felt the gooseflesh there. "I know it."

"You promise?"

"Of course. You're a Sinclair."

Kendra grinned and walked to the stage with Darin. The spotlight glowed on her skin, making her appear bronzed. Her head turned toward Darin, and she rested an arm along the piano. The purple and red scarf draped over her shoulder wavered. Darin played the opening notes to "Stormy Weather," and Tandy closed her eyes to hear her sister's smoky voice.

"Wow, she *can* sing." Clay breathed in her ear as they swayed on the dance floor. "She'll have no problem getting into Joe's office after this."

"Mmm." It was all Tandy could manage. She was working too hard to let the husky timbre of Kendra's tone, combined with the flickering candlelight in the room, wash away her fear of what would happen in nine days.

Seventeen

The air in Grace Christian church was as stuffy as an undersized casket on a four-hundred-pound man this Sunday morning. Tandy waved the church bulletin in front of her face in a spirited attempt to rid the air in front of her of its old-woman perfume. Someone had decided rose water was the perfect compliment to a church service. If only they'd thought to stop at one dab. Or even two. Tandy's nose wrinkled as she staved off another sneeze.

"It's Mrs. Simmons," Kendra stage-whispered.

"What?"

"The rose water. It's Mrs. Simmons." Kendra nodded her head toward a white-haired woman three pews up. The lady wore a red hat with a bright purple feather and was briskly moving a matching fan back and forth. "I wonder sometimes if she doesn't bathe in the stuff."

Tandy stifled a giggle. "Hush, she'll hear you."

"She hasn't heard anything more than six inches from her ear in a decade."

"Maybe someone should say something to her."

"Like what? 'Mrs. Simmons, you're making everyone

around you nauseous with your rose water. Mind not doing that?' Yeah, that's the way to share the love of Jesus."

"When did she start coming here? I don't remember her." Tandy thought she'd know everyone at Grace Christian and had run into a lot of familiar faces. But there were more new ones than she'd anticipated.

"She switched her membership from the Baptist church on Elm."

"Why?"

Kendra shrugged, then leaned over to talk to James on her other side who was pulling on her sleeve.

The windows of the little sanctuary were open and, before the room filled with people, a nice breeze had been blowing through. Tandy had skipped Sunday school to sit in the pew and feel that breeze across her face. She'd needed the quiet like the *Titanic* needed more lifeboats. Clay was her iceberg.

Sitting on the edge of the pew closest to the middle aisle, Tandy wondered why she hadn't made certain to sit on the other end, by the window. She gazed down the row of heads to her left. Kendra still talked with James, who had gone back to coloring a dinosaur in yellow and red. Savannah sat by his side, kicking her little patent-leather shoes against the pew in front of them.

Meg and Jamison sat tall on the other side of their children, Joy and Scott on their other side. They barely all fit into the pew, but there would be more room when Savannah and James went off to children's church after the first couple of hymns.

A deep sense of gratitude came over Tandy as she saw her family lined up beside her. They were each so unique yet so much a part of her. Scrapping with the sisters had provided a place to talk, to air out her thoughts and get feedback, to just relax and have some fun—all things Tandy hadn't fully acknowledged until now were missing from her life in Orlando. As soon as she got back, she'd need to go to the scrapping store and see if there was a group to meet with on a regular basis.

It wouldn't be the same as scrapping with the sisters in Momma's studio, but it might be a nice substitute. She wondered how other scrappers found like-minded people in their communities. If there wasn't a scrapbooking store, then how did women know who the other scrappers in their area were? Or did they just scrap alone all the time? The thought saddened her, that other women were missing out on the camaraderie of scrapping time with girlfriends.

Ms. Scarlet sat down at the piano and began to play. Conversations teetered off and, within a minute, the sanctuary got quiet except for the melody Ms. Scarlet's hands coaxed from the old upright. Tandy closed her eyes and drank it in like a marathon runner in her last mile. Even the rose water couldn't detract from the truth in the clear notes.

The song came to an end, and the new music minister approached the podium and told them all to turn to page 253 of the hymnal. Tandy's smile quirked a bit. He was opening with an oldie but goodie, "I'll Fly Away." Fast enough to wake everyone up, yet old enough to keep the traditional contingent happy.

As they stood to sing, Tandy resolved to enjoy the family of Grace Christian for the next hour, adding it to her memory banks as well.

A little over an hour later, the last amen sounded and the congregation began moving to the doors. Daddy stood in his customary place at the back of the sanctuary, shaking the hands of his flock and issuing a warm welcome to the few visitors. Tandy caught snatches of conversation here and there, mostly about the upcoming Iris Festival. She'd been so caught up in seeing Clay this weekend, she'd almost forgotten about the festival.

If this year was like every other, the celebrations would begin on Monday with community events scheduled every day. Tandy noticed a stack of brochures on the back table and wound her way through the people and pews to get one. A purple iris decorated the front of the program. Tandy perused the listing of events. Just as she'd suspected, the week kicked off with a prayer breakfast tomorrow morning at 7:00 a.m. An event was scheduled for nearly every hour between now and the parade.

"Planning out your week?"

Tandy turned to Kendra. "Yeah. Which of these are you going to?" She grabbed a short, stubby pencil from the Styrofoam cup on the table and began making stars by some of the events.

Kendra picked up a program and traced one red-lacquered nail down the page. "Hmmm. I'll take the sculpture to the contest booths in the morning."

"You finished it? When?"

Kendra smiled. "Last night. When I got back from our date. Let's just say I was inspired."

"Ah, Darin has a good effect on you?"

Kendra tilted her head in thought. "I'm not sure if it was Darin or singing soul music or seeing you and Clay together." She shrugged her shoulders. "Whatever it was, I'm grateful for it. I was up until five this morning, but the thing is done!"

"Good!" She focused again on the program. "What else are you going to? I was thinking about hitting the art show on Tuesday."

"Mm-hmm. Sounds good. And I'm sure Meg will take the kids to the street fair to ride the rides on Thursday since that's wristband day."

"Sounds like a scrapbooking moment to me."

Kendra nodded.

"What about the car show tomorrow?"

"Darin told me he and Clay were going to it."

"Then I guess we'll go, too!"

"Okay—" Tandy's eyes scanned the program—"looks like Pig-Out in the Park is on Friday night before the band plays." She made a star by it. "We'll definitely go to that."

"Oh yeah, all the barbecue you can eat and men walking around toting trophies the size of station wagons declaring them the best pig roaster in the county? Good times, good times." Kendra nudged Tandy in the ribs, making her laugh. "I'll bet Charles Dennis is going to be there."

"Oh, man! I haven't had barbecue like his in *ages*. You just can't find that in Orlando. They *slice* their barbecue."

"Slice it? Like ham? You're lying."

"I wish. Threw me for a loop the first time I saw it." Tandy looked back at the program.

"I think I'd have sent it back. That's like the time Joy made the hot-dog-and-biscuit casserole instead of just rolling them up and calling them pigs in a blanket. Some things should not be messed with."

"I'm with you. Okay, we've still got the quilt show, the library sale, and the pet show. Are we going to any of those?"

"James will be showing Tootsie in the pet show."

"Then we have to go and see that." Tandy penciled in a star. "Are either of those dogs better trained?"

Kendra shrugged. "Tootsie is as headstrong as ever. You know Welsh Terriers. They can be as willful as Britney Spears, and Tootsie doesn't disappoint. Belle, though, is still just as sweet as apple pie."

"She always was a cuddlebug."

"That's her."

"It looks like, then," Tandy ran her pencil down the stars she had drawn, "we'll have the car show on Monday, art show on Tuesday, pet show on Wednesday, street fair on Thursday, and Pig Out in the Park and then music on Friday."

"All culminating in a fabulous parade on Saturday morning!"

Tandy folded the program and stuffed it in the side of her Bible cover. "Now for the important question. What's for lunch?"

"We could go to a certain diner I know. Serves great burgers and the scenery is nice to look at." She grinned devilishly.

"I know you're not checking out my scenery."

"Nope, wouldn't dream of it." They walked out the church doors, and the bright sunshine made them squint.

Tandy reached up to shade her eyes. "What time does he open on Sundays? And when did you start eating anything but a veggie burger?"

"Noon. He goes to early service and then opens up the diner for the lunch crowd." Kendra was digging in her oversized purse for sunglasses. "And I've been eating burgers for about three months now."

"Seriously? What happened to all veggies, all the time?"

"I got bored. Needed some variety."

Typical Kendra. "What church around here has early service?"

"The Baptist one over on Elm."

"Since when?"

"Since their congregation aged so much that eight a.m. became a regular time for service."

"You're kidding me. Eight in the morning?"

"Aha!" Kendra found the glasses and put them on. Tandy rolled her eyes at the pink and lime-green rhinestones in the corners. "Yeah, eight in the morning. They don't even have a late service anymore."

"And they didn't lose members over that?"

"Sure they did." Kendra waved her arm back toward the church. "Didn't you notice we're full here?"

"That explains it."

"That's why we're putting up with rose water overload every Sunday morning."

"You are shameless."

"That's me." Kendra tossed her head as they continued on to the parking lot. "Did you ride with Daddy?"

Tandy nodded. "I'll run let him know I'm with you. Should we see if he wants to come to lunch with us?"

"He's got plans."

"With who?"

"Zelda. They have lunch every Sunday afternoon."

Tandy tried to ignore the frisson of alarm that ran through her. "Exactly how often do they see each other?"

"About as often as I change fingernail polish."

"Please tell me you're joking."

Kendra gave her a sympathetic look. "Sorry, sis. Things happen while you're off in the big city."

"I know things happen, Kendra. I'm not an idiot."

"Whoa, sister." Kendra held up her hands and backed away a few steps. "Can I have my head back?"

"Sorry. I didn't mean to bite it off. It's just that I'm sick of hearing how I'm so bad because I'm in the big city."

"Nobody said you were bad because you moved."

"No, of course they don't say it outright like that. But people mean it."

"What are you talking about?"

"Like when Daddy tells me to spend some time with Clay because it might make me move home and he misses me."

"I didn't hear a commentary in there on your lifestyle."

"Or when you tell me not to fall hard for Clay because I have to go back to the city."

"I *so* did not say you had to go back. I said if you *were* going back that it would be harder the more you fell for Clay again."

"Same thing."

"Not the same thing." Kendra shook her head, and her dangling silver coin earrings jangled. "Not even close to the same thing, sister."

Tandy sighed and squeezed her eyes shut, hands forming fists at her sides. After a minute she opened her eyes and smiled at Kendra. "Okay, fit time over."

Kendra looked at her with wide eyes. "Good, because I was getting ready to go therapeutic on you."

The girls laughed. "I'll run let Daddy know I'm riding with you." Tandy turned back toward the church.

"You do that. I'll go get the car and meet you up by the door." Kendra stopped at her red Rav4. "And try not to go crazy on me in the next two minutes!"

Tandy nodded, already walking back to the front door of the church. She found Daddy in the sanctuary and let him know she would be going to the diner with Kendra.

"Guess I'll see you there."

Tandy tried not to hurt at the twinkle in his eye. "So I hear."

Daddy quirked an eyebrow. "You hear? From who?"

"Whom, Daddy."

"From whom, Miss Grammar Queen?"

"It doesn't matter. I'll meet you at the diner." She pivoted on one heel and exited the sanctuary before he could nail her down about her feelings. Daddy had a way of peering into her soul that would make an amoeba on a microscope slide grateful for the glass.

She went back out into the sunshine and spotted Kendra's car idling by the front door. She slid in and flipped the visor down to check her makeup.

"You look fine," Kendra assured her. "He doesn't see anything but stars when you're around anyway."

"I could probably say the same about Darin when you're in the room."

"You think so?" Kendra's voice was hopeful.

Tandy rolled her eyes. "Um, yeah. Me and every other person at Joe's last night."

Kendra giggled and checked her own makeup in the rearview mirror. "You think he'll be at Clay's?"

"No idea."

Tandy turned on the radio, and sounds of the Miles Davis Quintet flooded the car. Kendra shot her a guilty look. "I thought maybe some jazz on the way to church would get me in a worshipful mood?"

Tandy burst out laughing. "You are the most transparent person on the planet, and I love you for that."

"I love you, too."

They rode the rest of the way to the diner nestled in the croon of John Coltrane's sax.

Kendra found a space on Lindell two doors down from Clay's Diner and parked. Tandy reached over and put her hand on top of Kendra's, stopping her. "Do you think we should go in there? I don't want him to think I'm chasing him or anything."

"Tandy, get your big-city self into that diner." Kendra shook her hand free, grabbed her purse from between the seats, and exited the vehicle.

Tandy joined her on the sidewalk. "What? I'm not being unreasonable. You know how Momma was about us calling boys or chasing after them."

"I don't think Momma would tell you not to eat in a diner owned by the man who goes gaga every time you walk in the room."

Now it was Tandy's turn to giggle. "Really? He does that?"

"You're smart enough to not act like a crazed schoolgirl, and yet—" Kendra pulled open the glass door, and the smell of hot burgers and ice cream wafted out of the diner. "He's into you, you're into him, and both of you are too dumb to do the right thing about it."

"I thought I was smart." She followed Kendra to a table on the far side of the room. People packed the diner, and the hubbub of conversation filled every nook and cranny. Tables full of well-dressed Stars Hill citizens fresh out of church gave a homey, community atmosphere. Tandy loved that Clay had created a place like this.

`"You are, but not when it comes to him." Kendra pointed behind the counter to Clay, who was smiling at a little girl with a short black ponytail and polka-dot ribbon as he took her order. "When he's in the room, your brain goes on hiatus faster than Lindsay Lohan from a movie set, and you start asking people if he's into you."

Tandy didn't have much to say to that since it was true. As soon as she believed Clay was as hip deep in this as she, reality intruded, and she flashed back to that little girl she'd been, living on the streets of Orlando. Too many nights in a cardboard box with stolen flashlight in hand to ward off monsters had made their mark on her heart, indelibly printing the word *unworthy* on it. Momma and Daddy had made enough marks of their own to cover it up most of the time, but not always.

Clay caught her watching him and jerked his head up. He stood before their table in three seconds. "Tandy! Hey, how was church?"

"Good. A little, um, perfumed." She waved her hand in front of her face and wrinkled her nose.

Clay looked to Kendra for explanation.

"Mrs. Simmons."

"Ah." Clay's face relaxed. He tapped his pencil on a notepad in his other hand. "What can I get you ladies today?"

"Burger and fries for me," Tandy said. "I hear this place has the best in town."

Clay leaned down near her ear. "You better believe it. We've also got a few other things you might be interested in." Tandy playfully shoved him away, and he beamed at her.

"Before you two make me lose my appetite, I'll have a burger and fries, too."

"Two burgers and fries, coming right up." Clay shoved his pencil behind his ear and headed off toward the kitchen.

Tandy and Kendra talked about the upcoming Iris Festival events until their orders arrived. Just as Tandy was about to take her first bite, in walked Daddy and Zelda.

"What?" Kendra said, her mouth full of burger.

Tandy wiped her face of reaction. "Nothing, nothing." She went back to her food. "I'm still not used to seeing them together."

Kendra shifted in her seat to see the front door. "Oh, Daddy and Zelda?"

"Who else?"

"It doesn't mean he's replacing Mom, Tandy."

"I know that. But seeing him with another woman, laughing, putting his hand on her elbow like that, my brain can't go there."

Kendra reached across the table and patted Tandy's arm. "It wasn't easy for me at first, either, but you get used to it."

"The day I get used to that will be the day I quit my job and move to Stars Hill."

"Stranger things have happened." Kendra took her hand back.

"Not many."

"Oh, I don't know. I wouldn't rule anything out at this point."

"I thought we weren't going to have this conversation again."

"You're right. We weren't. Let's talk about something else. Me. Do you think Darin had fun last night?"

"Hmm, let's find out." Before Kendra could stop her, Tandy jumped up from her chair and dashed behind the counter into the kitchen. Clay leaned against a counter cutting a tomato, his big hands moving like quicksilver.

"Hey!" He nearly cut himself as his eyes moved from the tomato to Tandy. "Give a guy some warning." He set the knife down on the counter and came over to her. "Something wrong with your lunch?"

"Yes, something's horribly wrong."

"What?" He moved to pass her and she grabbed the tie on his apron, pulling him back to her.

"You weren't sitting beside me while I ate it."

She would have sworn his smile lit up the room as his hands came around her waist. "I'm so sorry you've had a bad experience here." His eyes were full of mock concern. "Let's see what I can do to make it up to you." He dipped his head and touched his lips to hers.

Her world tilted. Here she was, standing in a public diner kissing Clay Kelner. Anybody in town could see them through the window if they were standing at the right angle. Shoot, one of the people out in the dining area could walk back here, wondering what the holdup was with their food.

But the warmth of him, the rightness of his hands on either side of her face, fingers buried in her hair, his black curls brushing her forehead, outweighed her fear of being found out, and she kissed him back. If Daddy could have lunch with Zelda in front of God and country, then she could certainly kiss Clay Kelner in the back of his own diner.

Clay eased away from her and took a deep breath. She looked up, her lids heavy with the haze of falling into him. "Something wrong?"

Clay cleared his throat and went back around to the cutting board. Picking up the knife, he pointed it at her. "You are a dangerous woman, Tandy Ann Sinclair."

She tucked her chin and batted her lashes at him. "Little ol' me? Surely not."

He shook his head, eyes on the knife now slicing through a tomato. "If I don't watch out, you'll have me closing this place up and heading to the beach for the rest of my days."

Her breath caught in her throat. Him moving to Florida hadn't really seemed like an option. *Was* it an option? Clay was Stars Hill. He just was.

"You'd move to Florida after three days with me?" The people in her head stood up and cheered again. She shushed them.

His eyes were serious as he looked up at her. "Three days? Tandy, I've known you forever. This—" he waved the knife between them—"is just a reminder, not a new thing."

Tandy bit her lip, needing time to think about this turn of events. "I should get back to Kendra. She's going to wonder what I'm doing back here."

"So's your dad. Scoot."

She left the kitchen and went back to her table.

"You look like you're in another world," Kendra said. "Did he say something about Darin? What happened?"

"Clay Kelner happened, that's what." She chomped down on a French fry.

"Did he say something?"

"Yeah. He said I could get him to move to Florida."

"What?!" Kendra's yelp caused Daddy and Zelda to look their way.

"Hush, hush." Tandy patted the air. "Finish your burger, and we'll talk about this *somewhere else.*"

Kendra tossed her fry back onto the plate. "I'm done. Let's go." She dug around in her purse and tossed some money on the table.

"Hey, I've still got some food here," Tandy protested.

"You know the owner; you can get more later." Kendra stood up. "Let's go."

Tandy sighed and followed her out of the diner, waving at Daddy as she left. He'd wonder why they had hurried out. Wonder what he'd say if she told him what had just happened in the kitchen?

The doors were barely closed when Kendra turned on her, eyes blazing. "Spill."

"Nothing, nothing."

"Nothing doesn't make you look like somebody promised you the Sears Tower."

"Is the Sears Tower even still standing?"

"Tandy." Kendra's voice held a warning note.

"What? I'm just saying you might need to update your references."

"Sister, you've got about five seconds to tell me what that man said to you, or so help me, I'll tell Joy and Meg it was you that ruined their roller skates."

"You wouldn't dare."

"Three seconds, two, one." Kendra reached for her cell phone.

"Clay offered to move to Florida." It came out in one big rush.

Kendra's fingers stilled on her phone. "Come again?"

"It's true. He said if I didn't watch out, I'd have him moving to the beach for the rest of his days." Tandy still couldn't believe it. Had he been serious?

"Was he serious?"

Tandy did a double take. "Get out of my head."

"So you don't know? Didn't you ask?"

"No, he kissed me and then—" Tandy squirmed in her seat—"it seemed like a good time to exit the scene."

Kendra gave her a knowing look. "Wise move if you don't want to know the answer." She sat back in her seat and crossed her arms. "You're going to have to ask. If he's willing to move to Florida, then this thing just might work."

"Kendra! I am *not* asking that man to give up his business, his home, and move eight hundred miles away just for me." *Though I'd like to.*

"Why not?"

"Because it's a selfish thing to do! He loves Stars Hill. And they love him, at least the him he's become. I don't want to ruin that."

They sat in silence for a second, then Kendra reached for the ignition and started the car. "Then you're either going to be very alone in Orlando, or you're moving here."

Tandy sighed and buckled her seat belt as Kendra maneuvered out of the parking space. "Knowing Momma, she knew all this would happen, and *that's* why she decided on Orlando. It would keep me away from Clay."

"I thought *you* decided on Orlando?"

"I did." Tandy's eyebrows scrunched as she fought to remember her conversations with Momma about the future. Exactly which of them had first said 'Orlando' wasn't clear. "At least, I think I did. Or maybe it was Momma." She threw up her hands. "Who knows? It doesn't matter. All that matters is my dreams are there."

"Except for one tall diner owner with black hair, green eyes, and a mean two-step."

She sighed again. "Yeah. Except for that."

They rode the rest of the way to the farm in silence.

Eighteen

Tuesday morning's skies held dark gray clouds swollen with rain. Tandy stood at the window in her bedroom, watching them build and shift, like orchestra members shifting in their seats before the conductor's baton fell. Cooper lay curled under his chair, tail tucked, worried eyes on Tandy. Each time thunder rolled across the field, he whimpered.

"I know, buddy. Storms are scary. But I won't let anything happen to you. You're safe." She skirted the bed and knelt down in front of Cooper. His velvety ears felt soft under her fingertips, and she scratched until he finally laid his head on his paws in resignation. "Good idea. There's no stopping the weather, so you might as well sleep through it."

She stood and stretched, checking the clock on the nightstand. Still a good hour before the art show would open. Kendra was a basket case, the same as every other time she'd unveiled one of her works for the public. Tandy didn't know how she did it, baring her inner thoughts like that for all the world to see.

Her own thoughts intensified in tandem with the tumult outside. It was growing harder to imagine her life without

Clay Kelner in it. Two amazing nights of dancing close, whispering secrets, sharing their thoughts and feelings, awakening old memories and forming new ones, had gathered like rain in the cloud of her future. Sooner or later the cloud would either dissipate and move on or come crashing down in a deluge. She wasn't sure anymore which result to wish for.

Running her hand over the stitches of the Dutch doll quilt, she wondered if Clay would really move to Florida and if considering the option was a betrayal of Momma. They hadn't mentioned Florida or the future at all yesterday when they'd met at the car show. Asking him to leave Stars Hill didn't have the ring of rightness to it. Besides, even if they ended up in Orlando together, she'd still be leaving the sisters behind. And Daddy. And her faith.

She cocked her head at that last one. Where had *that* come from?

The sisters meant more to her after this trip. Playing with Meg's kids, sitting at Joy's beautifully laid-out table, going on double dates with Kendra, and hearing Daddy's feet on the stairs gave her a surety of being, a solidness that was too elusive in Orlando. Here she belonged, had a history and identity that felt true. The idea of a God who gave her purpose and watched over her seemed more plausible. Odd, since this was the place from which he took Momma.

Every day, walking into the BellSouth building and riding that brass-gilded elevator up to her office, a small part of Tandy knew she was playing at her life, filling a role carved out for her from the rocky stone of her childhood. Each time a hawk hit her window, she wondered if they knew how much she beat her head against the wall of her existence as well. Or worried about the silence of her faith.

And yet the fighter in her, the part that would not let her beginnings dictate her endings, refused to back down. Life, dreams, *becoming* someone—these things required sacrifice and determination. Stars Hill couldn't let her rise above the years on the streets. It would only be a small town she'd run to and hidden in for the rest of her life. Wouldn't it?

Momma, with her wisdom and vision, must have known that. Why else would she have told Tandy not to let fear dictate her future?

Thunder rolled in the distance, making Cooper open his eyes and look to her.

"It's okay, boy. You're safe." Cooper closed his big basset eyes.

She wandered back to the window, the gray gloom of the atmosphere a perfect nest for her bewildered thoughts. The clouds hung closer now, and sheets of rain were crossing the field. Pretty soon everything around them would be soaked through and through.

Daddy's footfalls on the stairs broke the oppressive silence. She turned as he entered her room.

"Morning." He was in a striped button-up shirt and khakis, the blues and greens of the shirt faded from years of wear. His sleeves had razor sharp creases, though, and Tandy knew he'd used heavy starch. Momma was not a fan of ironing and Daddy, believing the outside to be a reflection of the inside, had ironed their clothes instead. His loafers, which she knew were at least fifteen years old, shined with new polish. He rocked on his heels, hands in pockets. "I've got some waffle batter ready downstairs if you're hungry."

"Thanks, Daddy."

"Why the long face?" He came into the room and sat

down in the chair over Cooper. Reaching down, he patted the dog's head.

"Oh, I don't know. Probably just the weather." The bed creaked again as she sat back down in her spot.

He chuckled. "You always were a gloomy Gus when storms rolled in."

"Was I?"

"Oh yeah. Some mornings we'd wake up and see those clouds and your Momma would say, 'Tandy'll be a handful today.' And she was nearly always right."

"Nearly?"

"Okay, about that, maybe always right."

"She was right about a lot of things." Her soft voice sent sad words into the gray air.

"That she was." Daddy nodded. "But not about everything."

She raised an eyebrow.

"It'd be easy to remember her as perfect, Tandy. That's a temptation when we lose someone as good as your momma. But she had her moments, same as the rest of us."

"Daddy, do you think I should have stayed in Stars Hill?"

He sat back in the chair and thought for a second.

"I can't answer that, honey girl."

"Why not?"

"Because your life is yours." He spoke gently, trying to take the sting out of his words. "Not your momma's or mine to decide. We tried to teach you about the important things—God, prayer, right from wrong, wise from foolish. You've got free will just like we do. And that means applying the knowledge you've got to the life you lead."

"Then why did Momma tell me to go to Orlando? That sounds more like telling me what to do than making me figure it out."

"I don't know that she did, Tandy." He looked at his hands. "I heard her tell you to refuse fear's leadership. She was right about that. I don't know how that applies to your present. I can tell you this, though—" he held up a finger— "your momma wanted you to know your worth and not let the things of this world force you onto a path not of your choosing. She taught all you girls that."

Tandy nodded, a tear trickling down her cheek.

Daddy got up and came to sit beside her. He put an arm around her back and hugged her to his side. "You're smart, and you've grown into a woman I'm proud to call my daughter, Tandy Ann Sinclair. You know what's right and what's wrong and who to talk to when the path ahead isn't too clear. I rest in that, honey girl, in knowing that your life is led by God."

Tandy remembered the day she'd walked the aisle at Grace Christian, meeting the God her daddy preached about.

"Daddy, you know I believe in God. But I'm not like you and Momma. I don't go around asking people if they know where they'll spend eternity or if they have a personal relationship with Jesus." She slumped further.

Daddy chuckled. "Tandy, do you think you could make a sculpture like Kendra?'

She turned her head to see his face, her forehead wrinkled in confusion. "Of course not."

"What about making a four-course meal like Joy? Think you could pull that off?"

"Maybe, but it wouldn't be as good as hers, and some of the food might be underdone or burned."

"How about Meg? Homeschooling one child while raising a three-year-old and an eight-month-old at the same time. Is that your life's path?"

"If it is, I'm way behind."

He laughed again. "That's the point, honey girl. You can believe and not be like every other believer. What you believe in doesn't change, but how you live out that belief is very different from how I do or your momma did. I worry because I don't see a lot of room in your life for God or your faith in him down in Orlando. I hope it's because we don't talk a lot, not because you've given up on him or pushed him away in anger."

Had she? "I was mad at him for a long time, Daddy. A long, long time. For a lot of reasons, not just Momma." She sniffed. "But I didn't have the time to dedicate to anger anymore, so I let it go."

"When?"

"When what?"

"When did you let go of your anger?"

"Oh, I don't know." She ran her hand over the quilt. "I just realized one morning I wasn't angry anymore."

"Are you still going to that church you told me about?"

"Most of the time, yeah, I go. And I *do* pray, Daddy. Not like I used to. Not like before Momma. But more than those years just after she died." She sniffed again and Daddy waited. "It's hard to feel. Does that make sense?"

"It does. If you feel, then you can get hurt. And when your momma died and Clay left, you had to hurt a lot. I don't blame you a bit for shutting down awhile. Makes perfect sense. But Tandy," he put a finger under her chin and tilted her face, "you have to feel again at some point. I know it's hard, especially for you. Lord knows you've had more reason than most to stop feeling. But don't do it. Don't give in to that. There are still lots of us who are here and who feel love for you."

He hugged her, and she buried her face in his shoulder, longing for Momma. The sheets of rain finished their trek across the fields and pounded her window, giving voice to the ache that battered within. Thunder cracked, right along with her composure, and she clung to the surety that was Daddy.

Nineteen

Tandy dashed from her Beamer to the front door of the civic center, puddles of rain splashing up around her jeans. The rain hadn't let up much and seemed to steal another degree of warmth from the air with each passing minute.

She stopped in the lobby and collapsed her umbrella. Droplets of water leaked from it as she wound it up and secured the Velcro strap. Looking down, she took stock of her jeans and realized they were soaked from the shin down. She shrugged. Not much to do about that now, and her hair was probably curled up tighter than a pair of skinny jeans after Christmas pies and cookies.

Her tennis shoes squeaked on the tile floor as she crossed the lobby and followed the signs to the art show. Entering a room that had hosted the high school prom every year for the past two decades and the town meetings every month for ten years, Tandy glanced around in search of Kendra. Her eye took in the myriad displays, from sculptures to paintings, while the room buzzed with conversation.

"There you are!" Kendra's voice behind her made her turn around.

"Hey! Where is it?"

"Over here." Kendra hustled her two aisles down. "I've checked everything out here, and I think there are two others giving me serious competition. Oh, and before I forget, I made a hundred dog biscuits for Cooper."

Tandy stopped and closed her eyes. "Okay, wait. Let me see the competition first, then yours. That way I'm not biased. And why did you make a hundred dog biscuits when you own a cat?"

"Because I needed something to do with my hands. I couldn't sleep worrying about this, and I had already made Kitty a hundred treats. Those things don't freeze well, so Cooper got lucky." Kendra spun her around, and Tandy opened her eyes as they walked the other way. "We'll go down the other aisle and back up this one. You'll see their sculptures before mine."

They passed painting after painting of irises in every color. Purple ones growing by a river. White ones lining a fencerow. Yellow ones encircling a maple. It was as if every painter had thought to win using the most obvious subject.

"Can't someone paint a rose or something?"

"I know." Kendra chuckled. "It's like every artist went iris crazy."

"Were they told to paint an iris?"

"No, but this *is* the Iris Festival Art Contest."

"Seems predictable."

"That's what I thought."

They rounded the end of the aisle and walked up the next. Tandy saw sculpture after sculpture of the flower. "You're kidding me."

"Nope. There are forty-seven embodiments of the iris on this aisle alone."

"I didn't know there were that many sculptors in Stars Hill."

"There aren't. Some people entered more than one thing."

"Did you?"

"No. Just the one. Here's one I think is good."

They stopped in front of a table draped in black. On its center stood a white stone sculpture in the shape of a lamppost.

Tandy turned to Kendra. "This is your competition? It's a lamppost."

"Yeah, but where have you seen this lamppost before?"

Tandy thought about it, then snapped her fingers in recognition. "This is the new Stars Hill lamppost!"

Kendra bobbed her head. "Yep. And guess who's on the judging committee for the art contest?"

"Not Tanner."

"Bingo."

Tandy looked at the sculpture again, noticing it was identical to the ones on Lindell. "Okay, you're right. This *is* competition. How hard did Tanner fight for the street lights?"

"A forty-five-minute monologue on our responsibility as citizens to uphold the historical value of Stars Hill."

"You might be in trouble."

"Don't I know it. And there's one other one." Taking her elbow, Kendra steered Tandy three tables down to a wooden image. The smooth oak was polished to a shine that now reflected the lights. It took Tandy a minute to catch on.

"Is this the caboose?"

Kendra nodded. "It's almost exactly like the one over in the park. And you know how Tanner loves that park."

"'The oldest public park in the State of Tennessee,'" Tandy quoted.

"If Tanner's said it once, he's said it a million times. He's proud of the park, and he loves the streetlights. I didn't think about that."

"Okay, show me yours."

Kendra crossed the aisle and walked past five tables. "Here."

Tandy's eyes grew wide and her breath caught. A woman's figure leaned forward over the edge of the base, her elbows pointed, hands clenched into fists, hair flying. Small strands of stone wound around her muscular legs. Tandy bent closer but couldn't find where one tendril ended and another began. They were hopelessly wrapped around her thighs, tangling around her shins and ankles. Her bare feet were free, some-how making her appear vulnerable. Tandy's eyes followed the cords as they grew thicker and ran to the other side of the sculpture. There, though they were made of stone, the thick bands appeared to writhe in a muddled, seething mass.

Tandy looked back to the face of the runner, shocked to find so much emotion on this small portion of the work. The woman's eyes were wide with fear, but the set of her brow seemed to indicate a resolve. Her head was tilted down, giving the illusion that she was plowing forward. The lips were set in a grim line of defiance, and tiny little nostrils were flared. This was a woman desperate to reach beyond the coils binding her.

Tandy took a breath, realizing she'd been holding it while staring at the art. She looked up at Kendra, whose gaze was full of indecision. "It's astounding,' she breathed, looking back at the sculpture, certain the woman would have broken free by now.

"Really? You think so?"

"I had no idea you could do this. I mean, your paintings are great and your articles are wonderful to read, but this—" she took in that face, literally set in stone—"this is unbelievable."

"You like her?"

"Like her? I want to *be* her."

Kendra opened her mouth to respond, then closed it and smiled over Tandy's shoulder. "I think I'm about to lose you."

"What?" Tandy looked over her shoulder and saw Clay walking down the aisle.

He grinned as he approached and planted a quick kiss on her nose. "I was beginning to wonder if someone had thought you two were art and snatched you up."

They groaned. "That was such a line," Tandy teased as he slid his arm around her waist.

"Maybe, but the best lines are grounded in truth."

Tandy leaned into him. "Has the rain let up?"

"A little. It's supposed to stop by tonight."

"Good, because getting this thing in here through the Great Flood was hard," Kendra said. "I'm not too keen on getting it back in the car."

"You don't have to leave it here when it wins?" Clay said.

"Thanks, but I'm not so certain about that."

"I've looked at everything, and I didn't see anything even close to competition," he said.

"Did you see the lamppost?"

"Yeah, but Tanner isn't the only judge. You'll be fine."

"Here's hoping," Kendra crossed her fingers.

"Is Darin coming?" Tandy said.

"He's here somewhere." Clay looked up and down the aisle, his head easily scanning the tops of the crowd. "Must be on another aisle. Come on, we'll find him."

The trio headed off, Tandy glancing back once at a sculpture that now seemed lonely without its audience.

Two hours later the foursome stood at the front of the exhibit hall, watching Tanner at the microphone.

His paunch had grown the past few years but was still covered by a bright red sweater vest. Rumpled gray pants ended in sneakers that were popular five years ago. He patted the air to quiet the crowd. "Before we announce the winners of the Iris Festival Art Contest," the buzz of conversation came to a halt—"let me say how difficult this decision was for the judges. We have a wealth of talent in our little community of Stars Hill, and the entries were no less than I'd expect from a citizenry proud to call this little patch of earth their home. I remember when we first began this art show, seventeen years ago . . ."

Clay leaned down and whispered into Tandy's ear, "The man never passes up an opportunity for a history lesson."

She giggled and swatted his arm. "He just loves Stars Hill."

"So do I, but I don't go around spouting off about its history every chance I get."

Her laughter was muffled behind her hand but drew Kendra's attention anyway. She leaned around Darin and whispered, "Bet the lamppost won."

That set Tandy off into another fit of giggles, earning her a disapproving glare from Tanner, who cleared his throat.

"At any rate, I'm sure you didn't all come here to listen to my reflections on days gone by." He looked at the crowd hopefully, as if wanting someone to contradict him. When no one spoke, he continued. "So without further ado, I give you the head of our judging committee this year, Ms. Sara Sykes."

Sara came to the microphone and adjusted the stand down to her height. "Hi, everybody. I won't delay this moment since you've all endured Tanner without comment." Chuckles sounded through the crowd. "The third place overall winner of the Eighteenth Annual Iris Festival Art Contest is Bradley Gallimore, for his replication in stone of the Stars Hill lamppost."

A smattering of applause accompanied Bradley's approach to the stage for his award. Tandy saw Darin take Kendra's hand. Surely her sister wouldn't lose to a caboose. Sara leaned back into the microphone. "Second place overall winner is Shelby Bentley for her oil painting *Sunful of Iris.*"

Tandy spotted Shelby weaving through the crowd, a hand over her heart as if shocked by the announcement. One glance at Kendra revealed her surprise as well.

"Guess irises may have been the way to go," Kendra whispered as Shelby ascended the stage.

"And the Grand Prize winner of this year's Iris Festival Art Contest is—"

Tandy held her breath. *Please . . .*

"—Kendra Sinclair for her sculpture, *Unbound.*"

"*Yea!*" Tandy jumped in the air and nearly knocked Darin over to get to Kendra, who looked a little stunned. "You won!" she squealed, squeezing her sister in an embrace. She let go and nudged Kendra toward the stage. "Get up there!"

Kendra approached the stage to receive her award, and Tandy slid back between Darin and Clay, keeping her gaze on her sister.

"I'm not sure what to say," Kendra said into the microphone. She looked at the winner's plaque in hand. "Tanner was right, this room is full of beautiful works of art." She paused and met Tandy's gaze. "And I'm grateful for those who inspired us to create it. Thank you."

The crowd broke out into applause as Kendra left the stage, and Tandy clapped until her hands burned.

"Let me see! Let me see!" she said, taking the plaque from Kendra.

Engraved into the brass plate was the phrase: *For art that speaks volumes without words, please accept this award.* Beneath that, in bigger letters, it read *GRAND CHAMPION, 18TH ANNUAL IRIS FESTIVAL ART CONTEST.*

"It's gorgeous!" Tandy handed the award back to Kendra. "Where are Meg and Joy? And Daddy?"

"I told them to leave about half an hour ago. Didn't want them here in case I didn't place."

"You nut!" Tandy slapped her hand on Kendra's arm and pulled her cell from her pocket. "We've gotta call and let them know." She hit the memory key for Meg and put the phone to her ear. "You call Joy. I've got Meg."

She listened to the ring, then relayed the good news to Meg. Clay and Darin shook their heads as Kendra and Tandy squealed into the cell phones.

Tandy finished her call first and slapped the phone shut. "This calls for a celebration."

"Definitely. How about burgers and pie all around?" Clay said.

"Oooh, good idea." Kendra shut her phone. "Joy thought we needed to get together anyway. How about burgers and pie now and scrapbooking tonight?"

Darin held up his hands. "Hey, watch it, lady. I'm way too macho to scrapbook."

She poked a finger in his chest and stood toe to toe with him. "Don't worry, nobody invited you."

"Oh, man, that was harsh." Clay laughed at Darin's wounded look.

"The woman breaks my heart." Darin captured Kendra's hand in his and kissed it. "But who can trust an *artiste?*"

Kendra grinned. "I don't think I ever said you should trust me."

They laughed and migrated toward the door.

"So burgers and pie now, scrapbooking tonight?" Tandy pushed through the double doors.

"Sure. I'll call Meg on the way to the diner. You call Joy."

"Got it. See you there."

She watched Kendra and Darin walk off arm in arm, Kendra holding her plaque out in front of them.

"They look good together," she said.

"Yeah, who knew?" Clay turned her the other direction, took her hand, and began walking toward the diner three blocks away.

"Thanks for coming."

"Wouldn't have missed it. Thanks for telling me she was entering."

"I don't know how she does it, putting herself out there like that."

They crossed the street.

"What's the worst that can happen?"

"Somebody laughs at her. Or rejects her."

"Not putting yourself out there won't prevent that from ever happening." He stepped over a small puddle.

"No, but it would sure cut down on how often it happens."

"And would that make it hurt less?"

"I don't know." She considered it. "Maybe. Maybe not."

They reached the end of the first block and went down two steps to cross the street. Climbing back up on the other side, he said, "Isn't that like letting other people tell you how to live?"

"No. It's protecting yourself."

"From what? You just admitted that rejection will come anyway. Maybe it won't hurt the same way, but it will still come. And if it's inevitable, why go out of your way to avoid it in the first place?"

"When did you get all Yoda on me?"

He looked at her, flashing a smile. "Amazing what a year in a sand pit will do for your perspective."

She accepted that. "In the grand scheme of things, then, it's dumb not to open yourself up for rejection? That seems counterintuitive to self-preservation."

"Okay, lawyer woman, save the legal speech for the courtroom. I'm saying that if protecting yourself doesn't really protect you, then wasting energy on the effort may not be the wisest move. It's like this time my unit was stuck in the middle of a road in Iraq. Our engine quit and we were sitting ducks, just waiting for some insane terrorist bent on blowing himself up and meeting seventy virgins to appear."

She shivered at the image.

"What'd you do?"

"We decided that we could just sit there and try to protect ourselves, but the odds were pretty high one or all of us would end up hurt or dead in the trying. So we abandoned the vehicle, radioed for help, and took cover until our backup got there."

"Seems smart."

"It was." He looked down at her. "It's pretty simple, really. You don't stick with a course of action that will likely get you killed if there's a way to live and maybe even win the battle."

They arrived at the diner, and Clay held the door open for her. She looked into his eyes, seeing the wisdom there mix with his feelings for her. "Would you really move to Florida? For me?"

He ran a finger down the side of her face. "If there's no other way to win the battle, yes."

She stared at him, trying to decipher his meaning and wondering if he had another option that would work. "Is there another way?"

He lifted a shoulder. "That's up to you, I think."

She saw Kendra and Darin getting out of his car and was grateful for the distraction. "Better get to work on those burgers."

He looked at her a second longer. "You bet."

Twenty

When they were all seated in a booth, burgers half eaten and pie on the way, Kendra leaned back into Darin's arm and patted her belly. "That burger was huge. I'm not sure where to put the pie."

"Should have brought your hollow leg," Tandy said.

"Very funny. Is Joy coming to scrapbook?"

"She wasn't sure. She'd told Scott to expect a nice dinner tonight. Scrapping would pretty much nix that."

Kendra nodded. "Meg wants to work with James some more before the pet show tomorrow. Guess our scrapping plan didn't work out too well." She shrugged. "Hey, we can always drown our sorrows at Sara's. I'm sure acquiring product will alleviate my disappointment to a certain degree."

"Good idea. But you'll need to be able to move if we're going there."

Kendra groaned. "Ugh. Cancel my pie. If I eat it, you'll have to roll me out of here."

"I know a couple guys who don't have plans tonight," Clay said.

"Man, I already told you. I don't do scrapbooking."

"Me either!" Clay looked offended. "I was thinking a night of bowling might be in order."

"Hmm. I don't know," Tandy picked up her glass of tea. "Daddy may have something planned."

"Ask him to come with. I'm sure Zelda wouldn't mind a night of bowling."

"Go on a date with my dad?" Kendra wagged a finger at Clay. "No. As fine as I am with him having Zelda, I don't need it on display during my own date."

"I second that," Tandy said.

"Then call and see if he has plans."

"If I ask him, then he'll know it's because I want to make plans. Which means he won't tell me if he *did* have something planned."

"Wow, you guys really play three balls ahead," Darin tossed the last bit of burger in his mouth.

"I tried to tell you this already," Kendra said.

"I know, I know. Just didn't get it until now. Remind me not to play pool with her." He pointed to Tandy.

Tandy grinned. "That'd be a smart move, right, Clay?"

"I refuse to comment on the grounds it might incriminate me."

Darin chewed and looked from one to the other, "Okay, what am I missing here?"

"You mean you didn't tell your closest buddy about having your rear end handed to you by a girl?" Tandy smiled slyly. "Can't imagine why not."

"You barely beat me."

"And yet, still, the words 'beat me' cross his lips." Tandy looked at Kendra and took a sip of her tea.

"You won because you cheated."

"*Moi?*" Tandy splayed her hand across her chest, fluttering her lashes. "Never."

"Come on, man, might as well tell me." Darin took a long drink of Coke, stopping when the slurp signaled the end of his drink. "If not, I'll get the embellished version from her later." He pointed his straw at Kendra.

Clay sighed and laid both hands flat on the table. "She told me she'd never played before."

"I did not. You assumed that."

"And you didn't correct the assumption."

"All's fair in love and war, soldier."

"Turns out she'd been playing since she was five. Five! The game was over before it started."

Darin studied Tandy. "I thought you didn't move here until you were seven."

"I didn't. Hustling kept my mother and me in a halfway house for six months. Nobody suspected a kid who was shorter than the pool stick could win. They were easy marks."

"How'd you even see the table?"

"I stood on a chair."

"Wait, you moved a chair around the whole game? How'd you know where to put it?"

"I watched where Mother looked. Put the chair where her eyes told me and took the shot. Nailed it nearly every time." These were among the few nice memories she had of Orlando, partnering with her mother, working as a team.

"That's unbelievable."

"Judging by the way she beat me in high school," Clay grimaced, "believe it. I haven't played her since."

"Poor male ego." Tandy rubbed Clay's head. "Took years for the bruising to heal."

"No pool. No bowling." Darin leaned his arms on the table. "Any other ideas?"

Clay slid out of the booth and snagged plates of pie from the counter where the waitress had set them. "We could drive to Nashville."

"No!" Tandy and Kendra spoke in unison.

"Okaaaay." Darin looked from one woman to the other. "No Nashville. Our options are dwindling rapidly, ladies."

Kendra sniffed. "It takes work to date the likes of us."

Clay set the plates on the table. "Don't I know it."

"Watch it, mister."

Kendra crossed her arms over her chest and huffed, "I wanted to scrapbook."

"I wasn't kidding, woman." Darin assumed a mock-serious tone. He splayed his hands and wiggled his fingers. "These hands do not go near a scrapbook."

"Not even for me?" She tilted her chin down and looked at him through her lashes.

"Especially not for you. All I need is your head filled with an image of me and some froufrou ribbon or something. You'd never look at me as a man again."

Kendra threw back her head and laughed. "You are too much."

"Spoken by a lot of women." He took a bite of his banana-cream pie.

"Maybe Kendra and I should just scrapbook by ourselves tonight. If Meg gets done with James, and Joy finishes dinner early, they could still come over."

Clay took her hand. "You don't want to go out tonight?"

"It's not that. It's just that I like scrapping in Momma's studio, and I wanted to get some more time in there before . . ." The words stuck in her throat.

Kendra noticed and jumped in. "Right. So we'll have some girl time tonight." She turned to Darin. "Absence makes the heart grow fonder, right?"

Clay snorted. "Amen to that."

✄ ✄ ✄

LATER THAT NIGHT Kendra and Tandy sat in the scrapping studio, heads bowed over their layouts. "You and Darin sure seemed happy with each other today."

"He's a cool cat." Kendra clicked an eyelet into place. "But don't sign us up for china just yet. You know it takes them a few weeks to get tired of me."

"Kendra, that is not true."

"Of course it is. I'm a hard woman to handle." Her tone told Tandy she was comfortable with this. "It'll take a strong man to stick around."

Tandy went back to her own pictures of an Orlando Magic game. "You make it sound like you're hard to love."

"I am." Her voice was matter-of-fact. "But the right man will know how to love me, and I'll know how to love him. It'll happen at some point."

"How do you know?"

"I don't. But allowing otherwise would drive me insane, so I choose to believe."

"Hmm." Tandy picked up a small stamp pad and distressed the tan-colored paper in front of her.

"I asked Clay if he'd move to Florida."

Kendra looked up from her work. "And?"

"He said he would if there was no other way."

"Doesn't sound like he wants to move."

"I don't think he does. I think he *would*, but only if I asked."

"And you're not going to ask."

"No." She was sure of that the moment she said it.

Kendra pulled ribbon off a roll and snipped it. "Did he ask you to move here?"

"No. I think he thinks that would be selfish on his part."

"Would it?"

"Maybe."

"Do you love him?"

"Yes." She sighed and put down her eyelet setter. "I do, Kendra. How dumb is that? I love a man who left me ten years ago and lives eight hundred miles from me."

"Yoo-hoo!" Meg's voice floated up the stairs as her footsteps sounded. "I heard there was scrapping going on in here."

"Hey there! I thought you were working with James tonight."

She waved her hand. "Jamison's handling it. I couldn't miss a chance to scrap." She pulled her photo box off the shelf. "Did I miss anything good?"

"Tandy's in love with Clay."

"This I know. Is she going to do something about it?" Meg pulled pictures from the box, then went and took the Becky Higgins sketchbook from its holder.

"I'm taking suggestions."

Meg looked at her quizzically. "I see. Oh, Kendra, before I forget, here." She took a card from her purse and slid it across the table to Kendra. "James and Savannah made it for you when I told them you won the art show."

"Oh, look, it says 'Congratulations' and it's spelled wrong. How sweet." She turned the card around for Tandy to see. "You've got the best kids."

"Every now and then they do remind me why I had them." Pages rustled as she thumbed through the sketchbook.

"Are James and Tootsie ready for the pet show?"

"I think so." Meg's cell phone rang, and she unclipped it from her jeans. "So long as Tootsie behaves." She flipped open the phone. "Hello?"

Kendra and Tandy could hear the wail of a child all the way across the table.

"Did you give him VeggieTales snacks?" Meg said. "How about a video?" She waited. "Jamison, I just got here."

Kendra gave Tandy a knowing look.

"Fine, fine. I'll be there in a few minutes." Meg ended the call and stood up. "I swear that man couldn't multitask to save his hide. James is crying because Tootsie won't cooperate, which made Savannah cry, which upset Hannah, and now he has a mess. The man is hopeless." She walked over to the stairs and waved over her shoulder. "'Bye, girls, duty calls!"

"Suddenly, singlehood is looking a little better," Kendra said.

"I can't believe Jamison can't handle the kids for an hour."

"He's hilarious with them. 'Helicopter parent' doesn't begin to cover it. Meg's the only thing that keeps him from cracking up."

"She *is* devoted to her family."

"Yeah, more power to her. I don't know how she stays home with them all day."

"Me either. Some of my clients act like children, but knowing they're paying by the hour prevents a lot of wasted time whining."

"I hadn't thought of that." Kendra cocked her head. "Maybe I'll start charging the editors I work with an hourly fee instead of an assignment fee."

"Does wonders for the bull factor." Tandy picked up a pen and began journaling.

Silence fell on the room, broken by the scratching of Tandy's journaler or Kendra's cutting board. Tandy resolved again to find some scrapping friends when she got back to Orlando. "Hey, how do you think scrappers find each other?"

"What?"

"In other towns." Tandy glanced up at her sister. "Do you think they get together like this and scrap?"

"I hope so. It's a whole lot more fun when you have people to talk to or bounce ideas off of."

"That's what I was thinking. But then I realized I scrap with you, Meg, and Joy. If I didn't already know you, how would I find you?"

"You'd go down to Emmy's and ask where the other scrappers were."

"But let's say there was no Emmy's."

"Then you'd be up a creek."

"Without an oar."

"Paddle."

"Whatever. I'd have a hard time finding people to scrap with."

"Yep."

"Hmmm, that's sad." Tandy finished her layout and slid it into sheet protectors. "Should I start another one or call it a night?"

Kendra leaned back on her stool, stretching her arms overhead. "My back is starting to hurt, so I'm going to stop when I finish this layout."

"We should have told the guys we'd go out tonight."

"Nah, this was fun."

"And we'll see them tomorrow, right?"

"I'm sure you'll see Clay at the pet show. I don't know if Darin's coming or not."

"Clay's not coming to the pet show. He's got to be at the diner."

Kendra sighed dramatically and, tossing back her head, placed the back of her hand on her forehead. "Whatever shall we do without our men?"

Tandy erupted into giggles. "I suppose we'll have to make do without them."

Kendra straightened. "Or we could go surprise them. It's only seven o'clock. We can pick Clay up and make him give us directions to Darin's."

"Have you forgotten Momma's rules? We don't chase boys."

"I'm thirty-three years old, and the man chased me first. My turn."

"Well, when you put it like that . . ."

"You better believe it." Kendra put her finished layout in sheet protectors. "You ready?"

"Let me run check my hair. The rain's wreaked havoc on it today."

Kendra followed her down the stairs. "I think it's cute when it's all curly like that. Makes me wonder if we don't share a blood ancestor somewhere down the line." She fingered her own spirals.

"Wouldn't that be a kick? I doubt it, though. You've got those gorgeous spirals, and I've got—" she pulled one of her burnished corkscrews—"these."

"Oh, stop. You look like Nicole Kidman before Tom Cruise sunk his fangs into her."

"Don't I wish."

They walked through Tandy's bedroom to her bathroom. "Where's Cooper?"

"Probably downstairs with Daddy. He curls up at Daddy's feet and, after a while, Daddy rubs his belly with his toes."

Kendra pulled a face. "That's disgusting."

"You'd think, but it's really quite cute." Tandy snagged a big hair clip from the vanity and twisted her hair up. She secured it and turned her head side to side to gauge the effect. "Up or down?"

"Up. That looks great."

They freshened their eye shadow and lipstick and were heading down the stairs to the living room in ten minutes.

Daddy smiled as they entered the room. "Where are you girls off to?" Cooper was lying at his feet.

"We're off to kidnap some unsuspecting victims," Kendra said. "We'd tell you who, but then you'd be an accessory, and we love you too much to make you an accomplice."

Daddy looked over the top of his reading glasses. "Is this something I'm going to hear about at church on Sunday?"

"No, Daddy," Tandy reassured him. "I'm pretty sure our victims will come willingly and without much fuss." She stepped on Kendra's toe as they stood behind the couch facing Daddy. Kendra winced but tried to hide it.

Daddy went back to his book. "It's times like this I'm happy you're over eighteen. Have fun."

"We will." Kendra pushed Tandy out of the room before Daddy could ask more questions.

Her hand on the doorknob of the front door, Kendra looked at her sister and grinned. "You ready?"

Tandy grinned back. "Absolutely."

More ready than she'd been in a long, long time.

Twenty-One

"Your car or mine?"

"Mine," Tandy said.

"But your backseat is the size of a lima bean."

"You can drive after we pick up Clay. I'd hate to make you cram yourself back there with Darin."

"Oh, no you don't, sister. You may be the lawyer, but I'm older and wiser. We'll take the backseat and *you* can have fun switching gears."

They got into the car and fastened their seat belts. Tandy shot a look at Kendra as she started the engine. "Do we know what we're doing with our kidnap victims once we have them?"

"Not a clue. But we have about five minutes to figure it out before we get to Clay's."

They bumped down the gravel driveway. "What about a movie? We could rent a DVD and take it to Darin's."

"That could work, but movies don't let you talk to each other, and I haven't known Darin long enough to be tired of talking to him."

"Good point. Cards?"

"I like that idea. I wonder if Darin plays cards?"

"We'll ask Clay. Let's make a backup plan just in case. Is Darin's place on the way to Nashville or in the other direction?"

"I think it's on the way."

"Then let's go to Nashville." Tandy shifted and glanced over at Kendra.

"We told the guys we didn't want to go to Nashville."

"That was lunchtime. We're women. They expect us to change our minds as often as our shoes."

"Okay, Nashville it is. We can be there by nine-ish."

"Good time to hit B.B. King's." Tandy adjusted the air-conditioning.

"They'd love that."

"Yeah, they would. Let's do that. Hey, I like making the dating decisions."

"It has its advantages." Kendra reached over and switched on the radio in time to hear Carrie Underwood's "Wasted."

Their voices blended as they sang along, putting their hearts into the sentiment about not spending life waiting, not waking one day to find they'd wasted years. The song came to an end as Tandy pulled in front of the diner.

"It just occurred to me that if I go in there, everyone's going to know why I'm there."

"Tandy, seriously, go get your man and quit worrying what this town is going to say about it."

"Right. Of course, you're right." Tandy took a deep breath and stepped out of the car. If he wasn't in the diner, she'd have to go through the kitchen to the back stairway and up to his place. She prayed he was in the diner so the whole town wouldn't hear she'd gone up to his apartment. Daddy *might* hear about *that* on Sunday.

She stepped into the diner and scanned the room for his face. Her heart hit her toes when all she saw were the faces of Stars Hill looking back. Smiling, hoping they'd go back to their conversations, she scooted to the counter, circled it, and went for the kitchen.

"Tandy!" Clay was stacking glassware on a shelf above the sink. He came to her, wiping his hands on his apron and taking her hand. "Is something wrong? What happened?" His skin was soft from the dishwater, she thought, so thankful he was here.

"Nothing's wrong. I'm fine. I just . . . it's just . . . Kendra and I, um . . ."

"A verb, Tandy. I need a verb." A smile played at the corner of her lips.

This was going well. Her first time asking a guy out, and she couldn't get an entire sentence to pass her lips. "Well, we're women, so we can change our minds."

He chuckled, rubbing her hands between his. "Try that again? Less words, more complete thoughts."

Her cheeks flamed. How did men do this all the time? "I'm kidnapping you."

"Not to look a gift horse in the mouth, but may I ask why?"

"So you can tell me how to get to Darin's."

"Come again?"

She pulled her lip between her teeth and looked him in the eye. Facing down a jury and telling them what to think, what to feel, was nothing compared to baring herself like this, letting him know she wanted to be with him. *Get it together. You've done harder things than this.* Not that she could think of one right now.

"Kendra's in the car. We're done scrapbooking, and

we're going to Nashville to B.B. King's. We thought you guys might want to come with us, so I'm kidnapping you."

"Ah, the lightbulb is on."

That wasn't a yes. "But I can see you're busy and you've got customers, so never mind. I'll see you tomorrow sometime, or Thursday. You know, whenever."

He pulled her close and kissed her. She forgot about her nerves and kissed him back, grateful for his arms around her waist telling her she hadn't made a fool of herself just now. Her fingers threaded through his thick black hair and his hands tightened, bringing her closer, removing any breath of distance between them.

His lips turned from demanding to endearingly soft, until she could feel the absence of heat and opened her eyes. He was staring at her, a look on his face that spoke volumes. He was so close she felt his warm exhalation and breathed it in. "That's a yes?"

"If I wasn't clear, I can try again."

"I'd hate to misunderstand."

He closed the gap between their lips, covering hers with a kiss that made her heart race. She stood on tiptoes to meet him, to give back as good as she was getting, to make sure he knew she felt just like he did.

"Ahem."

They jumped apart and turned to find Kendra in the doorway. "I hate to interrupt but . . . "She tapped on her watch.

Tandy smoothed her hair. "Sorry. Sorry. I was making sure he wanted to come with us."

Kendra's lips curled. "I think you got your answer."

"Yes, she did," Clay said. "Let me tell the help I'm

leaving and go throw on a different shirt. I'll be right with you ladies."

"Don't you call and warn Darin," Kendra pointed at his retreating back. "This is a covert operation."

Clay waved over his head and ducked into the back stairway.

"I guess we can wait for him in the car." Tandy made her way out of the kitchen.

"Good idea. You can give me all the juicy details there." Kendra pushed her in the back, prodding her out the door.

Once they were safe in the car, with Kendra now behind the wheel, Kendra turned and drilled Tandy with her eyes. "That didn't look like a love-'em-and-leave-'em kiss to me."

"Didn't feel like it, either." Tandy reached her fingers to her lips and felt them, certain they'd have changed shape or something in response to Clay's touch.

"Maybe you're rethinking the idea of getting him to move to Florida. If you get kisses like that every day, he can make do without Stars Hill."

"But then I'd have to make do without you." Tandy's wide eyes turned to Kendra.

"Aw, thanks, sweetie." Kendra fiddled with the gear shift. "I miss you, too."

"I really do miss you, Ken. I didn't realize how much until this trip."

Kendra nodded. "It's easy to push my missing you to the back of my mind when you're not here, but I'll confess I'm dreading Sunday when you go back. It'll be lonely around here."

"A fine pair we are," Tandy said. "Can't find friends outside of our family."

"I beg your pardon, sister dear. I have plenty of friends."

Tandy looked at her, not even trying to hide her disbelief.

Kendra slumped a little in the seat. "Okay, not friends like *we're* friends. But I'm okay with that."

"Me, too." Surprisingly enough, Tandy meant it. "It's hard enough keeping you in line. Imagine if I didn't have the family connection to lord over you!"

Kendra laughed and pointed to the diner. "Here comes your man."

Tandy looked up and, sure enough, Clay was loping toward them. Tight jeans and a dark-brown turtleneck sweater made him look like he'd stepped off the pages of a Ralph Lauren ad in *Town & Country* magazine. "Is he as fine as I think he is?"

Kendra squinted her eyes and peered out the windshield. "You're probably blinded by love, but he's definitely hot."

Tandy grinned and winked at her. "Darin's not bad on the ol' peepers, either."

"Honey, Darin is so hot, he scorches the air around him." Kendra licked her finger and held it up in the air, making a sizzling sound.

"You're hopeless."

Clay tapped on Tandy's window, and she opened the door.

"Can we help you?"

"In case you do this again sometime, I think the kidnap victim is supposed to be hauled away, not come looking for you."

They laughed as Tandy got out and pulled the seat up, allowing room for him to get in the backseat. "Little did you know I implanted a chip in your brain back there. I can control your movements with the smallest word from now on." She climbed in behind him and Kendra started the car.

"Make him tell me where Darin lives," Kendra said to Tandy, pulling out of the space and onto Lindell.

Tandy placed one hand by her mouth as if sharing a secret and said in a low voice, "Clay, you will now lead us to the lair of your friend, Darin."

Clay opened his eyes wide and sat up as straight as the bucket seat would allow, appearing for all intents and purposes to be under hypnotic suggestion. "Go to interstate 65N and take the first exit."

Kendra sped up and headed toward the highway. Tandy spoke in the same low tone. "You did very well, thank you. You may now resume normal activities."

Clay burst out laughing and swung his arm around her. "Have I told you how crazy you are?"

"Not today, no," she shook her head.

"You're a lunatic." He kissed her, a fast, quick peck, and she felt a spark of heat within. "Good thing I like craziness in my life."

"Yeah, good thing."

Twenty minutes and three "hypnotically given" directions later, they pulled into Darin's apartment complex.

"I had no idea these were out here." Kendra indicated the redbrick townhomes. Their doors varied from navy blue to brick red to a sunny gold. Darin's was a dusky plum. "Are they new?"

"Got me." Clay shrugged and adjusted his sweater after getting out of the car.

Kendra fluffed her hair and walked toward the door. "Time to snag our next victim."

Tandy giggled from her place in the crook of Clay's arm. Kendra pushed the doorbell button, which set Tandy to laughing again. "Um, sis, I don't think kidnappers ring the doorbell."

"Sure they do." Kendra looked over her shoulder at the two of them waiting on the step below her. "Gives us the element of surprise when he answers."

The door opened, and Clay joined Tandy in her laughter as they took in Darin's appearance. His UK sweatpants had more holes than a Clinton alibi, and his shirt—complete with torn out sleeves—read "I ♥ Bass." It was covered in pictures of green, scaly fish, and some of the gold flakes were still on in places. His hair was plastered to his scalp with sweat. Stained socks and shoes that looked like they came from Tanner's closet completed the ensemble.

"Kendra!"

"Um, hi." She gave a little wave. "We're here to kidnap you."

"We?"

Clay looked around Kendra and burst out laughing again, and Kendra turned and shot him a glare.

She focused again on Darin. "We're going to B.B. King's and so are you." She finally gave up the pretense. "*What* are you wearing?"

That set Tandy off again.

Darin looked down at his clothes and smiled sheepishly. "Workout clothes."

"I see," Kendra sniffed her disapproval.

Clay calmed down and tried not to look at Darin again. "I think you're supposed to invite the lady in, my friend."

"Right! Right!" Darin leapt into action. "Come in."

They entered his apartment, and Tandy took in the room, surprised to find it mirrored Kendra's tastes to a certain degree. Rather than Kendra's white carpet, Darin had Pergo floors, but his furniture was the same sleek leather as Kendra's. A black wood entertainment center dominated the far wall and appeared to hold more technology than Tandy would figure out in a lifetime. A basket of remote controls was on the glass coffee table.

"I'll just go grab a quick shower and be with you in a minute." Darin raced up the carpeted stairs, and they heard a door slam shut.

"I don't think he was expecting a kidnapping tonight." Kendra walked around to the couch.

"Um, no, I'm pretty sure we interrupted something." Tandy tried not to laugh again, for Kendra's sake.

Fifteen minutes later Darin was back downstairs in soft gray pants and a navy silk shirt. He held out his hands. "Kidnap victim, at your service."

Kendra walked over and circled around him.

"What?" He followed her as she walked. "Something wrong?"

"Nope." Kendra sighed, completing her circle and stopping in front of him. "Just trying to figure out how you can go from loving fish to this in fifteen minutes."

His forehead creased. "I don't love fish."

"Oh, come on. That shirt had fish all over it."

Understanding dawned on his face. "That shirt was an ill-conceived Christmas present too many years ago to count. My niece thought I loved bass fish, not bass guitar."

"How old is your niece?"

"She was five at the time."

"Are we going to stand here talking about T-shirts or go hear some blues?" Clay said.

"Hey, you're a kidnap victim," Tandy said sternly. "Hush up or no one will ever see you alive again."

"That was weak, sister."

"Sorry. This is my first felony."

They hustled out the door and to the car.

"Did you girls check to see who's playing tonight?" Darin adjusted the air vent and looked over at Kendra. She made eye contact with Tandy in the rearview mirror.

"We thought it'd be more of an adventure if we just showed up and enjoyed whoever was playing," Tandy said.

"I see. So this is a well-planned crime, I take it."

"Premeditation would get years tacked onto our sentence." Kendra turned up the radio. "No more talking from the prisoners."

They sped down the highway, and Tandy snuggled in to Clay's side, memorizing his feel and dreading the day she'd need a memory to keep her warm.

Twenty-Two

The rumble of a tractor engine awakened Tandy on Thursday morning. She opened her eyes to a room just beginning to glow with dawn's light. The clock on the nightstand read 6:02. Groaning, she rolled over and stuffed a pillow on top of her head. The drone of the engine permeated through the layers of feathers. Sleep wouldn't return now.

Sighing, she swung her legs out of bed and went to the window. Daddy was on his tractor, a mower attached to the back. He'd made one pass around the yard already and was halfway through the next. The first streaks of sun lanced across the sky, separating night from day. Tandy went to her bag and snagged the camera, recognizing a scrapbooking moment when she saw one.

She pointed the lens at Daddy and realized the glare of the window glass would ruin the picture. Cool wind, at least ten degrees warmer than Tuesday's rainy self, floated through the room as she raised the window and popped out the screen. Years of sneaking out had made her a master at removing and replacing window trappings without a scratch.

Leaning out the window, she waited for Daddy to round the bend again, then pointed her camera and clicked, capturing an image that defined her home as well as anything else she could think of.

After replacing the screen, she left the window open and went to the bathroom. A morning shower would clean the dreamy cobwebs from her mind and help her focus on the day.

Today was the street fair, Tandy remembered as she turned on the faucet and waited for steam to heat up the shower stall. Lindell would be closed to traffic and clogged with vendors hawking everything from funnel cakes to shoes. She stepped into the warm water spray and lathered up her hair.

The breeze she'd felt had that hint of summer to it. The bite of cold was gone, replaced by a promise of growth and new birth. By mid-day, she'd bet they would easily hit seventy degrees. Maybe a pair of shorts instead of jeans today.

Rinsing the suds from her curls, she wondered about Daddy and Zelda. An image of them at the pet show yesterday, clapping and cheering James on to second place, flashed through her mind. Kendra said Zelda made Daddy happy, and Tandy could admit that after seeing it with her own eyes. But that didn't mean Zelda belonged or was good for Daddy. Her fire-engine-red spiky hair and big hoop earrings confused Tandy and annoyed the snot out of Joy. What did Daddy see in this woman? Was it that she was so different from Momma that there was no chance he'd get them mixed up in his head? Or was it that Momma wasn't the kind of woman Daddy liked anymore? Had he changed?

Tandy lathered and rinsed, then stepped out of the shower. The whole idea of Daddy with someone besides

Momma felt foreign. Granted, it'd been ten years since Momma went on to heaven, but those ten years had lulled Tandy into a false sense of security of knowing that Daddy was just waiting out his days until he joined Momma.

If Daddy had begun dating again, and the sisters said he'd been seeing Zelda for quite some time, then that meant he had decided to have a life outside of Momma. And Tandy did not approve of that.

Wrapping a towel around her wet hair and tucking it into place, Tandy wiped the steam from the bathroom mirror and peered into it. Soft lines around her eyes reminded her that a lot of time had passed since Momma died. She'd spent ten years since then chasing after her mission of becoming a successful attorney in Orlando. Was Momma pleased with her? Did she look down from heaven and nod in approval at Tandy's choices?

Cooper plodded into the bathroom and woofed at her.

"Heaven knows, she'd think *you* were the laziest canine this side of the Mississippi."

Cooper woofed again.

"You need to go outside?"

Cooper turned and trotted to the door.

"Hang on a second. I can't go out like this."

She went to the closet and pulled a pair of khaki shorts from her suitcase and a long-sleeve T-shirt. Cooper woofed again.

"I'm coming, I'm coming. I've got to find my shoes." She dug around in the closet and, spying her flip-flops at the bottom of the pile, jerked them free.

She hopped on one foot, sliding on her shoes and reaching for the leash.

"Okay, here we go."

Cooper pulled her down the stairs and to the front door. Once outside, he dashed down the porch steps and stopped short at the sight of Daddy on the tractor.

"It's just Daddy cutting the grass, Coop. You're fine."

Cooper waddled off and did his morning business, never letting his eyes stray from the tractor. When he finished, he tugged her across the yard, intent on investigating this foreign sound. Daddy saw them coming and waved. Tandy grinned and waved back.

He cut the engine as they drew closer. "Did I wake you up?"

"You did. But I needed to get up anyway." The sun hung high in the sky now and bathed the farm in a golden light.

"Sorry about that. This grass was looking like nobody lived here, and with the street fair today and the parade tomorrow, I knew I wouldn't get to it anytime soon if I didn't do it this morning."

"Really, it's fine."

Cooper sniffed the tires, his stub of a tail wagging.

"Did you find enough volunteers for the ice cream giveaway?"

Daddy nodded. "Zelda's taking care of all that."

Tandy's chest tightened. "Oh? I didn't realize."

"Yeah. She's a social whiz, I tell you. Had a list of volunteers a mile long last week. All I had to do was sign the check for the ice cream and talk to Clay about storing it."

Tandy swallowed around the lump in her throat. "I'm glad she's such a help to you."

Daddy's gaze softened on her. "I know this isn't easy for you, honey girl."

Tandy waved that away. "That doesn't matter. You have

every right to have a . . . friend." She prayed he wouldn't feel the need to reveal it was more than that.

"All the same, I want you to know she isn't a replacement for your mother. Nobody could replace her, and Zelda wouldn't be dumb enough to try."

Tandy nodded, backing away from the tractor, not ready to have this conversation about a woman she barely knew. "I understand. I need to go put my face on. You want to ride downtown together?"

"Sure." He stared at her a minute. "If you want to talk about this, about Zelda, you'll let me know?"

She bobbed her head and looked away. "Yes, sir."

"Okay."

He turned the tractor key, and the engine rumbled to life. Cooper skittered back and began barking. "We'll leave in half an hour or so," Daddy called over the noise.

She nodded and walked back to the house.

It was time to learn more about this Zelda woman. Daddy wasn't a rich man, but he also didn't rank poorest in the county either. He had a big farm and a steady income from Grace Christian. If Zelda thought she could hook a bill payer, she had another thing coming.

Tandy veered into the kitchen and snagged the phone from the wall. She dialed Meg's number.

"Hello?"

"Meg? It's Tandy."

"Hey, girl. You ready for the street fair? The kids are going nuts about it."

"I'll bet. Daddy and I are leaving in about an hour. Listen, I need to ask you about something."

"Shoot."

"Tell me about this Zelda woman."

Meg's sigh crackled over the old phone line. "I can't say I know a whole lot about her. Daddy's been seeing her for several months. She's a widow. Moved here a year ago, I think."

"You didn't check her out when he started seeing her?"

"I tried, but I didn't get very far. She's only been here a year, and she doesn't reveal much about herself. I know. I asked around."

"Clay says she's okay."

"How would he know? Forget that, *why* would he know?"

"Long story. But he says he checked her out and she's not a hussy."

"Make him tell you how he knows. If she's okay, then I'd like to be sure. Daddy's spending an awful lot of time with her these days."

"I know." Worry tightened Tandy's voice. "He just assured me she wasn't a replacement for Momma."

"Well, nobody could do that. But he is lonely, Tandy. I worry about him all by himself in that big house, just rattling around." A child screeched in the background, and Meg hollered, "Let go of your sister's hair this instant, James!"

Tandy smiled. "World War III erupting over there?"

"You'd think." Tandy heard the smile in her sister's voice. "Ever since he got that ribbon at the pet show yesterday, he's been dangling it in front of Savannah's face and daring her to take it. As soon as she does, he yanks it away. She screams, he pulls her hair, they get in trouble, the wheels on the bus go 'round and 'round."

Tandy chuckled. "I don't know how you do it, sister."

"Me, either, most days. I wish I had more to tell you about Zelda."

"Me, too. Does Joy know anything?"

"Nothing more than what I know. I think your best bet is to have a chat with Clay and find out what he knows and how he knows it."

"I think you're right." Another screech sounded in the background. "Go break up the battle. I'll see you at the fair."

"See ya." Tandy heard the click and replaced her receiver. She briefly considered looking up Clay's number and grilling him over the phone but decided it'd be better to wait and do that in person. Then she could watch his face and know if he was holding something back.

She snagged a biscuit from the cookie sheet on the stove, then stared at it in her hand. Daddy *had* gotten up early. She dropped the biscuit and went upstairs to put her face on.

An hour later, with Cooper panting in the backseat and Daddy humming an old hymn, Tandy parked her car three blocks over from Lindell. "I can't believe this crowd."

"It seems to get worse every year." Daddy unhooked his seatbelt. "I should go check on the church booth, make sure they don't need anything."

Tandy knew he was going to see Zelda and decided not to mention it. "You go on ahead. Coop and I will catch up."

Daddy exited the car and walked off toward Lindell. Tandy sighed, seeing the spring in his step and praying Zelda was worthy of putting it there. "Cooper, we need to do some digging," she said, getting out of the car and raising the seat to allow Cooper to exit. She grabbed his leash as he passed by and shut the door. "First stop, Clay's Diner. Just follow the scent of hamburger."

Cooper's ears swayed back and forth as he padded along the sidewalk, sniffing the ground, then the air, then the ground again.

Tandy took in the people milling about, red balloons bobbing on strollers, toddlers on parents' shoulders, various leashes pulled taut just like hers as canines followed the confusing array of scents carried by the breeze. She smelled funnel cake and knew she'd have to have one before the end of the day.

The birds chirped and a squirrel darted across her path as Tandy and Cooper neared Lindell. Cooper froze at the sight of the squirrel's furry tail, and Tandy tightened her hold on the leash. "No, boy. We're not chasing animals today. You be good."

Cooper watched as the squirrel zoomed up a tree and out onto a branch. He turned his attention back to the sidewalk, and Tandy relaxed her hold a bit.

"Good boy."

Hoping no one would be offended at Cooper's presence inside the diner, she strolled in with fake confidence and stood at the counter. A long minute went by before Clay saw her through the opening and came out of the kitchen. "Hey." He came over and gave her a peck on the lips. "You two headed over to the street fair?"

"In a little while. I need to talk to you as soon as you have a second."

He sat down on the stool and motioned for her to join him. "Is something wrong?"

"I'm not sure." She glanced around the room and caught a few people looking away. "I'd rather talk about this somewhere else."

"Can it wait a few hours?"

"If it has to, sure."

"I've got some help coming in here in," he checked his watch, "two hours. If we're not packed, I can meet you somewhere. I don't know what it's going to be like with the fair and all."

"Okay. You've got my cell number. Just call me when there's a break, and I can meet you over in the park."

"Okay." She stood to go, and he stopped her with a touch. "You're sure everything's all right?"

"I hope so, Clay."

"If I need to, I can step out back for a few minutes."

"No, no. You go ahead and take care of things here. Between the fair and Emmy's scrapbooking section, I can kill two hours easy."

"You're sure?"

"Yeah, no problem."

The little bell over his door tinkled, and they looked up to see Zelda Norman walking in. "Morning, Clay!"

Tandy's face froze as fast as Cooper at the sight of a squirrel.

"Just need to grab another bucket of ice cream. It's going like crazy out there!"

"Sure, Zelda, you know where it is." He nodded toward the back. "You need help?"

"Nope, I've got it. I'll just borrow another dolly, if that's all right with you?"

"Help yourself." He turned back to Tandy. "So I'll see you in a couple of hours?"

Tandy blinked. "What's she doing in your kitchen?"

"I thought I told you. The ice cream for Grace Christian is in my freezer. It's easier than them going back and forth to the church."

"No, I don't think you told me that."

"Oh." He studied her face. "Is that a problem?"

"Uh, no. It's really nice of you." She tugged on Cooper's

leash, and he stood up. "You need to get back to work. See you in a couple of hours." She weaved her way through the tables as fast as a plodding basset hound allowed and exited the diner, not daring to look back.

Outside the sunshine had warmed up the day, and she was glad for her choice of shorts. The Iris Festival had grown in the past three years, and she let herself be pulled into the slowly moving throng. Vendors called to lines of people crowding the walkways between green and white tents. Wares of every size, shape, and color were being offered. Tandy paused at a display of handmade jewelry and admired the artist's work on a heavy pendant. Layers of glass had been burned together so that, no matter how she turned the pendant, it reflected a color. Gingerly, she laid it back on the black velvet and walked on.

The sharp scent of eucalyptus wafted from a stand of flower arrangements and wreaths, making her nose wrinkle. Momma always sneezed at this scent. Tandy spotted the source on a table at the back of the booth. Long stems of the round green and purple leaves were woven into an arrangement of cattails and tiger lilies. A pretty effect, but Tandy knew she'd never be able to have that smell in her home.

She continued down the line of booths, checking out clothes and purses, plants and pets, waving to the occasional Stars Hill resident who recognized her. Cooper barked at a cage holding a floppy-eared rabbit, making her laugh. The rabbit hopped to the edge of the cage and stared at Cooper, its nose twitching.

"I don't think he knows what to make of you, Coop."

The standoff ended when the booth owner dropped a lettuce leaf into the rabbit's crate. Coop gave the rabbit one last sniff and moved on.

They kept going, stopping to see anything of interest, until at last they reached the end of the line. Tandy pulled Cooper around and began walking back up the other side, amazed again at how many vendors were here. The familiar Flippen's Orchard sign two booths down caught her attention, and she pulled Coop over. Their apples were better than any she'd tasted here or in Florida. Pulling a bag mixed with golden delicious and red delicious varieties from its wooden crate, she paid the booth worker and trudged on.

"Aunt Tanny!" Savannah was on Jamison's shoulders, her little face lit up, arms stretched out toward Tandy.

"Savannah!" Tandy hustled over and handed Coop's leash and the bag of apples to Meg. "Look at you!" Reaching up, Tandy caught the little girl as she slid from Jamison's shoulders. "Where'd you get such a pretty dress?" Daises covered the spring frock and a ruffle of white bustled around the hem.

"Mommy got it."

"Your mommy has good taste."

James pulled on Tandy's shorts. "I'm handsome."

"Yes, you are. And a master dog handler, too." James grinned, revealing a gap in his teeth. "Did you lose a tooth?"

"Uh-huh. Dad says the toof fairy will bring me something if I put it under my pillow. But I don't want to yet."

"You don't? Why not?" She hefted Savannah further up on her hip.

"'Cause the toof fairy takes the toof, or she won't leave the surprise."

"You don't want her to take your tooth?"

"Uh-uh." He shook his head. "It's mine. I growed it and everything."

"You *grew* it," Meg corrected. Her hair was pulled back into a low ponytail, and Tandy noticed she looked tired.

"Hey. How long have you guys been here?"

"About half an hour," Jamison said.

"Long enough to be the proud owners of every type of sugar here." Meg held up a bag of cotton candy and a giant sucker.

"Not so. I smell funnel cake."

"Funnel cake!" James jumped up and down. "I want funnel cake!" He paused and turned to Meg. "What's funnel cake, Mommy?"

The adults laughed. "It's something that's going to wait until after lunch at least," Meg said. "How about we go find the jump-a-tron?"

"The what?" Tandy said.

"It's a big inflatable room the kids can go in and jump to their hearts' content." Meg leaned forward and whispered. "Wears them out like nothing else."

"Oh, good strategy."

"I think I saw it over by the library," Jamison said. "It was near Broadway last year. Here." He pushed the stroller so that it was in front of Meg. Tandy saw a sleeping Hannah inside. "You take her, and I'll go with them over to the rides."

Relief flooded Meg's face. "You are the most wonderful man." She leaned over and kissed him.

"I love you, too." Taking one child in each hand, he steered them off in the direction they'd come.

"Bye, Aunt Tanny!" Savannah waved with her free hand.

"Bye, cutie. See you in a little bit!" She turned to Meg. "You look exhausted."

"I'm a little tired. They've been a handful this morning." Meg stuffed their bags into the bottom of the stroller and turned it so they could continue perusing the booths.

"Do you ever wonder why you had three?"

"Sometimes." Meg's smile turned wry. "I don't regret having any of them, but I *do* get tired and need some peace and quiet."

"I think I'd pull my hair out."

"Oh, it's not bad. A little harder this year with James starting school, but I'm grateful I get to stay with them."

"How's the homeschooling coming?"

"It's not as hard as I thought it'd be. James catches on quickly to just about anything I show him. I'm sure it'll get harder as he ages, though."

"Let me know when he's ready to learn law."

"You bet." They stopped at a booth and considered some painted lap desks. Deciding the price was too high, they continued on. "Did you talk to Clay yet about Zelda?"

"He's over at the diner. I stopped in this morning, but he couldn't get away right then. We're supposed to meet over at the park in a bit."

"You think he'll tell you what he knows about her?"

"Yeah, I think so. I just don't know if he dug deep enough to find the dirt on her."

"Maybe there isn't any."

"Everybody has dirt, Meg. We're living proof of that."

"True."

"Do you know how Daddy met her?"

"I think it was in church. She went to the Baptist church for a while but then moved over to Grace Christian."

Tandy's eyes narrowed. "Hmm. Sounds like a calculated move to me."

"We don't know that," Meg defended. "Let's hold off on the judgment until we know more about her."

"You're okay with this whole Zelda-Daddy thing?"

"Not okay, no." Meg sighed and looked away. "Like I said, though, I worry about him. Can you imagine how lonely that must be? Night after night, nothing to keep him company but a book or the television?"

"Or a dog," Tandy muttered.

"What?" Meg blinked and looked down at Cooper. "Oh, Tandy, I'm sorry. That was awful. I didn't mean to imply—"

"No, you're right," Tandy rushed to assure her. "Being single has its downside. I hadn't thought of Daddy like that."

"Whether Zelda turns out to be okay or not, he needs someone to talk with, to share his life with."

Tandy stuffed her hands in her shorts pockets. "Can't he find a buddy?"

Meg snorted. "You sound like Joy."

"She may be the baby, but she has good ideas sometimes."

"That she does."

Tandy's cell phone rang.

"Hello?"

"Hey." Clay's voice sounded in her ear. "I'm walking to the park right now. Where are you?"

Tandy looked up and got her bearings. "A couple blocks away. I'll meet you at the picnic tables."

"Sounds good." He clicked off and she turned to Meg.

"Clay?"

"Yep. You want to come?"

"No, I think I'd rather enjoy the fair with a sleeping baby."

Tandy hugged her and blew a kiss at Hannah. "I understand. Enjoy your peace while it lasts!"

Meg nodded, and Tandy pulled her bag of apples from the stroller. She trotted off, tugging an increasingly tired Cooper behind her.

By the time they got to the park, Cooper was exhausted and his big head drooped.

"I think he's going to keel over of a heart attack." Clay stood as she approached the picnic table.

"He might. This is a whole lot more walking than he's used to." Meg sat down on top of the table, dropped her bag of apples on the bench, and looped Cooper's leash around her foot, knowing he wasn't going to take off anywhere. Cooper flopped in the dirt and closed his eyes.

Clay sat next to her, resting his elbows on his knees and looking out across the park. "So, what'd you need to talk about?"

"Remember when you said Zelda Norman was okay?"

He nodded.

"I need to know everything you know."

"Tandy, come on."

"Don't 'come on' me. This is Daddy we're talking about, and if he's falling for—" her throat squeezed at the words— "some woman, then I need to know all I can about her."

"I already told you, she's fine."

"Yes, you did. And I want to know how you know that."

"I did some digging, asked around."

"Dug where? Asked who? Meg says she's only been in

Stars Hill for a year. There can't be that much to say about her."

"No, but she lived in South Carolina before here. I knew her when I went through boot camp on Parris Island and then, by some fluke of fate, she and her husband ended up on another base I was sent to."

"You knew her when she was married? How?"

"She worked on base at the grocery store. Made flower arrangements and inflated balloons, that kind of thing."

"So what happened to her husband?"

"He was killed during a training exercise. I came in the store one day and there she was, arranging flowers with tears rolling down her cheeks. I asked her what was wrong and found out it was her husband who had died." He shrugged. "She's a good person, Tandy."

"Why'd she move to Stars Hill?"

"I was as surprised to see her as anybody. It had been years, but she remembered the stories I told her about this place and wanted to come see it for herself. She loved it so much, she picked up and moved here."

"What about her family? She couldn't go live with them?"

"She doesn't have any children and, as far as I can remember, only has one sister who lives out in Arizona somewhere. Her husband had a brother. He was killed in Desert Storm."

Tandy digested that information as the birds sang overhead and the breeze rustled new leaves on the trees.

Clay reached back and took her hand. "When she came to town, I was surprised but happy she'd found somewhere to fit in. And the first time I saw her with your dad, I had a talk with her. Even called some buddies who live around the base to see if anything had happened while I was gone. She doesn't have ulterior motives, Tandy."

She took a deep breath, blew it out. "I had a feeling she wouldn't."

"Then why the third degree?"

"Because she's spending a lot of time with Daddy."

"I think he's okay with that."

"He is."

"But you're not."

"I don't know if I am. It's . . . weird."

"Weird how?"

"Just weird. She's not exactly average looking."

"I'll give you that."

"Joy's ready to tie her down to a chair at the salon and fix that hideous red hair. And Daddy, well, I wouldn't have pictured him with a short, big-jewelry-wearing woman."

"Have you ever pictured him with anybody besides your mom?"

"No."

"Then Zelda's as good an image to plug in as any other."

She focused on his thumb tracing circles on her hand and listened to Cooper snoring. Anything but why she was struggling so with this.

"I suppose."

She tried to open her mind to the possibility of Daddy and Zelda. It was like tasting a new food—strange texture, odd experience, but perhaps acceptable.

"Does your dad date?" She readjusted the leash on her shoe.

"He might. We talk about once a month, and if he does, he doesn't mention it."

"Do you ever go out to visit him?"

"I flew out there last Christmas. New Mexico in the wintertime, though, isn't Christmas. I stayed a few days, met some of the folks who live there, came home."

"Is he doing well? I just realized I haven't asked you at all about him."

"It's okay." He let go of her hand and leaned back, bracing his arms behind. "He and I never had what you and your parents had. Most of him died that day in the car with my mom."

She didn't know what to say to that, remembering their long talks in high school where he shared with her the pain of starting junior high without a mother. It was what had made her cling to him when Momma died. Only someone who'd walked the road knew the pain of the loss.

"He's good, though. In an assisted-living community, only has to punch a button and someone's there to help if he needs it."

She scooted toward him. "Thanks for telling me about Zelda."

He turned his head, meeting her eyes. "You're welcome."

All the things they wanted to say, needed to say, *couldn't* say hung heavy between them. Today was Thursday. In three days she'd be going back to Florida. But the sunshine, the breeze, the perfection of the day, couldn't be marred by talk of decisions.

"Let's go get some funnel cake."

He blinked in surprise. "Okay, but I think Cooper might have a thing or two to say about that."

They glanced down at the snoring dog. A bird hopped a foot away and he didn't even twitch.

"Hmm, this could pose a problem." They stared at the dog for a few seconds.

"We could leave him at my place for a while."

"Is your place dog-proofed?"

"There isn't anything I'd mind him chewing on, if that's what you mean." He stepped onto the bench seat of the table and climbed to the ground. Dusting off his hands, he said, "Come on. We'll hook him up with a big floor pillow and go see what this fair has to offer."

She took the hand he was holding out and let him help her down off the table. "If he tears something up, I'll replace it."

"Deal." He stopped and looked at her for a second, then cupped his hand under her cheek. "Tandy Ann, you are the most beautiful girl here."

A blush crept up her neck at the blatant desire in his eyes, but she couldn't look away. Stepping toward her, he murmured, "What will I do when you're gone?" and kissed her.

She knew everyone in the park could see them but for now didn't care. His question broke something inside her, and she felt a tear trickle down as she kissed him back, straining to imprint this moment on her memory.

"Hey, none of that," he whispered, wiping her tear with his thumb.

"I'm sorry," she whispered.

"Don't be." He kissed her again, then guided her head to his chest. His arms came around her, and she closed her eyes, resting in his nearness, allowing a few more tears to fall before summoning the courage to stop. Momma's face, pale from sickness and swollen from medications, flashed through her mind. She couldn't stay here. Daddy had already left Momma behind for Zelda. If Tandy came home, where would that leave Momma? Or her, for that matter?

She straightened and stepped away from Clay. "I can't wait to hear what the busybodies have to say about this." She swiped at her cheeks.

His tender look told her he knew she hurt, but he let her change the subject. "Come on, let's get this lazy dog to my place."

She tugged on Cooper's leash and he stood up, stretched, and began plodding along behind her.

Twenty-Three

That night Tandy walked into the living room and sat down in Momma's old recliner by Daddy. A still-exhausted Cooper could be heard snoring upstairs from his chair in her bedroom.

"How'd the ice cream giveaway go?"

"Fine as frog hair, split three ways." He set down his book. "We have half a bucket of vanilla left. I put it out in the chest freezer if you want some."

"Ugh, I made myself sick on funnel cake." She reached for the recliner handle and flipped the footrest out. "That's enough sugar for one day."

"How's Clay?"

"He's good. The diner was nuts with all the visitors to the street fair. We didn't get much time together."

"From what I saw in the park, I'd say that could be a good thing."

Tandy's face turned bright red. "You saw that, huh?"

"I did." He didn't sound mad. "You still leaving on Sunday?"

"Yeah." She'd thought about staying longer, but that

would only make it harder. "If I call Mr. Beasley, he may let me come back in early. I'd guess the worst of it has blown over by now, and I'm going to have cases in court soon."

The tick of the clock competed with a creaking spring in Daddy's recliner as he went back to his book.

"Daddy?"

He looked up at her. "Hmm?"

"You and Zelda? That's, um, that's okay with me."

He set his book down on the table at his elbow. "Want to tell me why?"

"No, I don't think so." She nibbled her lip. Daddy waited. "I know that this—" her hands swept out to encompass the room—"can feel empty after a while. Can get lonely. I don't want you to be lonely."

"Are you sure you want to go back to Florida?"

"I can't stay here, Daddy. What would I do? I worked hard to be an attorney, and in a few years I'll probably make partner. Can you imagine? I'll be a partner in one of the biggest firms in the city whose streets used to be my bed."

"Will that give you what you're looking for?"

She turned to him. "What?"

Wisdom filled his sparkling sea-green eyes. "I remember when we first saw you, honey girl. You were dirty and thin, so thin, and sitting on a sidewalk off of I-Drive. I asked you where your mother was, and you told me she'd be right back. Do you remember that?"

She did. Unbearable heat had radiated from the pavement, scorching her feet through the holes in her shoes. Her mother hadn't come back to her the night before, but that didn't mean she wouldn't be back soon. "I do."

"So we waited with you, and when your mother finally

did come back that afternoon, she told us to take you and raise you."

Daddy made it sound better than it was. Her mother had asked them if they wanted to buy her. She was that desperate for money to fund her next high.

"And we did. Your momma and I held our breath every day in this house until the last paper was signed and we knew you were ours. And then we determined to teach you how worthy you are in our sight and God's."

Over twenty years later she wasn't sure the lesson had kicked in. If it had, why did she lash out at a client over his remarks about a man she didn't even know?

"I hope we did, that, Tandy." Daddy's voice was soothing. "I hope you know how very special you are to God and to me and your mother and sisters."

Did she know that? Searching her heart and mind, she knew they loved her, but were they proud of her? Had she given back to her parents by rising above the childhood they pulled her from? Did her present justify the sacrifice of their past?

She was on track for that. Making partner, succeeding— these things would give them something to point to and say, "See, we knew she could do something outstanding." She'd wracked her brain trying to find a way to do that in Stars Hill but had come up empty. There was no other way than going back to Orlando. It might seem dumb to some people, but the responsibility of proving herself weighed heavy on Tandy's shoulders. And having spent the first seven years of her life with a woman who wouldn't know duty if it slapped her in the face, Tandy wasn't about to turn her back on hers.

"I know, Daddy. I know." Picking up the remote from

the side table, she clicked on the television before he could reply. Talking about it wouldn't make the next few days any easier.

✂ ✂ ✂

FRIDAY MORNING TANDY worked with Daddy on the farm, harvesting the acres of winter wheat he had planted earlier and fixing various parts on the equipment. The corn seeds were in the ground in the back fields, and pretty soon the first sprouts would peek out of the dirt.

By lunchtime she was covered in sweat and dirt—and happy as a pig in slop. The hard work made her muscles burn, and she felt better than any time she'd spent in a gym. Knowing that in a few months her Daddy would have fields full of crops made her smile. Farming was a tough life, but seeing those first shoots of green appear was a thrill unlike any other. The miracle of life.

She trudged across the front yard, tugging off her gloves and smoothing back the curls that had pulled free of her braid. If her coworkers could see her now, they'd laugh themselves silly. She hightailed it up the stairs, shedding clothes on her way to the shower, anticipating the cool water on her sweaty skin. Pig-Out in the Park, or POP, would be starting right about now, and she didn't intend to miss any more of it than it took to shower and change.

Clay, Darin, and the rest of their band would be playing tonight, too. Kendra was as curious as she to see if they were any good.

She hurried through her shower, put on her makeup, and left her hair to air dry. The open moon roof of the Beamer could have it dry before she hit town and wouldn't frizz her hair like the blow dryer would.

Since there wouldn't be time between POP and the night's festivities, she decided a skirt would probably be best. Her fingers thumbed through the hangers in the closet, stopping at a sleeveless light-blue dress. It was cotton, which made it casual enough for POP, but a band of ribbon around the waist dressed it up enough for the evening. Perfect.

She pulled it over her head and slipped her feet into sandals. Good enough. Every minute preparing meant another minute missed at the park. Glancing at the sleeping Cooper, she decided to leave him here. He'd get too tired before nighttime, anyway.

"Be good, boy!" She left the room. "Daddy! I'm going downtown! You ready?"

Daddy stepped out of his bedroom door. "You go on ahead. I'm going to pick Zelda up on the way." He wiped shaving cream from his face. "Thanks for your help today."

"No problem. See you at the park!" She twirled and went for the door.

"Tell Clay hi for me," Daddy called down the hall.

She all but skipped to the Beamer, not positive of the reasons behind her lighthearted feeling but determined to enjoy it while it lasted. She slid into the soft gray leather and shifted into reverse. As the car bumped down the driveway, she opened the moon roof and smelled the country breeze.

By the time she'd arrived in town, her hair was dry for the most part. She closed the moon roof and switched on the radio, realizing she hadn't listened to the news since coming back to Stars Hill.

"Mr. Governor, are you saying you had no knowledge of the theft?"

Tandy rolled her eyes and moved to change the station when she heard the voice of the governor of Florida.

"I did not. I am deeply saddened by this turn of events and ask the good citizens of the state of Florida, and particularly those of the great city of Orlando, to hold their judgment until all the facts are known."

What on earth . . . ? Tandy turned up the volume.

"Does that mean you have information not known to the public at this time?"

"I have known Levi Walker all my life. If he says he didn't do this, then he did not do this."

"There you have it, direct from the governor," the newswoman said. "For those of you just tuning in, we've been talking with Florida's governor about the recent discovery that Lieutenant Governor Levi Walker embezzled more than forty million dollars from Florida taxpayers over the past three years. As you'll recall, Walker was instrumental in the creation of the new stadium in Orlando during his time there as mayor. Walker has not released a statement, and his attorney's office, Meyers, Briggs, and Stratton, did not return calls for comment."

Tandy pulled over and dug her cell phone out of her purse. Flipping it open, she nearly panicked when it showed twenty-one missed calls since she'd switched the ringer to vibrate last night. Why did she always forget to turn the ringer back on? Ignoring the voicemail icon, she dialed Anna's direct line.

"Meyers, Briggs, and Stratton, how may I help you?"

"Anna, it's Tandy."

"Tandy! Where have you been? We've been trying to find you all day."

"I know. I'm sorry. I turned my phone on vibrate and didn't turn it back. What's happening with Levi?"

"He's in Mr. Beasley's office right now. They're trying to draft a release to the press."

"There's no point in doing that now. It's the end of the work week. Let the networks rehash their old stuff all weekend, and we'll release something on Monday, then control the flow of information all week."

"How about I put you through to him?"

Tandy sighed, feeling the pull of her life in Orlando and seeing Stars Hill shrink away. "Go ahead."

She heard the hold tones click and then Mr. Beasley's voice. "Tandy?"

"Hi, Mr. Beasley. I understand Levi is there with you?"

"Tandy, I swear I did not do this." Levi's voice hadn't lost its power, but she detected a touch of panic.

"Of course you didn't, Levi." She ignored a twinge of doubt. She'd thought that about Harry Simons, too. "I'm out of state right now, but I'll be back in the office on Monday. We'll have a press conference that afternoon, in time for the evening news feeds. Can you be at my office at eight a.m.?"

"Of course."

"All right. Stay home this weekend. Do not go out. Do not answer the phone. Do not talk to the press."

"I can do that."

"I'll see you Monday, and we'll get this thing handled. Mr. Beasley?"

"I'm here."

"I assume it will be all right for me to be back on Monday?"

"Of course, of course. No need to bring that up. We'll see you Monday." He ended the call, and she dialed Anna.

"Meyers, Briggs, and Stratton, how may I help you?"

"Anna, it's me. Can you set up a press conference for Monday at three p.m., please?"

"Sure, Tandy. You, Mr. Beasley, Mr. Walker, and who else?"

"The usual. Get the partners in if you can. Walker's wife, Theresa, their kids. We'll need to make him look human instead of like a money-grubbing bureaucrat."

Anna laughed. "I sure have missed you around here, dear."

"I've missed you too. I'll be in on Monday. Try to keep Beasley from having a heart attack until then, all right?"

"Now that you're handling this little upset to his calm waters, I'm sure he's fine. Have a safe drive back."

"Bye, Anna."

She closed the phone and looked down the road, her lighthearted feeling gone. Even if she'd wanted to stay awhile longer, it was impossible now. Levi Walker had been one of her very first clients, back when he served as mayor. She didn't know him well enough to believe in his innocence, but he'd always been kind to her. When he moved to the lieutenant governor's office, she'd expected him to ask for a partner to handle his legal matters, but he'd never done so.

Now she almost wished he had. She checked her mirrors and pulled back onto the road.

She managed to push Levi and his legal troubles to the back of her mind. Tonight was POP. Tomorrow was the parade. She could leave after that and be back in Orlando by early Sunday morning. Plenty of time to rest, get a handle on the situation, and be ready for Levi Monday morning.

She swung the Beamer into a parking space and killed the engine. One look at her and Clay would know something had happened. He may have even seen it on the news, though she doubted he'd connect the scandal to her. Should she tell him? Or shield their last two days from the intrusion of her other life?

Playing it by ear had worked in the past, and it would have to work now. She got out of the car and took a deep breath. Smoothing the wrinkles in her dress, she walked toward the park. Clay had closed the diner in honor of POP and was meeting her at their table.

The leaves rustled overhead and the scent of barbecue hung heavy in the air as she entered the park. Smoke from the roasters rose into the trees and blended with the gray branches.

"Hey there, Taz." Clay ambled over. "Hungry?"

"Starved."

"You look beautiful." He hugged her close, then let her go. "Have fun with your dad today?"

"I did. He worked me to death, but we got a lot accomplished."

"Then you, madam, deserve a reward." He snagged a glass of iced tea from one of the vendor stalls and handed it to her. The best part about POP was that everything was free.

She took a sip. "Thanks."

He stopped and looked closer. "What's wrong?"

"Nothing. Other than my aching muscles, that is."

"You sure?"

"Positive."

"You know I'm going to get it out of you sooner or later."

"Can we make it later?"

"Will it get worse if we wait?"

"No."

"Then we can make it later."

"Thanks."

He looked at her a second longer, then let it go. "Kendra and Darin are holding our spots over there." He pointed to the picnic table, and they began walking. "We've got you a plate, but if you want to walk around first we can."

"Nah. I'm sure you got me the good stuff."

He faked an offended look. "Of course."

They reached the table and Darin started to stand. "Sit, sit. How's the barbecue?"

"Fabulous." Kendra smacked her lips. "I foresee a gain of at least five pounds tonight."

"That good, huh?"

Kendra nodded and drank her tea. "Charles outdid himself this year. I've got ten bucks that says he takes home the trophy."

"Have you tasted Corner Bar-B-Q yet?" Clay asked. "They won last year, remember."

"Only because Charles sat out the competition."

"Okay, I'll take that bet. Put ten for me on Corner."

Tandy bit into her sandwich and smoky flavor exploded in her mouth. "Mm-m-m. Ten bucks on this." She pointed to the sandwich.

"That's Charles's." Kendra's grin was triumphant. "How about we make this easy? If Corner wins, you boys win. If Charles wins, we girls are the victors."

"What do we win?"

"Whatever you want." Kendra batted her eyelashes at Darrin.

"Within reason," Tandy added in a rush.

Clay and Darin spoke in unison. "You're on."

They finished their sandwiches and cleaned up the trash, sparring about whose food was better.

"I need to walk." Kendra patted her stomach. "I can feel my arteries hardening the longer I sit here."

"I told you to stop at two sandwiches," Tandy said. "But you wouldn't listen."

"Does she ever?" Darin received a swat on the arm for his efforts. "What? That was a compliment. You're a woman who knows your mind and doesn't let others tell you what to do. That's a good thing, right?"

"When you put it that way . . . okay, thanks." Kendra looped her arm through Darin's as they left the park and walked down Lindell. The street vendors were still up, getting in every sale they could before dusk when they'd have to tear down and pack it in.

Tandy smiled, just glad to have time alone with Clay. "What are you guys playing tonight?"

"Little of this, little of that."

"You won't tell me?"

"A guy's got to have some secrets." He took her hand in his. "Wouldn't want you to get bored with me."

She saw Kendra and Darin stop at a booth and pulled Clay into the alley. "Hey, I told Daddy I was okay with him and Zelda."

He tucked a curl behind her ear. "I'm glad."

"If she hurts him—"

"He'll live. Your dad's a big boy."

She sighed. "You're right. But I still may break her kneecaps."

"Remind me not to get on your bad side." They shared a laugh. "You going to tell me what's on your mind?"

His hand was so warm around hers, she considered not telling him at all. Why ruin their last days? But running from the problem wouldn't solve anything. "A client got in some trouble."

He stiffened. "Do you have to go back?"

"Not until tomorrow, which we already knew. I've got a meeting with him Monday morning."

"What happened?"

She told him about Levi and the embezzlement, the weight of dread settling back on her shoulders.

"Did he do it?"

"I'm not sure. If you'd asked me that a few weeks ago, I'd be positive he was innocent. But I thought Harry Simons was innocent, too, and look where that got me."

"Here with me." He kissed the top of her hand. "I'm okay with you assuming things."

She smiled. "Anyway, this is going to be a media feeding frenzy, so we have a press conference scheduled on Monday."

The sadness in his eyes nearly broke her resolve.

"Hey, you two lovebirds, come on."

Kendra shushed Darin. "Can't you see they're having a moment?" Tandy laughed at her sister's reprimand. "We'll just be over here when you're ready," Kendra called to them and Tandy nodded.

"Tandy, can I ask you something?"

"Of course." *As long as it's not asking me to stay.*

"Do you like what you do for a living?"

She blinked. "What? I don't understand."

"It's a simple question. When you heard the news today about Levi, were you excited to help him? To get back to Orlando and defend him?"

"No." The word escaped before she could stop it. She put her hand over her mouth before anything else could get out.

He gently moved her hand and ran a thumb over her lips. "Then why do you do it? I'm trying to figure this out, Tandy, because if I can, then I think it will be easier to let you go. But you've got to help me out. When you talk about Orlando, you don't seem happy. When you told me, just now, about Levi, that gorgeous smile went away."

She didn't know what to say to that. Here, with people milling everywhere and plenty of ears desperate to pick up any tidbit of gossip to share, she didn't want to tell him. Didn't want to tell herself. Levi's problem was easy. Her own life was another story entirely.

"I can let you go if what you're running toward is something that makes you happy, that makes you feel inside the way I feel when I look at you. I won't like it, it'll wreck me; but I can do it, and I will for you." He pulled their joined hands up and held them to his chest. "But I can't seem to get to the place where I can let you go without a good reason. So I need you to tell me you *want* to go."

His eyes searched hers, and she saw the desperation in them. Felt her heart breaking into pieces. Knew it would never be whole again. But also knew that she couldn't be her mother, running from the duty she had toward her parents, her sisters. Meg was raising a beautiful family. Joy had built a lovely home and garnered a reputation for her hospitality. Kendra won awards for her amazing art. There was nothing in Stars Hill that would let her do something like that, *be* something they could be proud of.

And even if there was, she'd have Clay and a thousand emotions crashing around in her life all the time. That didn't sound as bad as it did a week before, though. Maybe the emotional mess was worth having him close, holding her hand, talking to her again. But taking that felt selfish, felt like a betrayal of her commitment to Momma and their dream.

"Tandy, look at me." His voice washed over her and she closed her eyes, unable to see the honesty of him. "Look at me, babe." Warm knuckles grazed her cheek, and she opened her eyes. "Just tell me you want to go."

She considered it, but lying to him now when he'd been so real with her didn't seem possible. She loved him. Had never really stopped, if she wanted to be honest. The cheering section in her brain went into overdrive again, and she tamped it down. It didn't matter if she loved him or he loved her because she had a duty to perform. And that duty didn't allow for an existence in Stars Hill. She shook her head at the irony—finally, her heart had melted from the deep freeze of mourning, but it came about ten years too late. The luxury of loving him, of living here in Stars Hill, was not a possibility. It wouldn't let her be successful. And she had to be successful to prove her worth and the enormity of the price of Momma and Daddy's sacrificial love.

"I *have* to go." Tears formed in her eyes, and she blinked.

"I don't understand that."

She shook her head and the tears traced tracks down her cheeks. She swiped at them. She hadn't cried in the last ten years as much as she had the past nine days. "You don't have to."

"I *do*."

"Why do you have to go back there? Is this about your mom? Tell me."

She shook her head harder. "It won't help." She gulped. "And it won't change things. I can't do this now. Kendra and Darin—"

"Are fine."

"Are waiting." She sniffed and looked down. His big hands enveloped her own and were rubbing those small circles again. She burned the sight in her memory banks and tried to force her heart into deep-freeze mode. It would make this so much easier. "I can't do this now."

"If not now, when?"

"I don't know, Clay. Not now." She pulled away from him and went to find Kendra.

They were stopped at a booth of toys, Darin demonstrating yo-yo techniques. Kendra looked up at her approach and hurried over.

"Are you okay? You look like someone just died."

"Someone did. Can you cover for me a second? I just need a minute."

"Yeah, yeah, go." Kendra pushed her on, and Tandy ran to her car. Her flip-flops slapped the pavement, their clapping mocking the cheering in her mind. Panic rode on the edge of her brain, but she pushed it away, hanging onto her crumbling composure until she fell into the car in a heap. Leaning over the steering wheel, she let the tears come in a rush. They poured down her face, and she wondered if a human heart could break twice. Leaving him was so *hard*. For the first time she began to understand her birth mother.

If she'd loved Tandy's dad like this, then no wonder she'd numbed herself with drugs. A sob escaped, scaring her with its wild sound.

It wasn't going to get any easier between now and tomorrow to leave. It would only get harder. Every second with him made leaving harder. Might as well go back to the house, pack up her stuff, and hit the road. Clay would be hurt—her tears intensified—but he'd be hurt just as much tomorrow as today. She put her hand on the keys but couldn't bring herself to turn them in the ignition. The selfish part of her, the one that wanted to tell Levi Walker to handle his own problems, wanted to run back there, find Clay, and hold him until she died.

But that wasn't enough. Another sob escaped, and she bit her lip to keep them in. The metallic taste of blood touched her tongue. She didn't care. Loving Clay was not enough to justify her existence in Stars Hill or the work Momma and Daddy put into her life. She couldn't be big enough here.

The reality of what she was leaving behind, not just Clay, but the sisters and Daddy, melded into one in her mind. Where in Orlando would she find the steady friendship like her sisters? Were there women who got together to scrapbook, poring over life's minutiae in a scrapbooking studio? Going to Orlando wasn't just the end of her and Clay; it was her return to an existence that revolved around Meyers, Briggs, and Stratton. To attending basketball games by herself, to taking pictures of Cooper so she'd have something to scrapbook, and then scrapbooking by herself while she watched TV. To eating lunches at her desk.

Loneliness, a familiar foe, crept into her car. It seeped into her bones and wrapped its tendrils around her heart, suffocating her, stealing her ability to cry. Her eyes dried, and after a while she sat up. She dug in the glove compartment and found a pack of tissues and repaired her damaged face as best she could.

This wasn't a surprise. Nine days was nine days. It was always going to end. This was nothing new. She'd see Clay tonight, watch his band perform, and laugh with Kendra. She'd hold his hand tomorrow during the parade between bouts of running with James and Savannah to scoop up candy. And while she wouldn't get to scrapbook with her sisters before she left—there simply wasn't time—she'd made some memories with them on this trip. When this Levi Walker thing was handled, maybe she could come back and scrap with them again.

The thought comforted her a little. She opened the car door and stepped out.

Kendra was leaning on the car behind her. "You okay?"

She nodded and sniffed.

"Yeah, sorry I ran out on you back there."

"Not a problem. Clay didn't look any better than you. Care to tell me what happened?"

She shrugged a nonchalance she didn't feel. "Reality. Same as ten years ago."

Kendra came over and put her arm around Tandy. "Anything I can do?"

"Not unless there's a big law firm in town I'm unaware of." Her laugh sounded shaky.

"You could start one."

"No." She shook her head and sniffed. "I don't think so. Not enough business to justify it here."

"Then start something else. I know a certain owner of a diner who would be open to having a partner."

She gave a wobbly smile. "Did he say anything to you?"

"No. He came out of that alley, and Darin went to him. I didn't think I should go there."

"I'm glad he's got Darin."

"I think he'd rather have you."

"I know." *Me, too.*

They leaned against the back of her car. "Kendra, do you ever think about how much Momma and Daddy did for us?"

"Every day. It's why I work so hard at my art."

"Exactly. That's exactly it. It's like we have to give back to them or something."

"Prove ourselves worthy."

"Yes."

"Is that why you're going back to Orlando?" Tandy nodded, and Kendra squeezed her shoulder. "So you *do* love him."

Why pretend? "I do." She wiped an errant tear and looked up at the perfect blue sky. "How dumb is that? I love a man I can't possibly be with."

"It's not ideal, I'll give you that." Kendra patted her shoulder. "But it's a relief you're loving him again. I'd seen enough of frozen Tandy to last me a lifetime."

Tandy smiled. "Yeah, me too."

"I can't stand in the way of you justifying Momma and Daddy's sacrifice since I'm on the same mission. But are you sure there isn't a way for you to do that here? In Stars Hill?"

"I've wracked my brain, Ken, but I can't come up with anything. The two little law firms here have all the business sewn up, and I don't know how to do anything else."

"You can scrapbook."

"Yeah, I thought about that. But Emmy's got a good thing going, and I wouldn't want to compete with her."

"There's got to be *something*. We're smart women. We should be able to figure this out."

"You're assuming there's a solution to find. There isn't. I know. I've looked."

"You're like that story about the fish and the bird."

"What?" Tandy rubbed her nose.

"You know. Momma read it to us. A fish and a bird fell in love, but they couldn't be together because the fish can't live in the air and the bird can't live in the sea."

The impossibility of the situation hit her again. "I wish he hadn't pushed until tomorrow."

"Why?"

"We could have had another day."

"You still can."

"We could, but I'm not sure he wants that."

"Well, you're not going to find out by standing here. Let's go hang out near the diner until we see them."

"What if he doesn't want to see me?"

"Then I'll help you pack."

Her heart felt like a hot knife had sliced through her chest. Pack. Leave.

They walked down the sidewalk, arms around each other's shoulders like they'd done in grade school. "You're a good sister, Kendra."

"Back at you."

"What do other women do?"

"You mean if they don't have sisters? Find friends, I suppose."

"But how? I've been in Orlando three years, and I haven't found someone like you or Meg or Joy."

"That's because there's nobody like us. God wouldn't have done that to the world."

Twenty-Four

They arrived at the diner and sat down on a bench. It was a short wait. Three minutes later Darin and Clay came up the sidewalk. Kendra went to meet them. Tandy couldn't move. She saw Darin and Kendra walk off together and watched Clay approach her. Blood rushed through her ears, and she wondered if she might faint. If her brain would just refuse to have this much emotion coursing through it and shut her down.

He sat down beside her, folding his hands in his lap and crossing his ankles.

People milled along Lindell in front of them. Some vendors had begun packing it in, putting unsold items into crates and tubs. Tandy watched it all with a detached air. She couldn't let herself be present right now. It would hurt too much.

"I'm not going to pretend to understand, Tandy. But if you want to tell me, I'll try."

She heard that, knew he was as good as his word. Knew, too, that no matter what words she chose, he would not—could not—understand. He had never owed anyone anything in his life. Hadn't ever been rescued from a desperate situation or had someone sacrifice for him. Just like he was the only one who knew her hurt when Momma died, only someone who had been given a gift like hers could understand this need to give back.

She touched his hand and he looked at her. "Can we have tonight? Let me see you play with your band, enjoy the music and the dancing, and leave it there?"

The muscles in his jaw worked, and she understood his struggle. If he could know her heart, she'd share it in a beat. But he couldn't.

"We can try." He turned his hand so he could grasp hers. Turning back to the view of Lindell, she leaned sideways into him, soaking up his warmth, her hand clasped in his.

They sat there for an hour. Twice he started to speak but never did. As the sun moved across the sky, it seemed to ridicule her, shifting the shadows, choosing whose way to light and whose to leave darkened.

When the last of the vendors had carted his goods off the street, she stared at the empty road. A few stragglers were still walking about, waiting for the promised music in an hour. Clay watched his bandmates set their gear up on the stage. She wondered if he would go to them, but he didn't move.

Just sat with her.

Breathing.

Feeling.

Being.

Finally, Kendra came over. She didn't speak, and Tandy was grateful for that. Mourning didn't leave much room for words. She held out her hand, the sun kissing its caramel color, and Tandy took it. Let herself be pulled up from the bench.

Clay squeezed her other hand, and she turned to him. He gave her a crooked smile and stood. Kissed her hand and let it go.

She stood with Kendra, watching him walk down the street to the stage. Saw Darin clap him on the shoulder and hug him. Saw how he needed that. The chairs in front of the stage were filling up now, called by the sound of the occasional mike check. Meg's blonde hair shone, and Tandy watched her look around, no doubt searching for her sisters.

She held Kendra's hand and went to join Meg.

"Hey, sis," Meg said when they arrived. "You doing okay?" She hugged Tandy.

"Yeah. I just hate to leave all of you."

"We hate to see you go."

Tandy and Kendra sat down in the folding chairs. "Have either of you seen Joy?"

The return to conversation brought a sense of normalcy back to the day. "No," Tandy answered. "You're sure she's coming?"

Meg nodded. "I called her before I left the house. Oh! There she is." She waved her hand until Joy noticed and came toward them. "I thought the sisterhood might be a good idea tonight."

"Where are Jamison and the kids?"

"At Jamison's parents' house. If they all have a meltdown, his mom can pick up the pieces."

Joy sat down on the other side of Kendra. "What'd I miss?"

"Nothing yet," Kendra said.

"Tandy, how are you?" Joy's concern filled her words. "You holding up?"

"I assume Kendra clued you both in?"

They nodded.

Meg shifted in her seat to face Tandy. "Is there anything we can do to make this easier?"

"No, it's enough to know you guys get why I have to go back."

"I just wish we could figure out something for you here," Joy said. "We could start a catering business if you want."

"Thanks, Joy, but you know me in a kitchen. I'm a danger to everyone within a five-block radius."

"Remember that time you tried to make quiche?" Meg shook her head and looked at the sky. "And you set off the fire alarm and there was smoke everywhere."

"And Momma came running in with a fire extinguisher." Tandy stared into the distance, the memory a vivid image.

"And Daddy saw the smoke from the barn and nearly had a heart attack," Joy joined in.

They laughed, remembering Tandy's attempt at cooking. "Yeah, maybe a catering business is a bad idea," Kendra said through her laughter.

A chord sounded through the speakers, and Tandy looked at the stage. Clay was looking at her, and the ache in his eyes was so real she couldn't breathe. She turned away, another part of her breaking inside.

"We want to thank all of you for coming out tonight." As Darin spoke, the girls sat back. "We're happy to take your requests if you've got them, and if you need an invitation to dance, this is it. There's a space right up here—" he pointed to a grassy area directly in front of the stage—"or at the back. This first number was chosen by a clever lady I recently met." He flashed a grin at Kendra. "We hope you enjoy it." He stepped back and strummed a chord on a shiny black guitar that hung at his hips. The other guys took their cue, and the opening notes of "Stormy Weather" sounded.

Tandy watched some couples rise from their seats and make their way to the dance area. Her heart longed to be with them, safe in Clay's arms, but her head kept her feet planted on the grass in front of her. His voice mesmerized as he crooned into the microphone. She hadn't known he could sing like this, but it didn't surprise her.

Song after song, minute by minute, darkness descended on them. The stars came out and they played. The crickets chirped in the park and they played. The new street lamps came on and they played.

Her heart broke and they played.

Meg's arm came around her back. Kendra held her hand. Joy held Kendra's. They lifted her up, kept her from drowning in the tears she held inside. Anchored her to the reality of being a Sinclair sister. Her eyes stayed on him, drinking him in, capturing his voice and hording it away like the food she'd found as a child. He didn't look at her often, and she understood that. But when he did, Kendra's hand tightened on hers. Meg's arm squeezed her shoulders. They held her together while everything in front of her fell apart.

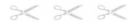

THE NEXT MORNING Tandy stuffed another pair of shorts into her suitcase and zipped it up. She'd leave as soon as the parade was over. No need to come back this way, to prolong the good-byes. She'd thought about leaving last night but knew that she couldn't disappoint James and Savannah that way. They were expecting her to help them snatch up candy as it rained from the floats.

"How's it coming in here?" Daddy stood in the doorway.

"Just finished up."

"Here, let me take that." He lifted her suitcase from the bed, and Cooper looked up.

"Don't worry, buddy, I'm not leaving you," she said, and the dog laid his head back down.

"I think that dog speaks English." Daddy huffed a bit as they went down the stairs.

"I've wondered that myself."

"Yesterday, I told him to get off the couch, so he jumped down and then got in your mother's chair."

Tandy laughed. "Well, you didn't say stay off the furniture."

"That's what I thought. I didn't have the heart to make him get down again, it took so much effort for him to get up there."

They went outside, and she opened her car trunk. He sat her suitcase inside, and they walked back toward the house. "Is your cell phone charged?"

"Yes, Daddy."

"When's the last time you had the oil checked in that thing?"

"It's fine, Daddy."

"How old are those tires?"

"Daddy, the car will make it to Orlando." She smiled, loving his protection of her.

"We'll see. One of these days you'll get something made in America, like my Dodge."

"Daddy, half the parts in your truck probably came from Japan."

"And all of yours came from Germany."

She rolled her eyes at him, pushing down the part of her that knew she'd miss this banter in a few short hours. "Whatever, Daddy. Are you coming to the parade?"

"I'll meet you down there." He patted her shoulder.

"Picking up Zelda?"

"Maybe."

She shook her head and climbed the stairs to get Cooper. "We'll save you a seat. Don't be late!"

"Yes, ma'am." He saluted her and went to his bedroom.

"Come on, Cooper. Time to hit the road." The dog jumped down from his chair and waddled over to her. "You are the cutest dog in the universe." She knelt down and scratched his big, floppy ears. "And pretty soon, it's just you and me again. Let's go."

He followed her out to the car, and she turned for a last look. How long would it be before she came back? Tears welled up and she swallowed hard. The thought was too much. She got into the car and drove down the gravel driveway, glancing no less than three times in the rearview mirror.

Twenty-Five

People packed the downtown area like bees in a honeycomb. Wedging the Beamer into a space better suited for a motorcycle, she avoided the end of Lindell where his diner sat and walked instead to the end by the park. Meg stood, waving her hand to get Tandy's attention. Tandy waved back and pulled Cooper in that direction.

"Aunt Tanny!" Savannah shrieked and launched herself at Tandy's legs.

Tandy scooped the girl up, tossing the leash to Jamison.

"Savannah!" She threw the little girl into the air and caught her. "You're getting so big! Pretty soon, I won't be able to hold you." Savannah giggled and touched Tandy's earrings. "Are you ready to score some candy?"

"Mm-hmm. Not too much." She waved a short finger back and forth in front of Tandy's face.

"Did Mommy say you couldn't have too much?"

Savannah nodded, her eyes serious. "Makes us sick."

"You must have one smart Mommy." Tandy winked at Meg. "Maybe we can get her to put some of your candy up for later."

Savannah looked to Meg for approval. "I think we could do that." At their mother's words, James and Savannah squealed.

Joy held Hannah, bouncing her on one knee while Hannah clapped in pleasure. Scott made googly faces at her.

"Do you think it might be a little loud for her?" Tandy nodded toward Hannah.

"I'm not sure. If it is, I'll just put my hands over her ears. The only things I'm worried about are the fire trucks and police cars."

Tandy put Savannah down. "Where's Kendra?"

"On her way. She overslept."

The wail of a police siren sounded, and Savannah's eyes grew wide. Tandy sat down on the pavement and pulled the little girl into her lap. "It's okay. That's the policeman. He starts the parade."

Savannah clapped while James jumped up and down. Kendra came running through the park just as the police car rounded the bend. "Sorry! Sorry! Got here as fast as I could. Where's Daddy?"

"Picking up Zelda."

Joy looked at Tandy. "Are we okay with that?"

"I think so. For now, anyway. She's good people." Tandy saw them coming down the sidewalk and waved. Zelda waved back. "She keeps him company."

The sisters watched Daddy and Zelda approach. The smile on Daddy's face was unmistakable. Meg's gaze softened into acceptance. "Yeah, she can stay for now."

"But pretty soon she's going to have to let me do something about that hair." Joy peered at Zelda's short red spikes and shuddered.

"Aunt Tanny! Canny!" Savannah said. This year's Hostess Princess and her court sat on a float covered in irises of all colors. The younger court members were throwing candy to the crowd. "Let's get it!" She held James's hand on one side and Savannah's on the other as they rushed into the street to snatch up the candy.

Float after float passed by, and the kids' stashes got bigger and bigger.

"They're never going to eat all this," Meg said.

"Sure they are." Tandy dashed into the street again, James and Savannah hot on her heels. "Just give them half of it and send them to their grandmother's."

"Oh, I'm sure my mom would love that," Jamison said.

All too soon, the parade was over.

"More canny?"

"No, sweetheart, we got it all," Tandy hugged Savannah, then James.

"You heading out?" Meg asked and Tandy nodded.

"Be careful."

"Buckle up," Joy said.

"And stay safe."

"Yeah, yeah, I got it, sisters." They came together in a group hug that had Tandy near tears again. "Love you."

"Love you back," they chorused and she turned to leave.

"Call often," Daddy said, handing her Cooper's leash.

"You've got it," she whispered, hugging him.

"Bye, y'all." She waved and headed off to the car, Cooper trotting along beside her. He woofed and they turned the corner.

"Just you and me again, Coop. Ready for a road trip?"

Cooper woofed and climbed into the car, settling himself in the backseat.

She was on the highway in less than ten minutes, speeding toward Orlando.

Twenty-Six

The reporters will be here in thirty minutes." Anna laid a stack of papers on Tandy's desk. "They've been calling all day, but I told them we had no comment until the press conference. How'd it go with Levi?"

Tandy rubbed her temples and sat back from the computer. Her deep-purple suit felt constricting, and she'd long ago kicked her heels off under the desk. A pair of boots would feel like heaven right about now. "I'm not sure. I can't tell if he's innocent or scared."

"Maybe both?"

Tandy nodded. "Is he still upstairs?"

"Yes. He and Mr. Beasley had lunch delivered. The way they're laughing, you'd think they just finished a round of good golf."

Tandy popped the top off a bottle of aspirin and poured three in her hand. "They're up there having a good time while I'm down here trying to figure out a way to get his rear end out of the sling he put it in. Tell me again why I do this."

"I have no idea." Anna left the office.

The echo of Tandy's words bounced off the walls. The past two days hadn't given her much time to think about Stars Hill, but she had anyway. Cooper, tuned to her like a winnowing fork to water, whined more than usual. She'd coached Levi on his statement for two hours this morning. He was ready for just about any question the media threw at him. All they had to do now was keep him behind closed doors until the press conference.

Tandy walked across the office and hit the PLAY button on her CD player. Sinatra crooned, "*I did it my way . . .*" So much had changed since she listened to this CD two weeks ago. Had someone asked her then if she did things her way, she'd have said yes in a heartbeat. But the fact that she sat in this chair behind her desk in Orlando served as proof that she didn't always do things her way. If she did, she'd have found a path that kept her in Stars Hill.

Her phone buzzed and she hit the flashing button. "Yes."

"Producer from *Hannity & Colmes* is on the line. Will you take the call?"

"Sure." She picked up the receiver and waited for the connection. "Hey, Sebastian."

"Tandy Sinclair. In the middle of a mess, it looks like."

"No bigger than yours back in law school."

"I did *not* cheat on that test."

"If you say so."

"I do. But that's more than your boy Levi can say, I hear."

"He didn't steal money, Sebastian. Why would he?"

"Greed, Tandy. It's a big motivator."

"So is self-preservation, and stealing that money certainly didn't contribute to the preservation of his career.

Come on, give the guy some credit. He's not dumb enough to commit this kind of political suicide."

"Then why's he ducking the cameras?"

"Because his attorney told him to and he's smart enough to listen to her. Will I see you at the press conference?"

"I'd rather see him in a studio with an exclusive."

"Hmm, we'll see how you treat him at the five and six news hours. Call me then, and we'll try to set something up."

"Unless I get the governor's commitment before then."

"If you get the governor to speak ill of his own lieutenant governor on air, thereby implicating himself legally and killing any chances of reelection, then more power to you. 'Bye, Sebastian."

She hung up and massaged her temples again. The throbbing increased. Levi wasn't her only iron in the fire. Most of her cases were coming up for trial within a few weeks. And she was two weeks behind. Miranda, the attorney who'd taken over her cases while she was gone, should have filed continuances but hadn't gotten around to it.

A hawk flew into her window, and Tandy jumped. "Dumb bird."

Her phone rang, and she let it go to voice mail. Rain clouds were gathering on the horizon, and she longed for Cooper and a long nap on the couch. Instead, the fight of the press conference lay before her.

Her intercom sounded. "Tandy, Mr. Beasley and Levi have some questions for you."

"Be right up, Anna." She grabbed a legal pad and left the office. Riding up in the plush elevator, Tandy wondered what they could want. Levi was probably panicking again. How had the man made it this far in politics with such a fear of cameras?

The elevator dinged and deposited her on Mr. Beasley's floor. "They're waiting for you." Anna motioned her on in.

"Should I be worried?"

"Only if Levi having a heart attack wouldn't make your day. Beasley's on cup number two. Levi's still on one."

Tandy grinned and entered Mr. Beasley's office. Levi sat before Christopher like a child in front of a principal, his tall, gaunt frame folded awkwardly into the chair. His mouse-brown hair was thinner on top than it'd been a few months ago, and a dusting of white particles lay across his shoulders.

Beasley sipped coffee, his eyes focused on Levi.

"Gentlemen." She sat down. "What can I do for you?"

"Tandy, are you sure a press conference is a good idea?"

Tandy groaned inwardly, wondering how many more times Levi would ask this question.

No, Levi, I think it's a horrid idea. I think the person who suggested it should be fired. That's what she wanted to say. Instead, she smiled demurely.

"Levi, you have to give them a story, or they'll make one up. Right now they're running with the idea that you're a greedy bureaucrat who stole money from the citizens of Orlando. If we don't give them an alternative, you'll be tried and convicted before you ever step foot in a courtroom."

"You're right." Levi wrung his hands. "I know you're right. But those reporters can be vicious."

"Only when they smell blood in the water. And you aren't going to give them that. You'll go in, tell them you didn't do this, answer a few questions, and get out of there. No time for an attack. Where's Theresa?"

"She's waiting in the boardroom with the kids," Mr. Beasley said.

"How about you go spend a little time with them before

we get this underway?" Tandy pulled Levi from his chair and steered him toward the door. "I'll be in to check on you in just a few minutes."

Levi allowed himself to be taken out of the room and directed down the hall to the boardroom.

Tandy looked for reinforcements. "Anna, could you see if Mr. Walker's family needs anything, please?"

Anna smiled and nodded, prodding Levi on down the hallway. Tandy closed the door to Mr. Beasley's office. "What happened to our confident client from Friday?"

Christopher held his palms up. "I have no idea. My guess is that the endless stream of phone calls wore him out. He said the phone hasn't stopped ringing since Friday."

"Why didn't he just unplug it?"

Christopher blinked. "I don't know."

Checking her watch, Tandy saw they had less than half an hour until the press conference. "I can't put that man in front of a bank of cameras. He looks guilty."

"Then go make him look innocent, Tandy."

She stared at him. Did he know she didn't actually have the power to manipulate situations to her advantage?

"You're one of the best attorneys at this firm. If anybody can save him, it's you."

Apparently not.

She huffed and left his office, knowing his endorsement of her performance should matter—and puzzling over why it didn't.

✂ ✂ ✂

THAT NIGHT, WHEN the sun had set on another day and the traffic jam on I-4 had thinned out, Tandy turned off her computer and laid her head on her desk. The press conference had been brutal, and, despite her best efforts, she feared the media didn't buy the story of Levi Walker, humble servant, upstanding family man, serving the citizenry of Florida.

She picked up the phone and dialed Kendra's number. *"Hey, you got my voice mail. Leave a message."*

Tandy hung up instead and dialed Joy. *"You have reached the home of Scott and Joy Lasky. We're sorry to have missed—"*

She disconnected the call, dialed Meg. *"This is the Fawcett residence. We're not around right now—"*

Tandy hung up and looked around her office. Outside her window, cars clogged Orange Avenue in both directions. In a city of over one and a half million people, she should be able to find a girlfriend or two. How did other women find friends around here? Church? Clubs? Work? She walked back to her computer and looked up the phone number for the scrapbook store.

"Savvy Scrapper," someone answered.

"Hi, I'm trying to find some scrapbookers around here."

"We have a class on Thursday night."

"No, I don't want to come to a class. I'm just wondering if you know of a group of women who scrapbook together?"

"We have an all-night crop next weekend."

"Right. I mean something not happening at your store. Maybe some girls who scrap at someone's house?"

She listened to the hum of the phone line.

"Never mind, thanks anyway."

She dropped the phone in its cradle. Cooper would need to go out soon. Gathering up her purse and shoes, she couldn't get the thought out of her mind that there had to be a way to find scrapbookers in her area. Some way to connect with people of like mind. Women who knew how to talk and share and laugh.

Whatever it took, she would find a way. She had to.

Before loneliness drove her utterly and completely crazy.

Twenty-Seven

Two weeks later the media frenzy surrounding Lieutenant Governor Levi Walker had reached a fever pitch, and Tandy still had not found any scrapbookers. She'd managed to talk to Kendra once and tried to be happy when she learned things were going great between her and Darin. But Darin meant Clay, and it was hard to pretend where he was concerned.

Her intercom sounded. "Tandy, Sebastian on the line for you."

She sighed, knowing he'd want to discuss Levi's latest slip of the tongue. Her client looked more and more guilty every day. Either that, or incredibly stupid.

"Hi, Sebastian."

"Tandy Sinclair. How's our buddy Levi today?"

"No better for the media wringer he's being put through. Is there something I can help you with?" She had neither the patience nor the inclination to deal with media today, even if they were old law-school classmates.

"Ouch. Touchy, touchy."

"Just tired, Sebastian. Did you have a question for me?"

"On the record, can you tell me what Levi's defense strategy will be?"

"You know I'm not going to give you that. I tend to refrain from handing the prosecution its case."

"Unless the client is Harry Simons."

Her headache, which had regressed to a dull pounding the past few days, jumped into high gear again. "Excuse me?"

"The Hope House case. Come on, did you think we wouldn't find out?"

"Considering there's nothing to find out, I'm not sure what we're talking about here. Harry Simons was given a good defense."

"That's not what he's telling media reps."

She held her sigh in. Harry was just another flare-up in a week full of eruptions. He'd go away when his fifteen minutes were up. "Mr. Simons is free to say whatever he wants to the media, Sebastian, though I'd be careful about aiding and abetting someone intent on defaming someone's character through libelous or otherwise criminal actions."

"We're not carrying it here, Tandy. But those guys over at CNN are starting to make some noise."

"Thanks for the warning. Anything else I can help you with?"

"Give me an exclusive with Levi. He hasn't done an interview yet."

That was because the man had no business being in front of a camera.

"Either he talks, or you get raked over the coals, Tandy. You know they're going to carry whatever story they're given."

"You understand that you are a part of *they* right?"

He chuckled. "Right, right."

She thought about it. Either Levi could give an exclusive to Sebastian, with her in the room able to stop him at a moment's notice, or she could lose control of this story with the media. It didn't seem to be a difficult decision. "He'll be here tomorrow at three p.m. Our offices, not your studios. And I'll be in the room the entire time."

"We'll be there with bells on." He hung up, and Tandy stuck her tongue out at the phone. She dialed Levi's new home number and waited for him to pick up.

"Levi Walker."

"Levi, we're giving an exclusive to FOX News tomorrow at three. Can you be here at 1:30 to prep?"

"Do we have to?"

"It's either that or lose control of the story. Up to you, sir." She tapped her pen against the legal pad on her desk, almost wishing he'd refuse and give her reason to cancel on Sebastian.

"I'll be there."

She heard defeat in his tone and noted on her legal pad to work on that next day. "Good. Chin up, Levi. You'll get through this."

"Thanks, Tandy."

She hung up the phone and pulled up a search engine on her computer. She typed in "scrapbook club Orlando" but got nothing useful. She knew women were getting together; that was just the nature of the hobby. But was no one organizing them?

She fiddled around with the search engine, finding a club listing here and there, sometimes on a church Web site, sometimes at a library. She never ran across one meeting in someone's home, but she assumed these groups must do that occasionally. Working in a legal world of precedent and over referencing everything, it astounded her that there didn't seem to be any directory of these groups.

An idea began to form in the back of her mind, and Tandy smiled—really smiled—for the first time since leaving Stars Hill. She leaned over the keyboard and continued running search terms.

✂ ✂ ✂

IT TOOK HER three days to get Kendra on the phone and talk about her idea and what she'd found in, of all places, Nashville. Kendra squealed and jumped on board before Tandy had finished describing it.

"You are the smartest woman on the planet!"

"I don't know about that. But if I have to deal with Levi Walker and his ilk for the rest of my life, I think I might go insane."

"Have you called Clay?"

"No, and he hasn't called me. I thought I'd get things settled here, make sure this idea of ours will float, and then go see him. Have you talked to him?"

"No, but Darin says he's hurting. They went out last Saturday, and Darin said he was just down. Not into anything they were doing."

"I know the feeling."

"Why don't you call him?"

"Because, Kendra, I don't want to get his hopes up and then have to dash them if this thing doesn't work out. Plus, if I hear his voice, I'm not sure I'll be able to think straight." Or think at all.

"Have you talked to your boss yet?"

"Have a meeting set up with him tomorrow. He's going to flip, but he'll get over it."

"Talked to the woman in Nashville?"

"Yep, yesterday. Her name is Jane Sandburg, and she's more than ready to hand this baby over to us."

"What about Daddy?"

"I wanted to tell you first. I'll call him as soon as we hang up."

"He's going to be over the moon."

"He ain't the only one. Listen, I should get off here and get to packing. I'll see you in a few days, okay?"

"You bet."

"And, Kendra?"

"Yeah?"

"Don't tell Darin."

"Mum's the word, sis."

"Bye."

"Bye."

She hung up the phone and scratched Cooper's ears. Why she hadn't thought of this sooner she couldn't figure out, but it was perfect. A company she could build and run from anywhere—including Stars Hill. She had two months to prove it before she ran out of money and started hoofing it to Nashville to beg for a legal position.

The excitement hummed through her like juicy news through Stars Hill. She'd found another way to win the battle! Clay wasn't the only smart soldier around here. And once everything was up and going, she'd have time to scrap with the sisters and go to gymnastics meets with Meg and hang out at Joy's for five-course meals. And Daddy!

Her cheeks hurt from grinning.

Pulling a box from the heap in the living room floor,

she began filling it with books from her bookshelf. "You're not very much help here, Coop." He wagged his stubby tail. "You want to go home to Stars Hill?"

"Woof!" He recognized the name of the town.

"Me, too. And the faster we get this stuff packed, the quicker we can hit the road."

Twenty-Eight

One week later Tandy opened the door of her car and pulled the seat up. Cooper climbed into the back, settling into his place on the seat. This trip would be a whole lot different from the one nearly two months ago. Because she wasn't coming back. The movers had already left with her stuff, which would hopefully meet up with her in Stars Hill at Daddy's house. Moving back home at thirty years old had required a ton of ego swallowing, but she had to save on expenses until the company was up and running.

She got into the car and closed the door, waved good-bye to her Florida apartment, and hit the road for Stars Hill. The weight that had settled on her chest when she'd crossed the Florida state line lifted, and she took in a deep lungful of air. The tangy taste of salt soaked the back of her throat.

Ocean air.

None of that in Stars Hill.

She let the thought roll around her mind for a minute, trying it on, testing its impact. Nope, it didn't hurt. And why should it? The sweet smells of turned dirt, tasseled-out corn, and fresh-cut grass were waiting in Stars Hill.

Her phone rang and she flipped it open. "Tandy Sinclair."

"Left yet?"

"Hi, Kendra, how are you? I'm fine thanks."

"Yeah, yeah, we're all good. Have you left yet?"

"I'm pulling out of the parking lot now. Does Darin know?"

"Not a word. I think he thinks something's up, but I haven't confirmed one way or the other."

"Keep him in the dark for eleven more hours. I'm stopping at the diner before I get to the house." The smell of frying burgers. That was another one she'd have in Stars Hill.

"You go, girl."

"You think he's moved on by now? It's been five weeks."

"Not if Darin's telling me the truth. The man mopes around like a lost puppy."

Tandy's heart hurt at that, but thrilled to it as well. "Let's hope I can fix that for him."

"I don't think there's any doubt about it."

"Your lips to God's ears, sister."

"Be careful."

"Will do."

She shut the phone and turned up the radio, dreaming about what was at the end of eight-hundred miles.

When she reached the Florida border, her phone rang again. "Hello?"

"Where are you?"

"Hi, Meg, I'm good. Got everything packed up no problem. Thanks for asking."

"I've got fourteen kids running around here on sugar highs and about thirty more seconds before one of them thinks it's fun to unplug the phone. Where are you?"

Tandy laughed. "Just crossed into Georgia."

"Ooh, careful of the Tifton speed trap."

"Right." Tandy adjusted her speed. "Why are there fourteen kids at your house?"

"Because I have issues with telling people no."

"In some universe I'm sure that makes perfect sense."

"Gabriella! *No!*"

Tandy listened to the mayhem that was Meg's house. It sounded as if someone had decided Kool-Aid would make a nifty floor wax. Meg yelled for Jamison and told the kids to stay back. Tandy grinned. She'd get to be part of the pandemonium soon.

"Hey, sorry about that."

"No problem. Crisis averted?"

"For now. Kendra says you've talked to the Nashville woman and we're good to go?"

"Yep. I'll drive up there tomorrow and sign the papers."

"I can't believe we're doing this."

"Have you told anyone?"

"No, you said I couldn't."

"Just making sure."

"I need to go referee a scuffle. Be careful, T."

"Will do."

Tandy closed the phone and turned up the radio. In a little over six hours, if all went according to plan, she'd be standing in front of Clay. Was he mad at her? He hadn't called once since she left. Then again, she hadn't called him either.

The memory of his face had kept her going through the craziness of the past five weeks. She prayed he'd be as excited about this new venture as she and the sisters were. If not, then she was going to feel really, really silly.

Spotting a police officer in a parking lot, she checked her speed and waved. Tifton police officers loved to catch speeding drivers. They were always on patrol here at the border. "Not today, boys. I don't have time to stop."

Three hours later the Beamer was awash in a sea of cars and trucks in downtown Atlanta. No matter what hour she hit the city, the roads were always full of people. Her cell phone sounded out the notes for "I'll Fly Away," and she couldn't stop a grin from forming when she answered it.

"Hello?"

"In Atlanta yet?"

"Hey, Ken. I'm in the middle of it right now."

"Ugh. Call me when you're out of it."

"'Kay."

She closed the phone and concentrated on the cars weaving in and out of lanes in front of her. Nobody in this city used turn signals. It was nuts.

A little while later she swerved the Beamer onto an exit ramp, and Cooper lifted his head.

"Ready for a quick break, buddy?" The BP looked to have the best grassy area for Cooper, so she pulled the car into a parking space there and cut the engine. Snapping a leash on Cooper, she exited the car with phone in hand and tugged him over to the grass.

"Do your business, boy." She dialed Kendra's number.

"Hello?"

"It's me. Mark me down for another successful Atlanta crossing."

"The Red Sea may not have been that hard."

Tandy chuckled, warmed at the sound of Kendra's laughter. "Hey, I had an idea and wanted to run it by you."

Tandy tugged a bit on Cooper's leash. "Shoot."

"I was over in Sara's store today and noticed she's not using her entire space. It's not huge, but I think it'd be big enough for us, and we'd be right by Emmy's, which fits in well with us."

"How much is it?"

"I didn't ask since she'd want to know why I was interested, and it's right there by Clay's. Didn't think you'd want me to chance it."

"I love the idea. Call Sara and see if we can meet with her in the morning. We can talk to her, then go to Nashville to meet this Jane woman."

"Good deal. See you in a few hours!"

Tandy closed the phone and pulled Cooper back to the car. "Come on, boy, we've got three more hours to go, and then you can have the whole farm to run around." Her heart beat faster with every hundred miles traveled. Stars Hill—home—was so close.

Cooper woofed and wagged his stubby tail.

✄ ✄ ✄

COMING BACK TO Stars Hill was a strange experience every time. Seven weeks ago she'd had no idea how one little trip would change the course of her life. As she drove the Beamer down Lindell, she saw it all now with fresh eyes. The eyes of someone who lived here. There would be no sign stretched across the street for her this time. That would have given everything away.

She parked the Beamer a block away from Clay's diner so he couldn't see her until she walked up. Praying he was there and not off on a date with some hussy, she opened her door and pulled Cooper out with her.

He sniffed the air, recognized its scent, and barked.

"Hush, boy, you'll give us away."

The new lampposts glowed a welcome. No breeze blew, as though the town waited for her to make a move. She walked down the street, seeing his red and navy sign hanging above the door, below the navy awning. A few of the tables held couples, but the place wasn't too full.

She stopped on the corner across the street, staring through the window at his world. A world she hoped he would invite her into when she walked through that door. Cooper sat down and waited with her.

After a full minute in which she convinced herself he wasn't there, he exited the kitchen and stood behind the counter. The light didn't let her see the details of his face from here, but his shoulders and head were bowed. He looked tired. Defeated.

Cooper saw him, too, and made a beeline across the street. She let herself be pulled along, then opened the glass door.

He looked up at the sound of the bell and froze. Unsure, unsteady, she threaded her way through the tables, skirted the counter, and came to stand in front of him. It felt like every eye in the room was on them, and for once she didn't care.

"Hi." It came out breathless.

His Adam's apple bobbed as he swallowed. "Hi."

Cooper settled back on his haunches, eyes going back and forth like he was watching a tennis match. "I wasn't sure if you would want to know, but I didn't want you to hear it from someone else, so . . ." If only she could read his eyes. They hadn't left hers since she'd walked in. "I'm moving here."

Life sprang into those green depths watching her. A slow grin grew across his face, and the steel band around her heart began to loosen again.

"You're what?"

"I'm moving here. I'm here, actually. My stuff probably beat me to Daddy's."

"Yes!" Before she knew it, he had picked her up and swung her around, showering her face with kisses. She dropped Cooper's leash before strangling him and reveled in the joy of Clay, in the feel of those thick black curls on her skin again, in knowing he still loved her. His strong arms around her waist were all she'd thought of for several hours of the drive. Shoot, for the last two months.

She heard clapping and wondered if that was in her head or if the Stars Hill diners were congratulating them. When Cooper woofed, she had her answer. Clay's adoration came to an abrupt halt, and he set her on her feet, his eyebrows scrunched. "Wait, what changed?"

"I—"

"Not that I'm saying you shouldn't move here." He tightened his hold on her waist again. "I just want to make sure I understand."

She glanced back at the room, at the side she could see of it, blushing when she saw that everyone waited for her answer.

Clay saw it, too. "Show's over, folks. We'll be right back."

He tugged her into the kitchen, and Cooper's nails clicked as he followed. "Now, you mean you're going to *live* here, right? Not going back to Orlando?"

She nodded and grinned.

"What happened to the need to prove yourself, to be a big attorney, to make partner, to give back to your parents?"

"I found a way to do that here."

"But we already have attorneys. Which I can go maim right now if you need me to, but—"

She put her fingers over his lips. "When I went back to Orlando, I was so lonely. I thought it would help if I could find some girlfriends like the sisters. You know, girls to scrap with and talk about life. I searched and searched, but I couldn't find a way to find those girls. And then it hit me: If *I* was looking for these groups, then there were probably lots of other women in the same boat. Needing friends, wanting them to be scrapbookers, and not having a way to find them. So I called Kendra."

"Uh-oh. This can only get crazy from here."

"Exactly. We found a lady in Nashville who owns a company called Sisters, Ink. She had this vision of creating an online database of scrapbooking clubs and got her girlfriends to start the company with her. But then the whole thing fell apart. She's getting married, and one of the owners is pregnant and just adopted a little girl from Chile. Another of them is going through marriage counseling. They didn't have the time to devote to the business. So Jane decided to sell it."

"Enter you and Kendra."

"Yep. We're going to Nashville tomorrow to sign the final papers, but it's pretty much a done deal. We'll be the new owners of Sisters, Ink and, hopefully, provide a resource for women to find other women in their local communities with whom they can scrap and share friendship."

He shook his head. "You are the most brilliant woman I've ever met."

"I'm not sure about that, but as Momma always said, 'Where there's a will, there's a way.'"

"Pretty smart woman, your momma." He leaned in and kissed her, and heat and joy flared inside her. This wouldn't be the last time his lips touched hers. She didn't have to walk away from him. Not ever again.

Cooper woofed, and they broke apart to look down at him. Tandy bent and patted his head.

"You were doing all this and never thought about calling to tell me? I've been in agony here, woman!" He pulled her back up to stand against him, and she saw the ocean she'd left behind in his eyes.

She ran her finger down his strong jaw. "Poor baby. I didn't want to get your hopes up—*my* hopes up—and then have it fall apart. Leaving you once was hard enough. I didn't think I could do it again."

He slid his hands up her side and held her face. "I love you, Tandy Ann Sinclair."

"I love you back, Clay Michael Kelner."

"You know, lots of women would have been happy just to be in love."

"Hmm. Maybe. But I'm not one of them." She leaned her head back and looked at him. "I need you to understand that. I do love you, more than I knew a woman could love a man, but I don't want my whole world to center around you. It'll suffocate you and me and us. Momma and Daddy sacrificed so much for me, and Momma was right when she told me to go to Orlando.

"I didn't realize until the past few weeks, though, that she told me to go there because she knew it was the one place I was afraid of. I don't think her dream was for me to go to Orlando and live the rest of my life. It was to chase after whatever God made me to do and not be afraid if that purpose took me to a city I was scared of." She stopped and took a deep breath. "I almost missed that, but I get it now." She shook her head. "I spent a lot of years fulfilling an expectation that no one had of me."

His eyes softened as he watched her, and the tenderness there made her heart race.

He tucked a coppery red curl behind her ear. "You are such a smart lady, Taz. I'm not sure how I got this lucky."

She kissed him and pulled back. "Just remember that in the next few weeks when I'm running around like a chicken with my head cut off trying to get a business going."

"I can help with that. Starting this place was no piece of cake, but it's doable. Are all four of you doing this thing?"

"Yeah. Meg and Joy won't be too involved, but they're co-owners. Kendra and I will mainly run the place. We're talking to Sara tomorrow about some store space she has between her shop and Emmy's."

"So you'll be right here near me every day?"

She hadn't thought of that. "Yep!"

"This just gets better and better."

"Hey, you two—" Kendra stuck her head around the corner of the doorframe—"any chance we can get some drink refills out here before Jesus comes back?"

Tandy laughed and went to hug her sister.

"Can't a guy have a moment in his own diner?" Clay made a move to pull Tandy back into his arms. "I've been waiting for this for weeks."

"Sorry, man." Darin came into the kitchen as well. "I tried to stop her, but you know how it is."

"She's a force to be reckoned with."

"Hello?" Kendra waved her hand in the air. "I'm right here in case anyone wants to talk *to* me." She put her hands on her hips in playful exasperation.

Clay glanced at the clock on the wall. "We're closing up in ten minutes. Let me run settle the tabs, and we'll all go out and do something."

"Yeah, like unload my moving truck. Daddy's going to have a conniption when he sees how much stuff is in there."

"We'll figure it out." Clay sounded happier than she could ever remember. "Be right back."

He walked out of the kitchen, and Tandy looked to Kendra, who grinned.

"That seemed to go well."

Tandy nudged her sister's arm. "When did you get here?"

"We were over in the corner when you came in," Darin said.

"I wasn't going to miss this!" Kendra said. "Did you think I would just sit at home, waiting on you to call me with the details?"

"Now that you mention it, no."

Kendra held up a small digital camera. "And you'll be happy to know I captured your perfect scrapbooking moment on film."

"You didn't!"

"I did." Kendra gave a satisfied smile. "Somebody had to make sure you didn't crop any more Cooper photos."

At the sound of his name, Cooper barked, making them all laugh.

"Thanks, sis."

"You bet."

"Did you call Sara?"

Kendra nodded. "We're meeting her tomorrow morning

at nine. Joy and Meg said to do whatever we thought was best, that worked with the budget."

"Great." She ran her hands down her jeans. "Let's get over to Daddy's and start unpacking. Whatever doesn't fit in the house we can put in the barn for now, I guess."

"Sounds good. We'll meet you there." They made their way out of the kitchen, and Tandy watched as Kendra and Darin left the diner, Darin's hand on her back. She had no idea if her sister would manage to stay with Darin longer than the usual couple of months, but it was nice to see her happy for now anyway. She turned back to tell Clay she was leaving and noticed everyone had left. He turned out the lights.

The glow from Tanner's streetlights spilled into the windows, giving just enough light to catch the sparkle in his eye.

She'd almost missed this.

Her breath caught at the thought, then eased as he walked over to her, steps steady and slow. She watched his shoulders move, smiled at the shadow in that little spot between his shoulder and neck, where her head fit so well. She had a place to fit. To really fit.

A tear traced its way down her cheek, and she couldn't decide if it was happiness at belonging or pain for all those who didn't have this. For all the years *she* hadn't had this.

Clay stopped in front of her, blocking part of the light. She shivered at his nearness. "Ready for some unpacking?"

"If it involves being with you, I'm ready for whatever." He put his arms around her. "Thank you." His voice was low and husky.

"For what?"

"I know this had to be hard for you."

Cooper gave voice to her sigh, and she smiled. "It was and it wasn't. It was hard when I thought I had to give up one dream to get another. It was easy when I figured out how to have them both."

"You are—" he kissed her—"the most—" he kissed her again—"wonderful woman—" another small kiss—"I have ever met." His last kiss was deeper than the others, telling her how much he loved her, wanted her, and treasured her.

When he raised his head and searched her eyes, she took a deep breath and locked her gaze to his, letting him see the love there in its entirety. For one brief, desperate moment, it felt like she'd jumped off a giant cliff and hung suspended in thin mountain air. But then he smiled and tightened his arms around her, and she knew that he knew. No, she *felt* that he knew.

After a long moment, he stepped back and held out his hand. "I think we need to go unload some boxes. If we stay here much longer, I'm pretty sure I'll be dragging you up those stairs and ruining this before it ever gets off the ground."

She shivered at his words, wanting the same thing and grateful that he was man enough to both admit it and avoid it. "Right. I'm parked outside. Want to ride with me?"

"Sure."

She tugged on Cooper's leash, and he hauled himself to his feet. They walked out the door, and she stood with Cooper while he locked it. When he turned back, she took his warm hand and held it as they crossed the street.

A man on one side. A dog on the other.

And a heart that could feel again.

Momma's Buckeyes

(Serves four ladies for three hours)

Ingredients:
- 2 sticks soft margarine
- 1½ boxes of confectioners (powdered) sugar
- 2 c. peanut butter (16 oz.)
- Large package chocolate chips
- ½ stick paraffin

Mix first three ingredients together by hand. (Get those fingers good and gooey!) When all ingredients are thoroughly mixed, roll into balls about half as big as a golf ball. Place balls on wax paper.

On stovetop, melt chocolate chips and paraffin in a double broiler over medium heat. Stick a toothpick about halfway in a peanut butter ball and dip the ball into the chocolate. Place back on the wax paper to dry.

Hint: If one falls off the toothpick and into the chocolate, you've just created a great excuse to eat your mistake. Grab a spoon!

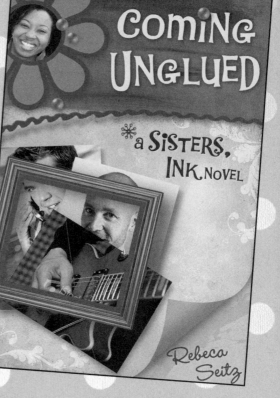